THE HOPE OF YOU

IN THE STARS

BOOK ONE

S.L. ASTOR

First edition September 2022

Kindle ASIN: B0B85QF9D4

Paperback ISBN: 9798843207571

Cover Designer: Murphy Rae www.MurphyRae.com

CONTENT WARNING

Please be advised that this is a work of fiction. It contains explicit language and content, and explores sensitive subjects surrounding mental health, cumulative and integrated grief, parental abandonment, and loss of a parent—off the page/in the past. It may be triggering for some readers, and is intended for audiences 18 years and older.

RORY'S CHAPTER SONGS

1. Here Comes the Sun, Sheryl Crow
2. Unwritten, Natasha Bedingfield
3. Black & White, Sarah McLachlin
4. Try Everything, Shakira
5. Landslide, Fleetwood Mac
6. Fight Song, Rachel Platten
7. Dreams, The Cranberries
8. The Ocean, Mike Perry, Shy Martin
9. Human, Christina Perri
10. Keep Breathing, Ingrid Michaelson
11. Ocean Eyes, Billie Eilish
12. The Writer, Ellie Goulding
13. Everything Has Changed, Taylor Swift, Ed Sheeran
14. Heart's Content, Brandi Carlile
15. Sunrise, Norah Jones
16. Fallin' for You, Colby Caillat
17. Honest, Kyndal Inskeep & The Song House
18. Now I'm in It, HAIM
19. Same Changes, The Weepies
20. Somebody, Dagny
21. The Trouble with Wanting, Joy Williams
22. Run to You, Lea Michele
23. Head Above Water, Avril Lavigne
24. Poison & Wine, The Civil Wars
25. Light Me Up, Ingrid Michaelson
26. Heart and Shoulder, Heather Nova
27. Can't Help Falling in Love, Landon Austin, Landrey Fulmer
28. Chasing Cars, Fleurie, Tommee Profitt
29. Feels Like Home, Chantal Kreviazuk
30. My Immortal, Evanescence
31. Alone, Heart
32. I'll Remember, Madonna
33. I Never Told You, Colbie Caillat
34. War of Hearts, Ruelle
35. Greatest Love of All, Whitney Houston
36. Breathe, Faith Hill (and) Unconditionally, Katy Perry
Epilogue: When You Say Nothing at All, Alison Krauss & Union Station

REED'S CHAPTER SONGS

1. Head Full of Doubt/Road Full of Promise, The Avett Brothers
2. The Wish, Josh Canova
3. Hemorrhage (In My Hands), Fuel
4. Dancing in the Dark, Imaginary Future
5. The Sound of Silence, Simon & Garfunkel
6. Wildflowers, Tom Petty
7. It's Time, Imagine Dragons
8. And Then You, Greg Laswell
9. Falling Slowly, Glen Hansard, Markéta Irglová
10. Shallow, Bradley Cooper and Lady Gaga
11. Green Eyes, Coldplay
12. Turning Page (Instrumental), Sleeping At Last
13. Bloom, The Paper Kites
14. Changes, Langhorne Slim & The Law
15. Broken, Seether, Amy Lee
16. You Are Enough, Sleeping At Last
17. Far Too Good, John Smith
18. Song for Someone, U2
19. Fix You, Coldplay
20. Pretend, Paper Route
21. Cross That Line, Josh Radin
22. Hanging by a Moment, Lifehouse
23. Hold You in My Arms, Ray LaMontagne
24. Never Say Never, The Fray
25. Ghosts That We Knew, Mumford & Sons
26. Need the Sun to Break, James Bay
27. Whataya Want from Me, Adam Lambert
28. Chasing Cars, Fleurie, Tommee Profitt
29. Without You, Parachute
30. Hands Open, Snow Patrol
31. Anywhere But Here, SafetySuit
32. If Your Light Goes Out, The Maine
33. If You Only Knew, Shinedown
34. This Woman's Work, Greg Laswell
35. Missing Piece, Vance Joy
36. All This Time, One Republic (and) Once in a Lifetime, Landon Austin
Epilogue: Home, Phillip Phillips

To the inner child.

&

To my children—stay curious, keep creating, be you.

"It's in the space between the love we've lost and the love we hope to find, where we meet ourselves."
—Mark Groves

1

— : —

RORY

"Everything you can imagine is real."
—Pablo Picasso

Second chances don't show up every day. And they definitely don't show up in mailboxes on Saturday morning with my name attached to them.

The envelope rattles in my grasp, edges curling against their will. I triple-check the label from Eden Books, then hold it up to the sun in hopes of discovering a hint of its contents, a single clue, but the brutal rays force my eyes to the ground, where flecks of silver and opal embedded in the pavement dance around in my vision.

There were hundreds of applicants. I'm sure it's a standard courtesy letter, rejecting my submission and encouraging me to try again next year. But for me, there is no next year. There is only this one.

I force a deep inhale to settle the shaking, half-expecting to exhale myself from one of my lucid dreams.

Typical brunch traffic in Boston competes with a pounding pulse in my chest, alerting my system that this might not be a drill. On the off chance this is actually happening, there is no way I'll look back at this moment, where my life changes forever, and replay some sad story about how the sole witness was a weathered mailbox in front of my apartment with its mouth hanging wide open.

Sorry, mailbox, it's not you, it's me.

I sprint across the street to Memory Lane, the café my best friend Kat owns. The racket of welcome bells and steel crashes in my wake. It takes all of two seconds to spot Kat behind the counter. Her platinum wavy hair with lavender ends piled on top of her head bounces as she bops along to classic rock music playing throughout the café.

Waving the envelope in the air like a white flag, I rush to the counter, practically knocking a latte from her hand.

"Goooooood morn—" Kat says, leaning over the counter. She takes in my state from head to toe—last night's leggings and messy bun, her eyes saucers of concern. "Are you," Kat lowers her voice, "having an anxiety attack? The kitchen's clear if you need a quiet place. It's all yours."

Kat's lips keep moving, but whatever she's saying isn't computing. I woke up this morning as ad sales Rory. Rory with a journalism degree collecting dust. The same Rory with the same coffee order, who spends her days in the same four-block radius.

I didn't let myself believe I could be chosen. Not for something this competitive or prestigious.

I'm potentially a signature line away from being a full-time writer.

My hands shake as I slam the envelope down on the counter in front of a bewildered Kat. "I can't open it."

"Can't open what?" Kat shoots me a quizzical glance.

I'm waiting for Kat to tap into her BFF radar and read my mind, because all I'm coming up with are jumbled consonants and vowels flashing in neon. I wipe the stray hair away from my face while spilling the unfiltered contents of my head.

My tongue scrapes like sandpaper, from the sprint and apprehension.

"The answer to whether I've been selected as Eden's debut writer is in this envelope. Whether I'm going to finally finish my book, and query agents, and commit to my dream." I'm nearly shouting now, riding an escalator of elation, making pit stops for shock and relief along the way. "And I'm too scared to open it and find out."

Kat's eyes pop open like cash registers. "I sure as shit am not!" She swipes the envelope from the counter, loosens a pencil from her hair, and rips right through the seal.

My stomach plummets. I steady my other hand on the counter.

At first, she stares intensely. Her brows pull in and her lips hold a straight line.

After counting five Mississippis in my head, convinced I can't wait another second, as if on cue, Kat's lashes lift and her expression slowly reveals a smile. She's smiling. Kat is smiling. At me.

"Congrats, Rory, you're officially—wait, let me read it—here we go, EB Publishing's Annual Aspiring Author Mentee! Well, that's a mouthful."

"I got in," I choke out. "I got in," I repeat in disbelief. "Wait, but I wasn't supposed to."

"Ha. That's what she said."

"C'mon, I'm serious."

"I am too. Dead serious," she points out.

Kat is laughing and flips the letter to face me, pushing the hard evidence into my trembling hands.

"Dear Ms. Rory Wells. Welcome to Eden. Accepted. Writing Mentorship. Reed Ashton." The words I'm reading escape in whispers as I race through the details.

Kat's voice grabs my attention. She's raising a brow at the paper to-go cup in her hand, giving it a hard stare. "Alta . . . lune, your mocha is all set." She leaves the cup on the pick-up bar and comes over from behind the counter. "These double names kill me," she sighs, shaking her head. "I swear, at this rate, I'm gonna need to order thirty-two-ounce cups to fit them."

She yanks me into her cinnamon-infused embrace, with her signature squeeze, genuine and strong. Waiting for this decision has been eating at me for months. I've made wishes on every star in the sky.

When we stop hugging, Kat catches me off guard in a rare moment of seriousness, saying, "Don't look so shocked. I knew you'd get it."

I wipe my hoodie sleeve gently across my eyes. Kat's confidence in me is something I've never gotten used to. I swear she laces her lattes with loyalty and support, maybe a splash of courage too.

It was terrifying to subject my writing to be judged, and I told myself that if this didn't work out, I'd take it as the final sign it was time to put the pen down, let go, and accept reality.

I'm thirty, which isn't a death sentence for dreams, but I also know that when something isn't working, you don't hold on tighter.

"Thank you for pushing me to apply and for being my friend."

She waves my affection off with a brush of her hand, like her steadfast friendship is no big deal and thanking her for it is almost an insult.

"You know what this means? I'm marching into Doris's office on Monday with a fuck-you-very-much resignation letter."

"You're absolutely recording that." She scans the café tables. The place is half-full, mostly regulars. "Seriously, this is the best news for my best non-paying customer."

I deadpan, both of us familiar with our established friendship charades. She's been my best friend, and also my barista, for close to a decade.

Kat strides over to the shelf of vinyl records in the corner, lifting the needle off the run-down record player. She's been talking about getting a replacement for forever.

The music stops. The music never stops at Memory Lane.

"Hey, listen up, everyone," she commands. The handful of patrons scattered around the café stop their conversations and look up. "This ridiculously talented romance writer is gonna be a bestseller-list-making household name."

The silence is deafening, followed by a few halfhearted claps. I feel thirteen again, eating in the bathroom, avoiding the riotous lunchroom at all costs.

Kat drops the needle back down. The music kicks on. The regulars, and my heart rate, return to business as usual.

"Hot pink's your color," Kat says, with a winged-tipped wink.

I touch my cheeks. They're on fire.

"C'mon, we're celebrating." She raises her voice again. "Lattes on the house."

The room erupts in applause. Sharp whistles startle me. I turn to see Kevin Donnelly, a retiree with a head of silver hair that sticks out from his navy and red ball cap. He peeks up from his paper with a pleased grin that is his full smile.

"Hey, hey. That's what I'm talkin' about."

"Dad, you don't even drink lattes," Kat remarks.

"How about ah dahk roast then? One sugah."

She sends a smile over her shoulder. His grin slips behind the crisp shuffling of paper.

"Grab your spot," Kat directs and passes me a bottle of water.

When she returns behind the counter, Mr. Donnelly starts chatting.

"Rawry, how's yah faucet workin' these days?"

"Haven't had a leak since you fixed it," I reply. "Thanks again."

"Don't mention it."

"Fitz is still terrified. I had to move his litter box away from the bathroom."

Mr. Donnelly chuckles. "Bet he is. That cat of yahs was soppin' wet."

Poor Fitz caught the brunt of a pipe burst. Luckily, Kat's dad was on the scene to help, like he does with all the neighborhood residents.

"Congrats, kid. When will I get to read yah book?"

"You read romance, Mr. Donnelly?" I ask, concealing my shock.

"Yahs will be my first."

"Thank you. Well, you'll be the first person on my advanced copy list." I knock on the wood table in front of him, not wanting to get too ahead of ourselves here.

Kat returns, dropping off her dad's coffee and linking her arm through mine. "I want all the details."

We make our way to the best view in the house. I sink into the ruffles of a matted-down velour armchair, positioned behind a large storefront window. "Memory Lane" is painted in swooping powder blue letters that mirror the sky's soft edges when they blend into low-hanging clouds. The street is lined with triple-deckers, foot traffic, and at a distance, the lights at Fenway Park are visible at night.

"Hello, neighborhood," I whisper.

It's quintessential fall in New England. The postcard kind, with hints of burnt orange and apple yellow foliage. A nipping invitation in the air to step outside and be a part of it all.

This is my favorite season in Boston—distinct flavors, hometown pride, traditions and trophies—a potion crafted of nostalgia and that intoxicating feeling of connection I've got to every sight, smell, and sound. And it's not solely about its incredible, rich history etched in every brick, on every building, on every street.

It's a city I can get lost in and still call home.

"I'm gonna grab our coffees and scones." Kat hops up and heads back to the counter. It doesn't take long to hear the frother sputter and hiss.

When Kat bought this place, she turned the key to a dump. Wall-to-wall red shag carpeting stained from winter street slush. Where I would've lit a match and never looked back, Kat saw potential. She gutted the space and restored its original flooring. She added mismatched chairs, tea tables, and a collection of vintage cups and plates. The walls are decorated with postcards, concert stubs, and photos. A low bookshelf with the sign "bring and borrow" rests against the right side of the wall. It operates on the honor system. Kat says, "Books are meant to be shared." I think her memories are too.

Shortly after I settled into my place on Chelsea Street, I'd walk by construction on my way to work, inhaling the fumes of paint sticking to summer air. Until one day, the magical scent of dark espresso roasting wafted all the way up into the tiny kitchen window of my third-floor apartment.

I ran into Memory Lane much like I did today, ordered a cinnamon latte, and fell in love with a bulletin board with a few scraps of paper tacked on. These days, those scraps overlap in a mosaic of pastels and permanent ink, displaying a collection of lyrics, one-liners, and words to live by.

Sometimes, I reach to reorder them, like a curator, so that they can be fully appreciated. Yet, I know there's something in Kat's cluttered chaos that makes this wall of quotes a piece of art, and altering it would be like removing a wild animal from its natural habitat, a travesty.

The iron table base wobbles as Kat places our scones and lattes down.

"Hey, when you get all fancy and famous, we'll take a trip to Ireland. We can check out the scone scene and pub hop our way across the island. Kiss the Blarney Stone."

"You had me at scone," I say.

Kat laughs. "Yeah, maybe even find ourselves lucky."

"Can you imagine meeting *the one* in such a romantic country?"

Kat pauses, holding her breath.

"Finding my own happily ever after." My lashes bat over my latte.

"I think the lack of caffeine has caught up to you."

"Perhaps," I confess, in a daydream of hand scenes and meet-cutes.

"I'm talking about a guy to grab a Guinness with, maybe shoot some darts. Definitely not ride off into the sunset material."

"Hazard of the job," I rationalize, defending the fairy tale fantasy tendencies I often find myself in.

"I'm so excited for you, Ror. Let me check out this letter again."

I pass it to her, wondering if living in my head for most of my life has skewed my view of romantic relationships.

Ideas start off in your subconscious and become aspirations over time. I'm not naive, but I also believe in something I can't define, so writing is how I work through it. And I'm not the only one. There's a billion-dollar industry looking for answers.

"We've talked about this so many times. Love in real life," Kat grabs her latte off the table and leans back, "is like baking. You can't throw random ingredients together. It has to be the right mix of timing and chemistry and compatibility. And the kiss. The first kiss has to be hot. None of this pecking nonsense like my parents do." Kat nods over at her dad drinking his coffee and finishing his paper.

"You also can't break it down like that. Love isn't fixed. Love is the variable." I cut my scone into quadrants, picking up a quarter, and add, "*The one* describes a feeling. Like slipping into the most comfortable sweater, it simply fits better than the rest."

Kat's blank stare says what she's thinking.

I consider reaching over and rolling her eyes for her.

She places her cup on the table and leans in closer into me. "Tillie let you watch too many princess movies growing up. Love is not always romance. Relationships are work." She pauses for a bite of her scone. "You better be taking notes, so you can use all this in your book."

"Well, if your theory is true, I don't have to write any of your realist relationship tips, because I'm writing fiction." I shove a piece of scone into my mouth and chew in pride, while my foot rattles under the table.

The mid-morning sun is warm on my legs, and my cinnamon latte is perfection. The steam coaxes a genuine smile from my lips, and for the first time since I held the letter myself, my shoulders relax too.

I've read about the places I want to travel to. As a kid, during recess, I'd make wishes on weeds, plucking petals. *If only I could be invisible, left to my imaginary worlds and words.* That's all I wanted then. To escape into stories.

I do think perhaps I made that wish one too many times. And I can't help but wonder if maybe we spend our entire lives on the receiving end of all that we ask for.

"Hey, so have you told your mom yet?" Kat asks.

"I will," hesitating, "tomorrow night at dinner."

"Can I tag along?" She's salivating for the free entertainment. "I'd never say no to her cooking and a Rory-Tillie showdown."

Because she knows—my mom will have a reaction.

"She's going to flip out. Maybe I shouldn't tell her."

"Maybe she'll be supportive."

"Maybe the sky is orange."

"Maybe she'll surprise you."

"Who's spinning fairy tales now?" I tease, shaking my head.

"By the way, this is amazing," Kat says.

She nods her head. "You're gonna be working with a mentor who also writes romance. So, are we excited about your match?" She peeks under the table at my feet rattling the base. "Nervous?"

I push my shoes firmly into the floor.

"He's a really big deal," I reply, chewing on my lip.

"And that's bad?" she questions. "And we don't like this because?"

"I wasn't expecting my mentor to be that guy. One whose books I've read too many times. I mean, they're all bent spines in my bedroom, Kat."

"And?"

"Stories I know by heart." My thoughts sound irrational. My eyes dart around the room.

"And?"

"I guess I wasn't prepared to be matched with an author of his caliber . . . you know, with so much," I stumble over my uncertainty, "experience."

"Isn't that a good thing?" she presses, as I continue to dance around denial. "So what if you fangirl a little? I'm sure all authors are used to that. You could totally get him to autograph those books by your bed."

I want to come up with an equally sarcastic retort, but I'm running on post-adrenaline empty.

The bell on the front door chimes. Kat checks and waves goodbye to the people leaving. There's only a few of us left in the café.

"I'd be more comfortable talking to a woman. You know, about certain scenes."

"You mean sex scenes, Rory?"

I roll my eyes.

"Well, my guess is you gotta get real comfortable, real quick. And so what? He's a professional. I'm sure he's done this a million times."

Kat starts vigorously typing into her phone.

"What are you doing?" I ask, shifting in the chair.

"While you're busy taking all your nerves out on the base of my table, I'm taking action."

I pry over her shoulder and see she's pulling up a browser with Reed's name in the search engine. "You're cyber-stalking him?" I spit out.

"It's the age of digital research. It's not like I'm driving by his house."

As Kat scrolls, my insides twist. I turn back to the window.

Vetting someone online before meeting them has never settled with me. It feels invasive and meeting someone naturally and discovering who they are, layer by layer, is where the magic exists.

There's not much in this world that we get to be surprised by anymore, but slowly learning about someone as they choose to expose themselves to you feels like one of the last sacred rituals on earth.

But she's right. It's the twenty-first century. It's simply research.

Anyway, it's probably smart to know a little bit about the person I'll be working with, aside from his jacket bio.

"I see what's really going on here," Kat says, and I scooch closer to get a better look.

It's a photo of Reed Ashton by a lake, crouched down next to a golden retriever.

He's wearing a navy blue and gray plaid shirt. The sleeves are rolled up to his elbows.

His eyes are covered under a faded Red Sox hat. A warm smile nestled in the middle of shadowy stubble.

Kat side-eyes me and returns her attention back to the screen. "This guy could grace the covers of his books. You're not worried about his bestseller status. You're freaking out that Reed Ashton has Rory Wells written all over him."

"You're so off the mark." I see her radar has finally switched on. I chug my coffee.

She raises her eyebrows at me, not buying a word of it.

"Obviously I see what he looks like. But I only care about how he can help my book."

"Maybe he'll come and rescue you from the depths of the writing trenches."

"You need to stop right now," I beg, swallowing amusement I shouldn't be entertaining.

"I've never seen you at such a loss for words. I bet that he's—"

"I'm not into him." My voice cracks and is unconvincing at best.

"With a face like that, he could sell me thin air."

I throw my head back in defeat. "It's fine. It'll be fine. I'm fine."

She puts her hand on mine. "Listen, you've wanted this for so long. You're not going to let a hot guy or me giving you grief get in the way. Anyway, it's all online, right?"

"Good point." I stretch my legs. "I bet that's why their previous mentees land agents so quickly too, because of how awesome their mentors are."

"His last post is dated two years ago. That's odd," Kat points out.

"He hasn't published a book since then either. It's like he fell off the map."

Kat hops up and takes our empty cups to the counter.

She returns with a paper sack and places my half-eaten scone inside it. She rolls the top down and hands it to me.

"You may have hit the mentor jackpot. Think about Stevie," she adds, gesturing to her concert tee. "Her mentor was Tom Petty."

"A true collab made in the music heavens."

The bells chime again. Two men in charcoal suits head to the counter.

"Talk to ya later," Kat says.

I get up and give her a hug. "I don't know if I'm prepared enough."

"This is your moment, and sometimes it's good to go off-script. Hey, especially with a costar that looks like that."

"You're never going to stop, are you?"

"Probably not. Love ya."

She might not extract the admission she's looking for from me, but she definitely earns a smile.

I wished for this opportunity and everything it comes with. I'll write until my fingers fall off. I'll eat, sleep, breathe this story. Nothing else matters but finishing, and nothing will get in my way this time.

I wave, then step outside. Traffic has picked up. My eyes close. I tilt my face toward the sun, soaking in what's left of morning.

I count on an inhale, *one, two, three, four*. Kat always finds a way to remind me that I won't lose my balance if I look up every once in a while. I release the breath, *five, six, seven, eight*, and check both ways before crossing.

2

RORY

"What's past is prologue."
—William Shakespeare

Boston suburbs on a Sunday are pin-drop quiet. Families tucked safely in their colonials, where Volvos and minivans live.

The walk from the train station to their house takes ten minutes. I use the time to rehearse my pitch.

I know my sudden life change is going to come as a surprise, but I didn't want to say anything until I knew it was a sure thing.

Being an author had always seemed like an unreachable dream meant for the lucky few. So, I went to college for cultural newswriting and reporting, while flirting with fiction in my dorm room. I knew I wanted to travel and write. To immerse myself in other countries, live multiple lives in one, and journalism was my ticket. It was my one brilliant plan.

During my final year at college, I was assigned a feature article on how terrorism changed tourism in New York. That one quest to uncover the truth sent me down a rabbit hole of crash statistics and indisputable facts.

The stricter regulations and preparedness didn't comfort me at all. I knew once I stepped on that plane, I surrendered my safety to someone I didn't know. Sometimes, having all of the information is the worst-case scenario. The fatalities and funerals. The missing persons. The randomness and risk. The roulette of it all.

I've tried a few times to fly. Bought the ticket once, even made it as far as the gate, but never got on. It didn't take me long to learn, as I watched my savings account deplete, that plans don't always lead in the direction you steer them toward.

So, the summer I spent after college living at my mom's, having to endure her daily lectures about the importance of security, sent me straight into the arms of the first job I was offered that paid enough to get me out from under her scrutiny. The job at Down & Route had a desk, health insurance, and a vending machine. It got me my own place.

Plan B became plan A.

It was supposed to be temporary. It wasn't writing, but the ad team did share a copy machine with the writing department, so sometimes I'd linger and catch the news.

I make my way up the stone walkway right at seven, clasping the iron knocker on the cherry-red door, before remembering I have a key. Whatever her reaction is, I'm going to stand my ground.

It also wasn't always like this. Me, keeping secrets from Mom. Existing in a routine without creative expression. I wasn't always uninspired. I had words. Words were my first friends.

I slip inside the house, working to remove my layers, hanging them on the mahogany hall tree's highest hook. My oversized scarf drops to the floor in an uncontained pile. I found it at a second-hand store down the street from Kat's, and couldn't resist it in a bin by itself. It deserved a good home.

The house is warm and autumn scented, like one of those teasing seasonal candles you want to take a bite out of.

I head to the bathroom, passing by the main staircase and wall of paintings, where large frames of coastal towns, vineyards, and food reside. I can hear Mom in the kitchen. She lives in the kitchen. She used to work in them too. That's how she met my step-dad, Arty Barron. He was the first person to give my mom a serious job, running the desserts at one of his hotels on the Cape. He found Mom's fervor for pastries and presentation, amongst other things, undeniable.

A year later, he gave Mom a new last name and a permanent address in Waverly, Massachusetts, a historic town outside of Boston, littered with manicured lawns and white picket fences. Arty's been in my life as long as he wasn't. He's the closest thing to a dad I've ever had. He's a caring and good man who quietly loves Mom and is happy to let her shine in every situation.

"Aurora, honey, is that you?" Mom calls in a sing-song voice.

"Yeah."

"Dinner's almost ready."

Bright pink cheeks and glassy eyes stare back at me in the mirror of the tiny powder room off the hallway. I pump two squirts of soap into my hands and warm them under the water.

Rory, you've got this. Rip it off, just like a Band-Aid.

State the facts. Facts don't have feelings.

I splash some water on my face and breathe into the soft hand towel on the wall, holding it in place. My inhale halts in my chest at the sound of knocking. If I keep pressing, I might accidentally cut off my air supply, pass out, and miss having to tell them. Seems like a reasonable backup plan to me.

"That train must've been late today," Mom whines behind the door.

I press harder. "Can you please grab me some Advil? I have a bit of a headache."

"I'll bring them to the table. Lexie is setting out the napkins and placemats." Mom's heels click down the hallway.

Her life now is unrecognizable from the nomadic diet she raised me on. I grew up eating off of roadmaps, not placemats.

I was sixteen, with a new house, a new life, and a new version of Mom. Everything about her grew louder as I disintegrated into a whisper, left to the safety of make-believe.

My hand glides along the smooth dark wood banister on my way into the dining room. The walls are royal blue and a brass chandelier hangs above an eight-person formal rectangular table, fit for the royal family.

I take my seat to the right of Arty, who's sitting at the head of the table. Mom and Lexie are across from me. On the wall behind them is one of our annual family portraits. We're in the garden surrounded by peach roses, coordinated in matching denim, contorted in positions that look more like a bag of giant blue pretzels than poses.

I pop the Advil.

"Rory, good to see you, kiddo," Arty remarks, picking up his fork. His salt and pepper hair is smoothed down and shines like a silver dollar. His skin stays tan well into the winter from summers spent on the golf course.

"What a day." Mom sips her chardonnay.

"Hey, Ror." Lexie's voice slips into the mix of people greeting me all at once.

I smile hello and start eating. Saving my energy to fight this headache and prepare for battle, wondering which will prevail.

"Tillie, aren't you going to enjoy this lovely meal you prepared?" Arty gently suggests since Mom hasn't picked up her fork yet.

I'm not entirely sure if he's genuinely concerned with her daily caloric intake or if he's trying to do us all a solid by keeping her mouth occupied. My mother is petite and doesn't need much to keep her going. I swear she runs off enthusiasm and a daily word quota.

Like her preference for talking over eating and any of her pint-sized genes, I didn't inherit much from my mom. I don't ever ask her if I look like my biological father. I assume by default I must have been the dumping ground for his chromosomes. Chestnut hair and prominent features, as opposed to Matilda's fair and delicate ones. We're opposites in every way possible.

I take a bite of roasted potatoes.

"Mom, this is so yummy." Lexie shoots me a silly face across the table.

"Thank you, Lex. Are you enjoying your dinner, Aurora?" she asks. "Butternut squash is the first of the season. I picked them up from the farmer's market yesterday."

"Rosemary." I smile.

Her food could win awards. Her mother taught her, and over the years she's tried to pass it on to yours truly. She once bought me a cooking class in the North End after I managed to ruin a simple lasagna one night. Don't ask me how those noodles didn't cook. It's a running joke now, *Oh Aurora, she can't even boil water.*

"We could try out the recipe together. It's easy."

My knife stills inside a potato.

"Yeah, maybe." She's always pushing. A pulse pounds twice between my eyes. She won't accept there are some things I'm not good at.

Arty places a hand on my left arm. "How's work this week?"

I'm grateful for Arty's ability to read the room. His kindness invites me right out of my pounding head and into the present moment, where I'm confronted by the elephant in the room I need to address.

I face Arty's gentle turquoise eyes.

"Well, I'm giving my two-week notice tomorrow." Not how I planned to say it, but there it is. Nothing I can do about it now.

The room stops breathing. I can hear Mom's blood bubbling beneath the surface.

I open my bag, pulling out the acceptance letter. I lay it on the table. Arty picks it up and gives it a once-over.

"So, I applied to a writing program this summer and found out yesterday that the spot's mine. It's an intensive six months working with a mentor, and then my manuscript will be ready to query agents." I take a drink of water. "So that's my news." I throw up jazz hands.

Lexie does too.

I dive back into eating. Safer to fill my mouth at this point.

"That's your plan?" Mom interjects.

I place my fork down. Chew. Swallow. "It's a plan, yes. Why?"

"Well, for one, you don't leave your job without securing another one first. Tell her, hun." Mom wiggles her free fingers in the air. Her other hand remains firmly on the stem of her glass.

"I need to have my submission ready by March. It's October."

"Submission, what?" she asks.

There's no point in trying to explain any of this to her. The ceiling's stark white and sterile. I count down in my head like I'm laid open on the operating table, waiting for the anesthesia to kick in.

I mutter, "Five, six, seven, eight."

"Are you seriously grounding? Aurora, I'm asking you questions because I—"

"That's so exciting, Rory," Lexie chimes in. "Can't wait to read it."

This isn't supposed to be happening this way. I was going to say my piece, they were going to be disinterested or minimally invasive, and then I was going to take my warm apple crisp home and digest it in peace.

"Lexie. I do not appreciate being interrupted, and Aurora," she looks from Lexie back to me, "am I hearing you correctly that your plan is to have no consistent income?" She claps her hands together. "You're not twenty-two anymore. You haven't said a word about writing a book in a decade. You have responsibilities and you need health insurance for stuff, your stuff," she emphasizes.

"Do I need to know this exact second, like over dinner," I reply, straining my voice, activating my inner six-year-old.

I've still got this. I'm in control.

Adult Rory gets back in the driver's seat.

"The plan is to get through the program and see where I'm at, and maybe I'll get a book deal with an advance, or maybe I'll work for Kat part-time. Then, I'll purchase my own health insurance. But none of that can happen if I don't have a query-ready manuscript. I have to start at step one. And thanks for having zero confidence in me."

I shove a heaping spoonful of food into my mouth, not even caring what it is, and hold back vomiting it all over the ivory linen.

Mom's face freezes like one of her still-life paintings hanging in the hall. Even her smile lines are frozen in a frown.

"Rory," Arty says, cautiously stepping into the line of fire, "we all know you'll knock it out of the park. I think what your mom is asking and what we'd both like to know is, how can we help?" He stops, then adds, "Do you have enough saved up?"

I pull in a deep breath and let it seep out. "I'm good, thanks. I've been saving since I knew I was going to apply. Should be enough for—"

"Should be?" Mom scoffs. "You cannot quit your job you've been at for years. What if one of those feature spots opens up and you miss your chance? You haven't thought this through."

She pours another glass.

My salivary glands promptly die. I release my lock grip on my fork, placing it down on the plate.

Has she just met me?

That's all I've been doing—thinking—about this. I've weighed the pros and cons. So I didn't map out health insurance, an oversight on my part, but I'm also a pretty healthy person and I've been in a stable place.

"I want to commit to this full-time and give it my undivided attention. It's exhausting working and trying to squeeze writing in," I add, twisting my napkin in my lap. *One, two, three, four.* "I don't need you discouraging me, telling me that I'm setting myself up to fail." *Five, six, seven, eight.*

"Here we go again." Her voice escalates and a hand waves for effect. "How many times have we gone over this? You can't blame your feelings on everyone else. Your fears only have the power that you give to them. If you think you'll fail, that's on you."

Did I miss my off-ramp?

How are we now talking about the things she knows I've worked so hard to recover from? My hands push into the tops of the table, slipping along its waxed surface.

"How about," and I use air quotes to drive my point home, "'my anxiety' doesn't work like that. It's fruitless to fight. It's never going away. It's who I am. It's a part of me that I live with. And naming my feelings and validating them is what takes their power away. When those feelings are heard, I'm able to regulate."

"Aurora, I simply meant—"

"Honestly, you have no idea how competitive this program is to get into or what it means that they chose me."

I stand up fast, battling the pressure in my head.

Lexie freezes, calculating Mom's next move, which will determine hers, alternating glances back and forth between us. I can't bear to look at Arty.

"Thanks for dinner," I project with absolute sarcasm, grabbing my plate and walking away from the remnants of my outburst, which I've left behind on the table.

Each step to the kitchen sink is excruciating. I couldn't even hold it together for one meal.

I should be able to manage varying degrees of conversation after years of therapy. I knew telling her would be disastrous. She's like a predator. Inviting smile, playing to your senses, and then she gets a whiff of any vulnerability and attacks, jumping on her prey, asking a million questions, drawing conclusions, and making assumptions.

A cool hand touches my cheek. The plate slips from my soapy hands and shatters at the bottom of the sink.

"Are you kidding me?" I don't know whether to laugh or to cry. I reach my hand in.

"Don't." Mom yanks it out. "You'll cut yourself. Let me get my rubber gloves."

I step aside and dry my hands on a kitchen towel. Mom's gloved up and already sweeping shards of porcelain from the sink into the trash.

"Aurora, you need to listen to me," she asserts, staying busy.

"So you can tell me how you don't approve of my decisions. Got the memo loud and clear five seconds ago."

"It's impossible talking to you when you're in a loop."

"Right. I'm the problem. You know, I came over here excited and with good news, and you shot me down before hearing me out."

"I support you wanting to write a book. It's the how to get there part I'm asking you to consider."

The kitchen towel chokes in my grasp. I close my eyes.

She doesn't trust my decision-making, that's what this is all about.

No publisher is going to come knock on my door because of a blog I sometimes update. The market is saturated with writers like me, trying to put their stories out into the world, and now I have a real shot at getting closer to being the one percent.

"I see those stars in your eyes. I know those stars, and I don't want to see you make the same mistakes I did."

The stabbing pain in my head returns.

When I abstain from replying, she fills the silence with more of the same, which isn't an apology.

I know she's speaking, but I can't hear anything past *mistake*, and it's a slow rickety Ferris wheel in my head.

Mistake, mistake, mistake . . . I'm not her, and before I know what I'm saying, it's out and I can't take it back.

"I'm not nineteen and pregnant."

She pauses, then drops the last of the broken pieces in the trash can and leaves me in the kitchen, reeling in place.

I rush to the door to grab my coat. Mom's footsteps disappear up the stairs.

"See you later," I call out to Arty and Lexie, avoiding facing their reaction to my episode, and close the door behind me.

Once I'm down the block, I sprint as fast as my legs will go and turn onto Chestnut Street.

I lower my shoulders enough to pull my coat on. I wait for the D train under the streetlamp glow.

"M-i-s-t-a-k-e."

It couldn't have been easy raising a child when she was only a kid herself, and I know I didn't fit into the life she chose with Arty, having a new baby, starting over, but I never once allowed myself to believe that she regretted having me.

I'm finally pursuing something I might actually be good at. I'm going to show her, prove to her, that nothing will stop me from finishing this time.

She's right, I'm not twenty-two anymore. Maybe I should get on a plane, but that's not the priority. My book is. And writing doesn't require a passport. Writing is the passport.

✳

When I'm tucked under the covers, my confidence from earlier wanes, and is replaced by a revolving door of questions I don't have answers to.

I make a mental list of what I know and what I don't. Fitz is nestling beside me. I pet his tuxedo coat and close my eyes to the high and low range of his purring. It vibrates against my skin.

Though the program has a successful track record of pairing mentors and mentees, I don't know if I'm capable of sharing thoughts, the kind you delve into during the creative process, with a man, and a stranger to boot. Intentionally, I've opted not to have a single male doctor. If I'm not comfortable having a man look at the outside of me, how will I ever handle having one intimately acquainted with the parts of me I don't show anyone else?

Ms. Healy, the program coordinator, did recommend being proactive about time management and communication.

Even the thought of typing "hello" to Reed Ashton leaves my fingertips tingling. They are bracing themselves at the starting gate, ready to sprint off to the finish line.

As apprehensive as I am about him being who he is, beneath the surface is a whispering excitement, an impatience to begin.

Impulsively, I hop up and grab my laptop from the desk before I can talk myself out of it. "I'm just doing my homework," I convince myself, and type his name, *Reed Ashton, author*, into the search engine.

The results return a handful of articles and social media platforms I scroll past. I select a link.

It's been two years since Reed Ashton, bestselling romance author, published his last book in the Cupid *series. Fans want to know, is he laying down his bow & arrow for now or for good?*

I scan the article, reading select lines.

Mr. Ashton is a poignant storyteller who captures his readers' hearts with his sweet and sexy style. A sprinkle of naughty throughout his books, you can't help but want to be on the top of Cupid's nice list.

A surprise snort and giggle escapes from the apparent teenager who lives inside me. Followed by an eyeroll from the thirty-year-old.

Next, I check out his website and stare at the only photo on the page.

My pulse quickens as I enhance the image—a man typing at a desk in a room with one window.

Aside from a head of full hair, his profile is barely visible. I squint to see if I can make out any of the words he has typed. Somehow, he's saying something here and a wave of desire to uncover its truth washes over me. His strong jaw and pensive gaze, and his fingers touching keys.

That one simple act that I know contains everything.

Next to his picture is a list of awards, *#1 Bestselling Author; Romance Novel of the Year, 2014, 2016; Eden Books Debut of the Year, 2012; Regional Book Critic Award, 2012; Readers Choice, 2013;* and a brief personal message to his readers. I follow along with my finger like I'm learning to read for the first time.

As a curious eight-year-old, I liked to play in my Uncle Lew's office, cloaked in dark intrigue, trophies, and books.

The smoky concoction of old books and dust invades my senses. Eight-year-old Reed immediately forms behind my eyes, tucked away, insulated from the outside world.

I'd create my own imaginary tales under his expansive desk. Hours would pass, lost to characters that I knew as friends.

Those moments built me into a storyteller. Along the way, I discovered that writing isn't a profession that I chose. It chose me.

In a world full of things that break, I want readers to feel whole when reading my stories. And if they blush along the way, I'm okay with that too.

I bring both of my palms to my cheeks.

Stepping away from financial security, possibly not finishing my book, having to find some other life-strangling desk job, proving my mom right, all these fears threaten to take over, but I'm resolved that this will be different.

I have a mentor invested in seeing me succeed.

And if an author I admire can show up for some rookie, I need to summon the courage to show up too. Like pledging an oath, but to myself. One I plan to keep at all costs.

3

REED

"WHATEVER CAUSES NIGHT IN OUR SOULS MAY LEAVE STARS."
—VICTOR HUGO

OCTOBER USED TO BE my favorite month up North.

Summer relented, taking with it the seasonal crowds, their traffic, and their noise. The lake quieted itself too, concealing the evidence of being abused all summer by boat engines and litter.

My hands are wrapped around the warmth of my cerulean blue coffee mug, a failed piece of art and my only attempt at a ceramics class.

As I look out the kitchen window at dawn over Berry Lake, there isn't a single ripple or sign of the thunderstorm that hammered our small New Hampshire town late last night.

The euphony of jays busy themselves, and the crisp air greets me through the cracked window.

I miss those early mornings—me, my kayak, and the water. Some of my best ideas came to life on our lake. I like to think the undisturbed expanse used to whisper inspiration to me as a reward for being gentle and kind to the habitat I knew I was merely a visitor in.

Its silence has become screams I can't shut out. *Ever.*

The coffee burns on the way down.

My phone vibrates inside my pocket. I swallow a small shudder before it escapes. *No one calls me this early.* Something must be wrong. My breath halts as I hold the receiver to my ear.

"Hello."

"Reed, hey, it's Cal," my agent says. I pull the phone away and squint at the screen to confirm. My breath releases with disorienting force, like a hostage running out of a building.

"How's my favorite romance author doing? How's the fam?" he asks. His high-pitched questioning lacks complete awareness of its decibel level. I set the phone on the kitchen counter, opting for speaker.

"We spoke two days ago," I remind him.

His labored breathing indicates to me that he's pacing the room. Unlike how Fenway, my golden retriever, alerted me to a storm coming, Cal is that storm.

"Right, we did. Well." He's stumbling, unlike him. "I have a favor to ask of you."

I cradle my mug in one hand, and pick at the peeling paint on the cabinet above me with the other. The inside of this house needs attention. Everything from the wood to the appliances is original. It's a time warp to my childhood. Shit, to Pops's childhood. I need to bump this up on the priority list of projects around the property.

"So, what do you think, Reed? You in?" Cal's voice breaks my mental catalog of lumber costs and stain swatches.

"Repeat that?" I close my eyes to hear him.

"I know it's a big ask, but it's only six months and it's all online. You'll guide the mentee through the drafting process and help get her query ready. Set her up for success and all that. Nothing we haven't done together. You could do it with your eyes closed."

My eyes snap open.

Fenway lays his entire sixty-five-pound frame at my feet. I reach down and rub his ears. Cal keeps talking, but I don't think I follow. Her? Mentee?

"I think you'd be a great fit for the task. You're made to mentor."

The last word sticks somewhere between my lungs and my ears. "Did you say mentor? As in a human being."

"Exactly. Eden's in a bind. Their slated author dropped out last-minute and they need a romance author for a romance writer."

Oh, there is absolutely no chance that person is me. "Cal, I'm not—"

"Listen, this is a zero-pressure situation. The program is short-term."

"I've got Emerson twice a week and the house. And what does it even matter to you if Eden's in a bind?"

"So, iron out a schedule that works for you," he counters.

I groan.

"They asked for you, and since they've been generous with us, I think this is a good move on our part to stay in their favor. Might make things smoother when you decide to get back in the game."

That's not going to happen. Aside from my commitment to my niece, no, just no. "Listen—"

Cal cuts me off from my third attempt at a pass. "Consider it a personal favor? You know, it would really help this girl out." He goes for the jugular.

I place the mug on the kitchen counter next to the phone and rake my hands over my face.

My eyes squint at the lake's reflective light, the surface resembling the top of a smooth river stone.

His voice softens. "I know how impossible this period has been for your family."

I blow out a short, hard sigh, pulling my fingers through my hair.

Cal's sympathy is genuine, and though it's appreciated, sympathy has become my least favorite of the well-meaning gestures over the past two years. Take the casseroles and the cards, leave the pity.

"The program has a stellar reputation, as you know. It's a good cause, Reed, with minimal effort on your part."

I shove my hands into my side pockets while Cal presses on.

"My understanding is that she shows real talent and promise. I mean, she was selected out of hundreds of applicants regionally. You could make a difference here." He tries to break me down until I bleed out.

Cal's been a great friend and agent for years. He supported my family through our hardest season and didn't push when I told him I wasn't writing anymore. Even when he thought all I needed was some time, he's never once made me feel like my responsibilities weren't important.

"What constitutes minimal?" I tread lightly, stepping over Fenway, dragging my mug along the exhausted lemon-chiffon colored counter to the coffeepot, and topping it off.

I lean against the metal edging, running out of reasons why I can't help.

"Emailing mostly. You'll proof chapters and provide feedback. Set up a timeline to get her on track to meet deadlines. It'll be like at LITA when you taught those writing workshops."

"Love in the Air was a lifetime ago." I laugh at the absurdity.

"So, you'll brush up first. Maybe run into inspiration of your own."

"Not interested," I grit out through clenched teeth. They fight back—*all lies, Reed, all lies.*

"I need verbal confirmation other than a grunt."

I'm definitely going to regret this. "Yeah, I'll help."

"Fantastic, man. I'll send over the info. Take care of yourself, and say hi to your mom for me. I dream about her blueberry scones all the time."

"You could've kept that last part inside."

Cal loves my mom—everyone does.

"Probably," he laughs. Not a single ounce of shame in his admission. He hangs up and I slide the phone back into my pocket.

"Let's go walk off that disturbing image, Fenway."

I pull on my hoodie and step onto the all-season porch. Fenway sprints through the front door, across the grass, and down to the water. My line of sight follows at a slower pace. Cal dreaming of my mom isn't the only thing I need to walk off. What the hell did I get myself into?

When we get back, I fill Fenway's water bowl, placing it by his spot on the oval rug in front of the door. Worst spot ever, but he's claimed it, so we make it work. "Here ya go, buddy."

The living room couch is backed up against a large window. The mid-morning sun heats the cushions, inviting me to give in to a nap. I put my glass on the end table, next to a stack of suspense and romance hardbacks. My body stretches the length of the couch.

This room is held together by stories. Some line bookcases, others are scattered on tables, the mantel, even the floor.

Outside of Saturday morning cartoons, in place of a remote, Mom put either a book or a bat in my hand and told me not to return until supper. She kept things running while taking care of me, and my younger sister, Carlynn. She managed the house, the garden, and the blueberry patch.

My father worked as an attorney in Boston, and lived in the city during the week. He came back home on weekends. He did what he had to do to provide for his family. Our life was simple. I was taught to not want for more than I already had.

I make a mental note to save a pile for Emerson and donate the rest to Berry's public library. No sense in them sitting here to be door stops. I check my phone for Cal's follow-up email, hitting the main points.

Good talk today. See program info below. I've also attached the draft the mentee submitted in her application.
Thanks again, man, and keep me posted.
Cal

Eden Books Mentorship Program, 2018:
Your mentor will see you through the revision process, act as your coach in voice and skill, and offer critique feedback. Your mentor will help you complete your manuscript on deadline and assist you in polishing your query letter for submission.

"Minimal involvement feels a lot like a massive undertaking right about now," I call out to Fenway in the kitchen. "I think Cal has lost his damn mind." I'm halfway through cursing Cal in my head when a name at the bottom of the screen stops my train of expletives. *Rory Wells.*

I curiously follow the link into Eden's portal. It takes me into a space that looks like a messaging app with Eden's tree logo designed in vines. There's an unopened message. My fingers hesitate over the keys.

Fenway appears at my side, nudging my knee, and rests his head on my leg.

Sometimes, I wonder which one of us is really comforting the other. I update the notifications to forward directly to my personal email.

"Wish me luck." Not even convinced it will help.

His playful brown eyes frown at me like he doesn't recognize the pessimist in front of him. I don't blame him. I hardly recognize myself.

How am I going to help this girl? I'm stale. My knowledge of the industry isn't relevant anymore.

Fenway's bark pulls me off the couch before I can read the message. I close the browser and head to the door.

My Uncle Lew and his black lab, Gunner, are lugging up the gravel drive with full hands, as usual.

Uncle Lew hands me Tupperware with a dozen blueberry scones. Fenway takes off and the two pups chase each other across the lawn.

"She knows I'm only one person here, right?"

Lew chuckles through closed lips, shaking off dirt that's collected on the hem of his navy trousers from the walk down the hill. "You're her only son. Plus, we can't keep up with half of what she bakes as it is. Convenient you live so close."

I take a seat in one of the four oak Adirondack chairs on the patio. The wood creaks beneath my weight.

"Still my favorite view in this part of the state," Lew remarks. The lake in front of us spans the entire width of our land, encompassed by sixty-foot pines.

I don't comment on how much I hate the view now. How deafening the silence is.

He uses his boot to grind fresh dirt into the cracks between the stones.

"Can't stand here and not think of him." Lew smiles, lost to a memory, and I kick at the firepit, actively avoiding one. "Your Pops, on his hands and knees that whole summer. There was a heat wave and he wouldn't quit, not till it was done."

Uncle Lew and Pops were best friends and neighbors growing up. They were also partners in their law practice for thirty years. On Saturday mornings, Uncle Lew, Carlynn, Pops, and me would take to the water before dawn. Mom and Shira, Lew's wife, would stay back to chat small-town gossip over strong coffee and blueberry scones.

Whether we were playing marathon gin rummy games on rainy afternoons or learning how to tie slip knots and fly kites in the wind, Uncle Lew and Aunt Shira were a permanent fixture in my childhood, and I can't think of any memories without them. We were family.

"Would've liked to see that," I reveal, thinking about how Pops spent his life building things that lasted.

"Yeah, well, you were where you were supposed to be. Enjoying all that Italian vino and living your life like a twenty-year-old should be."

I roll my neck from shoulder to shoulder and get up to crack a beer.

"You want one?" I ask, pulling a lager from the mini fridge on the porch and sliding back into my spot. Lew passes. I nudge around some loose dust with my unlaced boot, looking at uneven rows of stone and cement. "I haven't kept up with it enough."

"He'd be happy to see it being enjoyed. Can't believe it's been twelve years."

"Yeah." His absence weighs like a kettlebell in the center of my chest. I shake my head absentmindedly, but it doesn't go unnoticed.

"You know, Junior, no one ever knows shit. Not at eighteen, not at your thirty-two, hell, not even at my ripe old retired age. But if I may." He pauses, settling into the adjacent chair, facing me, waiting until my eyes are locked on his. "Time is the greatest gift, and not a single second past this one is guaranteed."

Lew's forgetting I didn't know that at twenty. Thought I had all the time in the world to figure it out. We lost Pops a few years after losing Shira to breast cancer while I was in college. I tried then to give up my plans to study abroad, but Mom pushed me out the door and said she wouldn't let me back in the house without a stamp in my passport and a couple of pasta pounds packed on my pitcher's frame.

There should be some kind of trading rules in the Universe, where you can't draft from the same team within back-to-back seasons. We barely were catching our breath from one loss.

"You remember the letters I wrote you?" I ask Lew, pulling another swig from the bottle. The crisp carbonation rips down my throat.

"How could I forget?" He leans his head to the left. "I had a good challenge working through all that Italian. Some of your best writing, if you ask me. It was like I was right there in Tuscany with you."

Like the lake, Italy lost its magic for me.

Somewhere between my taking a bite of hand-rolled cannelloni and swallowing, Pops had a massive heart attack in bed while sleeping. There was nothing anyone could've done. That's what everyone said to us. But grief wraps around your mind and twists the story to make room for any scenario in which something could've been done.

I tore myself apart for years, looking for missing details. Ransacked his medicine cabinet, had the house tested for mold, even saw a therapist for a while where I asked impossible questions, like does anyone pay close enough attention to know the exact second their lives will change forever? Are there signs, clues? Or is it all just random and meaningless?

I didn't feel any warning signs with Pops. I was simply eating across the world, happily joking around the dinner table, talking with my host family on a pleasant night, under a clear sky, illuminated by candlelight and a peppering of stars.

The therapist said some questions don't come with answers. I didn't find that helpful, so I stopped wasting my time and I stopped asking other people questions.

"You working on anything now?" Lew asks, shifting the conversation.

I use the sleeve of my hoodie to wipe along the rim of my eyes. "Nope."

A light wind picks up. "No point."

After we lost so much, Lew would come down the hill to check on Mom every day. She'd weep while weeding her vegetable garden, while doing dishes, or any mundane task. Sometimes, Lew would sit with her in silence. Other days, they'd have Arnold Palmers on the patio, nestled in these chairs, surveying the tree overgrowth.

As time went on, like it does unapologetically, they'd talk about the old days and keep each other company. I think mostly they were keeping the memories alive.

They live together now, as companions, and I wonder if you ever find that spark again after you've lost *the one*? What am I even thinking? *The one*. I drain my beer and toss it in the barrel.

Lew hands me a journal I hadn't noticed he was holding.

"What's this?" I ask, thumbing over the weathered binding.

"It's a lump of coal." He gives me the side-eye. "You know the rule in this family. Ask a throwaway question . . ." he advises, trailing off.

"You get a throwaway answer."

I wasted my breath on a pretty obvious question because I'm distracted. It's like my body is itching and I know the point of origin, but the target keeps moving and I can't get relief. How did I let myself get roped into this mess? I didn't have to come to the rescue. Who is this person I've become?

The minute anyone sends up a smoke signal these days, I rush to the call, working odd jobs around town.

I'm with my niece a few days during the week, and whenever my brother-in-law needs an extra hand at the brewery, I'm there tapping a keg. Busy keeps me standing.

"Stop by later, let your Mom get a good look at you." Two hard pats land on the back of my shoulders.

Lew whistles for Gunner and they leave, disappearing around the drive.

Fenway beats me through the door and back into the warm house. I drop the journal and scones on the counter. It has that loved exterior I know well. Someone kept this close. It lands next to the clutter—a bowl of keys, a Red Sox hat, a mason jar full of rocks, and a stack of unopened mail.

A ping notifies me that I have a new email. I'm eyeing my phone like it's a detonator. I need a plan, fast.

Mom always says, the simpler the ingredients, the better the food tastes. I'll keep it simple. Set clear boundaries, a mere transaction.

Mr. Ashton,

Hello. I'm Rory Wells. Nice to meet you.

I'm looking forward to this program and can't wait to get started. Currently, I'm working at an outdoor adventure magazine, and my last day is Friday, so I'm all yours after that. I have to tell you how much I admire your writing. I've read all your books. Your *Cupid* series is my favorite. The characters are complex, funny, and relatable. I think you create endings that are unpredictable, which makes them satisfying.

In my welcome packet, there's a list of twenty "Ice-Breaker" questions to get to know each other better. Did you want to try some of those first?

***What inspired you to write romance and what inspires you today?* Technically, two questions in one.**

Best regards,

Rory

Fenway's eyes stalk my laps around the room as I chase my thoughts. I'm breathing heavily, raking my hands through my hair.

I shoot up the stairs, two at a time, tossing my phone onto the nightstand. I blast the CD player in an attempt to hemorrhage the sweetness of her words from my head. I try to suffocate my conscience while I'm at it too, but not even the blaring sound of crisp, sharp rock music can drown out the impact of her question. How she managed to knock me on my ass is beyond me. Somehow Cal forgot to inform me that Ms. Wells also drinks liquid sunshine. Is she serious about those ice-breakers? Stopping the fantasy train this girl has hitched herself to is the only way.

After a few songs, I switch off the music and pick up an advanced copy of "Crafting" that my buddy self-published. I'd be envious of his collection of stories about brew culture, if I gave a shit about writing anymore. I close the book and drop to the floor for pushups. I'm working my way up to fifty in a row. Focusing on each strain and pull of my forearms, while my core engages and my thighs tighten, the forward lunge of my body stops me from slipping into the past.

Cal wants me to be a mentor? What a joke. I can barely focus on reading. I walk the three steps it takes to cross the room and pull open the top drawer of my dresser.

I see Pops's Sox jersey he'd wear all season long during home games. It's tucked away, inside a plastic bag. When I feel strong enough to miss him that deeply, I break the seal and breathe in. It destroys me every time.

That's not going to be today. Instead, I pick up the only story I can stomach reading. I glide my hands along the cover, which has faded into a gentle grayish purple. Whenever I hold it in my hands, the same thing happens. The summer sun greets me. I'd never seen anything as bright as that dress.

I carry her over to the rocking chair by the window and settle in. These pages are a world I can retreat to, like catching up with an old friend whenever I need one. And I need that, right now, to distract me from Rory's words, which haven't stopped playing on a loop in my head.

What inspired you to become an author? A question about a life I'm desperately trying to forget. I knew this mentorship was a terrible idea. My inspiration was swept away years ago, and there's no turning back to claim it.

4

RORY

"THE BEST WAY OUT IS ALWAYS THROUGH."
—ROBERT FROST

"THERE SHOULD BE A hard and fast forty-eight-hour turnaround on email replies." My frustration hits the pavement along with my running shoes, trying to keep up with Kat's sprinter's stride.

"It's not like an office. Maybe he operates on island time," she suggests, making our final loop over the Montgomery Bridge.

We collapse onto a grassy area, prime real estate, with a view of Boston's most beloved college campus. The sprawl of brick buildings and the gold clocktower as the backdrop to Kat's favorite landscape, the collegiate crew teams out on the river.

My breath syncs to the rhythm of their oars. *One, two, three, four . . . five, six, seven, eight.*

"Rory, hell-oooo." Kat swipes a hand in front of my innocent and obvious gawking.

I redirect my focus to her barely flushed face. "How do you do it?"

"Do what?"

"You run a few miles, chug some water, and manage to come out looking refreshed."

She drains her canteen.

"I, however, have the 'in need of medical attention' look."

Kat shakes her head at me, attempting to mask her laughter.

"What? You know it's funny. Seriously, on a scale of peach to tomato, what do I look like?"

"More beet than tomato. Magenta." She winks. "What's your deal anyway? You're in Ror-Ror-land more than usual."

My cheeks sting in the cool air while I run my fingers through blades of grass.

"I had vivid dreams last night."

"Oh yeah?" Kat leans her arms over her perched knees, covered in lime green. "Tell me," she breaks out into a sultry voice, "was it about a clothing-optional writing session, perhaps with a certain romance author?" Her face lights up like the one kid who cracks open the pinata. She stretches her legs out, folding into them.

"Stop it," I laugh, burying into my shins. "You're guaranteeing that I'll never be able to look at Reed Ashton."

"Hey, it wouldn't be the worst thing in the world. A little eye candy inspo. Isn't this writing gig supposed to be . . . fun?"

"Forget fun; I need a queryable manuscript. Anyway, I'm pretty sure Eden frowns on mounting your mentor."

"Well that escalated quickly, Rory. And I like where it's going."

"Kidding!" I push her arm, and she throws her hands in the air. "Katherine, can we focus on my dream?"

"If we must." She sighs.

"Thank you." I twist my body left and right, reaching my arms above my head.

"I can't believe you're still having those dreams, honestly. It's been a long time."

"Eight years. Replaying the same nightmare. Over and over again," I sneer, ridiculing myself.

Kat crosses her legs and looks out onto the glistening water. I know she's giving me space to vent and I'm grateful.

A quick sear inside my chest catches my heart off guard. All these years later and I still think about it, the first public anxiety attack I ever had, in the middle of hundreds of authors I admired.

"It was so embarrassing, running out of the ballroom like that," I recount, following the oars as they rise from the water.

Joggers pass in front of us, weaving through couples, strollers, and the occasional suit. The city has a distinct collective white noise that I find comforting.

"They were probably concerned. I don't think the average person notices anxiety attacks, not the way you think they do. Like the first time I saw your teeth rattle, I assumed you simply needed a cup of hot coffee."

I bring my thumbnail up to my mouth, and Kat swats it back into my lap.

"The dream always starts off with excitement, just like that day. Then it spirals into me waking up drenched in sweat, and screaming out for help, like a piece of myself has been stolen, something essential like a limb or major organ." I pause, realizing that the dream plays out with an alternate ending every time. And always is the farthest thing from what happened. *I never screamed for help.*

My eyes flood as my words transport me back to that brutal summer day, the kind that sticks to your skin. This is the part that hurts.

"An hour. That's all it took." My face warms with guilt. "I'll never forgive myself for being so careless."

Kat rubs my back in circles. "I know how traumatic that was for you, but you're here now, moving your body, getting all that out. Not letting the past dictate your future."

A natural smile breaks through the regret. "I am, aren't I?" I sit up straighter and wipe the moisture from my face. The heat from our run has worn off. "If Mr. Ashton would get back to me, I could maybe see a glimpse into that future."

"He's Mr. Ashton now? Those are some role-playing words, if I've ever heard any."

"You're never going to stop, are you?"

"I'm having too much fun." She smirks. "Hey, you do know that you have a voice in this situation. This is, after all, your mentorship."

I've been coloring in the lines my whole life. It didn't occur to me that I could do something other than wait and worry.

"They look good out there," Kat notes. She's not wrong.

I shove the aftershocks of reminiscing back into their compartment. I need to focus on the things that do matter, like finishing these edits before my money runs out and I have to find another full-time job or beg for my current one back, which would be excruciating.

My mom reminds me ad nauseam that living in a fantasy for too long can permanently distort reality.

In therapy, I've learned that reality is the safest place for me.

All I know is that I'm starting to experience racing thoughts. I shake out my hands and dig my sneakers into the ground. "I have to figure out why he seems to be more of a ghost than—"

"A real live boy," Kat interjects, making me laugh. "I'm impressed. It's been three days."

She leans into me. "I'm shocked there aren't actual sirens coming from your person."

"You can't hear them?" I tease, leaving out that I can feel them lurking. "I hate to come across as impatient or start this mentorship off on the wrong foot, but I think I should email him again to make sure he's in fact my mentor."

"I'm sure there's a reasonable explanation or like a glitch in the communication system or something."

"Maybe I'll email the program coordinator and see what she thinks." I'm avoiding the thought that keeps creeping up, and what it would mean if his lack of reply were a conscious choice, not a glitch. What if he's read the original draft I submitted in my application and hates it?

"Listen, send another friendly yet direct message. I mean, maybe he's busy writing his own book or something. Writers are reclusive like that."

"Ehm." I mock-cough.

"You know what I mean. They each have, like, their own magic process, right? Maybe his bag of tricks includes a disappearing act." Kat jumps up and starts jogging in place again.

The teams have passed and the sun is directly above us now.

"Would align with his lack of a social media presence too." I look up at Kat, shielding my hand over my eyes.

"See, you're totally handling this so well, Rory. I'm proud of you."

I don't have the heart to tell her that I'm already coming up with every possible worst-case scenario.

I'm frustrated with myself for allowing those thoughts to even surface.

"He's the one who signed up to be a mentor." The words come out louder than I intended. "Theoretically, a mentor wants to help," my voice raises, "yet I have no direction." I'm trying to go with the flow and trust this process. "This is not what I was expecting."

"Waiting around isn't in your wheelhouse, but give him the benefit of the doubt, make another attempt, and if you get crickets again, then request a new mentor."

"I'll sleep on it," I say, standing up.

"I suggest dreaming on it, and while you're dreaming, throw some Henry Cavill in there for me, please and thank you. All right, I'm too sweaty and gross. I'll see you tomorrow morning."

There's a lot of things Kat and I share with each other, but sweaty hugs aren't one of them.

I add, "Hey, don't forget Friday night."

"Wouldn't miss it. Can't wait to celebrate the start of something great for you."

It's official. My last week at Down & Route has arrived. Since I submitted my notice, my accounts have been handed over to other sales reps, leaving me without a single ad to work on. I'm basically a sitting duck until five o'clock today, so I made lists, created character playlists, and bleached my cubicle, twice.

Any personal trace of my time here has been thoroughly wiped clean.

Unfortunately, all this sitting around is giving me time to think. It's been five days since my last email, so I sent a follow-up to Reed

Ashton this morning. I kept it simple, asking what our next steps were.

The silence on his end is gnawing at me like a well-worked-over chew toy. I don't mind exercising patience as long as I know there's a game plan. We're on a deadline and the letter said to create a schedule first thing.

Well, it feels like *first thing* has expired.

I spin around in my desk chair, surveying the cubicles for a final time. Sometimes, when our boss takes an early lunch, my office buddy and gossip hub, Gavin, and I do wheelie races down the aisle. He's been at the company since it opened and knows everyone and everything that happens here. I wouldn't mind a final joyride.

The whole week has somehow triggered residual feelings of instability. I'm doing all my grounding exercises to keep myself regulated, but fear is knocking.

If I don't start revising now, I may not have enough time to finish. And if I don't finish, I won't be ready to query, and I won't be a part of the ninety percent that Ms. Healy claims go on to land agents within the first round of querying, which will set my timeline back even farther, and if I don't land an agent . . .

I have to stop thinking. I grab the pack of bleach wipes and go at my desk again. My face floods with warm tears that spill down my cheeks. I can't believe I'm crying in my cubicle. I want to blame it on the cleaner fumes, but that would be a lie.

If this mentorship isn't successful, I won't write anymore. It hurts too much to keep trying and failing at something I love.

Over and over, I told myself it was fate the first time, reminding me where I didn't belong. I'd gone to that signing years ago with enthusiasm and quickly deflated like a defective party balloon, and then I freaked out, and left it all behind.

Maybe some things in life are simply save-the-dates, not actual invitations. Some things are like what Kat mentioned, a glitch, and maybe the universe is trying to show me something.

The building is extra quiet when the wall clock strikes five o'clock. I duck into the bathroom, splash some water on my face, dab some lipgloss on, and wrap my hair up into a messy bun. It's a quick skip down the street to The Harp, and Kat already has our bartop table snagged when I walk through the door.

The place is dark, especially at night. The bar itself takes up the length of one wall. Illuminated green, amber, and clear glass bottles, and a medium-sized flat-screen rests in the middle of the liquor.

"Hey, hey! How's it feel to be free?" She greets me with espresso-infused enthusiasm.

"It still feels like a regular Friday," I reply. Freedom hasn't sunk in yet.

I left the office like I arrived, empty-handed and without a fuss. I got a couple of cards and hugs, but mostly, it was uneventful, with a bit of bickering over who got my chair.

"Well, we need to fix this," Kat commands, handing me a bottle of Blue Moon with a slice of orange shoved into its mouth. She's wearing her hair loose, and it falls over both shoulders, framing her warm complexion and welcoming smile.

I thank her with an air-kiss, pulling off my layers and settling onto the barstool. I lay my phone on the table, face-up, and check it for any notifications.

"Are you checking for him?" She reads my mind.

"Obviously, I'd get an alert. But I can't seem to stop obsessively checking to see if he's replied," I admit.

"I was wrong about that guy. Mr. Jerk-Face." Kat reaches over and yanks a loose piece of my air-dried hair. I lift my phone up to her line of sight, opening my camera app.

"Smile," I say.

"Um, what's happening?" Kat leans as far back as she can without falling off her stool.

"Just making sure there's photographic evidence of you admitting you were wrong about something." I grin and snap the shot. Her middle finger is strategically placed in front of her grimace.

I lay my phone down on the table, face-up again—wishful thinking—and raise my Blue Moon to my lips and swallow. The sweet hint of orange lingers on my tongue. The initial sip is hands-down the best. Every time.

"Be nice to me, otherwise I can't guarantee I won't embarrass you in front of all these people here. I've got a solid congratulatory speech all prepared." Kat talks over the jukebox music so I can hear her.

"No speech," I plead and worry at my bottom lip.

The Harp is our favorite neighborhood pub. There's enough room to sit now, but in an hour, it will be standing room only, and the floors will get sticky.

Lucky for us, the two bartenders on happen to be Kat's cousins, so it works in our favor. We don't wait for drinks all night.

"Sean's gonna let me up on the bar to do your sendoff right."

I chug my beer to hide my smile.

"So what's your plan with Mr. Disappearing-Act?"

"Is that what we're calling him now?"

"Yeah, you know I like to change it up. I can go back to 'jerk' if you like that better?"

"I think I'm mad-ish, or something. Mostly frustrated and uncertain," I confess.

"You *think* you're mad?" Kat's eyebrows lift.

My toes are tingling.

My pulse is hammering.

The tips of my ears feel screaming hot.

I look down at my chest, and it's full of flushed splotches. Thoughts slam into one another, a somersault of tangled emotion.

"Technically, it's go-time for my mentorship, and I don't even know if my mentor has a pulse."

"Time to tell him you're going to ask for another mentor. He'll either shit or get off the pot."

"I can't do that. Can I?"

"Why the hell not? You said so yourself—there's a timeline. I'm sure you can talk to that Healy chick about finding a different mentor. Someone you know has a heartbeat and responds to emails."

I pick up my beer and take the last swig. It wobbles off-balance when I place it back down on the table.

"Kat," Sean hollers from behind the bar. "Another round?" He circles his pointer finger in the air. She looks back at me for confirmation.

"You're right. I don't need Reed Ashton. He doesn't want to mentor me? I don't want to work with him either." I project over the raucous bar crowd. A familiar Irish tune fills the room. The space is packed now, bodies bumping, elbows rubbing, everyone singing off-key.

"You in?" Kat confirms.

I hold up my middle finger. "One more." This is a celebration, after all.

She raises her thumb over the crowded heads. Sean nods and brings us our beers.

"Cheers to obliterating comfort zones."

Our bottles connect. The first sip is as good as it was hours ago, maybe even a little sweeter going down.

Keeping her word, Kat slides off her barstool and hops right on top of that bar. She holds her bottle in the air, and whatever she's saying is drowned out by the crowd. The music is playing, the air is electric, and I see the scene like I see my characters, a classroom full of vulnerable young minds, bright, inspired, and promising to seize the day. *Carpe Diem.* And that's exactly what I plan to do.

5

REED

"My motto was always to keep swinging."
—Hank Aaron

Embedded in my DNA are the backroads of Berry. The route around the lake to my sister Carlynn's house most of all. I know where to turn, pause, stop, and when to slow down. It's muscle memory.

My truck bumps and sways along the uneven dirt and rocks. I learned how to drive at sixteen when I was dating bubbly Misty Anderson. Her parents didn't enforce a curfew, so we'd take late-night cruises for skinny dipping and pints of black raspberry ice cream from our local creamery. Her platinum locks matched the bright cone of high beams, so when I'd kill the engine to sample how black raspberries tasted off her lips, the silhouette of blonde hair was the only visible thing for miles.

I switch on my wipers to clear off the moisture saturating the windshield. It's early, and visibility is limited by a haze of shimmering mist. The reflection bounces off cluttered rows of white birch trees, peeling in a way that makes them look silver.

Twists and turns are a part of small-town living. If you're unfamiliar with this terrain, you shouldn't be driving it.

The residents don't push for the state to maintain these roads. I've tried to advocate for rails around the lake, but it gets voted down with bullshit excuses like it'll ruin the aesthetic. Even if they voted for upgrades, the state has its hands full. Every summer, the only road that manages to see any construction is the main highway that connects all of the towns in Northern New Hampshire to one another. Each year, same road, new patch.

When I get to Carlynn's, she's already stepping outside. We have a routine that works, and Fenway enjoys roaming the undisturbed woods here.

"Emmy hasn't woken up yet, but the fridge is stocked and her meds are on the counter."

"Got it covered."

"I'll be back after the brunch shift. Tell her I had to go in early." She heads to her car.

My voice projects, sharper than I intended. "Visibility isn't great," I pause, then soften my tone, "around the bend."

We hold eye contact and speak without words, the way only two kids who grew up sharing a secret hiding place to stash soggy fish sticks and peas can do.

I carry an early morning chill into the house with me. A single soft light above the stove is on. I remove my boots and head to the sink, where I fill the kettle with tap water. I set out a mug and put the kettle on.

The open concept of this house makes room for natural light to filter in through every window, including the peaked ceiling, which has four sunlights. By nine in the morning, the main living area is a petri dish. I slink into a chair at the kitchen table while the kettle rattles and check my email on my phone.

I haven't looked in a few days, but it occurs to me as I open the app that I haven't looked at them in almost a week. There's one new message forwarded from Eden, from R. Wells. It's dated yesterday.

Mr. Ashton,

Hi. I wanted to follow up and see if you received my initial email? I'd like to know what the plan is moving forward. Thanks so much and have a great day.

Rory

The week flew by. I didn't intentionally not reply to her. I've been mulling over the guidelines and outline of this program, and I'm not built for it.

All of this wasn't a problem until a week ago either. No one messaged me. The few people I know who would need me, call. I like it that way.

Trying to manage and maintain communication online seems complicated, and the simplicity of my life is the only thing that brings me a modicum of peace.

And right now, my peace is protesting.

My forearms tighten and my stomach drops when I read over her email again. Her words are stacked, one over the other, like unpaid bills that I'm responsible for.

The kettle whistles loudly and pulls me away from the screen.

There once existed a time in the world, not that long ago, where you could be surprised by sheer luck and timing.

Where you could meet a person and not learn everything about them in a matter of virtual minutes.

There was magic in the mystery of discovering someone layer by layer.

We've come into an era of haste and impatience. We rush everything, from book deadlines to intimacy, swapping connection for swiping.

I sit back down, pulling off my wool sweater, tossing it over the chair. I meditate over the piping hot liquid. It burns a little going down, desperate to fill the pit in my stomach.

My jaw clenches. This is not what Cal sold me on.

I'm driven back to the first email, refreshing my memory. Is she seriously saying we should partake in "Ice-Breakers?" I laugh heartily at the absurdity of it all. The last time I sat around a circle was at Lake Berry summer camp. I was ten. Rocking tie-dye and friendship bracelets, marshmallow fingers and singing along to a campfire cheer.

"Mom, you there?"

Emerson's dry morning voice cuts through my amusement, and I leap out of my chair.

I walk down the hall and open her bedroom door. She's sitting in bed, buried in a sea of pink pillows. Midnight curls frame her round face, a sprinkling of freckles dust her nose, and her hazel eyes shine. She looks like Carlynn. She looks like my mom.

Though her complexion has paled.

"Uncle Reed, you're here?" she questions, brimming excitement in her expression.

I go to her side, picking up her magenta glasses from the nightstand. She slips them on.

"Better?" I ask.

"Much, thanks. Where's Mom? It's Saturday."

"She had to help at work. The opener called in sick." I sit on the edge of the double bed and place the front side of my palm against her forehead. "How'd ya sleep?"

"No complaints." She smooths down her fluffy comforter. It puffs right back up, refusing to conform. My insides push against the swell in my chest.

"Sorry if I startled you. I was reading something that made me laugh," I admit.

"Mom can leave me home alone. I'm twelve, not two." Emerson points to her dresser behind me. "As promised," she crosses her fingers over her heart, "I haven't read ahead since Thursday. Can you grab it, please?"

"I'm impressed." Emerson would miss a meal if it meant one more chapter. There's been nights where I've had to gently pry a book from her hands after she's fallen asleep with it. She's like my mom in that way too.

I smile and turn around to get the book.

My hands tremble as I face the wall now in front of me. An explosion of baby pink and promise, medals, hanging pointe shoes, photos of Emerson at recitals holding peonies, surrounded by beaming coaches and family, hugging friends, smiling with Shannon.

Shannon.

My eyes slam shut.

Throat constricts.

My heart leaps into a sprint, to drag me away.

I press my hand into my chest and force a deep inhale, hold it, and slowly release. And again. And again. And again.

Sensation returns to my hands and lips. My eyes lift open.

I back away from the dresser and return to Emerson playing with the fringe of one of her decorative pillows.

"Do you want to read first?" she asks.

"I'd prefer to listen today if that's okay with you." I settle on the edge of her bed, handing her the book. While she opens to where we left off, I reach for the stone in my pocket. I hold it firmly in my fist as Emerson's voice fills my head. The sound of scraping steel slips back into its compartment.

When Carlynn pulls up from her shift, Emerson's on the couch with her phone. And I grab my boots and coat, wanting to get a hike in.

"Where are you off so fast?" my sister asks, passing me on her way in.

"Taking Fenway up the peak before the day is gone."

"How'd she do?"

"She worked hard. We got through the exercises and she whipped me at Scrabble. Her strategy is ruthless. I'll see ya tomorrow night."

"Bye, Uncle Reed." Emerson throws me a wave.

"Couldn't do this without you," Carlynn adds, giving my arm a squeeze.

I disagree. She could've done so many things. She spent her entire childhood dancing. A dream that kept her on her tiptoes twirling around the house, ribbon and tulle permanently stuck in the sewing machine. She was destined to perform.

When she broke the news to Mom and Pops that she was going to stay in-state and attend the University of New Hampshire instead of auditioning in New York, we were all shocked. Pops in the silent way, that meant he needed to talk to Mom.

I never understood her decision, and it formed a microscopic crack in the foundation of our relationship. Like a shift beneath our feet that separated us. We had come from the same place, raised by the same people, and for the first time in my life, I couldn't relate to my sister.

Somehow I failed to notice when she decided to change. She made her decision and never looked back.

"Love ya, Reed. See ya tomorrow night."

"Love ya too. C'mon Fenway, let's go," I say, followed by a sharp whistle.

We hop in the truck and take down the gravel drive. I allow myself to try and feel her sentiment. For one second. Nope. It's still there. Still razor sharp. Still shredding my heart into tiny pieces.

I scoop the fragments up and bury them, like I do with everything else. What's one more scoop on the pile anyway?

I roll down the window as fast as I can.

The fresh air is shocking and necessary. I don't deserve the joy of innate freedoms like movement and breath.

Up the trail, my muscles tighten and strain against the path I've chosen. Normally, this is a moderate hike for me, but my mind hasn't found its way back to center since the email and the panic ambush this morning.

I don't even know this person and I'm letting her invade my thoughts. It never occurred to me that mentoring Rory would mean she'd actually depend on me to be regularly accessible. This was all supposed to be a clean transaction.

She'd send her draft, and I'd critique it. She'd land an agent, and I'd move the fuck on.

But apparently, this program is an immersive experience.

To make the situation especially cruel, we have a fast-approaching deadline and my mentee has an agenda that is wasting time. I know what she's looking for. She wants the illusion of Reed Ashton, romance author. She's going to be pretty disappointed when that bubble bursts.

This entire set-up is asking me to artificially manufacture creative sync. I don't see how that's possible when I'm completely out of touch with writing. Whatever she thinks she needs to know to feel ready to hand over her work isn't going to change the task at hand.

I start to jog back down the path. My calves burn. I'm being thrown into the deep end, and apparently, I'm the one who's supposed to provide the life vests should this ship capsize. Which it most definitely will. My lungs aren't keeping pace today, weary from the hostile adrenaline takeover earlier.

We hit the bottom of the trail, and Fenway hops in the truck to head home.

Like most local businesses outside of the village, BL Brews is tucked inside a lane of birch trees, a disorienting maze of stripped-down bark. Nature's way of weeding out trespassers.

That's the thing about seasonal towns—they have the on-season and the off-season.

People from all over, mostly Providence and Boston, come up, wear the shit out of Berry for a few months, and then, like an expensive tuxedo, return it back to its original owner when they're done.

We take back what is ours and restore it to its original condition, knowing full well that it will happen again next season.

Carlynn and her husband, Will, built BL Brews from the basement up. They moved back to Berry after college, to create a life in a town where people leave their doors unlocked and know your name. The brewery was our friend group's go-to spot. For a time, we were all blissfully unaware of how quickly the future would arrive.

I consider stopping inside, saying hello, and having a pint. Knowing what time of year it is, the place will be packed, and everyone will want to catch up, ask me how I'm doing. They'll want me to say I'm doing great, any response that makes them feel good about moving on with their lives.

That's human nature. We like progress. We are creatures of heading upstream.

I pass on the beer.

When I arrive home, I swipe a lager out of the fridge and drag one of the Adirondack chairs down to the shoreline. I dig my toes into the cold, wet sand.

This spot right here, before sunset, is the money shot, surrounded by one-hundred-foot red pines, wrapping around the perimeter and tapering off into a row of microscopic black lines. My neighbor's homes are pushed back away from the beach. From a distance, you can barely make out their wooden docks jutting out over the water.

I soak in the silence. For a moment my head clears. I close my eyes.

Carlynn's fists bash into my chest. She buries her wet face against my frozen skin.

The flashback ends and I release my chokehold on the bottle, carrying my boots and self-loathing back up to the house. *Fucking lake.*

Fenway eats while I run the shower to warm up.

I empty my pockets and remove my sweater and shirt, catching a glimpse of a reflection I barely know. His hazy eyes and dull skin. His wild hair and scruffy beard. It's been a while since I've paused to take a good look at myself.

And immediately, I remember why.

My phone buzzes on the counter with a notification. It's an email from Cal, checking in on how the mentoring is going. He signs off with a thumbs up. The worst of all emojis. The most dismissive for sure.

Fenway's at my feet now. I glide my toes along his soft golden fur. I better get this over with.

Keep it simple, Reed.

She's there. You're here. A few words.

"It's now or never," I whisper and type:

Ms. Wells,
We are s-c-r-e-w-e-d . . .

Backspace. Backspace. Backspace. *Too soon?*

Ms. Wells,
I apologize for the delay. Send me your most current draft, please.
Cheers,
Reed

My phone pings with an alert before I have time to put it down.

Mr. Ashton,
Hello. How are you? Thanks for getting back to me. The thing is, before we get to work on my manuscript, I'd like to build some kind of rapport first, if that's okay.
Call me Rory, please.

Her message churns in my head. I'd like to take an icepick to those ice-breaker questions.

Rory,
I understand you'd like us to get to know one another, but sending your most updated draft and having me critique it *is* how this works. Twenty questions wastes time and won't help me help you. And Reed is fine.

Ping.
How fast does this girl type?

Reed,
Hello again. The thing is, this is my dream, and I planned to work closely with a mentor, and a mentor, by definition, is a trusted advisor. How can you help me if you don't know me? I'm happy to request being reassigned. You're correct—I don't want to waste anyone's time.
Take care,
Rory

She wants out. Best news I've heard all week. I chuck the phone back onto the counter and hop in the shower. The steam and heat beating down my shoulders is a welcome reprieve.

I step out of the shower and wrap a towel around my waist. The tile floor is cool—a stark contrast to the steam rolling off my shoulders. I collect all my shit and head upstairs to change into sweatpants. Loosened up and lying in bed hasn't changed a damn thing. I'm right back where I left off—figuring out how to respond to Rory.

The bookshelf in front of me is full of all the books that have ever meant anything to me. Most of them are signed by friends. Some are from childhood. And some are mine. My debut romance amongst them.

I've been in her shoes. I remember that feeling of frustration and excitement, pouring everything I had into that first attempt. The grit and grief of revising and reading, filtering criticism and praise. How proud my family was of me. How authors I admired all of sudden became my peers who paid attention to me. How much it meant at the time.

Something about the first is special. The entire writing process and then the result.

Take this get-out-of-jail-free card . . . Pass Go . . . Collect your freedom.

I'm pacing the room now, chewing on her directness. It wasn't unkind or abrasive, but something about its urgency struck me. She's seriously ready to throw in the towel after a couple brief emails. That's like me walking away after two strikes. Who gives up like that? She wants me to get to know her over email by indulging in some fantasy game of twenty questions when we could be making actual progress.

Winter creeps along the floorboards like frostbite, claiming my ankles. I walk around Fenway, curled up on the oval rug next to the bed.

I scoff. Fenway raises his head and barks.

"I'm fine, buddy. It's fine. Everything is fine." He shakes his head at me. I'm not convincing anyone.

As much as I'd love to be rid of this mess, I made a commitment. I know where she's at, all the rookie moves, doubt and uncertainty, even some misguided confidence. I relied on a lot of people, eyes on my work, mouths to spread the word. Granted, I had met them in person, but still, I didn't do it alone. Publishing a book isn't a solo mission.

The sky tonight is lit by a sheet of twinkling stars. Like someone took a piece of black construction paper and poked thousands of tiny holes in it with the tip of a pushpin. The moon's reflection pours into the room, illuminating the edge of the bed and the bookshelf.

If her persistence on paper is any indication of what the next six months will be like, she's going to be as fierce as one of my headaches. My teeth ache thinking about answering a single one of those ridiculous questions.

"Should I let her go?" I send out a wish for clarity. I know he's there to receive it.

A star straight out the window, brighter than the rest, winks in the sky. One wink, two. A smile settles over my face at nature's nightlight. I pick up the bat resting against the wall and take a few full swings in the air. "Thanks, Pops. You always have my back."

6

RORY

"Everything that's worth having is some trouble."
—L.M. Montgomery

The weekend isn't a weekend anymore. It's become another day in the fold where I'm not working on my manuscript.

The welcome letter lead me to believe I'd establish some common ground with my mentor before tackling the revision process. I know Reed wants the updated version of my manuscript, but I'm not ready. I'm just not ready.

He's colder than I imagined someone who writes love stories would be. He's also not the one with a future on the line here, so maybe to him it's about the project, not the person.

After I toss my stuff onto the hall tree, I stomp to the powder room.

Wild hair, flushed face, and a nipped-at nose perfectly represent everything I'm feeling after trying to communicate with Reed. I need to go slowly. I take a breath and smooth out what I can to keep Mom off my case, and give up on the rest.

Everything feels off the rails, disorganized and messy, and now I'm spending a few hours with my mom, after a week's worth of silence, on both our ends. *Can't wait.*

"Oh good, Aurora, you're on time." Mom's voice rips me from the staring contest I'm having with myself in the mirror. "Can you run upstairs and grab Lexie's duffel bag? She'll need it to change after the match." Mom's carrying a giant white pumpkin, twice the size of her head, and a can of glitter spray paint.

I don't even want to know.

"Why couldn't I have met you at her school? Can we also talk about Sunday? I wanted to—"

"Aurora, my hands are full," she cuts in, and her perfectly penciled-in eyebrow lifts, as if it's a question in and of itself.

I roll my eyes.

"I saw that," Mom snaps, walking into the kitchen.

"You were meant to," I whisper, shaking off the interaction for the sake of making it through the rest of the day. I poke my head into Arty's study before going upstairs. He looks up at me from his recliner, a book nestled in his lap.

"Sorry to interrupt."

"Never an interruption, Rory. How's self-employment taste?"

I restlessly hover in the doorway, my hands worrying at the dark wood frame.

"Getting settled into this whole being my own boss thing, I guess."

"Feels great, doesn't it?" He smiles, bright and white, his wire frames slipping down his nose.

I surprise myself when I return his smile.

When I make it upstairs, my legs halt in front of Lexie's closed door. I reach for the knob, closing my eyes, counting on the inhale, *one, two, three, four*, and twist to the right, exhaling, *five, six, seven, eight*.

I step in, hesitant to look around, but it's unavoidable. Here lies all the evidence that Lexie and I grew up in alternate universes.

It's a completely different reality inside this room. Every square inch is cloaked in belonging. Posters and picture collages line the walls, a layer of nursery pink paint still visible beneath. This bedroom is a shrine of stability. Proof a childhood existed here. Its permanence feels like tiny cuts over the same wound, never allowing it to heal.

As I sit on the edge of her bed, my body and heart sink a little. Lexie doesn't understand what it means to live a life held together by painter's tape, growing up in a rotation of trailers and motels. She's been handed nails and a hammer.

In her effort to gloss over the uprooting that was our life, Mom portrays a picture of adventure, conveniently misplacing details such as missed moments, late nights, and cereal for dinner.

Lexie doesn't know Matilda Wells. She knows Tillie Barron, PTA volunteer, family meals, front row at every school event.

The person our mother became when she grew up herself.

Lexie has the security she feels and deserves in the version of our mom that she got. I would never want to take that away from her. Some truths aren't worth their cost.

"Aurora," Mom calls from downstairs, "we can't be late."

I'm officially annoying myself carrying on about this. It's in the past and I've built myself a good life. *Let it go.*

I hop off the bed, scoop up Lexie's duffel by the closet, and take one last spin around the shrine. Then I turn off the light and close the door behind me.

✳

The Waverly Ravens are playing at home. We find our seats in the middle of the bleachers, high enough for Mom to see the entire field. My phone pings in my jacket pocket, and my pulse speeds up when I see it's an email from Reed. I absorb each word methodically over the commotion of the crowd.

I've never mentored anyone before. Writing has been a solitary process for me. And we won't get to know each other in any helpful way by answering a random list of questions online.

Mom shoots up from her spot on the bleachers. "Go, Lexie! Woohoo!"

She sits back down, squeezing in closer as someone pushes in next to me from the other side. I noncommittally smile at the stranger and look back at Reed's email.

There are no guarantees this will work. That may sound pessimistic, but in my experience, creativity is organic, inspired. This whole manufactured set-up feels like a disaster waiting to happen. You see that, right?

I want to believe that this mentorship is important to him, even if solely on an altruistic level. I blow out a visible breath into the October air and watch it stick.

This makes no sense. He's had to have read the draft I submitted with my application. My heart plummets.

What if he means disaster because of what he's already read? What if he's hoping it's better now or something? I drop my head and put my phone back in my jacket pocket. Doesn't he want to give this a chance?

Mom nudges my side.

"What's wrong with you?" She turns her focus back onto the field.

I straighten up and follow suit. Lexie's in midfield, running defense against the other team. These players have endurance. Running for fun in the cold. No thanks. The only thing I know about field hockey is that it's a sport. I'm more excited about the snack game than the actual game. And the people-watching proves to be an unexpected bonus, collecting details like a shiny pair of red rain boots, kids warming their hands with cups of hot chocolate, their faces painted in team spirit, a huddle of maroon and black.

And there's something about the back and forth rhythm that my brain finds appealing.

I've learned to visualize a calming scene when a spiral approaches. Like the ocean washing onto the shore, birds singing, a warm breeze on my sun-kissed skin. It's not rocket science. Yet, it's not working this time. Instead, I'm grinning, almost unhinged, as I play out a scenario in which a confident Rory marches onto that field, taking hold of Lexie's stick and slapping the ball into oblivion. Everyone cheers, lifts me onto their shoulders, and we win.

"She looks great out there, doesn't she?"

"Hmm mmm." I search the field for number eleven. "Yup, looks great."

Lexie's laser-focused, calling out the shots. One minute she's in position and the next, she's down the field, passing to someone. I scoot to the edge of the bleacher to get as into the action as I can from the sidelines.

"I'm glad to see you're enjoying the match, Aurora." *Mental note—not a game, a match.*

"For having no idea what's going on, sure." My phone vibrates in my pocket. I open up the notification, and it's from Reed again.

I want to be clear. To be query-ready in the spring. Do you know how much focus that will take? Some mentees may pause their lives to fully immerse themselves, but I can't do that. My time is spoken for. Not to mention, this program's structure is everything I'm not. It subscribes to the philosophy that a compelling novel in a competitive genre can derive from following generic rules and guidelines. C'mon, have you read them all?

Now he's saying the entire program is a joke. My thumbs punch the keys.

Why are you here if you don't want to be? Clearly, we're both new to this, so there'll be a natural learning curve. I'm not exactly thrilled you've never mentored before. Does this way of writing a book bother me? Why would something with a track record of success be a disaster? It's what I signed on for. And honestly, as much as this all terrifies me, it equally excites me too.

"Just had to get you down here," Mom jabs, and I catch the accusatory intention behind her comment, but also not really able to process what she's saying either. I whip my head up toward her, while gripping the phone in my hands.

"I work full time and it's not like I live next door. I come to Lexie's games when I can."

"*Worked* full time," she corrects me. "Currently, you're unemployed."

She's bundled up in her black knee-length parka. It looks like a body bag. She calls out Lexie's name with the constant fierce sense of pride I'm always witness to.

I find Lexie immediately on the field this time. Same straw hair. Same spotlight. The teams are yelling directions, the crowd's cheering, my thoughts are battling for airtime, and the collective adrenaline is thick enough to choke on. All eyes are on number eleven. On Lexie.

I fly up from my seat when my phone pings again. Mom looks up at me like I'm causing a scene, shooting me "sit down" eyes before I embarrass her. I quickly glance at his reply.

They're prescriptive. I can see why someone writing their first book would cling to those bullet points like it's the only map to get to where you want to go.

I rip off my beanie and spit out my words.

I'm not clinging to anything. I'm following the rules.

"Your sister scored," Mom shrieks, jumping up, hollering. "Aurora, get off your phone. There you go, girls. Way to go, Lex. That's how it's done!"

The players join in a huddle and tap their sticks together. The flame which was my annoyance has spread to a wildfire.

Mom digs into me before my ass hits the metal bench.

"Your sister's really incredible out there, and you aren't even paying attention. You're never here and then when you are, you aren't. Why even bother coming, Rory?"

Mom has never called me Rory a day in my life. I fill my lungs. *One, two, three, four … five, six, seven, eight. One, two, three …* I try to pump the brakes. "What the fuck, Mom?"

"Did you just say what I think you said?" she questions in disbelief.

My phone rattles in my grip. Mom, stark white and silent, shakes her head at me.

"What's your problem?" I shout. "Yes, I agree she's totally dominating out there. Would you like me to skywrite it? Tattoo it on my face?"

Back to silent death darts.

I'm forced to fill the void. "Why are you looking at me like that?"

"Aurora, I will not dignify this scene by stooping to a juvenile level with you. All I'm asking is if you're going to come here to support Lexie, you follow through and act supportive."

"Are you serious right now? My being here to watch the game–*match*," I correct myself, hating myself, "is supporting her. I'm dealing with a work issue that can't wait."

"What work issue? You don't have a job," she announces to everyone within earshot. She'll never take my writing seriously. She doesn't believe in me.

When she breaks eye contact to check on Lexie, the chaos around me fades, sharpening every acute sound. The slap of the puck against solid wood becomes soft whispers scratching over blades of cold grass. The distinct shuffle of her coat turning away from me echoes in my ears. My anger combusts into tiny particles of scattered despair. The one person I should be able to confide in is sitting right next to me and miles away.

I read his next email through blurred vision, tucking my chin into my chest.

Think about how you want this to go. You want to publish a book—cool, I get that. I make no guarantees about how we'll work together. You want us to get to know each other so you can trust me with your writing, and I'm asking you to trust me now so we can get to your writing right away. Remember, deadline?

These lists don't take into account a writer's process. My point is, those rules you're insistent on following, where do you think they'll lead? I'll tell you where—into a pile of submissions that read like everyone else's.

Rules written for everyone become books that sound like everyone. And I have a feeling you're not everyone.

"I know what this is about." Mom's voice rings in my ear again, and I need the noise to stop. What's wrong with me? *I'm not like everyone.* His words and Mom's voice—everything is out of focus.

"What's that supposed to mean?" I demand.

"You know."

All I know is I'm itchy behind my knees and across my chest.

I scramble around in my bag, digging for my meds.

The phone slips off my lap onto the bleacher floor.

"You can be mad at me all you want." Mom reaches down and holds it hostage.

"But do not take your unprocessed anger out on your little sister, who does nothing but adore you. Now, if you're finished with this regression, I'm going to return to the rest of the match. No one is chaining you to this seat. If you have other priorities, go do what you want to be doing."

"You're asking me to leave?"

"That's up to you."

"Are you serious? Up to me. When's anything ever up to me?"

"Keep your voice down. This is not the time or the place. And I'm done with this conversation."

I'm fuming, because I know there's truth in what she's saying.

When I'm triggered, a part of me takes over, an impulsive and immature part, a child, a child who's been hurt. Mom also knows this is a part of my trauma work, and she's using it against me.

So yeah, I'm fuming.

I retrieve my phone from her grasp and storm off the bleachers, scanning the open space for my sister.

Luckily, I catch her attention, and there's a break on the field. She sprints over to me.

Lexie looks up at Mom and then back to me. "Leaving already?"

"Book stuff." I shrug. "Hey, you're killing it out there."

Her smile takes up her whole face. Her blonde hair curls at the edges of her temple in a sweaty mess. I need to spend more time with Lexie. It isn't her fault.

"Sister weekend soon? Marathon movies and mozzarella sticks?"

"Yes, please," she squeals. "I'm so pumped for you. My sister, the famous author. I can't wait to tell the team."

"Well, when you see my name on a jacket wrapped around an actual book, stocked on a shelf, and someone who isn't related to us purchases it, then we can spread the word." I pull her in for a hug. "For now, just between us."

"Deal." She waves on her way back to her teammates and camaraderie.

I received more affection in that one exchange than I did in the entire hour I spent with my own mother. Sitting next to someone you love and not being able to connect with them is a special brand of torture.

The train back into Boston is full. I luck out, finding an open seat two rows behind the exit. The orange pad still warm. There's an older man in tweed, legs crossed, fully immersed in a book. I pull out my phone, remembering I never finished Reed's message. This device is supposed to connect people, so why is it that the more time I spend on it, the worse I feel?

I scroll through Reed's last message, picking up where I left off.

If you decide you want a new mentor, I'll understand. If you decide you want to stay and make this the best story it can be, and you want to do that with my help, then we're going to have to bend the rules. I'm here. The rest is up to you.

I miss stars.

As the train moves past unlit corridors of trees between each suburban stop on its way into the city, I lean my head against the window, counting wishes on their way to someone.

He's asking me to make a gut decision. To implicitly trust him so we can get to work. How do I trust him when, most of the time, I can't even trust myself?

Reed Ashton is no longer this mythical author wrapped in my rose-colored writer aspirations. He's a living, breathing, opinionated person, my mentor, and he's testing me.

The tingling inside my stomach hasn't settled, and if I'm being honest with myself, it's been this way since the first email I sent him. It's like my mind dispatches flare signals to my entire nervous system, alerting it of potential danger. There was a plan. Now there is not a plan.

I stretch my jaw and roll my shoulders, relieving some of the tension that's been building up. I don't notice the tears until I taste them.

Failing is something I know how to do, and above all else, giving up on myself is no longer an option. Fine if my mom doesn't believe in me. Fine if Reed is reluctant to work with me. Fine if I'm scared.

What's not fine is quitting, walking away when it's hard.

Finishing this book is the only option. But if I run out of my savings, I won't be able to pay my rent. I can't go back to that life. Maybe Mom's right and it was irresponsible to quit my job. Maybe I'll ask Doris for my job back and then write at night.

Authors do it all the time.

Responsible authors.

My stomach flips.

Authors with their shit together.

I grip the rail, waiting for the tap-dancing teeth.

The events of today are the perfect storm for me to spiral.

One, two, three, four . . . five, six, seven, eight.

Then I replay his words, the ones that seemed to hint that I'm in control and he wants to be here. *I have a feeling you're not like everyone. If you decide you really want this. It's up to you.*

The train squeals to a stop.

I step through the sliding doors into the street, lightheaded from a flood of artificial light. The stars are no longer visible without the blanket of darkness holding them up.

I pull out my phone and jot down my thoughts before I lose them. *Light. Dark. Interdependent.*

On my walk home, I extract the imagery until it fully forms into an idea. Writing exposes me to risk.

The last decade has been a singular wash, rinse, and repeat cycle, my dream shoved in a drawer for long enough.

I might not understand exactly what I want here, but I know with full confidence that I don't want to go backward. I don't want my book to be like everyone else's, and Reed seems to understand that about me.

Maybe I've been mostly uninspired for nearly a decade, and this feeling in my gut that won't go away is in spite of fear, not because of it.

I might regret trusting someone I barely know, but my fear of not finding out what could be outweighs my fear of failing.

I have to make it work.

My pulse rushes with excitement, and the sixty seconds it takes to make it up the stairs to my apartment is like riding in the front seat of a rollercoaster, right to the top, on the edge of the big drop—hitting pause on the self-doubt and buckling up. I go into my bedroom and message Reed.

I'm in this if you are.

I'm in too. Let's start from the top on Monday, clean slate. One updated chapter from you. One ice-breaker answer from me.

Grinning, I toss my phone on my writing desk. Our agreement is in black and white now.

I stretch my arms above my head and freefall onto my bed, closing my eyes and barreling down into a dream, a twisted tunnel, each curve like a whirl of licorice, where a friendly face lingers, sweet and strong.

It's always the same scene.

The bench. The wet air. The brutal sun.

Like watching a channel with limited reception, it's a pixelated cone of static speckles, bright electricity smiling at me.

And then he reaches out and I run.

7

—— : ——

RORY

"THE ROLE OF THE ARTIST IS TO ASK QUESTIONS,
NOT ANSWER THEM." —ANTON PAVLOVICH CHEKOV

MY ENTIRE ROUTINE IS off, and though that was fun for twenty minutes this morning, like an unplanned snow day, reality is starting to sink in. I have no idea how to function in the chaos of uncertainty.

Good Morning.

I've never been a Monday person—or morning person for that matter—but I woke up well before my alarm clock.

Do you drink coffee? I exist on it. Luckily, my best friend owns the café across the street, so I haven't made my own coffee in almost a decade.

So, I'm attaching Chapter One. What happens next? Do we go through it together?

Full disclosure—this whole "not knowing the plan" thing is not easy for me, in case you didn't pick up on that. :)

I'd say have a nice Monday, but I wouldn't mean it.

So instead . . . I'll say, have a nice almost Tuesday.

Rory

Three chewed-on blue pen caps later, I've managed to revise two paragraphs and check my email for a reply from Reed five times.

Hard to get this show on the road without some direction.

I'm playing around with the lines, seeing if I can make what's not working work. If I measured how many times I've hit backspace in the last hour, I'd erase the entire document. My head hits this desk along with my motivation.

Though it isn't the same story, there is some carryover from the original story I'd written. It was too painful to go back and rewrite all of what I'd lost.

Fitz leaps onto my lap and nudges my chin for kisses. I pet his shiny, jet-black coat, giving him a snuggle. Animals just know.

"I'm going nowhere, going in circles like this."

He meows with uncanny timing, like a cat who's chased his own tail before.

I drop him off at my bed, throw on my hoodie, and meow back at him.

"Look, Fitzy, we're twins today."

In our matching tuxedo look, all black and a triangle of white on our chests. Dressing to match my cat definitely sounds "off the deep end" when I vocalize it. I need to pull myself together.

Step one, splash some water on my face. The bathroom mirror suggests there may be a few more steps ahead of me. Deep-set purple bags stare back. It's only now I see the party favor of a week's worth of neglected sleep.

When the glass fogs up from steam, I draw my name into it with my pointer—*Rory Wells, Author*—and immediately wipe it away with my palm.

I'm so mad that I've let my mom anywhere near my haven.

Writing is my realm. Not everyone deserves the key to enter.

I should've known better.

People don't change.

Maybe they want to, pretend to, dress the part, but the core, what someone believes or doesn't believe to be true—that stays the same.

A reflection of pasty skin and dull eyes confronts me. I stick out my tongue and spot-check for blue ink. I run my toothbrush over it for good measure, pinching some pink into my cheeks and shaking away these uninvited thoughts.

I'm tired. That's all.

I toss the towel onto the floor with the pile of dirty clothes I've been neglecting too.

Normally during this time, I'd be taking my snack break with Gavin. I decide to shoot off a quick text message to check in and see what's happening at Down & Route, instead of doing my laundry.

ME: Miss me?

GAV: Morning break was lame without you.

ME: Anyone steal my chair yet?

GAV: Didn't have time to. Your position is already filled.

ME: What? How?

GAV: Doris promoted Delaney from admin.

GAV: Delaney doesn't do wheelies or listen to The Beatles.

ME: That sounds terrible.

GAV: The worst. I haven't scoped out her snack game yet.

ME: She probably has a tuna pouch and beef jerky.

GAV: Hey, don't shoot the messenger.

ME: I know. Sorry. I didn't think she'd fill it so quickly.

GAV: Didn't even give us time to raid your desk.
GAV: Drinks soon?
ME: Yes to drinks. :)
GAV: Be glad you're gone from this hole.

Too early for a margarita and vent sesh with Kat? It's ten a.m. Okay, maybe that's hasty. I've been gone less than a week, a blunt reminder of how replaceable I am. Even if I was thinking of entertaining the idea of crawling back to my job, that option is off the table now.

Parched and discouraged, lost in the haze of my new normal, I rush to the kitchen for water and wipe out on the braided rug in the hall. Of course, I'm already on my knees before noon. *Typical Monday.*

I'm cursing Mom as I push myself back up, brushing a thin layer of dust off last night's leggings. I knew I didn't need that useless rug, but she insisted on buying it for me. I'm halfway to the fridge when my phone chimes in my room, alerting me that I have a new email. I sprint-hop to check it, scolding myself along the way. I need to chill out.

When I see it's from Reed, though, the smile on my face conveys I'm anything but chill.

You sound upbeat for being in the throes of a melancholy Monday. I'm not sure I want to know what Tuesday looks like. I do drink coffee, dark and hot. Is this your way of working the system, trying to get to know each other without using one of your allotted questions? Clever.

Thanks for sending Chapter One. Ready for lesson time?

These are some things I've thought about in my own process, and they may help you to get started.

Lesson One

Accessing your story is not some switch. It's an intimate connection to the self. It may be uncomfortable at times to sit in your own solitude while you get to know your characters, but it's a necessary practice. When you listen to your characters, the words will come. Make time today to practice listening.

There'll be times when you'll want to pull from the world around you, and then there are times when you'll need to withdraw from it. So if you've got family or a partner or anyone you care about, let them know you'll be unavailable for stretches at a time.

To be accessible to your fictional world, you have to limit access to your real one.

Here are some *rules* for writing.

#1: Find a home for your phone while you're writing.

#2: Stay hydrated.

#3: Stretch. Every hour.

#4: Have tools on hand.

Pens, notebook. Whatever it takes to be a diligent note-taker. I carry a baseball when brainstorming.

#5: Show up.

Per our agreement, here's my answer to your question: *If you could instantly be an expert in a subject, what would it be and why?*

The law. So I could have a few more healthy, rowdy debates with my pops about his love of rules and order.

I have a question threshold, for the record, and you have a book to revise.

Meow. I whip my head to Fitz's yellow eyes glowing.

"I think Mr. Serious made an actual joke." He starts purring as I pet around his ears. This feeling is *almost* as good as the time I earned a feature spot on the college paper. For someone who scoffs at ice-breakers, he seems to be warming to them.

Smile grows wider, check.

Non-existent chill factor increases, double check.

I decide to follow the lesson's suggestions. The overzealous journalism major in me is thrilled to have an assignment. Even if it's one that requires I stay silent.

My email may have sounded upbeat in an effort to begin from a "clean slate," as you suggested.

I also may have been overconfident when I sold myself on diving right into meditation this afternoon to practice clearing my mind before writing. Let me tell you, that was harder than I'd anticipated. My mind kept trying to fill the silence with anything and everything that wasn't my story.

Honestly, there's no way on planet earth that I'll abide by this "no additional questions" of yours clause. If you ask me to do this, I'll fail miserably. Because even though you may think my questions are unhelpful to this process, you also

say I should be a diligent note-taker. And the only way I can think to do that is by first asking questions.

Dinner isn't even substantial enough to distract me from not accomplishing anything this afternoon. Orange noodles flop around on my plate. My appetite has been waning all week.

I set the plate aside and grab my laptop, opening up my last email to Reed, compelled to say a few more things.

Hi, again. I know you haven't had a chance to respond to my last email yet—no rush. I had some ideas to run by you in the interim.

I tried to write more today and I hit a wall. I categorized my bookshelf, made dinner, and now I'm sitting here staring at the screen again, and I've got nothing. Is this a block or a lull? Do you have any suggestions?

Your answer to my question made me think about my little sister. She's sixteen now and wants to be a math teacher. It's a strange thing for me to hold a book and not be able to excavate it. When I'm in her presence and she's talking about numbers, I'm surrounded by a language I don't understand. So my response is, I'd be a math expert. They say math is the only universal language, and I want to know how to speak it.

Before I have time to worry that sending a second email was overkill, a familiar alert comes through my inbox.

My heart thumps.

Once, twice.

Hey. Math isn't so different from storytelling. There are patterns and relationships between variables. Both are an equation. You have to solve for x.

The researcher in me leaps at the possibility of being able to understand this concept more.

So are you saying that if math is the language of the universe, then writing is the language of storytelling?

Can we talk about the mechanics of how we'll make the most of the mentorship moving forward? I've got a calendar and some felt-tip pens burning a hole in my desk. :)

You mentioned Pops. Is he a relative? What kind of law does he practice? Or is he a teacher? Have a good night.

When my inbox pings again, I lay on my bed and curl up to read his response, anxious to get back into his head.

It takes time to adjust to meditation. Pops is my dad. When he was alive, he owned a law practice in Boston. We'd have these philosophical discussions about morality and the constitution. Sometimes, I have these dreams where we talk for hours. He'd always get me fired up to debate. Those are hard to wake up from.

It's okay to send me emails and ask questions, with the understanding that I might miss some.

Yes, writing is the language that you, the storyteller, have to communicate with the world. You're onto something here.

I'm not entirely sure where you're stuck or why, but I want you to stop thinking about it for tonight. You have a solid opening chapter.

Get some rest.

The apartment is pitch black. On the way to fill up my water, I pause at the narrow kitchen window overlooking the desolate street illuminated by a row of lit lamps. Even when the sidewalks are empty, the city speaks. I suppose we all have stories, pieced together by triumphs and heartbreaks.

The relationship Reed described between him and his dad sounds like a bond that transcends loss. I guess I've been luckier than Reed in that I can't really lose something I've never had. I don't grieve my biological father as much as I mourn the fantasy of who I wanted him to be.

While I wait for the ache to subside to a dull squeeze, I trace sideways eights along the windowpane until the tip of my finger is too numb to move any further.

Picturing a young Reed delivering his clipped and confident points of view helps me settle my spiraling thoughts. Reed exudes a sense of conviction I admire and wish I had, where he believes so strongly in what he's saying, as if, in his mind, being honest is simply the only way to be kind. I can't imagine not second-guessing every move I make.

I take everything he says to heart. The side effect is a nagging, growing curiosity about my mentor, to learn as much as I can, as quickly as I can.

He's impossible to peg, but today I was given a glimpse of the person behind the profile. I learned that though we are different in every obvious way, we share two things in common. One, we know loss. And the other, Reed Ashton has vivid dreams too.

I try to make sense of the math. Reed didn't have to tell me about his dreams. He told me because he wanted to. And that changes things.

8

— • —

REED

"WE WRITE TO TASTE LIFE TWICE, IN THE MOMENT AND IN RETROSPECT." —ANAIS NIN

IT DIDN'T MATTER WHAT I thought.

But that didn't stop me from overthinking anyway.

Since I quit giving my ideas pen and paper, it seems they're eager to find any place to land, without remorse. *A writer's curse.*

"What are you workin' on, Reed?" Lew stops where I'm kneeling in the dirt while Mom heads inside the house carrying stacked Tupperware.

"Digging out some last-minute weeds before it freezes over."

"Need a hand?" he offers.

"Nah, I'm good. Just a few more here." I tug tightly.

"You sure?"

"Enough." I growl into the hardened earth, then shift from the ground into a squat. I rest my arms over my knees, clapping my hands together. "Sorry, yeah, I think that's it for today." I wipe my sleeve along my forehead.

Lew helps me gather my pile. "What's on your mind?" he treads gently as we walk together.

"Nothing."

I don't dare to look at the man who's known me since birth. He'll see straight through whatever story I'm about to try and sell him.

"You look like you've been out here all day. And you're—"

"There's work around here. That's all. It needed to get done."

"Weeding for winter needed to get done? Hmmm, that's a new one."

He knows I'm not taking the bait today—by now he's used to it. He stops pressing. A small kindness on his part.

Lew lifts the barrel lid for me and I deposit the debris from my hands into the metal bin. The clang of the contact is harsh, shaking me from the fog I've been settled in since reading the round of Rory emails from this morning.

"What time is it?" The sun has dipped close to the horizon, leaving a disorienting pale pink glow.

"It's five o'clock. You okay?"

Had I really missed lunch?

There's something about growing up in a small town that's equal parts insulation and trap.

I owed it to Mom that I did not fall victim to the latter. She encouraged us as children to seek a world outside Berry, knowing we always had home to come back to.

I flip my hands over and feel the cool air biting at the small cuts.

"Let Mom know I'll be down in a minute. I've been in the weeds—weeding—all day."

Before I ramble my way into a confession, I head upstairs to wash off the hours I lost to unnecessarily digging out weeds that will freeze over during winter and die anyway.

For two years, I haven't left, haven't even entertained the idea.

And somehow now, the outside world, mainly Rory Wells, is pulling me into another hemisphere.

I find myself like a moth to a flame, back on my phone, rereading our conversation from earlier.

Sorry to hear about your father. I haven't lost a parent, not in the way you have, but I can understand the way a room feels emptier (like birthdays) without the people you want to love there.

I was raised by my mom. She left her home in Seattle and moved to Anchorage, Alaska at eighteen. Sometimes, I wonder what life would've been like had she said no more times than yes.

Isn't life so much a series of made and missed opportunities? One train stop too soon, one change of heart too late.

Next question: *Do you have a hero or your own mentor?*

P.S. When I have a tough time with dreams, I listen to the Relax app. It really helps.

She's right, the heart is often the caboose, and catches up last. I wonder if she's the type of person who spends more time on her phone than on her craft.

Hey. Thanks for sending the next chapter and for the kind words about Pops. Is your phone always glued to your hand?

No, I don't always have my phone in my hand. Sometimes, it's strategically placed next to me. :)

Her response makes me laugh. My shoulders relax as my thumbs type away. *Moth. Flame.*

Pops was larger than life in a subtle way. If you weren't looking, you'd almost miss it.

He had a quiet magnetism about him. Picture the guy who cheers the loudest from the bleachers and faithfully leaves half the crossword puzzle for my mom in the Sunday paper.

He was a provider. A good man. A great example.

Ever notice how the best people leave this Earth too soon? And somehow they manage to make the most of the time they were given. As if some part of them knew.

My father is my hero and, in many ways, was a mentor too.

What did you mean when you wrote, "like birthdays"?

You are prolonging this conversation, Reed, for no reason at all other than you're enjoying the back and forth, passing the dopamine hot potato.

Going to take a rain check on the answer to my hero.

We get those, right? :)

Me and my mom, we moved around. Every year on my birthday, I'd celebrate with her random coworkers, depending on the shift she was scheduled that day.

I guess I always imagined those vacant seats in the room were filled with people who knew my favorite color was periwinkle, that I'm allergic to almonds, or that books make me irrationally happy.

It must have been hard to lose someone you have memories with.

Memories surface as I read her reflection.

When we first lost him, they were painful, but then I valued having so many because they also kept him close. He's still everywhere in this house.

It has its hard days. There's this chair at the head of our table, it was his, and no one sits in it anymore. The memories are mostly comforting.

How many places have you lived? Often, inspiration is drawn from real-life experiences. Did you get any writing in today?

Seriously, Reed, I can't believe how many emails we've written today. Feels like an actual conversation.

To answer your question, I've lived in more places than I can count on both hands. It taught me to be an efficient packer. :)

Not sure how to tell you this, but I'm really stumped with my revisions. I took myself on a walk, listened to meditations, and even did some journal prompts. I'm kinda waiting for your direction on how to improve it.

What are you writing these days? Will we see more of _Cupid's Desire_?

Do you have a social media page I should be following for tips or anything?

A list of questions I don't want to answer is my cue to drop the potato. I strip and step into the shower.

The water's scalding against my back. My head hangs in the steam.

Talking about Pops isn't generally my go-to conversation with strangers, but somehow Rory's easier to talk to than I gave her credit for initially. And fuck, I like it.

She asked me who my hero was, and for a moment, I considered listing prolific authors or all-star players. She wouldn't have known the difference, but in doing so, I'd be denying Pops and the truth. And I'm not a liar.

Her questions, and this scalding water, hit like rounds of ammunition. Rory's transient history with her mom has also left me with more questions. Moving around like that—she's insistent about timelines and plans for good reason. Now that I've read her first chapter, I'm making connections between Rory, the person and Rory, the writer.

Thinking about Rory as a person was not on the agenda. I'm in no position to get to know her. Once these six months are up, we go back to our lives, and I get my quiet back. That's the plan. That's what I want.

Heat runs down my chin and chest, rinsing away the remnants of the day. I switch off the water and step out of the steam.

This friendly chatting between us can't continue. It will create false expectations.

Reading her draft chapter by chapter isn't going to help either. I need to get Rory on the same page so she'll send me her full draft and I can do my job. The ice has been broken enough. It's damn near melted.

I take a hard look in the mirror, my stinging hands gripping the edges of the porcelain sink.

My curiosity in the past has won over rational thinking. I won't chase that high again.

"There he is." Mom gives me her cheek to kiss. I grab a glass of water and sit across from her on the other side of the kitchen island. My fingers tap the Formica, impressively still in decent shape. The kitchen is the central point of most of our memories together. There was never any rush to prioritize fixing her up. Old lake houses around here are impossible to replicate or replace. They take shape throughout the decades of life being lived in them.

Mom chops away.

I lift the water glass to take a drink.

"Reed, what happened to your hands?" she observes, pointing to the gauze wraps I placed over them.

"Nothing, Ma—don't worry. I worked a little too hard. What are you making?" I put down my water.

She ignores my question, laying wet lettuce on a blue and white dish towel.

"Take off those wraps."

I give her a quizzical look which she returns. A warning signal. *She wasn't asking.*

I remove the gauze slowly and open my hands as far as I can, though the skin is tight and fighting back. A faint hissing sound scrapes between my teeth as air hits the fresh wounds.

"These will help those cuts heal faster." She lays bite-size cucumber slices over them. It's shocking at first, then soothing. I look up to thank her, confronted by the silent strength she's always had my entire life. She doesn't just profess her loves for a person; she shows it with all that she has.

"Thanks, Ma. Cucumbers really are magical. Who knew?"

She peels her steady gaze from mine and goes back to preparing mushrooms.

"Can I assume by how you're treating your hands that you're not writing much this week?"

Try the past one hundred and four weeks. I open my mouth and she tosses a mushroom into it.

"You can say that," I reply, chewing.

"Something you want to talk about?"

I swallow. "Nope."

"I'm heading into town tomorrow. How about I grab Genevieve's mail off the counter and forward it along for you?" She nods behind her to where the pile of proof that someone else used to live here has taken up residence.

"I'll take care of it."

"When, Reed?"

I hesitate with an answer I don't have.

Genevieve left after the accident. People in town, my own family, silently blamed her for leaving when things got tough, but they didn't know her leaving was inevitable.

The end of my five-year relationship was a symptom of unhappiness I'd ignored for too long. Sometimes, you have to let go of what you think you want to make room for what you don't even realize you need. It's been a hard two years around here, but it would've been harder had she stayed.

"What are you keeping it for? I know it isn't the same thing, but I had to release myself from the physical clutter before I could even address Pops being gone. If she couldn't handle being there for you when you were at your worst, she never deserved any part of you at your best."

When I told my mom Genevieve wouldn't be coming to our potlucks anymore, she did what any good mother does—she checked on how I was doing. When I told her I was okay but felt like I wasted five years of her life, she told me that Genevieve made her own choices. Then she did the other thing she does fearlessly—she baked me a blueberry pie.

"Mom," I whisper.

"It wasn't your fault. It hurts to see you punish yourself." She reaches over and places her warm hands over mine. One by one she flips the cucumber slices until I feel their cool surface seep into my soon-to-be blisters.

"I don't want her to come back. I don't know why I'm holding onto it. I just—"

Emerson cheers from the living room, "I got Boardwalk."

I continue, "I don't want to talk about this right now."

"All right, well, consider letting me forward this on, or at least let me use the industrial-size shredder Lew got me for my birthday this year. You know how much that thing can hold? It's like a barrel full of cathartic confetti." She winks at me and her cheeks rise, lifting her wireframes along the bridge of her nose. The lines around her mouth and eyes curve in delight.

She's enjoying her idea.

I pull the cucumbers off and reach out a hand. "I'll take the green peppers."

"You sure?"

"Yeah, I'm good. All healed." I wave my hands in front of her for inspection, like Carlynn and I used to do before supper.

With the sound of our chopping in the kitchen, and Will, Carlynn, Emerson, and Lew playing Monopoly in the living room, I find myself relaxing for the first time since this morning, which seems like days ago at this point.

"What's happening in your world?"

"I'm mentoring a writer." Another overshare from me today.

"Run that one by me again? And this time, include all the details." She takes a sip of her wine.

"Eden needed help and Cal called in a favor—me being the favor." I reach for Mom's glass and take a swig.

"First, Reed, go get yourself a glass. Second, pour me another."

I hop up and grab a small glass from the cupboard. When I return, I fill hers and then mine.

"And third, let's cheers to this new adventure."

Our glasses meet and I know she's making a silent wish. I do too. It's one of Meryl's momisms. Whenever two glasses, bottles, people are brought together in a toast, we send a silent wish into the world for good health and happiness or something more specific. Thirty-two years of wishing and I still don't know a single one she's sent out.

"What'd you wish for?"

"Not a chance in this life, Junior. So, what's his name?"

"Whose name?" I reply, tossing the peppers into the bowl.

"The writer you're mentoring."

Oh, right. I bring the glass to my lips. "Her name is Rory Wells." And drink.

"A woman," Mom confirms.

I nod and pick up radishes to slice.

The only women I talk to these days are Mom and Carlynn. Talking to Rory feels easy, which unsettles me. She's surprising, like when she asked to take a rain check on answering who her hero was. This girl has barely taken a breath since I met her, yet this question, she doesn't have an immediate response to.

My forearms tighten and my grip on the chopping knife locks as I draw the parallel to my own inability to answer Mom earlier. I can't answer a question I don't have an answer to. I shake out my hands.

"What's she like?" Mom turns around, stirring sauce and taste-testing. "Ah, this is almost ready," she adds, focusing her attention back on me.

I clear my throat, racing to collect some detail I can share. "I barely know her. She's bright. I guess. Inquisitive. She's got a lot to say," I conclude.

"Sounds like a perfect match to not let you off the hook." She winks.

The stool wobbles beneath my weight.

"What else aren't you saying?"

I sigh. "I get the feeling that she's not close to a lot of people."

"That's a shame. Well, I'm glad then that she has you."

Wait, what? No. I cough and chug a gulp of my wine, meaning to grab my water, and choke out, "She doesn't have me, Ma."

Mom's stare tells me I'm possibly overreacting. But she's mis-reading my curiosity for caring about Rory, that cheerful sparkle in her eye that somehow mentoring Rory will bring back her best-selling-romance-author son.

"Oh, Reed, I don't mean these things so literally. No need to fall off your stool. I simply meant she has you to talk to. And that might mean a lot to someone who doesn't have trusted people in her life."

My head is spinning, and it isn't from the cabernet.

I sit through dinner, half-checked out. Mom wasn't wrong in what she said—that wasn't the problem. The problem is that now that she's said it, I can't unsee it. While I've been avoiding Rory, she's probably been stretching well outside her comfort zone, trying to establish a good rapport with her new mentor.

Yes, you jackass. She's not trying to get personal, she's trying to get comfortable.

Which really, in many ways, should've been my responsibility to facilitate. *What a dick move, Reed.* I don't know if I'm motivated by guilt or a genuine intrigue to learn more about her now that I know it's not about her being starstruck or something, but after everyone's left, I'm at my laptop, again, Fenway at my feet, writing back to Rory.

Hey. How was your night? My family came over for dinner. It's potluck style, and we usually gather here since it's always been that way. Anyway, I wanted to follow up.

First, the Relax app sounds cool. I think some apps are worthwhile. Social apps are awful. So, you went for a walk, but that didn't help. Have you tried journaling as your characters?

I'll be up for another hour.

I look at the screen after I send the email and immediately feel tomato sauce and tannins churning in my stomach.

Sitting here is worry-making business, so I get up and walk to my dresser, seeking the consistent comfort that only exists within these sacred pages. I've read them so many times, the spine effortlessly bends. I gently open to a random page to hear her voice.

The quiet. They liked it that way. The ice in their drinks had almost gone, sweating under an unseasonably warm winter night. He knew what she was thinking. He always did. She wore her heart on her sleeve. Tears had fallen somewhere between the silence and his sweeping embrace. She was lost in the way his soft mouth had found hers, parting her shivering lips.

"I know I want to be with you, to not waste this," he whispered.

She pressed their swollen mouths together, capturing his words. She never meant to find him. She wasn't even looking. Their kissing waltzed to the rhythm of the intermittent breeze, torturously slow and teasing. This was their longest kiss. Not their first, never their last. Just the longest. One that made promises and kept them.

I follow her notes as they wrap themselves around the entire page. My chest squeezes. The ink is written with purpose. One spot has dried and wrinkled. If I had known what was in here, I would've waited longer. I would've waited all day.

My thumb flips the page to more lines.

I don't always feel invisible, but I do today. I was sick and Mom couldn't reschedule the family photographer, so they went ahead and took them without me. I don't know why I'm surprised. Or why I even care. Something as trivial as being absent from a card that will be distributed to hundreds of people I don't even know has me questioning my entire existence.

When I first read these pages, I was an engaged reader. The more I found myself in her mind, the more active of a participant I became, jotting down my own inspiration and ideas alongside hers. Creating a conversation between her words and mine.

** *I've had an independent life, and yet . . . I've always felt like something was missing. Maybe that's our cross to bear? We can't help but wonder who we'd be in spite of who we became.* **

My smile from the memory melts into bittersweet shards of shared gratitude and remorse. It doesn't take long for me to wonder how she's doing now, when an alert from my phone signals that I have a new email. I sigh and return the story to its safe place. Then, I check my phone.

My night's been okay. I don't really sleep much. Thank you for asking. You know how some people have a green thumb? My mom's the equivalent of that in the kitchen. I didn't pick up her love of cooking and entertaining even though I grew up in restaurants. I've taught myself to make a few things well. Most of them include two slices of bread and a piece of cheese.

A potluck sounds really nice. Is your mom a master chef in the kitchen too?

I don't sleep much either. We share that in common.

In college, we went full throttle one night over a grilled cheese. It was my sophomore year, and eight of us baseball players lived in a suite with a shared bathroom. I still shudder thinking about that bathroom floor.

Four of us came home from a party one night, and all we could talk about on the "walk off the booze" stroll to the dorm was the late-night grilled cheese sandwich in our future. The problem was, our rations were limited, and the town shut down by ten p.m., so this grilled cheese was our only shot at not ending the night wrapped around a toilet.

When we arrived at the suite, two of the other guys had beat us to it. I can still see the warm cheese dripping from their smiles. Pretty sure I cried.

Moral of the story: When you're dreaming of the perfect sandwich and you're drunk and stuck with a snack pack of stale pretzels, you learn to appreciate two slices of bread and a piece of cheese. It's comfort food. Now I really want one. Midnight snack of champions.

The grilled cheese hits the spot.

I fill Fenway's water bowl, put on classical music, and climb into bed. The lamp in the room is low, and an orange glow falls over the floor.

The sky is dark and the house has settled. Fenway's whistling tells me he's sound asleep. The stars glittering outside the window remind me that I should be sleeping too.

My nights mostly consist of alternating bouts of restlessness and wired exhaustion. This is a strange feeling not to be fighting a headache or straining through push-ups until I pass out.

I need to reel us back in, keep us on track. I have to remember who she is, a temporary place card in my life.

I check to see if Rory has replied, cautioning myself when I grin at what she's written.

I see your midnight picturesque small-town grilled cheese and raise you a two a.m. late-night slice of pizza hot off the street in New York.

It's not what she says about the perfect grilled cheese. It's everything it implies in between.

That image of a slice of pizza takes my breath away. And my mom—she's not a master chef, but she loves to cook for her family. We use a lot of local produce and ingredients. It's similar in Italy, smaller courses and the togetherness, but man, those dinners lasted for hours. Italians do good food and company and great wine, of course.

What do you do to shake things up? I ask because we can easily get stuck in consistency, like we get stuck in our thoughts or our writing. For the sake of creative inspiration, we need to change it up once in a while.

Predictability can be paralyzing to innovation. Writing is about testing and experimenting. It's about risk.

Here's my next lesson for you. Goodnight.

Lesson Two

Have you ever heard of an inspiration date? It's an opportunity for you, "the writer," to take yourself out. Listen to a new band play, try a new restaurant, order something you've never had. Check out a used bookstore—they're goldmines. Introduce your inner creative to new things. You never know, you may surprise yourself. Inspiration has a way of showing up when you least expect it.

9

— · —

RORY

"I WRITE BECAUSE IF I DON'T,
EVERYTHING FEELS EVEN WORSE." —LILY KING

MORNING COMES QUICKLY. I clocked five hours of sleep, thinking about the type of inspiration date I wanted to take myself on.
There's a new exhibit at the Museum of Fine Arts. But first, coffee.

The morning rush is in full swing when I drag myself through
the doors.

"Hey, friend, rough night?"

"Rough few nights. Haven't slept much all week, you know,
after the fight with mom, and the mentorship is—"

"Still not great?" she finishes my sentence over frothing and
Fleetwood.

"He speaks in full sentences now, so that's an improvement."

Reed definitely isn't who I thought he was a week ago. It sometimes feels like maybe he's a friend, but I don't even remember
what making a friend feels like. Kat and Gavin are the only friends
I've made since moving to Boston. I'm rusty.

"I'm learning," I add, feeling like I need to clarify. "I like talking
to him, but mentally he's all over the place."

She hands me my latte and we walk over to sit in our spot.

"You know how some people exist in clutter and still know exactly where everything is? He's had me throw all of the program timelines out the window. It's this digressive conversation with him. He's sharing helpful writing information, but we haven't actually talked about my book. I feel stuck with my writing, stuck with these non-rules rules, while my savings account keeps shrinking. What have I gotten myself into?"

I throw my messy bun back into the chair and blow out a frustrated sigh.

"I can see a lot is on your mind. Or should I say, a lot of someone is?"

"I'm not sure what to make of him. Is he really invested in this?"

"Invested in this? Or invested in you?" she challenges me.

"In my success. Obviously." I pull out the pen holding up my hair, letting it down.

Kat takes the pen from my hand and knowingly replaces it with my latte. I was about to destroy that cap with my teeth.

"We can agree that it started out rough and who knows why. Sometimes, we don't get to know the why. But it seems like you guys are moving past that, so my question for you is, do you want it to work?"

"Yes, of course I do. Why would you ask that?"

"Well, in the beginning, it was easy to blame him, but now that he's putting in some effort, you'll have to stop blaming him and trust him. I guess it sounds like you're creating reasons to have an issue with his mentoring style. Maybe try and loosen your grip a little. You know the whole adage, the risk is worth the reward?"

I chuckle. Risk seems to be the theme these days.

"Yeah, I know, cheesy but effective, right?"

"That's not it exactly. Reed's last email mentioned something about risk too."

"Ah, see, I'm already liking Mr. Finally-Returns-a-Fucking-Email."

We both laugh and it's the jolt I need to get out of my head.

"You're right. I'm feeding the anxio-beast." I drag my hands through my hair. "The thought that keeps bothering me is that he's got no reason to want my success. There's no real investment for him. I mean, if he doesn't care about—"

"Careful, Rory. I mean it. It can be all fun and games, but it can't be attachment."

"None of this is fun and games to me. It's about the book." I look out the window for no reason other than sheer paranoia that someone is listening in on our conversation or that, perhaps, I'm avoiding what I might care about.

"Yeah, Rory. The book. Okay."

"It's not about him, I swear. I don't . . . I barely even know him. He's a means to my end."

"Who are you trying to convince here?" she asks, putting a comforting hand on mine. "I have to go, but do yourself a favor: Let him lead the way a little, and come over tonight for margaritas."

"Your blood orange margs are strong competition against your lattes," I say, enjoying my drink on her deck. Our eyes are on the neighborhood kids playing catch in the street below.

"Don't make me choose between my children." Kat cracks a smile, stirring the ice in her rocks glass with a straw.

"So, how bad was the fight with Tillie?" she asks.

"You ever get that feeling when you're trying to be quiet but you're so fired up, your voice naturally amps up in volume and you realize you're screaming in public at your sister's high school field hockey match?" *Sip one.*

She nods. *She knows.*

"We both avoided saying what we meant. The fact is, when she doesn't approve of my choices, she withdraws her affection. Which is so hypocritical for a woman who lived the first half of her life on her own terms without a care for what anyone else thought." *Sip two.*

The same woman who was too busy looking in the mirror to see my shrinking sense of safety in the world. *Sip three.*

I fill Kat in on the details between sips and pauses until the streetlamps come on and the last pinch of daylight disappears.

"The thing is, being ignored, the way she acts like I don't exist, brings me to a place that I thought was extinct."

Kat tops my glass off. "By place, do you mean inner-child Rory?"

"Yes," I admit, swallowing my emotion along with my drink.

I don't let anyone else but Kat see all sides of me, but this realization is hard to face.

"I thought I was absolved of the pain and anger. I've made so much progress in therapy." I wipe at my eyes. "I was so disappointed in myself, by the intensity of my reaction to her rejection. I've tried to reassure myself that the past is in the past, but I wonder if you can ever really leave it behind when something is a permanent part of you?"

Kat looks directly at me, sensing my confliction. "The history between you two needs to be aired out like a prom dress, but, I mean, adulting in general isn't easy. At what point do we become completely self-reliant?"

"My timeline was kind of reversed. I guess when your parents aren't available, you become an adult, no matter your age."

"Healing doesn't happen because of a decision to one day let go of something or someone. It's a good thing you're a writer. Work that shit out on the page." She grabs our glasses and heads into the kitchen.

"I tried that once, remember? Didn't end happily," I call out from the deck.

I could've hugged my mother goodbye in that ridiculously large parka instead of storming off. It could've been different. I wonder who I'd be if my parents were different people too. Where I'd be had I not left my backpack behind.

Kat blows me a kiss and I head inside to curl up with a book—with his book. I've been rereading them since I found out he was my mentor. For research purposes, obviously.

"You have what you need?"

"Yes, thank you for today," I reply. Kat's the kite to my rock. She picks me up off the ground whenever my mind weighs me down.

"I was thinking." Kat transitions effortlessly into her deepest Southern drawl. "Rory Wells, do you have a schoolgirl crush on this Reed Ashton boy?"

I put my water down, spilling a little on my hand and the cover of his book. I watch the droplets bounce off its slippery surface. "He's my mentor." I shake off the remaining water from my hand. "My off-limits mentor."

"Interesting how you brought up *that* last part." She smirks.

"The only interesting thing right now is your wild imagination."

"Okay."

"What? I'm learning from him. That's what I'm supposed to do."

"Learning. Is that what the kids call it these days?"

"Clearly, I'm going to need to find a new place to sleep off my mother problems."

"Let me know how that works out for you." She closes the door to her bedroom with a betting-on-the-house variety of laughter in tow.

I switch off the lamp, abandoning reading.

My thoughts swirl.

Mom and I don't mesh. Not the way she and Lexie do. They like the same things, like action movies, being the center of attention, and winter sports.

The last time I tried to go skiing with them on a girl's weekend, they skied and I lodged with a cup of hot cocoa. There's zero reason in my mind to get cold on purpose.

Uninvited thoughts keep invading my intention.

She called me Rory. My mom, who makes this monumental ordeal about a given name, as if she has some secret language with my sister that I'm not privy to, drops my nickname in an argument like an explosive.

When I was in kindergarten, crying that a boy was being mean to me, Mom would say, *Oh, the boys who tease you actually like you.* I remember thinking how backward that was. They tease me because they like me?

So, if a boy likes me, he'll be mean to me?

That's right, Aurora. They tease you because they like to see your reaction. So don't let them see you react.

I've been negotiating *fight or flight* for a long time, from the oxygen deprivation to lashing out. My first instinct is to avoid being a burden or judged for the symptoms.

I wonder how my mentor would enjoy this version of me, thoughts racing a million miles a minute.

Living with a brain and nervous system that hyper-communicates is like sending a beautifully handwritten letter to your dearest friend and having it arrive with smudges on it. A tragic accident.

I don't hide that I have anxiety, but I'm cautious, often afraid of what someone will do with that information once they have it.

Unless they're trained in how to help, people, often with kind intentions and suggestions, make it worse. Even Kat, who's been my friend for ages, who's seen me have episodes before, knows she can't do anything but be there until it passes.

Maybe it was the tequila or the lack of food I forgot to eat today. With no scheduled lunch break to rely on, I've missed a few meals.

Inhaling deeply, I tap the center of my chest and chant, "I am safe. I am tired. I am hungry." Then I sip on my water and open my phone for a distraction. Kat has to be at work in a few hours, so I don't want to keep her up.

Compulsive thoughts are like traps. The longer I sit in them, the more power they have.

I know it's past business hours.

I know it's not the most sound idea I've ever had.

I'm in no condition to be anything other than fast-acting to ward off the symptoms from spiraling.

With cool shaky hands, I type a direct message to the only person I think may be awake.

ME: Hi there, mentor.
RA: Hey.
ME: So, this is different, the whole chat thing? :)
RA: I don't really chat in the middle of the night, Rory.

I shouldn't have messaged him. I'll apologize and go curl up in a ball of shame now.

ME: Sorry it's so late. I can let you go.
RA: We're here now, so what's up?
ME: I need some mentoring advice.
RA: I don't know if I'm the best person for advice.

I don't get it. Isn't that what mentors do?

ME: You're where I want to be. Living the dream.
RA: You're only seeing a snapshot of my life. Don't disillusion yourself that I have everything you want.

How do I explain what this means to me? How every time I think I'm making progress, my heartbeat, dry mouth, and cold hands remind me who's in charge. I'm working on believing anxiety is not a weakness, but then why am I so tired?

ME: I want my anxiety to go away.
ME: Overshare. :)
RA: What's it like?
ME: Last chance to back out.
RA: I don't ask questions I don't want the answers to.

I drain my water and lean back, holding my phone above my face. The black screen tempers the blue light. It's easier to write about the experience in a safe space.

ME: Remember ride-alongs in driver's education? You're driving with caution, aware of your surroundings. Then, out of nowhere, the instructor slams on her side of the brakes. Tires squeal, the car screeches to a halt, the seat belt cuts into your chest, you get whiplash and bruises to your chest. It takes hours for your heart rate to return to normal. Your arms are sore from gripping the steering wheel. And when your heart rate has returned to normal, the instructor proceeds to list everything you did wrong.

ME: There's a point in the middle of an anxiety attack where you know the end is in sight. It's a tunnel of darkness, and then there's light. You slowly submit to the way your body surrenders, leaving you in an adrenaline puddle.

RA: Is this happening now?

RA: Is there someone who can be with you? We aren't meant to go through everything alone.

That's thoughtful. To even ask. No one has ever asked me that before.

ME: I'm okay. I reached out to you before it got bad. I usually prefer to be alone during the height of one.

RA: I'm glad you're okay. Do you like being alone?

ME: I think so. I spend most of the time in my imagination. Even when I'm not alone. You?

RA: I could be completely settled in a Hemingway sort of way, but I know that's not sustainable. It's in direct conflict with our biology.

RA: Think about when you come into this world, right? You're welcomed into the arms of another person. Then on our deathbeds, we want the people we love most by our side.

ME: Sometimes, though, it doesn't happen like that.

ME: Sometimes, you're not welcomed into this world with open arms. Sometimes, when you die, it's alone at your home in the middle of nowhere while cleaning your firearm.

I stretch my fingers over my head, peeking at the clock. Maybe I'm imagining that we're having a genuine conversation here. Messaging can be misleading like that. One conversation, two perspectives. It's impossible to know.

ME: Have you ever taken yourself on an extended inspiration date? Like a writer's retreat or something? I think I need more than a few hours to shake things up. I think I need an earthquake.

ME: And thanks for listening to me. I owe you one.

10

REED & RORY

"When nothing is sure, everything is possible."
—Margaret Drabble

"Morning, Uncle Reed." Emerson greets me with her infectious smile as I pull off my boots at the door.

"Hey there. How's my favorite rockstar niece?" I grab an apple off the counter.

"All right, you two. I'll see you after my shift." Carlynn kisses Emerson on the cheek. "There's a breakfast casserole warming in the oven," she says, running out the door.

I brew fresh coffee, needing a little extra pep. I couldn't shake Rory's words last night. *I owe you one.* The phrase led me into my dreams, under the hot sun, where I finally got the chance to say what I've needed to say for all these years.

Emerson and I spend the morning quietly working on some exercises, strengthening her core and upper body.

"You're pushing hard today."

She finishes her set. "I'm getting tired. I think I'm done."

I bring Emerson a glass of water and sit on the floor, rolling my neck.

"Sorry I quit early, Uncle Reed."

Reflecting on the strength she has, the courage she doesn't even know she possesses. "You did great. You showed up and you gave it your best."

Her smile tells me I've gotten through.

"Did Mom share my new trick with you? I'm able to push myself up onto the bed, unassisted."

She's beaming with pride, and I hug her because words won't convey how much I love this kid. They'll only reveal my regret. My chest tightens. She deserves the life she had. One with walking, dancing, and normal adolescent trials. Not this.

My phone rattles in my pocket. Emerson opens a book and I get up to check the notification.

It's Rory.

Another message in our chat from last night. I walk into the kitchen, running a hand through my hair as I read through her message.

RW: Hey. Hi. Thanks again for last night. And I'd like it if we can move past it. I definitely wasn't my best self. Do you have time today to talk about next steps with my book? My life was prescribed every hour of every day until now and I need some of that to anchor me. Thanks, Rory

She sounds like she's still waiting for me to lay this whole thing out when I haven't made a plan past yesterday.

This is my time with Emerson. I slide the phone back into my pocket and grab my water.

"Something's different with you. Haircut? Beard trim?" Emerson persuades.

"Nope, same me," I smirk. "I see what you're doing, by the way. I'm just tired from a late night."

"Mom asked me to try and convince you. She misses your face. It's hiding under all that," she laughs, gesturing to my full beard. "So, was it a story-worthy late night?"

"Yeah, wild night at the house," I joke.

"You used to bring me the best stories. You can always make one up."

"Stories on the spot, I'll have to remember that. I was talking to the person I'm mentoring and the chat ran long."

She doesn't press and I'm thankful for that because my phone is vibrating again.

RW: Btw, have you had a chance to look at the chapters? Any feedback?

She's asking questions I don't have time to answer.

I start to type a reply, but every sentence stops short at my knuckles. What was I thinking? After two years of not writing, I could dive right back in? Talking about writing with Rory is like holding up a mirror to my failure.

The rain outside is tapping the roof. Carlynn comes up the drive. I shove my phone into my coat pocket and join Emerson in a game of cards.

My breaths are exaggerated yawns.

"Hi, Mom."

"Hey, girlie. How'd the day go?" she asks, removing her coat and kicking her boots off in the front entryway.

"Uncle Reed said I did my best."

"Always." I give her a wink and lay down three-of-a-kind, all eights.

Carlynn settles in at the round kitchen table and takes a sip of my water. "So, fill me in. What did I miss aside from Emmy kicking your butt over here at rummy?"

"Well, she worked like a champ, we read a little, and now you're seeing the takedown of my winning streak."

Carlynn notices the vibrating sound coming from my coat on the hook.

"You need to get that?"

I shake my head.

"Uncle Reed's tired today," Emerson quips. "Perfect time to sweep in and steal the title."

"Sneaky," I tease, trying to ignore the buzzing sound. Again. "You wait until I take a nap. It'll be game on."

"Oh, late night," Carlynn interjects.

I shoot Carlynn a you-must-be-joking eye.

"What? I'm not up on your dating life these days."

I stand and head back to the coffeepot, pouring myself a cup.

"Late night with the mentor person," Emerson unhelpfully supplies.

Carlynn and Emerson exchange a glance, which I catch out of my peripheral as I add sugar to my coffee.

"Um, brother, you do realize that you're pouring salt in your cup, right?"

I yank my hand away, flicking my wrist to see the damage I've done to my much-desired cup of coffee.

The buzzing sounds off again.

Carlynn side-eyes me and smirks.

"Well, it's been fun, but I've gotta get going." I dump the coffee and give them each a kiss on the cheek before grabbing my coat and boots and heading outside to put them on. Carlynn trails behind me.

"Wait, Reed. Stay and catch a nap in Emmy's room?"

"I'm good. I have some mentor things to take care of."

I struggle pushing my foot in my boot. The laces are too tight.

"How's it going, by the way? Everything with the mentorship?"

"Yeah, yeah, it's good. She's good. I mean, she's smart. I think she'll do well."

I'm actively avoiding eye contact. I don't want her to see that my boot isn't the only thing I'm struggling with. She's got that sister's intuition. I also can't blatantly ignore Carlynn and put her in my pocket, as she's standing right in front of me, watching me haphazardly lace up my boots. As if on cue, Carlynn commands my attention with one word, a sincere request.

"Hey?"

I look up. A navigational pull.

"She's a full-time job," I admit.

"Who is?"

I yank on my coat and take out my phone, holding up the hard evidence.

"Rory Wells, my mentee."

"Oh, I see."

"Yeah, I've been on the phone more in the past two weeks than I have in two years. I hate it. Her thoughts move at lightning speed. I know I miss half of what she's saying. We have these real deadlines and I made this promise to Cal, but something is missing trying to work like this. I barely know her."

"Well, get to know her. Could you video chat?"

"More technology? I'd rather take a bullet."

"That sounds reasonable," she teases.

And I blow out a frustrated sigh. "Conversation is an art, it has to be practiced in someone's presence. It's not this technical disjointed volley of information."

"Why not invite her up here?" she suggests. "There's plenty of room at the house, and you could get that face time in."

"Absolutely not."

Rory at my house? Give up my solitude and silence? Okay, maybe that's extreme, but no, you don't just invite people to stay with you. That's ridiculous. I'm working to convince myself while a small glimmer of something in Carlynn's suggestion excites me, like a butterfly I can't take my eyes off of.

I laugh at Carlynn's serious expression. *This is ridiculous.*

"That wasn't a joke." Carlynn snatches my phone. I drop my shoulders and look her in the eyes. "You know what Pops would say?"

The air is thick, cool, and my lungs inflate like a balloon.

"I'm in over my head." I smile, offering some levity to the situation.

She shakes her head. "Embrace the unexpected."

None of this has been expected. I keep that thought to myself like a souvenir.

Carlynn leaves me with more to think about, which is the last thing I want right now.

I get into my truck and open up our message thread. There are ten new messages. I don't even read them before shooting off a reply.

ME: Hey, I haven't had a chance to read your messages or the new chapters you've sent. I can't keep up with communication like this.

RW: . . . . . .

I see her replying, but I don't wait.

ME: It's not about our conversation last night.

ME: It's not you. Well, it is. But mostly, this is about me.

RW: Wait, you haven't read past the first chapter? Why?

ME: At first, I didn't want to. Then, I couldn't bring myself to.

RW: . . . .

ME: I need to get back to you later when I have my thoughts together.

"Fuck." I slam my phone down and chuck it into the glove box. I bring balled fists to my eyes and fall back. The air in my lungs wheezes on the way out.

At first, I was dismissive of her chapters because I was resentful about the forced situation I was thrown into. Then, I was hesitant to read them because I'm in no position to help anyone. I've only read her first chapter and I don't know if I can trust myself to support her the way she needs, when I can't even bring myself to connect to my own storytelling. I don't want to hurt her—her career—because I'm not me anymore.

A swift realization sucker punches me. If I don't connect with her work, then telling her will set her back even further, but telling her anything would mean exposing everything. She's like that therapist who won't get out of my head. How do I explain to her why I keep my phone notifications on at all times, or why I don't sleep either, or that I'm not writing anymore?

How do I say those things without revealing the reason behind them?

There's a real safety net in being able to log out of my email and walk away. But now I have this person depending on me on the other end, who never seems to sleep or stop talking, someone who can't even make her own coffee or decisions about her story, the same someone who has me opening up my email and talking about writing again, this person who I do not know yet somehow want to understand.

She makes me smile when no one is looking, and I haven't felt that tug in a really long time.

RORY

I find myself in a dream I have no intention of waking from, because I'm going to die from embarrassment. I thought my oversharing was bad—this is an absolute nightmare.

I sent too many messages while chasing my thoughts like I could trust them, and now I've possibly ruined what was starting to feel like progress.

I was tired from another poor night's sleep, but I'd woken up with a renewed sense of motivation after talking to Reed last night. I fed Fitzy, sent my thanks-for-listening email, and then hopped in the shower. I didn't feel like a million bucks yet, but I was clean and vertical so that was an improvement.

I've wanted this mentorship for so long. I let my excitement and nerves and my margarita say too much. Why do I do that? Why can't I slow down?

I grab my coat and charcoal wool scarf. It hasn't snowed and stuck yet this season, but I can taste the heaviness in the air. It's only a matter of time. And I'd welcome the insulation. Somehow, when it snows in Boston, the streets feel warmer.

I take the stairs down to the street, carrying on the conversation I'm having with myself.

I've always done a fair job at keeping the peace, gently side-stepping foreseeable conflict like a line dancing pro. But this is now unavoidable. He doesn't even want to talk to me. I walk through the door into Memory Lane in search of something familiar.

The morning rush relents and Kat eventually makes her way to my corner. She relaxes in her chair, leaning back into the teal plush velour, nursing her latte, piercing eyes peering over her cup, staring me down like a hungry stray.

"I'm here," she announces.

By the time I finish telling her what happened, Kat has both elbows propped up on the small round table between us, head slumped in her hands, jaw clenched.

"This is half my fault. I should've paused."

"Hold up, Rory. If there's one thing I can talk to you about with full certainty, it's business. You have a business arrangement with Mr. Might-Be-A-Mentor. He's supposed to read your work. Plain and simple. He's not doing that. So maybe you sent one or five too many messages, but he's not holding up his end of the deal here."

The more I think about it, the more I talk myself out of holding Reed accountable. I always do this. I turn into some kind of puddle that I let everyone splash through.

"If this had mattered to him at all, he would've had a plan, but he hasn't. How can I believe anything he says when his actions say nothing at all?"

"What a bag of celery sticks this guy is. Does he seriously think he can string you along?"

"Maybe it's not meant to be. This is a sign."

"A sign he doesn't have his shit together. And by the way, you're allowed to have feelings. I mean, how hard is it to read a few chapters and give you some feedback?"

"I think I got too comfortable. He helped me a little and I latched onto that like Velcro."

"You didn't do anything wrong, Rory."

"I hoped."

"Well, hope can be restored, but time cannot, and he's wasting yours. Did you ever ask him why he's been off the grid for the last two years?"

I shake my head. "I shouldn't have paused my therapy sessions." I close my eyes, willing my feelings to find somewhere else to go. "I was in maintenance mode. I thought that meant I was safe to stop going for a while."

"Maybe a good time to get a tune-up." She walks over to the quote board, flipping up scraps of paper in search of something. "Aha, here we go." She cackles on her way back to the table. "A perfect quote for the mystery which is your mentor." Kat smirks knowingly through her words and places a torn strip of paper in my palm.

"Scratch any cynic and you'll find a disappointed idealist."
—*George Carlin*

I attempt to give it back to her. She covers my hand with hers. "You keep it."

The street is fairly empty when I leave Kat's, taking the long way up and around the block. The sun has fallen behind me.

Movement is my trusted friend. I've always kept busy. In college, I stacked my schedule with internships, course work, and paying jobs. I knew then that adrenaline fatigue would knock me down if I stopped. And not functioning intentionally has never been an option.

When I wasn't writing for the paper or studying, I had people who relied on me to show up at the restaurant, customers looking for a person to place dinner orders with and air their grievances to.

I think about how working in restaurants gave me the original idea to write Chelsea's character. My whole life has been influenced by food in one way or another. Mom taught me to believe in food like a love language. So I gravitated to situations where I could feed that.

I've watched so many forevers form and break over a meal.

I knew I wanted to write about love, and food was a natural connection for me. Chelsea is a lot like me, avoidant and uncomfortable with praise. When I wrote her character, I'd recognize pieces of myself that I otherwise hid in my actual life. I consider a writer's inspiration and process. As if there's somehow something cathartic about telling a story with which you have experienced parts of yourself. If your main character resembles you in the way she wears her hair, what cereal she eats, or how she overcomes her inner struggle. And in some way, when your character heals, does a part of you heal too?

Maybe that's what writers do? We bury our own truth in the stories we tell.

These are the questions I'd optimistically believed would be answered in this mentorship. I didn't ever dream it could be so one-sided and cold. I wanted to have a mentor, and beneath that, I had let my imagination indulge in the idea that he wanted to be here.

My pulse quickens and I notice that my feet have picked up the pace. I'm almost stomping these questions into the unresponsive pavement. The air nips at my face in the wind.

When I was barely hanging on last night, Reed was there for me. He offered me understanding and an ear. He asked if I had someone with me. He stayed up with me until I was calm. How can he be both people at the same time?

My chest swells. I slow at the corner, somehow forgetting how to cross.

Expectations are happiness thieves.

The reality is they've never gotten me anywhere but disappointed. He was kind and that's all. He was present but not offering anything. I let my guard down and allowed myself to believe we were on the same page.

It's time to get back on track. I have a book to write, with or without his participation.

I'd try to schedule a session with my therapist, but I don't have health insurance and I need to be careful with my money and I already know what I need to stay regulated. I'll journal instead.

The sky floods in a canopy of spilled ink. A scuffle behind me reaches and alerts my amygdala. My pulse races and my legs instantly press forward. I'm fleeing from the sinking sun. My feet hit the ground, picking up speed, every possible noise closing in. I stay directly under the row of streetlamps near the edge of the curb.

I mean to slow down to steady my breath and heart rate because I'm a rational person and know I'm safe, but instead, my hamstrings burn into a sprint.

I run from my shame, from impulsivity, from all of this wasted time. I run from my pain, from the part of myself I left behind and never got back. I run from regret, from my mom, from all the voices telling me to quit. I run and I don't stop until I'm in my apartment, back against the door, spine sliding down to the floor.

Fitz greets me, purring at my knees, then jumps away and scatters, startled by the shriek of my phone ringing.

I answer, trembling, clearing my throat. "Hello."

"Hello, hey, Rory? It's Reed."

A flutter travels along my ribcage and lodges itself at the base of my throat.

Shit. I clasp my hand over my mouth.

His voice registers. *His voice!*

The deep way it hummed my name like a memorized lyric, has me throwing myself onto my couch to hide under a cushion.

"You there?"

I steady my voice. "How did you know it was me?"

"I called you," he points out, understandably confused. "Hey, are you all right?"

I'm shaking my head on a prayer that I can pull myself together enough to get through this call, to hear the inevitable rejection. I pushed too hard and he wants out. Couldn't he have emailed me instead?

Just get it over with.

"Yes, yes, I was startled by my own shadow, really."

He laughs, scratchy and low. My heart responds, kind of like panic, kind of like something I can't identify.

One, two, three, four . . . five, six, seven, eight.

"I want to apologize for, you know, how I handled things earlier, when—"

"I'm sorry for all my messages. I had so many thoughts I wanted to brainstorm and sometimes they take over and that's no excuse but—"

"My response to you, Rory, was entirely on me, and I owe you an explanation."

"Honestly, can we forget what happened and focus on what's next?"

Silence stretches between us like taffy.

"Reed, you still there?" I tread lightly.

"You kinda threw me off here. I had a whole speech planned."

Oh.

My feet shake beneath me. There's barking in the background.

"You have a dog?"

"Golden retriever. Fenway. He's all cuddles."

"I'm pro-cuddle. Well, I mean, you know, with animals, like my cat, Fitzwilliam Darcy. He's a great cuddler." *Oh my shit show, Rory, stop talking.*

"Austen fan?"

"That's putting it mildly."

"How would ya feel about the next lesson being in person?"

"Like a video chat?"

"I was thinking more like you coming up to New Hampshire."

The phone slips from my hand like sand and wedges itself in the couch cushion. When I reach to dig it out, I end up pushing it further into an abyss of foam and fabric.

"No. This cannot be happening." This might as well be a Venus flytrap. In a frenzy, I flip off the cushion entirely while scrambling for my phone. "Hold on, Reed. Sorry, one minute, please."

Worst timing ever.

I manage to grab hold of it, pressing it back to my ear. The receiver is molten lava against my skin.

I put it on speaker and sink on top of the discarded cushion lying on the floor and shake out my legs, riddled with nerves again. I acknowledge their mixed variety, images of me ending up in a body bag and the other kind, the rush of anticipation I try to deny.

My voice cracks. "As in, your house?"

"Yes, my house," Reed confirms.

"Um."

"There's plenty of space here, or you can stay up the road at my mom's or at my sister's if that would make you more comfortable."

"Well, at the risk of sounding confused, which, by the way, I am . . . why?"

"I think we need a reset, and I think being in the same space for purposes of creativity and efficiency will help us to make up for lost time. It's quiet here and there's tons of space to work. Sometimes, the change of scenery even helps with inspiration."

"You're being serious?" *He doesn't want to quit.*

"I promise you'll be safe here. I have some ideas and I want to share them. What we're trying to do isn't working for either of us, and I want it to work. Rory, I want to help you get your book done."

My eyes flood. My fingertips tingle. I bury my face in my hands.

"So, you'll come up? I'm still in this if you are."

"That depends," I say, stifling a sniffle.

"On what?"

"How's the coffee in New Hampshire?"

"Fresh and hot. And wait until you try my mom's blueberry scones."

11

RORY & REED

"THE MEETING OF TWO PERSONALITIES IS LIKE THE CONTACT OF TWO CHEMICAL SUBSTANCES: IF THERE IS ANY REACTION, BOTH ARE TRANSFORMED." —C.G. JUNG

"I'VE CLOCKED THE DRIVE. It's only two hours and thirty-five minutes door to door. You have a ten-minute pee-stop leeway and then I'm putting out a search party."

Kat's watched too many Cold Case Files.

"I won't be stopping." I've also watched too many episodes.

We went over the pros and cons this morning and agreed on two things. One, I have a book to write. Whether I like it or not, I'm behind now, and Reed is a part of the solution. Second, this can only happen if I agree to let Kat install a tracking app on my phone.

I pull away from my street, neck-to-neck brick and concrete, leaving the comfort of the city I love to chase my dream up Interstate 93. Beneath the bumps in the road, nothing has truly changed. My hopes are higher than ever.

"Thanks for keeping me company," I tell Kat over the phone, "and for this latte. Reed swears the coffee is good in New Hampshire, but it's obviously not yours."

"Damn straight." The clash of cabinets opening and slamming shut fills the car. "Where are Fitz's treats again?"

"In the drawer by the sink."

"Okay, cool. Got 'em."

"I was thinking, random thought, but why can't people come with warning labels?" I ask, nursing my latte. "Like, intellectual but emotionally unavailable."

"Oooh, I like this game. Let's play this out." She laughs. "What would your label be?"

"Hmmm . . . if you stay for the credits, you may wait forever." The heat is blasting and I crack the window.

"Speak nicely about yourself or else," she lectures.

"I know what you're thinking." She's always pushed me to book a one-way ticket to pursue anything other than my daily routine. And it's because planes are scary. I'm beginning to wonder if not living the life I want is scarier.

"Hey, you might know what I'm thinking, but you definitely don't know what I'm going to say."

"Oh yeah?"

"Will choose live music, coffee, and tequila over you."

We both laugh at that one. "Perfect, Kat."

"All right, I'm gonna go be a good kitty auntie and spoil the crap out of Mr. Darcy here. You focus on driving. Text when you get there. Love ya."

"Love ya more."

This stretch of highway is such a straight shot that I barely notice how far I've driven.

How did I get so lucky to have this friendship? Kat's watching my place and taking care of my cat. I'm borrowing her car and sipping on the last-minute cinnamon latte she made me. Even if I wanted to thank her, she wouldn't let me. I know friends are supposed to be there for one another, but I wonder if the bridge between us has become unbalanced. She's constantly crossing it to help me. The coffees, the pep talks, the favors, the car. I wouldn't be here right now if she hadn't insisted that I submit my manuscript.

I cross the state line, sweating through my sweater. I'm nervous, maybe. Excited, most likely. Anxious, the strongest contender. I squirm in my seat, unable to find a spot to settle in.

My phone rings and I answer my Bluetooth immediately, surprised I'm getting service and that Kat's checking on me. "Hey, that was fast. Can you name thirty-one flavors in thirty-one seconds? I'll start you off with vanilla, chocolate, and strawberry. Ready, set, go."

"Rory." His deep velvet voice greets me.

I slam my eyes shut. It's not Kat. *Ahhh.* It's Reed. *Oh, no no no. You're driving. Eyes on the road, Rory. Eyes on the road.*

"Hey, sorry. I thought you were someone else. Someone who really likes ice cream," I fumble, slapping my palm to my forehead.

He laughs.

I breathe.

"I like ice cream," he adds.

I smile.

"Wanted to check on how you're doing with time?"

Again, with the thoughtfulness.

"I just passed exit twenty."

"Okay, cool, you have another hour."

There are barely any cars on the two-lane route.

Another beat passes without a dial tone. My palms slide down the grain of the steering wheel. I guess I'll say something.

"Great, okay, well, thanks for checking."

"Call if you get lost or anything. The bend by the bridge can be hard to see. So go slowly around the lake."

"Sure thing."

Reed checking on me should make me feel relieved yet my mind is racing.

Two lanes become one once I exit the highway. The main road is sparsely populated with convenience stores and restaurants. I get giddy when I think of the poems Frost wrote inspired by the towns here. This is going to be the perfect place to channel inspiration. The car in front of me has a license plate that reads *Live Free or Die*.

Why does that feel like a warning? *Because you have an overactive imagination, Rory Wells. That's why.*

The steering wheel rattles in my hands, alerting me to the dirt road I'm on. I follow the single path slowly as instructed. The autumn colors are fading into a canvas of russet and red, marigold and brown. A rainbow forest. An artist's haven.

The closer I get to Reed's house, the faster my heart races. In a few minutes, we'll meet. I've had two hours to prepare myself and here I am, a sweaty, pulse-accelerating mess. My hands squeeze the wheel so forcefully that my knuckles blanch at the sheer will of my anticipation.

I find a clearing to pull over to take a few pictures and breaths. Kat has to see how beautiful this place is.

Unbuckling myself, I stretch my legs and roll my neck, then step out of the car into stillness, quite possibly the quietest place I've ever been. *I'm never going to fall asleep.*

The sun's peeking through tall trees and unmistakable fresh pine saturates the air. The magnitude of their shadows cast over the glassy lake. It reminds me of the time Arty and Mom took Lexie and me to Disney On Ice. During intermission we stood for a lithograph. The finished product was a cut-out of points and curves. This view is nature's lithograph. This moment is preserved in time.

After I grab the images, I shoot them off to Kat with an "in the woods" message and a smiley emoji. It's almost dark and his house is over the covered bridge. I can't see it, but I know it's there.

A few cleansing breaths and a wish later, I creep onto the gravel drive, parking behind a blue pickup truck. I preemptively steady my breath and adrenaline. *One, two, three, four . . . five, six, seven–*

My door swings open and a pair of boots lands in front of me. I sense his presence before I see him.

"Are you all right?" His voice projects sharp and sore.

I keep my hands locked on the steering wheel. Unsure what's happening and if I'm allowed to speak.

He steps back, which gives me room to exhale.

"Did you get lost?" he asks. His tone is still tense, tight, and its state of urgency activates my pulse. My body can't decide if it's cold and scared or cold and curious.

I bubble wrap myself in rambling words.

"I stopped to take in the view. Have you seen this place? Of course you have. You live here. What I mean is that it's breathtaking. That's all. I just had to capture it."

I'm disoriented by Reed's rush to greet me and now it's getting dark and my shoulders are up to my ears, waiting for his next move. *Why isn't he moving? Should I keep talking? Is he pissed for some reason?*

"Do you have a bag?"

Although his voice drops its edge, my pulse and imagination refuse to slow their roll.

"Yes, thanks." I turn off the engine and grab my purse and book off the passenger seat. "It's in the back."

"Cool. Follow me."

Cool? How is any of this cool?

This   is   heart-palpitating,   chewing-your-nails-till-they-bleed,   meeting-someone-you-admire-who-perplexes-the-shit-out-of-you, next-level, spiral-inducing panic central.

This is anything but cool.

But I'm not showing him an ounce of my uncool. I need to be guarded, aware. I never know which version of Reed I'm about to get.

I slide out of my car and lock it, noticing that I fit in the width of his shadow. He effortlessly lifts my bag and carries it with him.

The paint is peeling in some places around the exterior of the house. The green roof is dark, like a layer of damp moss has been strategically placed on top, camouflaging the camp-style cabin into its natural surroundings.

We walk down a stone path, up a wooden ramp, and through an enclosed porch. There's a door in front of me with a pane of glass large enough that I'm able to sneak a peek. Looking down into the room, there's nothing but undefined shapes. Another landing, six feet off to the right, holds a door with a smaller pane of glass cut in the middle. A warm glow is emitting from inside.

"Hey, this way," he calls over to where I'm frozen in an internal recitation of "The Road Not Taken." To get into Reed Ashton's house, there's a literal fork in the road.

Another wooden ramp leads inside.

Reed holds the door open for me, and I duck under his arm into the amber-lit open-concept kitchen, with a long farmhouse table in front of me and eight wooden chairs in varied designs tucked into it. The faux-tile flooring is cracked in spaces, held together by metal that's lost its shine. Reed's house is inviting, soft yellows and well-loved oak, warm like butter on toast.

Though it's inviting, I still shrink myself to blend in where I stand. Hyper-aware of the way my body next to his quickly fills up the entire space we're in, sandwiched between the refrigerator and a counter.

The door closes and now Reed's brown boots are directly in front of me with the laces undone. A loud thud hits the floor when he drops my bag.

"Plan to stay a while?"

"I like to be prepared."

If he can hear how unsettled I feel in this moment, he doesn't let on.

"Of course you do. You can come inside."

I push off the wall and move closer, holding the book to my chest. My eyes are glued to his boots, and the way the laces land accidentally in figure eights.

"What are you reading?" he asks, clearing his throat.

My gaze drifts up to his knees.

I pull the book away from my body and wince when I'm reminded of what I'm holding and how premeditated this appears.

He's obviously going to see it now.

Delaying the inevitable will only make it ten times more awkward.

I scrutinize the length of his arms, covered in a soft charcoal gray fleece. A tan hand presses against his thigh, the skin weathered around the knuckles. He slides both hands into his pockets.

"Rory."

My eyes snap up to meet Reed head-on, and my vision crystalizes. He says my name, and my heart leaps into my throat.

"*Heart for One*." Offering a tentative smile, hoping he'll be flattered, not nettled.

He's staring right into me, like a sheltering coastal oak on the shore, severe, bearded, and blue. His eyes are made of free-flowing waves against a setting sun. The deep center of the ocean, layered like crushed velvet, storm clouds, and spring.

His lips are sealed and I'm completely unprepared to be this close to Reed Ashton.

"It's one of my favorites in contemporary romance." I nod my head, knowing the chattering train is going full steam ahead. *Change the subject, ask him any question, just say something.* "Do you have a favorite book?"

The space between us is consumed by an all-encompassing rush and swell. Two sets of inhales and exhales, coming and going like the tide.

"*A Farewell to Arms*," he shares. "Hemingway."

I don't mean to lose my voice, but when he speaks, it echoes barely above a whisper, and my reply is drowned out by our sweeping shallow breaths.

Being in the same space as Reed forces me to face the one thing I've been dodging since finding out he was my mentor. The one thing that's been simmering beneath the surface. The one thing Kat called from miles away.

Well, it's too late now.

I'm in trouble.

Big, big, trouble.

REED

She's holding my book, shifting her feet, when a loose laugh escapes, remnants of an internal thought I don't have access to.

"I've read your series a few times." She rubs her fingers along the edge of the kitchen counter. When Rory speaks again, she talks to the middle of my chest. A grin hesitates on her lips, a golden light flickers in her eyes.

"It's good to meet you." She reaches out to shake my hand. Her shoulders fall and her whole face blossoms into a blushing smile.

Every muscle in my body strains against itself as her fingers slide into my grasp. I turn rigid from the contact while a piercing ache shoots down the cords of my forearm. The blast of heat that lands on impact between our palms forces me to rip my hand from hers, rescuing my scrambled thoughts and racing pulse. I run my hand through my hair to extinguish the shock.

"It's good to meet you too."

I study her jumping gaze as she surveys her surroundings. She's averting eye contact while I'm willing her to look at me.

Fenway finally gets with the program and lazily greets Rory, politely informing her that she's standing in his spot.

"This is Fenway. He's all beta. Likes long walks on the beach and wild salmon, and he'll let you rub around his ears all day long."

"Oh, this sweet boy, how can you get any work done at all?" She kneels down and goes straight for behind the ears. Hi, Fenway, I'm Aurora, but everyone calls me Rory," she shares in a gentle, inviting voice.

"Aurora?" I repeat, as a direct question. She looks up under thick glasses and lashes as her name jumps off my tongue again. "Aurora."

"Only my mom calls me that. Rory's good. Also, may I use your bathroom?"

"Of course." I walk her over to the door by the stairs. "I can show you to your room after."

"Great, thanks." She shuts the door.

With Rory safely out of my sight, I drop my head back against the wood paneling by the stairwell and breathe deeply. I work the inside of my cheek between my teeth. My eyes dance over the room. Layers of wood and linoleum, scattered mementos lining the counter. Generations have lived and passed in this house. Sweat and tears weaved throughout.

I can't look at the head of the table without seeing Pops. An unkempt mustache, stiff flannel hugging his shoulders, black coffee and newspaper permeating the air.

The iron latch to the bathroom door scrapes. I straighten up and kick off the wall.

In this light, I can see that Rory's cheeks are lightly freckled and visibly flushed.

I clear my throat.

"Follow me," I say, carrying her bag of bricks up the stairs.

The upstairs is true to its original log-cabin style. There's minimal natural light when the bedroom doors are closed. There are two on the left. To the right is a narrow hall that resembles a bridge connecting to another bedroom and a bathroom.

It's easy to get turned around if you don't know your way, so I map it out for Rory.

"The room I'm in and the bathroom are over there. Which is all yours. I'll take the bathroom downstairs."

She nods.

"That's my parents' room," I say, pointing out the first room we pass. I swing left into the next open door. "This is my room, where you'll be staying," I confirm, dropping her bag next to the rocking chair by the window, quickly scanning the space for the eighteenth time today.

Rory pauses in the doorway. "The room at the end of the hall, with the closed door—"

"It's another bedroom."

Seeming to accept my answer, she enters my room.

"It hasn't changed much from high school," I say, following along the trail of her sweeping path. She beelines to the bookshelf in front of my bed, trapping me by the window. She scans the stacks. Her face alternates between micro-expressions of approval and curiosity. "Feel free to borrow whatever you like."

"All these books. This room is like a mini-library. Is this *yours*?"

"Yup."

She crosses the room, finally giving me a clear shot to the door. Her fingers trace a poster of the solar system tacked to the slanted ceiling. "Back in the good ol' days when Pluto was still considered a planet. Your room, Reed, is like a time capsule." She throws a look over her shoulder that I can't interpret. "Are you sure I'm not putting you out? I'm happy to stay on the couch or something."

"There's extra blankets on the bed. I even fluffed the pillows. Sorry though, fresh out of mints."

"How domestic. A host and a bestselling author, what can't you do?" Her playfulness knocks at something inside of me. "Seriously, thank you. It's great."

This is my cue to end the scene. If I were writing this moment, I'd make my character exit immediately. But this is real life, there's no script, and I'm not moving a damn inch.

Her vanilla-bean-and-violet scent has replaced the oxygen in here. And this is a small room. Only so much breathing capacity left.

I need to get out of here. Right now.

"You can prop open the window if it gets stuffy. You know, from the heat." I gesture behind me.

When our eyes connect again, my pulse runs the length of my body. Not sure what this feeling is, but I can only liken it to the way Lew and Pops would stare each other down during intense games of chess, patiently waiting for their opponent to make their next move. Except this feels more like a hostile takeover of my senses and I'm about to be in checkmate.

"I'll start making some food," I add quickly, realizing I haven't even asked if she's hungry. "Take your time, of course. If you want to shower, towels are in the bathroom for you." I stop talking, reminding myself that this is business and to quit acting like a fucking concierge.

"Um," she giggles. "Okay, sounds good. Can I help with any-thing?"

You can help by not moving another inch until I leave.

"No." I hold out a firm hand like a stop sign.

I'd have to be living under a rock not to notice her full lips and bright eyes. She's attractive, but that doesn't give me the green light to be attracted to her. It would also help if she didn't smell like summer and night swimming.

I close the door behind me without uttering another word, flying down the steps, the banister burning the palm of my hand. I'm not convinced cooking will provide its usual diversion and much-needed distraction.

I rip a bottle of red from the liquor cabinet. Maybe wine will.

12

RORY

"IN LOVE THERE ARE TWO THINGS: BODIES AND WORDS."
—JOYCE CAROL OATES

ME: Made it. :)

KAT: I know. Remember, tracking app? Is he cute?

ME: That's seriously your first question?

KAT: Your answer determines my follow-up questions.

ME: It was awkward.

ME: He showed me my room and then couldn't get away fast enough.

KAT: Is he awkward and CUTE?

ME: Maybe this was a bad idea.

KAT: Going to NH?

ME: Messaging you! Byeeeeee.

KAT: Please at least tell me there's only one bed.

13

REED

"THERE ARE DARKNESSES IN LIFE AND THERE ARE LIGHTS,
AND YOU ARE ONE OF THE LIGHTS, THE LIGHT OF ALL LIGHTS."
—BRAM STOKER

WHEN RORY APPEARS AT the top of the stairs, I've roasted enough garlic and sage to perform an exorcism on my scent receptors. The scallops are sautéing and pasta water is boiling. I have our plates set out and half a bottle of merlot consumed.

Like a hyper-aware cat, she assesses the stairs, borderline skittish, conscious of every step, even the ones she hasn't taken yet. Both of us, for different reasons, I imagine, hone in on her approach. I observe in complete stillness to avoid possibly startling her. When she makes it to the landing, I exhale.

She's covered head to toe, wearing leggings and a gray hoodie with faded NYU letters stitched in purple and white across her chest. It looks like three Rorys could fit in there. A mop of wet hair is piled on top of her head. As she gets closer, that damn scent swirls back into the mix, threatening the shield of seasoning I've built. I take an intentionally large gulp of wine.

"You look relaxed," I observe.

"Decided to take you up on the hot shower offer."

"Good." I fill my mouth with merlot again, shaking the image of Rory in my shower.

"So, can I help you with anything now?"

Sure, can you start by telling me how you walked into my life when I was perfectly fine before?

"It smells incredible," she adds.

Pretty sure that's you. Get a hold of yourself.

"Wine?" I offer. "I have beer or seltzer. Coffee?"

"Wine is great, thanks." She reaches for the empty glass on the counter, holding the base steady while I pour. We raise our glasses at the same time. "Cheers to fresh starts," she toasts.

She either has a great poker face or I'm sorely out of practice. Attraction usually works both ways, in my experience. My thoughts are so juvenile. I've been around my family for too long. I've forgotten what it looks like to talk to a pretty woman.

"Cheers," I reply, swallowing more than my wine and sending a silent wish to make it out of this night with a shred of dignity.

In the spirit of starting fresh, I also make a vow. Rory is here—here for her book. I told her this was a safe space to write in. I gave her my word that I would provide mentorship and guidance. And I'll hold to that promise like it's my final breath.

Our plates overflow with penne, roasted tomatoes, and shaved parmesan, flavors that transport me to never-ending summer lunches in Tuscany.

"I'm used to you being...different...online. You're not entirely what I expected." She shares this with me as I spill the scallops on top of the pasta.

"Oh yeah, you're not entirely what I expected either."

She's luminous in the warm light of the kitchen. I grab both plates and walk over to the table.

There's an ease to the way we move in the same direction, an unforced togetherness. I notice our bodies are being respectful, yet keeping close, figuring out how to occupy the same space.

"Does this mean you'd like to continue your ice-breaker questions to get to know me better?"

"Not at all," she spits out, waving her free hand wildly. Her laughter is unshy as she folds down into it. The echo it creates in the room is feminine and uplifting. A sound I didn't know I was missing until now. A vise-grip squeezes inside my chest.

She adds through her fading laughter, "Please don't ever bring them up again. It's one thing to hide behind a screen when I need to take cover. But I can't hide from you here, can I?"

Feeling is mutual, Rory Wells.

"They were fun," I say, instead.

"Fun? Really? I got the impression you felt like you were being interrogated."

"It took me some time to initially warm up to the idea."

I shove food into my mouth faster than is appealing but necessary to shut my trap.

"Where'd you learn to cook like this?"

I'm still chewing and savoring. I sip my wine and lean back in my chair. I know it's common courtesy to look at someone when talking to them, but I'm finding it virtually impossible to take my eyes off her at all.

"My mom taught me to cook a bit. We have a lot of shared meals around here. Everyone ends up in the kitchen at some point. Though my passion for cooking came from my time living abroad."

Rory's eyes come alive like a standing ovation.

"The entire country and culture, customs and celebrations, at the heart of it all was cuisine. It's truly their love language."

She's smiling now. It encourages me to keep going.

I tell her about the simplicity of the ingredients. How most meals are prepared with meat and vegetables off the land, and always bread. Such good bread.

"When I returned to the States with what I had learned in Tuscany, I couldn't go back to eating the way I had. So, I began experimenting with making Tuscan dishes from what was available locally."

I'm swept away by the gift of Rory's listening. Can't really tell these things over email. She focuses on me with her entire body. From her glittering eyes to stilled fork, I know I have her full attention. She hangs onto what I'm saying like it's a sermon. Nothing rattles her focus. Not even the radiator as it hisses and settles. She doesn't flinch when my words stick as I strain to clear my throat. I've lost my train of thought the way she's tuned in, her face so close, warm from the wine. I feel seen, and it feels intoxicating to be seen.

I fill my mouth with wine, chewing on its tart cherry and chocolate notes.

Maybe this isn't about her at all. Maybe I want her looking at me like who I was before I ruined everything in my life.

"All of that sounds incredible. Exactly how I imagine Europe." She props her head onto her fist.

Rory's presence at this table flips a switch in my mind, a memory of the last woman who sat at this table who wasn't related to me. She scrolled on her phone, spoke over me, only saw around me. She'd interject the obligatory nod, but her focus was elsewhere. The disconnection became a real issue in our relationship. I began to despise technology more than I despised being ignored.

There's a clear social statement that we embrace when we refuse to put our devices down. It sells this story that you can stay connected to people from all over the world, while refusing to recognize that it also keeps you far away from the people directly in front of you.

Some people in life can be sitting clear across from one another and feel invisible. Then, there are certain people who shine a spotlight right on you, and you can't help but feel like the only star in the sky.

Rory's attentiveness has placed my past in front of me, *admittedly not the best timing*, but I've learned to accept that I can't control the timing of anything.

"What's your favorite country you've been to?" I ask.

She glances down to her plate, pushing around the penne. "I haven't actually been outside the country. My passport expired years ago. Gotta get that renewed."

Wait. She's moved around her whole life, but she hasn't traveled. The squeeze is back, tighter this time.

"I like living in this area. There's so much to see right here." I try to shift the conversation.

Rory lights up with enthusiasm, lifting her gaze to the original wood staircase. "I bet there's a ton of history in this house."

"Tomorrow, I can show you around. I thought maybe we'd take the afternoon before diving in. You said you write at night, right?"

"Yes, sometimes. I just, well, do you think that's a wise idea? Shouldn't we begin right away? I don't want to waste valuable time."

"Who says it'll be wasted?"

She pulls her eyes from mine, and I feel it, doubt and uncertainty, tugging at my gut. She doesn't trust me yet. *Good. She shouldn't.*

"You know what they say, all work and no play makes for terribly uninspired writing sessions."

"If that's what they say, I guess I better be prepared to play."

"First, I need to ask you something. So I can do my job." I raise an eyebrow, daring her to take an additional step outside of her comfort zone.

"Name it," she says, wide-eyed.

"Your latest draft. I need it. And then comes the hard part. You can't touch a single word until I give you revision notes."

14

RORY

"IT IS IMPOSSIBLE TO BECOME LESS OF YOURSELF BY DOING SOMETHING YOU REALLY WANNA DO. YOU CAN ONLY BECOME LESS BY NOT DOING IT." —TIFFANIE DEBARTOLO

I KNEW THE REQUEST for my manuscript was coming at some point. Just thought maybe I'd have time to unpack first.

My fingers grasp the duffel's handle and I yank hard, tossing it on his bed. It takes effort to get everything out. I organize my clothes into piles before putting them away in an empty dresser drawer.

Then I reshape the duffel, shaking off the dust, feeling like I, too, could use a good shake and reshape.

"Well, this thing has seen better days."

"What's the last decade you used it in?" Kat laughs through the bluetooth in my ear.

I blow out a long breath and sit on the edge of the bed facing the dresser and closed door.

This room is the vacation version of Lexie's. It has a life of its own like hers too. But the space doesn't feel like tiny cuts. It's magazine-worthy. With its memorabilia, earth tones, dark wood, and cozy light, it resembles a patchwork quilt stitched together by generations of Ashton family stories.

"Um, hello, Rory . . . are you still present?"

"Yikes, sorry. Anyway, the last time I used the duffel was when I broke up with Ben and moved my stuff out of his condo."

"Well, then that duffel was in desperate need of an adventure."

That makes two of us.

Ben was a nice guy. Stable. Secure. When he asked me to live with him, I froze. I wasn't ready to give up the dream of finding a love so special, the kind that inspires and ignites. There was no spark with Ben. We simply co-existed in the way the shallow part of a lake does with the sand. No waves, no current, just an even side-to-side sway.

He took my refusal as rejection. I tried to get him to see that I was inflicting a scratch, necessary pain now to avoid a gaping wound in the future.

Mom obviously loved him. When we broke up, she didn't speak to me for weeks, mourning whatever life she had mapped out for me.

"You ever hear from him?"

"Nah." I shake my head and toss the duffel under Reed's bed. "I heard he was promoted to vice president at his investment firm."

"How'd that come across your radar?"

"Mom mentioned it while passing the asparagus."

Kat bursts out in maniacal laughter. "She did not? That is some prize-worthy Matilda moves right there."

"He had a 401k. She really liked him, maybe more than she likes me."

"She liked that his security was one less thing you'd have to worry about."

Kat sometimes surprises me and knows what I'm thinking before I do, like she's doing now, in a witchy, premonition-y sort of way.

"Yeah, well, that ship sailed."

"So . . . do I get any juicy deets about the new ship in your harbor?"

"No ship. No harbor. And yes, I learned that he can cook. Like really cook."

"Right. Well, I'll say what we're both thinking—that's hot."

I'm grateful Kat can't see my full-on smile as I pull out what I want to wear tomorrow—an ivory cable-knit sweater and leggings.

The idea that we will be starting to work on my story sends my stomach somersaulting.

"He asked me to give him the updated draft, like tonight, so he can start making notes."

"Great news. Let's get this show on the road." Kat turns on the water and starts brushing her teeth.

"But what if he hates it? Or something happens to it?"

"Don't you have like ten backups?" she mutters through a mouthful of toothpaste.

"Yes."

The sound of water stops and Kat sighs.

"Rory Wells, send the man the damn manuscript. It's not like before. Untangle yourself from the past, or you'll be strangled by it."

"Welcome to my brain. It's a good time here."

"Yeah, we'll see in sixty seconds."

We both laugh in the face of that truth.

Even with the fear of not knowing what he'll think of my story, there's a part of me that felt comfortable being in his company. Like at dinner tonight. Conversation was easy. Listening to him speak was like reading one of his books—I was all in.

He's lived abroad and seen the world. Of course he has a well of experience to draw from, and I was riveted and shocked by the sheer volume of what he had to say. The wine. The food. Fenway at our feet. His mind is like some irresistible loveseat, with a footrest made for me.

"He's taking me out on some kind of property tour tomorrow. He seems to be eagerly awaiting it."

"Whoa, whoa, Rory Wells. I'm by no means sold yet on Mr. Changes-His-Tune-More-Than-I-Change-My-Coffee-Filters, but I have to say, I like what I'm seeing here."

"I have no idea what you're talking about." I place my clothes into the drawer.

"You sure? I'm happy to elaborate."

"My clothes should all fit," I deflect, inventorying out loud. "Wait, what is this?" I say, staring at the slinky fabric in my hands. "What did you do?"

"What do you mean?"

"Little. Black. Dress. Ring any bells?"

"Oh yeah, that needed an adventure too."

"Cocktail attire in the middle of the woods?"

"Humor me? What if there's a town ball or something."

"Nope. Definitely not," I say, half-laughing, mostly horrified.

"Heels too," she boasts.

"I see that, Katherine." Examining the sparkly peep-toes she managed to hide inside my bag.

The jitters are in attendance, amongst other fluttery feelings.

"Fine if you don't want to wear the dress, but for the sake of your future as an author, I removed *the* pants."

"Those are my emergency oh-shit-I-ran-out-of-pants pants," I gasp, defending *the* pants. "I love those pants."

"But they don't love you."

"Hey, they don't have to look good, just feel good."

"That's what she said, Rory." Kat exhales a triumphant breath. "That's what she said," she repeats. A sharp clapping sound, followed by laughter, penetrates the airwaves. "I know Mr. Your-Type-But-Clearly-We-Aren't-Admitting-That-Yet is your mentor. All I'm saying is, there's zero chance I was letting you wear pants that have to be secured around your waist with a rubber band, while staying under the same roof with a hot fellow writer."

"I'm going to have to duct tape your mouth now." My eyes dart around the room to make sure her voice is not carrying, somehow, someway.

I've had those sunflower lounge pants since high school, and they're still hanging on strong.

"You'll thank me for this later."

"It doesn't matter what I wear in front of Reed."

"Sure it doesn't." I can hear Kat's smirk on the other end. "Send him the draft."

"I am."

"Like right now."

"I will."

"There's plenty more material in my arsenal, if you're in need of further encouragement."

I fold the dress up and put it in the drawer. "I'm going to do it."

"I've got all the time in the—"

"Okay, okay." I open my laptop on the bed and power it on. I breathe, make a wish, and press send.

15

REED

WHILE THE COFFEE BREWS, Rory pokes around the kitchen with a sense of purpose. I welcome her preoccupation.

After receiving her draft last night, I printed it, made myself some ginger tea, and stayed up most of the night reading, *finally*.

I surprised myself with how effortless it was to get back into revising pages. Rory's also surprising me right now—she's more alert than I expected since declaring herself an anti-morning person.

Her hair cascades down her oversized ivory sweater, reaching the middle of her back. She's standing between the table on her left and the built-in buffet on her right. It stretches the length of the kitchen from Fenway's spot to the ramp by the staircase. What was once intended as a serving station has become a catch-all of clutter and family photographs.

Watching Rory scope out a new environment is like observing an artist approach a blank canvas. There's a silent contract being drawn up between the creator and the creation.

She holds each frame, evaluating them and drawing conclusions while she's at it.

No different than the conclusions I've been drawing about her since she arrived. It's unavoidable. The writer's way. We can't help ourselves. "So, this is you, and . . .?"

It takes a few beats for me to reach her bare feet. With caution and while holding my breath, I lean over Rory's shoulder to look at the particular image. "That's Pops." I sigh.

"Thick as thieves." She smiles. "You look alike."

I take the frame, careful to avoid grazing her fingers. Matching jerseys and ridiculous grins plastered on our faces.

"Yeah, this was the best game we'd ever been to, and that's saying a lot." The center of my chest squeezes hard. Inhales stop short in my lungs. "Game five of the 2004 ALCS. At home. Against the Yankees. Nail-biting energy. Concentrated chaos like a shaken-up soda can. Pops was snapping peanuts while the crowd silently prayed. Eight decades' worth of heartbreak and bated breath and unrelenting hope. It took fourteen innings, Rory. Six hours. Not a single fan in the park was on a cellphone. It was the stuff of miracles. It was magic."

Blinking away the moisture in my eyes, I hand the frame back to Rory, sliding my fingers into my pocket, rubbing the small stone inside with my thumb. He's still everywhere in this house and always will be.

"It ended up being one of the firsts of our lasts. He saw me graduate in the spring, we spent part of the summer at the beach, and then I went abroad, and a year later he was gone."

"This photo. It's incredible, really." Her voice is full, sticky, and her eyes expose her meaning.

She keeps looking at me like she knows where I've been.

I clear my throat and walk away to check on the coffee. The clouds out the window hang low. An early light peeks through across the water.

"I've got an important question for you." Rory's voice suddenly behind me.

"Okay." *Not okay.* I step to the side.

"How about that amazing New Hampshire coffee you sold me on?" She breaks into a gentle smile—too inviting, too close, too distracting. *What was I doing?*

"So, is that a yes on the coffee?"

"Yes." I cough, once, twice, leaning over the counter to open the cupboard. It creaks in my grasp. "Take your pick."

She's beside me again, reaching, gliding her bitten nails over the peeling paint.

"I've been meaning to sand it down and stain them."

"Oh, really? I love it, actually. They've had a good life." She pulls out her pick, placing it on the counter.

"Are you sure you want this one?" I gesture to the mug she's chosen.

"It suits me." She guides her fingers gently over the cerulean blue clay, and my fingerprints. "I like the way it feels."

This confined space is less than three feet from wall to wall. One of us needs to move, preferably not at the same time.

"By the way, how do you take your coffee?"

"Anything's fine." Her feet shuffle around to the other side of the counter.

This has become a line dance I don't know the choreography to. I scan the contents of each shelf with no direction, so I grab it all.

"Hey, so what about your dad? He ever take you to Fenway?"

"No."

I line up my haul on the counter. Milk, cream, almond milk, whipped cream.

Rory narrows in on one thing. "Whipped cream?"

"Anything means everything," I inform her, shocked she isn't one of those people with a complicated coffee order.

"Milk is fine. Thanks."

I fill our mugs and put all the shit I just set down back into the fridge. I crack the kitchen window, letting the vanilla and violets out and my composure back in.

Rory's eyelids close as she breathes in the steam.

Exhale, Reed. Exhale!

"Is it up to your city standards?" My teasing question interrupts what might be her ritual, and I momentarily feel bad about it until I see her lips rise into a smile over the lip of the mug.

"The first sip is my favorite."

"I'll take that as a yes."

She shrugs, then turns on her heel into the living room, leaving me thoroughly aware of her absence.

We've already blown through our ice-breakers, and at this point, she knows more about me than anyone has in a long time. I refresh Fenway's water bowl, then follow her trail.

Rory's chosen a spot on the far end of the couch, so I take the opposite end. She's alternating glances between the open book in her lap and the scenery out the bay window.

Sharing memories of Pops was not on my agenda. I'm going to have to rely on my rusty conversational skills moving forward, however excruciating small talk may be. "Whatcha got there?" I ask.

Two round cheeks flush above a timid smile. She pushes her glasses up the bridge of her nose. "Caught me. I'm rereading *Cupid's Desire*."

"Why read that crap? I've got plenty to choose from." I grab one and hold it up. "Austen?"

"Nice try, and you realize that you're saying your book is crap, right?"

I walk over and playfully pluck it from her hands. She reaches to grab it back.

"Oh, please don't look inside it," she pleads.

But it's too late. I've already scanned the page, noting the marked-up margins and highlights, some kind of color-coded shorthand in block lettering. "What's all this?"

"I'm an active note-taker. An old journalism habit from college."

I can't decipher a single word of it, but the organization, the system she's got going on, is impressive. My stomach flips as I hand my story—her book—back to her.

"Thanks." She rests it on her thighs and returns to the lake view.

"What do you think?" I ask, curious if her reaction will match my assumption.

"There are no words to describe it." Her eyes remain on the water. And my eyes remain on her.

I had a feeling she'd appreciate this view, and the nurturing way she's cradling my mug sends something familiar through me. Like a memory that hasn't even happened yet.

"I made that monstrosity in high school."

"Oh, really." She inspects it, and will soon discover the flaws.

"I failed the assignment, but not the class, and I needed it to graduate."

"You can't fail at art, Reed."

I reach in my pocket and rub the stone a few times. "I'll build from wood and dig in the dirt any day, but me and clay? Not compatible."

She turns back to me. The lake's reflection has brightened her emerald eyes into a shimmering gold. Her gaze becomes impossible to hold. I bite the lip of my mug.

"You can fail at plenty of things."

"But failure isn't necessarily a negative thing, right?" she asks. Her ears perk up, along with her posture.

"I don't know. Maybe failing only exists in the absence of an attempt?"

She pulls her phone out of nowhere. *Seriously, what part of her body did that come from?* This is the first time I've seen her with her phone. I'd anticipated it would've been hooked up to her like an IV.

"Do you need privacy?" I ask.

She laughs softly while furiously typing with one hand. "I'm writing down what we've talked about. I don't want to lose this thought."

"You take notes on your phone like that often?"

"Whenever I have an idea, which happens often." She smiles. "Like with my story, it started out as a bunch of random notes. I knew the characters and that the opening scene was at a playground. I saw all these snapshots before the big picture."

This might be a good time to bring up the notes I've made on her draft. I wanted to wait a day and let her get settled, but this feels like a good segue.

"I think your opening scene is perfect." I rub behind my neck. Exhale hard and long.

"You do?" She focuses all of her attention on me.

Her face is glowing and I'm pretty sure mine has been drained of all color. I don't want to answer her follow-up question. I didn't exactly prep what I was going to say about her book.

When I remain silent, she takes the reins of the conversation again, speaking through a slight yawn.

"I'm not used to all this nature." She sips her coffee. "It's like you could hear a snowflake drop out here."

I stand. "How did you sleep?"

She shrugs. "The usual. I don't really sleep much, ever." A crease between her eyebrows appears. "It's not about the bed or anything—it's a me issue."

"Same," I admit. "Sleep, that is."

Rory glances down at my pocket. I release the stone. "Hey, how about Fenway and I show you around."

She leaps off the couch like a jack-in-the-box, uncoordinated, and with a frightening volume of enthusiasm.

Coffee shoots through the air.

I reach out to steady her balance, and immediately retreat when faced with her wide eyes, reminding me where my hands should not be heading.

Fenway joins in the commotion, barking for attention.

"Um, your rug, I'm so sorry, let me clean this up. What a mess. Really, I'm so sorry."

Her hands shake. Her face is flushed.

"Rory, it's fine. This house can handle a spill. Easy fix." I grab a towel from the kitchen.

When I return, Rory's hunched over the spot, gentle laughter rolls off her shoulders, while she types on her phone. My jaw softens as I lay the towel down and press it into the rug.

I've witnessed multiple versions of Rory in the last twenty-four hours. Reserved, happy, optimistic, shy, nervous, funny, supportive . . . I can't keep up with who she is. Is she amused, taking notes again, or is there someone on the other end of that smile? Whatever it is, this unfiltered version might be my favorite thus far.

"Let me grab my coat and boots," she says.

Ten minutes later, Rory skips down the stairs, tugging at the ends of her hair. Her coat, scarf, and wool hat will work, but whatever she's got on her feet is hazardous material.

Brown and battered, hugging her legs up to her knees. I stop there.

"What are those?"

She turns to look around, confused.

"What are what?"

"Is that the only footwear you brought?" I ask, kneeling to lace my boot up.

"These are my winter boots."

"Those are not winter boots." I shake my head, not masking my chuckle.

"Um, they fit like a glove."

"You ever think about replacing that pair? They're worn-down and broken."

"No, I haven't."

"Why the hell not? If they aren't practical?"

"Do you ever have something that becomes too much a part of you to ever let go of?"

Sweat and sunshine. Pops's catcher's mitt sweeps away my sense of time and place.

Rory's hard stare, the way her breath shows in the rise and fall of her chest under her sweater, still pulling at the ends of her hair, and asking heavy questions. They feel like steel cages, and answering them honestly might be the only way to set myself free.

"Yes, Rory. I do." I finish lacing up my boots. "Maybe those death traps are suitable for salted, shoveled sidewalks in Boston, but all they'll guarantee you here is a concussion." I drag out a bin full of gear from the hall closet.

"What's this, like a Berry Lake lost and found?" She sifts through the mess.

"Overflow." I toss the boots at her feet. "Have at it. Take what you need and layer these socks over the tissue paper you're wearing."

"Thank you, I think." She squirms. "This is all very generous, but I don't think I should wear someone else's socks."

"Frostbite is option B."

She scowls at me through a stubborn frown. "Give me those." Her hasty hands rip them from my grip, and I ignore the tug at my lips and the rush of her thumb brushing against my skin.

16

RORY

"I GIVE YOU TRUTH IN THE PLEASANT DISGUISE OF ILLUSION."
—TENNESSEE WILLIAMS

I'M LIKE A KID in a candy store touring the property around Reed's house. He knows every nook and cranny of this woodland haven. We check out his mother's garden, rows of damp dirt this time of year, the blueberry patch (where, I'm told, all the magic happens), and an old shed full of equipment and tools.

My opening scene is perfect. He said those words.

I'm so pumped to get to work tonight, I skip down the dock and stop at the edge, next to two Adirondack chairs and a covered boat.

Peeking past my feet, I search for life under the water. The denim blue top layer blackens to brown beneath the surface. It would be so easy to fall in.

A ripple in my peripheral lands in my ears like a restrained gulp, catching at the base of your throat. By the time I scan the water, the lake is silent again.

As quickly as something was here, it's gone, swallowed whole.

"Even when it's freezing, it must be beautiful out here at night," I say. "I bet you can see every star."

"Nothing else like it."

"Alaska has skies like that. I don't remember much, we didn't live there for long, but I'll never forget how bright the nights were."

"Were you okay with moving around so much?" Reed asks, bending down, checking the ropes along the dock.

"It's all I knew. Commitment kinda epitomized confinement to my mom, so we were always on the road, seeking her next great adventure."

"What about your dad?"

"No, um." I stumble over my thoughts like a skipping stone. I've been asked this so many times before that you'd think there'd be no reason to pause, yet I brace myself for the unwanted sympathy masked as sweetness.

"My father left before he knew my name." I plaster an exaggerated smile on my face, edging the end of the dock. The memory surfaces much like the vision of this lake—still and opaque. "Every June leading up to Father's Day, I'd get all moody and reclusive, listening to kids talking about pancakes and barbecues. Maybe what stung the most was that while I was missing a father, I never knew if he was missing me. For years I waited for him to change his mind, realize he'd made this colossal mistake and return. I wished on stars and dandelions." *Like a homesick kid at summer camp checking the mail every day for that care package, proof someone back home hadn't forgotten them.* The wind shifts and I pass a glance over my shoulder at Reed. "By the time I turned ten, I gave up."

He steps up beside me. Our eyes return to the horizon of pines.

"Anyway, the man who chose to be my dad, Arty, he's amazing. So good for my mom. Had my father never left, I'd never have Arty. And that is truly unimaginable."

Reed's voice sticks then clears.

He nods once. *He understands some part of what I've said.*

"What about your name, Aurora? Is there a story behind it?" he asks, handling each syllable with care.

This man simply speaks—and my pulse kicks into high gear. My thoughts tumble around like an amateur wrestling match. The ideas are too close and too sloppy for me to figure out who's winning. What is happening to me? *Get out of your head, Rory! Answer him!*

"Of course there's a story. It's ridiculous, really. She believes that a name is your first gift, like a legacy to uphold or something. She'll tell anyone who'll listen—'I held Aurora under the northern lights that night, and her eyes lit up with the same green-gold flashes and flairs in the sky. My daughter was a newborn and her eyes should've been closed, but instead, they were wide open, ready to take on the world.' To my mom, there was some kind of synchronicity in that moment. She says she named me Aurora after a sky so magnificent, she knew I was destined for greatness."

His steady gaze scrapes down my spine.

"I warned you, it's out there." I laugh through the squeeze in my chest, the wave of cringe that inevitably follows when I say too much.

"Your mom sounds like she knows what she's talking about."

"Don't ever let her hear you say that. She'll never let you forget it." I swat his arm like I do with Kat. *Like that's okay.* He doesn't even flinch, but my stomach flips.

When he turns away from the lake, I roll my eyes at myself.

"On an off night, the lights can be undetectable. You have to take a picture in the dark and then wait to view them inside. It's all luck of the draw." Reed's head lowers as we walk down the dock.

"My mom never calls me Rory. In her eyes, it's like a shortcut, a cheapened version of the truth." My shoulders tense at my following thought. "Meanwhile, my younger sister, Alexis," the axis on which Mom's world spins, "is Lexie."

I sneak a glance at Reed, who's unreadable. As per usual.

Birds chirping remind me of how breathtaking this area is, and how I'm wasting this view with yammering on about nothing.

We continue our stroll, and I'm surprised when he keeps the conversation going. "Do you prefer Rory?"

"Um, well, it's hard to say. I've always been Aurora with my mom, and Rory with just about everyone else. In college, my roommate called me Rory, and when she did, I didn't correct her. Somehow, it felt like a term of endearment the way she said it. Mom wasn't around to make a scene. Anyway, I was tired of being Aurora. It felt like a fresh start. I could be Rory Wells, a girl with a ticket to anywhere." *A girl with a nickname and a friend.*

"And it stuck." He grins like it's his only job on planet earth. It makes me want to decode every micro-expression, every one of his unfiltered thoughts, like the time I saw his photo online. His face is fuller now, tanner, older, covered in a thick beard and hair that curls over his forehead. It's still Reed, undeniably him, but his eyes aren't as bright, and I think they might be sad.

"How many times have you seen the northern lights?" I want to know.

"Once. You?"

"Never," I confess.

He winces like someone stole his ice cream cone.

"It's on my bucket list," I throw in. "Where did you see them?"

"A few winters ago at Mount Washington. It was incredible."

"How many pictures did you take?"

"Not a single one."

"What?" I blurt out, shocked that he didn't take a single photo. "I wouldn't have put the camera down."

"Some moments, Rory Wells, are meant to be captured," he points to my hat, dusting the yarn by my temple, "solely in here."

He's halfway down the trail, hands shoved into his pockets and hunched inside his heavy coat, when it occurs to me that I've stopped in my tracks.

The quick sprint to catch up leaves me a little winded and a lot warmer.

"You know, you've got great stories. You could use them in your writing," he suggests.

We're walking shoulder to shoulder now, with Fenway hanging on my right.

"Use my own story. No, that's not an option."

"I don't mean write a memoir. I mean spin the details into fiction, until truth and imagination are indistinguishable from one another."

I reach for my phone in my pocket and take note.

"You could try to remember what we talk about." Reed picks up a stick and throws it for Fenway, who chases off after it.

"No way. Remember, I take diligent notes and notes for the notes. Safer that way." I smile. The air is infused with pine and promise. I want to tell Reed how much I value his experience but I don't want to sound too eager. "I think you're a natural storyteller."

He shrugs, bending down again, this time though he picks up a flat rock, and slips it into his pocket.

"I think they're bestsellers for a reason. People love the banter, of course—it's playful and funny—but they come back for the way your characters make them feel. When a reader puts your book down having learned something about life and relationships, that's the mark of a great story."

"I don't see exactly how my books do all that, but thank you. I appreciate it."

"Love," I reply, like it's the most obvious answer.

His side-eye tells me I've missed my mark. "Love?"

"Love is what people believe in," I reiterate, kicking at dried leaves and fractured branches.

"You mean what people want to believe in." He picks up another rock, examines it, and tosses it to the ground.

Our footsteps through crunching earth soften to silence. I turn around, facing him. The chill heats my cheeks.

Maybe it's the walk. Maybe it's all this fresh air that makes his eyes come alive, wild against a heavy gray sky.

We're standing so close now that I catch his wintergreen breath. I mean to ask him about the rocks. I mean to ask him why he chooses some over others. I mean to, but I don't.

Instead, my voice drops, almost cracking, as I lift to meet him at eye level. "What I'm trying to say, is that believing," my words fall to a whisper, "is proof of love."

His almost undetectable lips, hidden by his beard, shine as he runs his tongue over them. They descend closer and my teeth begin to lightly tap. One step forward and his mouth will . . . I shouldn't want him to kiss me. I shouldn't, but I do.

A twig breaks beneath my borrowed boot, snapping me from this pine-induced lust trance.

I lose my balance, dropping like it's a fire drill.

Reed's above me now, extending his hand. I keep my gaze on the ground as I push myself up on my own.

The boots are big. "The air is too fresh out here."

"Come again?" He laughs. "The air is too fresh?" he asks, perplexed.

"Yup, you heard me. I'm used to city air—street meat and industry." I hurry down the uneven path, not entirely certain if this is the right way.

He hangs back a few steps, and I chew on my bottom lip without regard for how bruised it and my pride will be later.

"Wait up," he calls out. "I want to finish this. You say love is the reason readers buy my books. But it's not actual love. I sell them the idea of love. I mean, they have to know real love is often messy and temporary, not neatly wrapped in a three-hundred-page package with a happily ever after at the end?"

I laugh, recalling Carlin's quote on cynicism. *Kat always knows.* But I'm not buying it either. I've read his books. If he doesn't believe in love, he can't write the way he does. I whip around, standing my ground. "Are you kidding? They call you 'Cupid's arrow.' You, of all people, should know that's when it's worth it. The messier, the better. The flaws. The imperfection. Your characters sure know it. Your books may be fiction, but your message about love is real."

"Has that been your experience? The messier, the better?" His redirection effectively halts my conviction. He's making this personal, and I don't know why. "Okay, so that's a no."

He's assuming my hesitation is denial. He's acting like he's got me pegged.

"Well, is that what you believe then?" he accuses.

I fumble over what I think and what I've read in books and what I want to be true. But they blend. They mix together and it's impossible to know what I believe for certain anymore.

"I'm not convinced love is something you can ever plan for," I finally conclude.

"This surprises me. To hear the woman who has a plan for her plan sticking up for anything that could deviate from it." Reed's face is alive with debate. He's enjoying this.

"And you?" is the only thing I manage to push out.

"About what? About love?" he laughs, confidently. *At my expense.*

I stomp ahead, then demand answers over my shoulder. "What about you, as in, what about your experiences? What about your books? And characters? What about your writing?" *The Rory train has left the station.* "Is that why you haven't published anything in two years, because you don't believe in love anymore?" *And crashed.*

His face gives away nothing.

"And you're wrong."

"How so?" he states, cool and unaffected. Meanwhile, my heart is pounding in place.

"You're wrong about me."

"Well, then. You know what they say about assuming?" His smile makes an appearance.

I do. Flushed, and feeling like a total ass, I try to gather my composure. Before I'm able to smooth things over, Reed points out that we aren't far from his house.

"Hey, Rory, want to race back?"

And now he's not playing fair. Because I've lost track of how this conversation even began.

"Do I want to run for fun in the freezing cold? I've never wanted anything less in my life, except that time I had mono freshman year of college. That might have been the worst."

He's been smiling, grinning, smirking since I arrived, and I had expected only cold, straight-faced, serious Reed. But this Reed, even when he's composed, is somehow playfully engaging, and permeating the air in his soapy, spiced scent.

Daylight makes its descent quicker than our pace back to the house. By the time we arrive, the sky is covered in silver swirls.

Reed reaches a door I haven't seen till now. I'm out of breath and drenched in sweat. He grabs my hand, pressing his warm fingers into mine, guiding me over the nonexistent step.

We fall through the doorway into a pitch-black room, crashing into one another. The absurdity of the two of us stumbling around, peeling our outer layers off, is the most ridiculous I've felt in some time. Our breathing is as loud as our laughter.

"I can't wait to take a hot shower and get to bed, so we can start early tomorrow," I say, through chattering teeth.

"I'll get tea going."

Reed leads me into the living room, and instantly I'm on fire. Actually, I'm not on fire, but I'm standing next to one.

It takes me a second to orient myself, distracted by the commotion we made coming inside, I missed the active sounds coming from the main rooms of the house.

It takes longer for me to register that all of the kitchen lights are on too. Muddled voices mix with crackling logs, and the smell of onions drenched in butter permeates the air. I'm starving now.

And then, I stop walking and breathing in one swoop.

I see her before she sees us. Cradling a mixing bowl in one arm and gripping a wooden spoon with the other. Her stirs are methodic and quick. She moves around the kitchen with confidence, the kind that tells me she does this with her eyes closed, stopping mid-stir because she senses us before she acknowledges us. Dark spirals fall to her shoulders and bounce like springs as she whips the contents of her bowl into submission.

"Are we in an alternate dimension?" I whisper, leaning into Reed.

"Hey," she says.

He ignores my question. I avoid her gaze and focus on the fireplace, full of fresh logs and smoke, orange and white flames that brush my icy skin and burn.

"Hey?" he questions, running his hand across the back of his neck, taking a noticeable step to the left, and widening the gap between us. The sides of my body are now two distinctly different temperatures.

I'm wishing Kat were here to make me laugh with one of her jokes. Something about side-stepping or line dancing. She'd call it as she sees it, and then we'd rush out of here driving a getaway car. I entertain this scenario long enough to distract me from the pairs of eyes on me. I clasp my hands against my damp clothes behind my back.

"Who's this?" Amusement lingers in her tone.

She might not know who I am, but I've scanned all the photos by the stairs—I know exactly who she is.

17

RORY

"Before we love with our heart, we already love with our imagination." —Louise Colet

I'd considered maybe we'd run into his family. But not while I'm standing in their living room, wearing their boots and socks, my thawing sweat and distress on full display.

I turn my gaze to Reed and expect to find him physically in the same heap of disarray. Aside from his deer in headlights look, the rest of him remains unmarred from our jog back. In fact, it seems to have invigorated him. He's glowing. *Is that an actual sheen on his cheekbone?*

Meanwhile I'm standing here looking like a deer after impact. No wonder he quickly put distance between us. I crook my head slightly, stealing a sniff. *I mean, not that bad.*

He turns to me with his head only. "I can tell them to leave."

"No." I have to stop myself from screeching. That would be ten times worse. "It's fine." *It's their house*, I think to myself.

His jaw tenses and pulses beneath its straight line. I refuse to go down in the Ashton storybooks as the random writer who once ruined Sunday dinner because my overactive sympathetic nervous system makes social interaction vomit-inducing.

"Recovering people-pleaser over here. I've got this." *Nope. That probably didn't help.*

I want Reed to believe me, and even though I'm anxious about meeting new people, I can adapt. "I've been in worse situations."

"Is that supposed to be encouraging?"

"It means I can handle a crowd."

At the same time that Reed goes to say something to me, his mom approaches us with open arms, speaking loud enough that their separate voices become one.

"Hi there, you must be Rory."

Does she know who I am? I look at Reed and back at her.

"So nice to meet you. I'm Meryl, and this one," she nods her head toward Reed, "calls me Mom. Welcome." She wipes her hands over her apron, moving closer to where we're standing. It's covered in bright marigold sunflowers, green ties wrapping around her neck and waist like vines.

"By the way, we hug around here, Rory," she announces with open arms.

When in Rome, I tell myself, stepping into her embrace. If she's willing to hug a total stranger in my current state, at the very least she deserves a hug back, and maybe a halo.

Her hug is fierce, aromatic, and genuine. *These are the hugs Reed has had his whole life?*

I pull away, rubbing my arms. The thought tugs at my gut.

"Are you cold?" Meryl asks.

I shake my head, painting a faint smile to assure her.

"Heya, honey. Out on the trail?" Her voice is as direct as it is sincere.

"Hey Mom, we made our way around the property."

His shoulders drop and the determined cross on his brows disappears. He sighs, and my lips part.

"Okay, well, everybody, this is Aurora Wells, the writer I'm mentoring. She's up here so we can get some distraction-free work in. This is my Uncle Lew; my sister, Carlynn; her husband, Will; and this kiddo is my pal and the coolest niece ever, Emerson."

Everyone waves from where they're scattered in the kitchen. I'm grateful for their restraint. I don't think I can handle hugging any more Ashtons at this point.

"Hello, it's really good to meet everyone. I'm Rory, the writer." *Oh wow, that hurt coming out.*

"I like that. Writer Rory, wanna come to our house for Scrabble while you're here?" Emerson asks.

"I'm sure they're going to be busy," Carlynn interjects, winking at Reed. All eyes turn to me.

Suddenly, I feel like a crystal ball everyone is looking directly into for answers.

I walk over to Emerson and kneel in front of her wheelchair. Her eyes are amber and wistful, her face full of youthful freckles, and her dark, rich hair matches her mom's and grandma's.

"We'll have plenty of time and I'd love to see your house. Name the day and I'll be there." Emerson's smile is affirming.

"Tuesdays and Thursdays are our mornings together," she replies, motioning to Reed.

I can feel his eyes behind me like bullets in my back.

Sure, I probably should've consulted him before committing a portion of our limited time together, but when a kid asks you over for Scrabble, you go to Scrabble. "We can fit that in, right, Reed?" I try to grab his attention. "Reed?"

He shifts his gaze to Emerson. "We'll figure it out." He doesn't look at me when he adds, "Don't let her fool you. Emerson's a Scrabble whiz."

I try and catch his expression to see if I misread the situation, but I fail on both accounts. These clothes now own me like a straitjacket. I'm going to need a SWAT team to peel me out of them.

Just like that, as if the entire room has been on pause and someone's pressed play, everyone resumes whatever they were doing before we waltzed in. Will and Emerson are talking at the kitchen table, Uncle Lew is adding logs to the fire now, and Carlynn is cooking.

Fenway is at his spot in front of the kitchen door.

Meryl and Reed both glance in my direction. Something transpires between them, a mother-child language I don't speak. I feel like a wet towel being hung out to dry.

"I'll be back down shortly," I announce.

"Take your time," Meryl insists.

"Grab a shower," Reed adds.

It must be worse than I thought if he's blatantly suggesting I shower.

As I head up the stairs, I attempt to be stealth, looking over my shoulder to where they're standing, like a teenager stealing a glimpse of her crush in anticipation of some silent reassurance that he's crushing too.

Reed doesn't look up. But Meryl does and waves. *Busted.*

Before I turn into the bathroom, I overhear her melodic voice—"Maybe you should take your own advice there, son."

I like her.

The tradeoff of not going to bed early tonight is getting a closer look into who Reed Ashton is, and maybe if I listen real hard, I'll find the answers on my own.

At Mom's house, there are four unfilled seats lagging at the end of the dining room table like dead weight. Dinner at the Ashton's, is a fascinating sight to behold.

I'm sandwiched between Meryl and Emerson. Lew is settled at the end of the table between Emerson and Carlynn, and Will and Reed are sitting across from me. The only empty seat remains at the head of the table. The ease with which they gather, genuinely enjoying one another's company, reaching over one another, completing each other's sentences. I observe Reed's family, looking in as if I'm not here at all. A snowglobe of what a family is supposed to resemble.

"What's your favorite game, Rory?" Emerson asks, breaking through an unfamiliar sensation rushing my heart.

"See, what did I tell ya?" Reed interjects, winking at Emerson. "Scoping out her competition."

"I'll share a little secret," I say. "I hate to win."

Emerson giggles. "What do you mean? Like, for real? You wanna lose?"

I lean over and whisper loud enough for everyone to hear, "I feel so bad for the losing person or team that it takes away the joy of winning. The only exception is Scrabble, of course."

Reed's expression is scrutinizing, so I force a tight-lipped smile at his unnerving response, and turn to a friendlier face.

"So, Rory," Meryl chimes in, "we'd love to hear more about you. It's nice to have someone new at the table."

Putting me center stage instantly presses the pulse-racing button in my head.

"Are you from the area?" she adds.

"Boston." *Keep it simple. They don't need your whole story, Rory. You just met them. Slow your roll.*

"We don't know much about the program," Carlynn notes. "Aside from telling us about you, Reed hasn't said a thing. Maybe you can fill us in." She passes a bowl to Emerson, and I linger on this new piece of information, that Reed's spoken about me to his family. It's not like he was excited to be a mentor, but he didn't hide me away like some secret, either.

Flooding with adrenaline, I exclaim, "Reed's books have been a source of inspiration for me. You all must be so proud of him." I glance over my glass of water at Reed, whose eyes are on his plate.

Meryl smiles. "Yes, we've always been proud of him."

"Uncle Reed writes the best stories, though I'm not allowed to read some pages," she says, sighing.

"Not until you're old enough to vote, Em," Carlynn replies in a playful tone, and directs the focus back onto me. "How do you like being a mentee?"

They all seem at ease, but I'm starting to question my place at the table and in this conversation. It never matters how many people are in a room—when I'm trapped by my fears, I am alone. Plus, I can't decide if Reed is comfortable with this conversation. Should I hold back? If he hasn't said much, should I say anything at all?

"Your brother's a great mentor. I especially appreciate his lessons."

The hard line of his mouth falters enough to show a sliver of amusement curving at the corners, and then they drop back in line.

"There's great trails here, if you're into hiking," Will contributes. "Reed's hiked all over the country."

"We're both homebodies," Carlynn adds. "Reed's the traveler in our family. What's your book about?"

"Um." My throat runs dry. I've practiced this a million times in my head, but aside from Kat and applying for the program, I haven't spoken to anyone about my story. I realize Reed and I haven't even prepared for this question. Is this something we should be doing? I attempt to explain what I've poured my heart and soul into over a plate of mashed potatoes, and I fumble.

"It's a love story." I take a deep breath, pushing my potatoes around on my plate. "About two people stuck at the hands of the universe's timing. It explores the relationship between the right people meeting at the wrong time or the wrong people meeting at the right time. And ultimately, can these two right people find their way to the right time, or is there a window in how many chances you get when it comes to love? Is it choice or chance, random or destiny?" Did that even make any sense? Wincing in embarrassment, I shove the potatoes in my mouth.

"Sounds interesting . . ." Carlynn trails off, and I become nauseated at her obvious discomfort.

The truth is, it's never easy to talk about this book because it can trigger memories of the moment I left my life exposed to the world for anyone to invade. Those flashbacks haunted me for years. I'd lost my will to write, crippled by guilt for even attempting to move on. First, I journaled, slowly reacquainting myself with my voice, then I started building scenes in my head. Sometimes, our own stories replay like broken records. Same old tune. This mentorship and this book are like throwing on a new record. I want to listen to it on repeat.

"She's a talented writer," Reed pipes up and I stop chewing. Was that a genuine compliment? My jaw drops open sans potatoes. He smirks, tapping his left temple, reminding me of what he said earlier on our walk. I've never been more grateful for a room full of strangers in my life.

Meryl places her hand over mine and squeezes. "Well, if Reed vouches for you, I know you must be a great writer." Everyone is casually eating and laughing across the table.

"How did you end up applying?" Carlynn asks, digging into her salad.

"My friend encouraged me after hearing me talk about it for years. When I turned thirty, I decided to finally put myself out there, as a final test, to see if I could make something of my writing." *One, two, three, four.*

"Wait," Reed projects from across the table. "What was the plan if you didn't get in?" He's all hard lines and urgency, and I don't understand his meaning or why he's looking at me with enough intensity to split a tree stump, or me, in half.

I lock my feet around the legs of my chair to keep them still. *Five, six, seven, eight.*

"There was no plan after that. That was my stop sign." I sip my water.

"You do know there's more than one path to publishing these days. That a no in one direction can be a yes in another."

"Yes, well, that direction would've been something other than writing for me."

"So, you'd give up?" he asks me in front of everyone.

The air between is slippery and numb. Reed's revulsion takes up most of the breathing room at the table, and no one else is speaking. I'm so embarrassed he's putting me on the spot. I should've known it wouldn't take long for him to run cold again. A stark reminder of what we are—strangers—and what we aren't—people who laugh together over a meal.

"You must be thrilled to have been chosen. What an accomplishment, Rory. Right, Reed? What great luck for us all to be here together now." Meryl's aware of her son, and whether she means what she's saying to me or not, I'm simply grateful for her.

"I'm so excited for this opportunity and to work with Reed." I smile hesitantly, peeking up at his intense eyes still locked on me.

Don't cry, Rory Wells. DO NOT cry.

As if on cue from the heavens, Uncle Lew breaks the direction of the conversation, sending us on a new course. "So, are you also a traveler like Reed?"

Except for that course. Am I wearing my regret on my face today or something? I wipe my mouth with my napkin.

"Step one is getting my book finished," I clear my throat and Meryl removes her hand from mine, "with the help of someone at this table," I take a sip of my water, wishing it was vodka, "and step two will be to see the northern lights."

"Well, that sounds like a great plan," Meryl adds. "And don't worry too much about pesky plans anyway. None of us knows what card we'll pull next, even when we think we can see our own hand."

"All right, enough questions. Rory is here for work, not to reenact her life story for our entertainment," Reed states, standing from the table and bringing his dishes over to the sink. "Emmy, how about you come take some of these books in the living room off my hands?"

"Sweet. Any fairy tales?" Emerson tries to back up but the wheel is stuck on the front of my chair.

I push back my chair and step around it. "Is it okay with you if I help get the wheel unstuck?"

"Yes, please. Thanks so much," she says, giving me permission. I pause, wondering what Emerson's story is. Then I pull her wheel-chair out of the jam. She speeds off into the living room. Reed waits for me to join him and we walk in together. He comes in close, and my body responds, erupting in tingles. I rub my arms to settle the shiver.

"Here, take this." He slides his black hoodie off and holds it open for me to slip on. I discreetly inhale as I pull up the zipper. Cedar, orange, spice, and soap. It's entirely unfair how good he smells. If I smelled like this, I'd bottle that up and sell it. Create a line of *Book Boyfriend* fragrances. I'd be able to retire off the concept after some company buys my idea. Then I'd find a small house under the stars and write all day and night.

I pull out my phone and make a note. I spend the rest of the night distracted by fantasies, enveloped in his smell, unable to shake the sense that everyone is avoiding talking about Reed's writing, especially him.

18

RORY

"WE LOVE BECAUSE IT'S THE ONLY
TRUE ADVENTURE." —NIKKI GIOVANNI

WHEN THE HOUSE IS empty, I linger by his family photos. I keep coming back to them, to the stories they tell.

Reed walks through the door with Fenway, the night air clinging to him. "Hey."

"Hi."

"I'm sorry for all the questions tonight. They can't seem to help themselves." He moves in closer.

"Don't be," I reassure him, clearing my throat. "They were being friendly." Curious if he'll acknowledge his role in the questioning.

"My family's interested in you, understandably, but they should read a room better, and honestly, I should've too."

He noticed.

"It was nice. Having them interested in what I had to say."

"I can't imagine you don't get that a lot."

"No." I shake my head.

Reed lands to my right. "Well, maybe you don't notice."

Maybe he should stop this guessing game. The idea that everyone was noticing me has me replaying everything I said.

He adds, "Because I sat in a room tonight with five people whose eyes were solely focused on you."

"Focused or horrified? Because I saw their faces too. If you ask me, it could go either way." I laugh.

"Do you always do that?"

I shift my attention to him, crossing my arms over my chest. "Do what?"

"Make light of things."

"Only when I'm especially uncomfortable," I try to joke again. "All right, stop looking at me that way. I guess it happens."

"So a deflection technique?" His stare pierces through me.

"Speaking of deflection, I'm going to very obviously change the subject now." I reach for a photo of what looks like an identical Reed and Carlynn sitting together on rocks in vintage swimsuits. "Are these your parents?"

"Well played." He takes the picture frame from me. His eyes soften and sparkle. A youthful smile appears, hidden behind layers of scruff. "This is the first picture ever taken of them, on the day they met."

"Really? That's incredibly lucky."

"Pops believed in luck. Mom believed in choice. He was a romantic. Together, they made sense."

"No wonder you're a romance author."

"What? No, not like Pops. I just make up stories."

"Are you saying that you don't believe in love?"

"I'm like my mom—I believe relationships are about choice."

"How so?"

"Simple. You make the choice to love someone. You show up, you do the work. Or you don't. Either way, it's a choice."

"You make love sound like a job." We're picking up where we left off earlier and it's infuriating. "You have to believe in what you're writing or how will anyone else?"

"People believe what they want to believe."

"I don't know how I can be holding a picture that embodies so much love, something you grew up witnessing every day, and accept that you don't believe in it."

"I didn't say I don't believe in it."

"But you—"

"Hold that thought." Reed lifts his pointer and smiles, strolling over to the stove where he starts the kettle.

I want the remote he's holding, pressing pause whenever he feels like it after I've asked him an important question. I chomp on his words, trying to find the place where Reed got turned around. It's not about losing his father, and it's not about a broken family. They are sitcom material—you end the half-hour happy.

He hands me the mug that I've appropriated while I'm here.

"Chamomile. Helps with sleep."

"Thank you." I wiggle from the heat, unsettled and unsure if this is a peace offering, a subtle gesture toward a ceasefire for this conversation. I'm straddling the line of being too curious to stop thinking and too tired to keep digging into his head.

I want to ask, but I know I can't dig deeper. There are consequences for that.

"Bedtime story?" He implies more than asks, as if he's made the decision for both of us.

I decide to let it go. He's clearly avoiding the subject and it's his house and he's my mentor. He doesn't owe me any explanation. "Is it a love story?" I ask.

That earns me a smile. "Aren't they all?"

Keep 'em coming, Reed Ashton. I'm collecting them now.

We settle in, side by side, on the stairs. Our thighs rest an inch from each other. I grip the misshapen mug, focusing on the heat between my palms, forcing my attention away from the places inside of me, hyper-aware of how dangerously close we are to touching.

"As you know now, not much changes around here. My parents met in Berry when they were kids. During the summer, droves of out-of-towners would swarm the lake. Pops was hanging with his friends at the Hollows, a hidden natural spring swimming spot, on his seventeenth birthday. Which also happens to be the same day as our town's Founders Day. Pops would tell ya that he couldn't have met Mom any other way than on a day dedicated to celebrating."

"It was fate," I mumble into the warm steam.

"Pops thought so. He couldn't take his eyes off her. Asked her to wish him luck as he leapt from a boulder into the water—showing off his cannonball, of course. Youthful pride. Anyway, she swore he was going to dive to his death and it would all be for nothing, but he was persistent and hell-bent on getting and keeping Mom's attention. He knew what he wanted."

"So . . . did he do it?"

"He did, and she peeked. She held her breath the whole way down. She knew if she felt that scared for a stranger, he might be someone worth getting to know."

"I think I just melted into a puddle, Reed," I whimper.

Reed's belly laugh is sincere and contagious. *Trouble.*

"She promised to meet him at the same spot the next day. That summer became a lifetime full of tomorrows."

"This should be a book."

"When Pops and Uncle Lew decided to keep their practice in the city, Mom chose to stay up North. It was home. It was where she belonged. They made it work. They made choices."

"And they really loved each other," I add.

Reed nods. His profile remains the same, stoic and broken and beautiful.

"She was right." He shakes his head.

"She was?" I ask.

"Yeah. It's just like how you know when you belong somewhere or with someone. The way you know the moment you have a great story idea."

"Can it be that simple?"

"It's always a leap, but yeah, it can be."

That sounds like someone who believes in love to me.

Reed doesn't break eye contact. "You're going to write an incredible debut, Rory Wells, and I'm going to mentor the shit out of you."

His declaration steals the air from my lungs. My throat constricts as I fight to stifle the emotion behind my eyes. The swell lasts for a moment longer than a full inhale and then releases.

He stands, reaching for a box of tissues, offering them to me.

"C'mon, Fenway. You're gonna sleep with 'Rory the Writer' tonight." He smiles and adds, "Just so you know, Fenway's a snorer." An echo of faint laughter disappears with him up the stairs.

"Reed?" I call out, almost desperately.

He stops and leans his head over the railing.

"Your hoodie." I go to unzip it.

"Hang onto it while you're here."

I wait until his broad steps above me fall silent and the door to his room latches shut. Then I let Fenway lead the way.

After I wash my face and brush my teeth, I'm still wired. The day is flipping through my mind. I step over a snoring Fenway to get into the bed. The whistling is a welcome sound in utter silence. *To live and love like a dog.* The simplicity appeals to me. It feels good to have a companion in the absolute stillness of this house.

I pull the blankets to my chin and try to find a spot to bury into. There's always something going on outside my apartment. I miss the hum of the city. I miss my weighted blanket and stick-on stars. I miss Fitz's paws kneading into my side.

I wonder how Sunday dinner went.

Whether Lexie is reading the book I recommended.

If my mom has thought about me at all.

It's temporarily disorienting stepping outside of your own world and into someone else's—as if I expected everyone in Boston to wait until I drove back over state lines.

But that's not how time works. It stops for no one.

When Carlynn brought up my book at dinner, there wasn't any mention of what Reed's working on. So I'm lying here hypothesizing again. When I exhaust that effort, I turn over our conversations from today. I'm not entirely sure what I've gotten myself into. I know we're entering uncharted territory tomorrow, finally diving into the work. I'm excited and also preparing myself for disaster, seeing as every time he enters my bubble, my heart starts racing in my ears and I forget why I'm here.

If I sleep, I dream. If I dream, I envision him. When I wake, I'm soaked—in sweat.

They're dreams, nothing I can control. He's attractive and unexpectedly thoughtful. Anyone with a pulse would be responding this way.

I rummage through my purse and find my guided meditations book. I set it down to read a few and turn on my phone. I haven't been on social media since I've been here. I've been completely immersed in the house and the lake, the people I've met, and each layered version of Reed I'm discovering.

I look at the time. It's only nine o'clock. I might catch her awake.

"Hello, stranger," Kat answers on the second ring.

"It's been two days."

"I miss you too. How's the coffee up North?"

"Not bad actually—not *yours*, but it does the job."

"Whatcha doing?" she asks.

"I'm in bed."

"Whose bed?" Something in her tone tells me she's looking for a certain answer.

"Um, the bed in the room I'm staying in," I reply vaguely. *Payback is fun.*

"Which room is that, Rory?" she persists. "Has he shown you the ropes yet? Whipped out his mentoring ruler? Fiercely followed your rookie moves with his ocean eyes and extensive romance-writerly knowledge?"

My chest is sweltering under my skin. My writer's brain is filling the plot holes and the star of it is my off-limits mentor.

I pinch my eyes closed. Think happy thoughts: puppies, cotton candy, road trip playlists, beach—noooo, *not* beach, Reed—Reed

Ashton is hovering over me on the beach. That damn oak tree . . . back up, reverse, cotton candy . . . puppies.

"Puppies!"

Kat barks into the receiver, "Um, what now?"

I slide under the covers to conceal our laughter.

"You can say it. You're in your mentor's bed, and you like it."

"Will you lower your voice?"

"He can't hear us. Unless . . . wait . . . are you telling me he's in the same room as you right now? I've got questions. How many beds are there? I need all of the information," she demands. "Wait, I'm grabbing a beer."

"No, he's not in this room, Kat," I scream-whisper. "He's down the hall. But this house, aside from being plucked out of a historical novel and gorgeous, its walls are also made of paper-mache."

"Well, that's disappointing."

"Reed's taking me on an adventure tomorrow."

"Does he know adventure is *not* your middle name?"

"I can be adventurous." I fail to convince both of us. "Anyway, he has a theory about getting out of my comfort zone for creative purposes or something."

"As long as discomfort ends up with your book on a shelf, he can call it whatever he likes."

"How's your week going?"

"Oh, you know, customers to caffeinate. I'd like to add that I'll apartment sit for you any day. You have the sweetest new neighbor on the first floor with an extremely large goldfish?"

"You mean Mrs. Leeman?"

"Yup. She invited me over to play in her gin group. I brought pastries."

"She hasn't invited me to play gin."

"Well, that would require you talking to people you don't know, and besides, I've got a strong baked goods game."

"Very true. How's Fitz?" It's a relief to know everything is taken care of.

"He's one well-fed kitty. Huh, Fitzwilliam, Auntie Kat is the best?" I can hear her pull a sip of her beer. "So, spit it out."

"How did you know?" I ask, listening to her munch on something crunchy.

"It's my spidey sense. It gets all tingly when you have something important to tell me."

"Really?"

"No." She laughs. "It's your tell—I know the quieter you are, the more you have to say."

"I'm pretty transparent."

"Only to those who understand you."

"He's really attractive," I admit.

"I figured as much. And?"

"And it's distracting. We're kinda doing exactly what I wanted, the get-to-know-you dance, but the more I learn, the more I want to know. I see this person forming in front of my eyes, a puzzle that's starting to make sense to me, and I can't afford any distractions."

Kat chuckles.

"This isn't funny."

"I mean, you don't see the humor here in this?"

"I can barely focus."

"You gonna make it?"

"It seems like all I do around this guy is feel."

"And?"

"He's frustrating in so many ways, and he's also kind and protective and loves his family. Kat, I met them today and his mom is amazing. They all are. This place is just," I exhale, "everything I've ever imagined it would be like growing up in one home."

"So you're getting exactly what you asked for and still freaking out? Rory," Kat lectures lovingly, "what if you tried to do that thing you learned in therapy to help you process your bio father not being around."

"Radical acceptance."

"Yup. Accept it all. The attraction. The mentorship. Your feelings."

"Isn't there some theory about creative chemistry too?"

"I've never heard of that."

"Maybe I made it up. It's the idea that some people mesh creatively."

"Yeah, I gotcha. Like a duet or something."

"Exactly. Sonny and Cher," I say.

"Dylan and Cash. Nicks and Petty."

"Gaga and Cooper." We both bust out singing lyrics.

"I like it, Rory. This chemistry stuff is creative fuel. Emotion is like writing juice, right? Embrace it as part of the process."

Kat's assuredness is motivating me. I can use all of these feelings in my characters. I bring the covers to my chin and breathe in.

The moon is high. The day is done. My fears have loosened their grip—for now. The sky here has more stars than I can count, so I stick with the brightest one and wish for the best.

19

REED

"Invisible threads are the strongest ties."
—Friedrich Nietzsche

After I leave Fenway in Rory's safe hands, I spend most of the night alternating between pathetic attempts at sleep and scrutinizing every idea I've come up with to help her manuscript shine.

I'm into what she's written. It's compelling, romantic, and the heroine, Chelsea, is well-developed. But her hero, it's like I'm reading something that isn't supposed to exist yet. He's flat, too zoomed out, and I can't reconcile the hesitation with his character when everything else is fleshed out.

I run my hands through my hair, pacing the bunk room, which is set up with two twin beds diagonally across from one another. Matching russet and royal blue quilts, my gram made when Pops was a kid, cover each bed.

There's a single dresser and a bed lamp on each wall.

At first, I thought maybe the discrepancy I was seeing in her story was all on me. My editing eye and instinct can't be as sharp as they once were. Then I read it again, and again.

Having deeper insight into Rory's family history, I'm pretty sure I know what's missing.

But understanding it and approaching her about it are two different things.

When I thought I could simply mark up the page and email it back to her, I had fewer reservations. Now that she's here, there's a level of care I must take.

Hearing that she was one possible rejection slip away from giving up tells me she's in a more fragile place than she lets on. I was pissed she'd so easily let go, but I stopped myself from pushing the issue, because what could I say without being a total hypocrite?

I thumb through her pages again, going over my notes for a final time, preparing how I'm going to deliver my feedback to Rory without crushing her spirit.

As I read her chapters, the raw emotion alone sent familiar feelings and repressed adrenaline coursing through my body. Her voice tethered itself around my wrists, dragging me out of the creative black hole I've existed in for the last two years. Her words were flickers of light, and I chased every last one of them until I crawled my way out.

I felt that sense of pride for Rory, knowing what it means to type "The End" for the first time, knowing a little of what it means for a writer to finish their novel, I was damn proud of her for that.

I'd borrow her imagination and get lost in it anytime. The story kept me turning pages. And there was this quality to her writing, not mechanical, but her style. So familiar and compelling. Some editor is going to have fun with it.

Her story in places reminded me of the journal I'd found years ago. My then friend, Genevieve, brought me to my first book signing in Boston. I'd felt shitty being her arm candy and missing Pops and found a reprieve outside, among the noise of downtown.

People fascinate me and there's no better place than a city street to be invisible.

So, when a frantic girl ran out of the hotel, I watched. She leaned her shaking body against the wall, eyes closed, chanting or counting out loud.

I should've turned away when I saw her bare shoulders heave up and down, but I didn't. That wall looked like it was the only thing holding her up. Then she moved to the bench. I'll never forget the coral dress she was wearing or the way her words ended up changing my life.

Guilt tugged at my gut as I stole a glimpse of this girl's private moment. But I've always been too curious for my own good, and she was someone I couldn't ignore.

I tried to talk to her that day. I said hello, wanting to make sure she was okay, but then she took off. When she didn't return, I grabbed the gold backpack she left behind on the bench, and gave it to Genevieve. My instructions were clear. I asked Gen to drop the backpack at the concierge desk while I attended a meet and greet event.

It was a disorganized time in my life. I was distracted with grief over Pops. When we got back to New Hampshire, I discovered Gen still had the backpack. She said she forgot, it was no big deal, and offered to donate it. There was no way I wasn't going to at least try to return it. I left my number with the hotel, and waited for a call back.

Why that girl didn't write her contact info in that journal still baffles me to the point of exasperation. Why she didn't get my number from the front desk and call me has plagued my dreams.

After three months, I opened the journal, expecting to find personal reflections. Instead, I found a handwritten draft, a love story about two lost people in the world, trying to find their way back together. Embedded in the heroine's character arc was a story of loss. The loss of her father. I didn't know if this was luck or destiny, maybe even Pops's way of playing a prank on me, because what are the chances? It was like this person knew everything I was going through.

Whatever its origin, it became my solace. This stranger's heart helped heal my own.

I highlighted in it, made notes in the margins, and eventually was so inspired that I drafted my own story about my relationship with Pops. I never did finish it. Once I started writing romance, the story of a father and son took a backseat to my publisher's plans.

I invited my mentee up here thinking it might guide her to her own spark. But then she showed up as Rory the writer and Aurora the woman. Two people who now occupy two distinct parts of my head. Any good intentions I had when she walked into this house, along with my resolve, flew out the fucking window when I laid eyes on her. I'm determined to mentor the aspiring author I've been entrusted with, trying not to think about the captivating person whose laughter lights up a room, and definitely not allowing myself to think about how she's currently down the hall sleeping in my bed.

Surprisingly, all this neglected sleep hasn't wiped me out. It's invigorating and I'm ready to help Rory finish her book. I won't berate myself either because I also happen to enjoy her company.

Mom's words squeeze their way into my thoughts. *It wasn't your fault. Stop punishing yourself.*

After I move past the guilt, for now, I opt to focus on what I know about Rory. She's stepped out of her comfort zone multiple times since arriving, even endured a family dinner while genuinely smiling through it. She listened to Emerson. She made fast friends with Fenway. She seems to want to be here. If she's experiencing anxiety, she's an expert at concealing it.

The house creaks. Once, twice, and the door to the room swings open. Rory's standing in the shadows of the hall in leggings and my hoodie. Her hair is over her shoulders and she's as pale as a ghost.

I jump out of the twin bed, throwing on a discarded white t-shirt and blue flannel.

"Hey, you okay?"

She nods and steps down into the room.

"Can't sleep. You too?" Rory's line of sight lands directly on the bed where her manuscript and the journal are on display. I rush back and compile everything, then shove it under the pillow.

"You can sit if you want." I hum a solemn *Simon and Garfunkel* tune Pops used to play on the piano.

She takes a spot on the edge of the bed, pulling her legs into her chest. She's doing that thing again, where she tugs at the loose ends of her hair. I lean against the pillow on the other side of the bed, facing Rory, a little jealous, okay, more than a little jealous, of her fingers.

"I like your flannel." She watches me, one button at a time.

"It's Pops's," I offer, grateful for busy hands.

This is a small room. And her presence takes up all of it.

"It suits you."

I clear my throat, and breathe in.

Mom was stripped down to bare bones and grief that day.

Whatever thread had been holding her together, dissolved.

"A year after he died, I found Mom by her closet, crumpled in a pile of his clothes. She held his faded flannels, squeezing them between her fingers. His dress shirts were laid out on the bed, starched and pressed. And on the floor was a shriveled version of my mother, her face buried in everything he owned.

"I asked her, 'Mom, what are you doing? Can I help you? Do you want me to get Carlynn?'

"She replied, 'No, no Reed. I'm fine, I'm fine. I was cleaning out the closet. I pulled out the work shirts, then his dress pants, but when I got to these . . .' She held up an armful of his favorite shirts, the ones with holes and missing buttons, soft fabric and memories attached to them, and she lost herself in grief. She choked out words, fresh tears and desperation spilled from her swollen eyes, down her face. 'These smell like him. They've been freaking washed,' she shrieked, 'and they still smell like him. I miss him. I miss him so much, every day, like a wound that won't heal. And when I try to make progress . . . they say, clean out the closet, make room for healing, that's what they say to do. So, I try, you know? I try and I try. I stand up, and one by one, I remove your father's existence from the closet, and each hanger weighs ten pounds, and it's scratching at the wound but it was fine—I swear, I was fine.'

"I kneeled on the floor next to my beautiful mother and listened as she held onto the only tangible thing left of the man she loved for almost five decades. Half a century of devotion, sacrifice, and compromise, stolen moments in the late afternoon us kids pretended not to notice. As I stayed beside her that morning, I became aware that my mom was holding onto every piece of Pops's clothing because it made the love hurt less. If she could hold enough of his shirts in the right way while breathing in deep enough for long enough, she could convince herself that he was holding her back.

"Eventually, all of the clothes went into boxes. They lost their grasp on Mom, or maybe she was finally able to let hers go. But before they found their way to another life in another closet, I kept a few for myself, including that Red Sox jersey in the photo."

Rory's face is saturated with fresh tears and silence. She's holding space for me. It's one thing when she's talking constantly—that I stand a chance against. But this silent, unwavering strength in her eyes? That Rory is pulling me under.

"Fuck." I gasp, dragging my hands through my hair, then laying them in my lap.

She slides her smooth fingers over mine.

I can't move. Her palms over my skin might as well be handcuffs.

"Reed." My name on her lips. Her pink and pouting lower lip.

I'm not positive I can hear anything other than the ventricles of my own heart slamming inside my chest. I shoot up from the bed and onto my unreliable legs. As I make my way across the room, my hearing and heart rate steady.

"I listen better when I move around."

Rory's eyes are like pinballs on me. A slight frown suggests she's turned off by the physical distance I've put between us. It pains me to think I caused uncertainty for her, but I can't think being touched in that way.

She increases the distance between us, walking up the two steps it takes to reach the landing. She pauses, then looks over her shoulder into the bunkroom—at me—my hands shoved in my pockets, eyes hot and heart racing again.

Her voice deflates. "Do you have any Tylenol?"

"In the bathroom cabinet. Are you okay?"

"Just a headache, that's all."

"Take whatever you need."

Rory drags her bottom lip between her teeth, and I forget my own name.

"There's so much love in this house," she points out, followed by a shy smile. "Goodnight."

✳

I catch a few hours of sleep before I'm dressed and ready to get this show on the road. It's a new day and we have a mountain of work ahead of us.

"You're up?" I observe, surprised. Rory's leaning by the kitchen window.

"Wanted to catch the sunrise." Her eyes are cruel mirrors against the early morning light, delicate and weary in a way I hadn't let myself see until last night. They are now eyes that have seen a part of me too.

She smiles lazily. This isn't something I should get used to.

"Are you always up this early, Mr. Mentor?" she teases, gliding across the scuffed vinyl over to the counter.

"Pops used to say the only things worth losing sleep over were extra innings or a great sunrise." I stretch my arms above my head, then open the container with Mom's blueberry scones. I pull raspberry jam and cold butter from the fridge and place them on the counter.

In the small space where I'm standing, she manages to do a choreographed dance behind me, reaching into the cabinet. She chooses the same mug as yesterday, fills it up, and twirls back around me.

"Excuse me," she sings, bending over into the fridge, taking out the milk, reaching around me again. I hold the sides of the counter to avoid disturbing what I'm witnessing. It's like noticing someone for the first time when they think no one else is looking. She ends on the opposite side of the counter, facing me. "I'm excited for today." She fills her mug with milk and adds a dash of cinnamon.

"You take cinnamon in your coffee?"

She smiles back over the lip of her mug. She didn't tell me the other morning. She's not comfortable. An involuntary shudder rolls through me.

"Are you cold?" she misreads.

"What? No." I run my hand through my hair.

"You sure? It's okay to admit you're cold." She smirks.

I top my mug off and put the milk back into the fridge.

"You start the fire?" I ask, noticing the snap and pop of dehydrated pine.

"I'm not completely useless. I even brewed coffee without burning the house down."

"I definitely don't think you're useless. You're full of surprises, though."

Her eyes beam with enthusiasm. "To be honest, I keep surprising myself."

"Want to grab a scone and follow me?"

I turn to see she's frozen in place.

"Well, what are you waiting for? Need a green light?"

"Oh, you mean follow you, like now?" she states, grabbing a scone, then trailing behind me. "Did you know green symbolizes new beginnings? My roommate from college once taught me these emotional regulation cues, and green can mean feeling happy, even ready to learn." *She's barely had a sip of her coffee.*

I push the stack of mail to the side as Rory observes every move I make. I shove my wool hat onto my head and collect my phone and keys.

"You've sure got a lot to say this morning, you know, for it being a Monday." I smile, recalling one of her first emails. I'm relieved to see Rory's back in full swing and doesn't require a round of ice-breakers after last night. It's time we make progress. It's time for some mentoring.

20

RORY

"Seven years would be insufficient to make some people acquainted with each other, and seven days are more than enough for others." —Jane Austen

Reed's truck isn't pretentious at all. It's understated and taken care of. I'm not sure what I was expecting, but I suppose "bestselling author" was synonymous with fancy toys and materialism in my mind.

There's loose change and a red folder in the center console. And much to my happy surprise, the seats have been heated. This is heaven.

I thought it might be awkward driving together after last night, when clearly Reed did not want me in his personal space, but he seems unaffected by it now. Like it never even happened.

Just because he's moved on doesn't mean I've forgotten about how Reed lost his father at an age when he was trying to figure out his own identity in the world, and how it shaped him into the person sitting next to me now.

The heat hisses through the vents and seeps into my legs. Reed turns on the radio to a classical station. His aversion to technology is becoming one of my favorite things about him. The arrangement moves along to the pace of the view out the window, like a premeditated soundtrack. I rest my cheek against the cold surface, mesmerized by thick woods and isolated clearings, snow-capped mountains, and narrow roads that twist and turn.

I haven't seen any recent pictures of Reed in the house. Some photos are from when he was a kid, on the lake, playing T-ball, and one of him and Carlynn on snowboards. In all of them, he's happy. I wonder if his beard has swallowed up some of his smiles.

I know he has his mother's kind smile and that Ashton signature unruly hair that's now peeking out from under his wool hat. The way it loops at the ends reminds me of the way my mom makes zucchini noodles using a spiralizer.

I absentmindedly trace over his face, trying to imagine what else I'm missing beneath all that winterization. Probably the absolute last thing I should be doing, so I return to the window, overlooking the passing mountain landscape.

"I didn't know the view could get any better?"

Mount Washington is beautiful. Rock and ice, winter frozen over fall, summer dried up from a wet spring. If nature can do all this, year after year, I can certainly rise to the challenge of finishing my story without falling for my mentor.

Spice and soap invade my inhale. His smell brings me to my favorite parts of fall. "This truck smells like you—nutmeg and cider, fresh air and old books."

He clears his throat.

Shit. *Inside thought, Rory! Inside. Thought!* I slam my mouth shut to deadbolt anything else from escaping. My panic wheel is swirling like cotton candy.

Reed's locked on ten and two, shaking his head at how ridiculous my existence is.

There was an intimacy in my admission that I hadn't intended for an audience. I don't want him to think that I presume to know him or smell him constantly, but truly it's unavoidable when you're trapped in a car with the heat on high. I'm certain his rational sense will also draw the same conclusion.

"So, have you practiced your elevator pitch before?"

He stretches an arm out, crossing the armrest and into my territory to adjust the heat. I look at the length, trailing down to his open palm, my pulse leaping and heart racing. How does he switch gears like that? Maybe he didn't even hear me. *Cool. I'm going with that.*

"You could tell how much I struggled with that." My voice cracks.

"It's not easy for anyone. You'll get there. We'll practice."

"Practice?" I ask, unsure if he means right now.

"Consider me the pitcher and you, the hitter. Ever go after anything with a bat before?"

"Only my own irrational fear in the middle of the night."

Reed's smirking at me while extending the same side-eye Kat doles out when she's calling me on a disparaging comment I've made about myself. Most of the time, I don't even realize I'm using words like *irrational.*

Somewhere along the line, I figured it would be better if I softened the blow before anyone else could get a swing in.

"What? I live alone. Sometimes, unfamiliar noises can be unsafe. So I keep a bat—a rolling pin—near my bed."

"Bet that baking utensil is terrifying." His smirk gives into laughter. The kind that shakes your core, peeling me free from my spiraling nerves.

I dig around in my bag to see if there's snacks. I've never been happier in my life to see a scone. I notice my feet, covered in slush and small pebbles, muddied dirt from yesterday's walk.

I return to my view, holding back from rubbing my entire face on the chilled window.

The scone melts in my mouth.

"Have you always run with a competitive streak?" I ask.

"I've always wanted to be the best at whatever it is I'm doing. In high school, it was baseball. In college, it was writing. With publishing too, it mattered to me, having my name on a bestseller list."

"So, you've always been the best at everything you do?"

Reed's hands grip the steering wheel, choking the leather. "You ask good questions, Rory. And I don't always have immediate answers. Sometimes, when you ask me something, it's the first time I've considered it myself." He pulls his hat off and runs a hand through his hair, then cracks the window.

The aroma of coffee, along with our honesty, is sucked out the window. Fresh mountain air penetrates our taut bubble.

"I don't know why I need to be the best. Some kind of self-validation. I watched Pops as a kick-ass attorney, husband, and father. My mom is the best person I know, and my sister was an incredible dancer. They never pressured me to be anything other than myself, but somehow I managed to put that pressure on myself anyway. I've always wanted my life to mean something significant. To leave a legacy behind. And the kicker is, even though I've won trophies and made lists, none of that made me happy long-term. I was always left chasing the next thing."

"Is that how you feel about writing now too?"

"Writing romance was a temporary solution to my life at the time. I'd like to write about other things. Broaden my scope. Romance is fun. But it's not where I'm at anymore. I don't like having to be a name and a face. I prefer my privacy these days, and I'm not inspired to write about something I don't have in my life."

My heart sinks, crushing my little crush. "I guess we aren't so different in that way. I've had trouble writing about some things that I haven't experienced before myself. Things you can't really convey simply by researching them."

After a few minutes, Reed breaks the silence. "Sometimes, I think I see parts of myself in you. Maybe it's that things are more familiar the more I get to know you. Maybe it's that I'm telling you things about myself that I've never told anyone before."

He keeps his gaze on the road but I feel his attention all over me.

We move in and out of conversation like there's no rush.

We're definitely passing the car-trip test, which gives me confidence that even though he's not inspired to write romance, we'll still make a good team.

"Grab the red folder."

"What's this?" I flip open the red file folder and see printed pages of my manuscript. My pulse quickens. I wasn't expecting to see his edits like this. Red pen. Yellow lines. Tabs.

"Read the parts I've highlighted."

"Like now?"

I take his lack of response as a yes.

My chest heats beneath my layers. The papers rattle. Maybe from the road. Maybe from me.

"His career is about to take off. With his steely eyes, seductive smile, and quick wit, not to mention his notorious fast-action skills behind

the line, he's the perfect face for the Food Channel's newest cooking show in the Bay Area."

My voice is shaky but quickly smooths out, knowing these lines by heart.

"He finishes his plated entree presentation in the kitchen and makes his way outside to the deck where the dinner party is in full swing. The sound of crystal and flatware scraping porcelain fills the air. He's not one to shy away from a compliment as he comes around to collect them one by one, schmoozing with the deep pockets at the table. Immediately, he finds himself intrigued by the blonde in the black dress, with a string of pearls safely wrapped around her neck, and without a date. She isn't paying attention to the mundane discourse. Instead, she's singularly focused on the food in front of her, methodically chewing and savoring every bite. Was that a moan he heard? She isn't simply tasting parts of her meal, she's devouring the entire thing, her bright red lips unmarred as she dabs the linen napkin to the corners of her mouth. He catches himself lifting his gaze mid-conversation as he makes his way around. He's simply fascinated, watching her eat his food."

I touch my lips, warm and dry, and when I drag my bottom lip between my teeth to soften it, Reed startles me by ripping the folder from my hands.

His exhale is a hard hush in my ear. I'm hooked on the harsh sound it makes, mixing with the rustling of the heater.

"So your hero, he's like this big, important guy. Full of ego, right?"

"Yeah, I guess so, at this point in the story." The suddenness of this conversation is unsettling.

"Tell me about him."

I drag my fingers through the ends of my hair. The truck is moving at a steady speed on an upclimb.

"It seems like you already know, I mean, you've read it, so . . ." I'm starting to worry. This feels like another lecture coming in hot.

"Sure, I know what I read. I want to know what you know about him."

"Okay, well, he's not the same person he was when they first met. He's lost that childlike wonder. But every time they meet, it's like he's still seeking that version of Chelsea out, maybe to get back to a time when he made sense to himself."

I push my glasses up the bridge of my nose.

Reed rolls his neck.

And I press my fingertips into the air along with the melody playing, as if I can feel the piano keys resist and give in.

"Do you play?" he asks.

"No. I'm focused on writing for now, but it doesn't stop me from imagining, though."

"Your story, you have an incredible sensory imagination. Don't lose that about yourself. Don't ever stop writing."

He's oblivious to how deep his words reach and wrap around my insides like a tetherball.

To him, they're direct observations. To me, they're confirmation that what I've been wanting is in my reach.

Knowing he thinks I have potential somehow makes it possible for me to believe it too.

I rest my head against the window, thinking about love and loss, about these two characters on the playground, swinging together in a thunderstorm, set on different life paths, trying to find a way back to each other.

"Their story led to so much separation. So much time wasted." I can't help but draw the parallel to how much time I've wasted, scared I'd leave another story behind. Scared I could never replicate what I had written. Scared that it was a sign I didn't deserve to dream. "The love they shared stood the test of time."

I know I've spoken. I just don't know if he's heard me.

Meryl and Pops. Their love stood the hardest tests any could.

What if what I see hiding beneath all of Reed's layers is simply years of grief? When I add up the inconsistency in his moods, his reserve, even his abundance of flannel like in all the photos of his dad, when I contemplate his thoughtfulness and gentleness, the picture becomes as clear to me as the bright landscape out the window.

My vision was obstructed before by my need to control everything. I want him to know that I understand what it means to lose someone.

"I read once that grief is love with no place to go. And I've never forgotten it because it means if you're grieving, you must've had something worth loving. Even when things don't last forever, it means that the love was real."

I don't notice the tears in my eyes until they've fallen, until the window has stopped moving and the change rattling in the center console has ceased. "It's something to hold onto." I begin my next thought.

"Hold onto what?" Reed cuts in, and I shift my body to face his sparkling eyes and the vulnerable way in which he has opened up to me.

He reaches over the armrest, crossing the distance between us.

The pads of his thumbs drag hot tears from my cheeks.

His fingers are soft and warm and bite at my skin when they leave.

Like the truck's engine, I've come to a complete stop. I've stopped thinking, stopped breathing, stopped hiding. All I want is to hold his open hands against my face and pull his mouth to mine. I want nothing more than to close this distance between us, forgetting who we are and why we're here.

When his touch doesn't return, I squeeze my eyes shut. I can't bear to face what he thinks of me now, unraveled in the passenger seat like a discarded pile of ribbons.

The only thing keeping me from throwing myself out of this vehicle is the seat belt, which won't give an inch when I try to tear myself away from his obvious discomfort. His arm grazes mine as he reaches past my line of sight between the armrest and my seat. He repeats his question, "Hold onto what?"

"Hope," I whisper with growing agitation and shame.

I catch my breath and draw in the courage I need to meet his eyes. "Maybe the love you've always felt for a person, even after they're gone, can't be lost. Instead, it's meant to grow . . . into something else. Wouldn't it be a remarkable thing to not lose that love? It's our stranglehold on love that causes us to hurt. Because we're terrified if we let the grief go, we'll let the person go too. But if we use that love and invest it, share it, maybe the loss will slowly hurt less and less. Maybe it might even help us heal. The idea that real love can never be destroyed, it can only be a part of new beginnings. And I, for one, believe in beginnings."

A sharp click and release of the buckle shoots the seatbelt across my lap. Before we step out of his truck, Reed asks me a loaded question. "Have you considered writing your story in first-person?"

"No, no way. I am not. Nope."

"Really? It's pretty standard in romance. You want to write romance?" he challenges, testing me.

"Hey, yes." I jump to my own defense, "It's just, well, that's Seth's point of view. I wouldn't know how to . . . and anyway, would you dive off a cliff if everyone else was?" Mom echoes in my ear, the time she asked me if I wanted to be myself or like everyone else. All because I asked to cut my bangs in seventh grade.

Reed grins at the suggestion of a dare. "Yeah, I'd leap."

"Well, that makes you—"

He cuts me off. *A wise choice.*

"Adventurous," he fills in the blank.

"How is conforming adventurous?"

"Sometimes it's not conforming to follow a well-lit path. Listen, I see how red your ears are getting, Ms. Wells. Let's take a walk."

"My ears aren't red. Another walk? Ms. Wells?"

"Got something against fresh air?"

"I've got something against wasting writing time. Wait, why are you laughing? That was not meant to be funny. I'm serious—we have a deadline." I'm a breath away from whining.

"Consider the path like a guard rail. It's there for a damn reason. Doesn't mean you have to walk it like everyone else," he growls in my direction, and not unapologetic about it either.

First, he advises against conformity, and now he's telling me to stay in my lane. The rules keep changing. I've never been more confused.

After a silent and moderate hike through light snow and heavily wooded trails, we slide back into his truck and its warming seats.

I blast the heat the entire way to his house.

When we pull up the drive, Reed kills the engine and leans his head against the headrest. Then he turns, clears his throat, and throws another curve ball at me.

"Have you ever cooked with a man before?"

"You know I don't cook."

"Ready for your third lesson, Rory the Writer?"

"Why do I have the feeling that I most definitely am not?"

21

— · —

RORY & REED

"Creativity is a combination of discipline and childlike spirit." —Robert Greene

Reed leans in the doorway between the living room and the kitchen with a spirited grin and a glimmer in his eye.

"We're having a working dinner tonight," he announces.

"I don't usually mix business with pleasure." I barely keep a straight face. "So, what's this entail and how do I get to eat?"

His slower responses used to rattle me, but I'm learning to be patient. When Reed finally does speak and say what's on his mind, it's worth the wait. And when Reed finally removes his coat, that's worth the wait too.

Beneath, he's wearing a simple heather gray cotton t-shirt with the word *Nantucket* printed in navy blue lettering across the chest. It hugs in every place I've pretended not to notice since laying eyes on him. And it's entirely unfair that he's this attractive all the time.

I firmly told myself, after our excursion today, that I was done entertaining any thoughts of Reed Ashton that were not one-hundred-percent professional. Our working relationship being a success is all that matters. I'm not going to throw away everything because the man looks good in a t-shirt, worn-in denim, and bare feet. This isn't going to be some short-lived showmance, writers edition. I'm in this for the long haul, for the book and maybe, if I'm lucky, I'll have made my first author friend.

I was fully prepared to brush off the small crush I'd flirted with in my head, but then he walks into the living room like a perfectly wrapped gift on the highest shelf before your birthday—taunting and out of reach—and Kat's advice takes over. *Radical acceptance.* I nibble my nails as he bends over, adding logs to the hearth.

"I got the ingredients to prepare a Tuscan classic. Your hero's a chef, so this will be a perfect opportunity for you to get into—"

"His pants," I quip, finishing his sentence, internally scolding myself, *kinda*. Reed's face is composed, but it's his smiling eyes that give him away. They're amused. "His head. Obviously, that's what I meant."

Where's Kat when you need a good "That's what she said" joke? I suck in my lower lip between my teeth and run my tongue along its center. Reed notices and leaves the room, only to come back five seconds later, tossing Meryl's sunflower apron at my face.

"Put that on."

I hold the ultra-soft cotton in my hands before placing it over my neck.

At the kitchen counter, Reed has a rainbow's worth of fresh ingredients laid out: rustic bread, tomatoes, basil, garlic, dijon mustard, and red wine vinegar. A pot of water is rolling to a boil on the stove. He's poured two glasses of wine and the room is lit in soft yellows.

Reed walks around me, popping a couple of green olives in his mouth. I'm fixated on watching him chew, then swallow, then smile. He's in his element here.

"You know, I can't even boil water," I remind him.

He ignores my statement with an eye roll, handing me a cutting board and tomatoes. He takes the garlic and shallots. We're standing side by side. I'm slicing slowly. He chops quickly.

His arm snakes around my waist as he slides me over to his cutting board, switching our places. I start chopping quickly. He slices slowly.

"So tell me, what's the hang-up with writing first-person from the male point of view? I need more than a nope. There's always a reason."

I sigh. Where to begin? I scrape what I've diced and put it into a ceramic bowl between us.

"I have this desire to craft an authentic character, someone readers will love but maybe aren't used to typically loving."

"So, no alpha male?" Reed winks.

"I mean, maybe a little alpha." I grin.

He hands me linguini and nods over to the water, which has come to a complete boil.

"Me?"

"The one and only," he motions to the pot.

I step to the stove, staring into the steam. He reaches over me, grazing my shoulder with his forearm, and the contact causes me to drop all the pasta into the pot. The scalding water splatters, catching my wrist and the exposed skin on my neck. Reed spins me around to face him. His grip is gentle on my arms, his eyes are everywhere.

"Rory, are you okay?"

"Yes. Burned for a sec, but I'm fine."

"Let's ice it."

"Really, I'm okay. I'm wearing long sleeves. Plus, these shallots aren't going to brown themselves."

"Are you sure?"

"It's not my first rodeo. I'll ice it later if I need to."

He looks at me, unconvinced, but I've made my point and am ready to move on.

"Here are mushrooms—we use baby portobellos. I've added some dry white wine, yellow onion, and garlic to the oil. Smells amazing, right?"

"I'd eat it just like this," I admit.

"Toss the portobellos in and babysit them. We want them to be almost soft. When they're done, we'll combine them with the sauce."

"I don't want to mess this up."

"You've got this," he encourages me. I breathe through the gesture. *One, two, three, four.*

He fires up another pan and hands me butter to gently place inside. It sizzles on impact. *Five, six, seven, eight.*

The kitchen is coming alive. With flavor. With ideas. With something else I won't define.

Reed hums a warm and upbeat tune, transporting us to the sixties and freedom.

We can't be more than a few feet from one another. I look up to see his eyes on me. We hold one another's gaze like the start of a conversation that we intend to finish later.

"Why don't you write him how you want him to be versus worrying about what a reader might want? Submission-ready is your first priority. The rest can be worked out in edits."

"I don't know how to be in his head."

"Draw inspiration from real life, the men around you." Reed hands me a spoon. "Stir."

"There's no men around me." I stir, following his instruction.

"Haven't you had relationships?"

I keep stirring. "Sure, but nothing inspiration-worthy. He also wasn't open about his feelings."

"Okay, what about characters in books or films? Mr. Darcy?" Reed holds out his hand. I place the spoon in it, and my fingers graze the soft edge of his palm. His eyes sweep over my face.

"Like this." He leans over me, pushing the shallots and browning slices of onion across the pan. "You have to constantly keep them moving, so they won't burn. You try."

The spoon slides from his fingers into my hand and I stop thinking.

Reed's frame has me pressing my body into the stove as garlic-infused steam rises to my face. His smoky voice tickles behind my ear. "Maybe the romance wasn't fireworks, but can you pull from the breakup? Breakups usually have a way of blowing things up."

The spoon rattles in my grasp. "Nope. No explosion or damage."

"No?" he asks. "Why not?"

"I didn't care enough to fight for him. Not like I was supposed to," I whisper. "I knew it wasn't the kind of love that was meant to last, because when it ended, it didn't feel like a loss—it felt like an exhale."

I can barely breathe when my eyes land on Reed's. His face is a mistake waiting to happen away from mine.

Though my hands are still shaking, I manage to return to the spoon and my task. Reed steps back, putting a foot of distance between us, and only then do I dare to inhale.

"I don't want to mess my book up either," I add, staring into the pan of thoroughly browned vegetables. "I've put so much work into it already."

"Listen, that work isn't wasted. It all serves the story. And a story isn't any different than what we're doing here. There's ingredients and recipes. You experiment and explore, and you taste. Here." He lifts a fresh metal spoon up to my lips.

I drag the contents of the spoon onto my tongue.

"Is the spice profile on point? Is it flavorful? Does it need something more?" His words land on the tip of my nose.

This moment feels like being a dutiful kid with my hand tucked behind my back during library time, restricting myself from touching the spines screaming to be read, so I say the first thing that pops into my head to avoid acting on the impulse I have to tear those spines from the shelves and make them mine.

"That dressing is drinkable. It doesn't need a thing." *Except to maybe be licked off . . . Rory, stop.*

Reed laughs like he can hear my thoughts. But he can't, *right*?

My eyes dart around the room, and then my glasses slip down the bridge of my nose. Reed pushes them back into place.

"I think I burned the veggies."

"Here." He guides me back with a gentle stroke of his palm cupping my elbow. We're looking at the pan now, but my thoughts are split down the middle. Half are here in the present. Half are stuck in the past, just a few moments ago. "Sometimes, Rory, when things get really close to us, we don't see them clearly. And sometimes, to understand a thing better, we have to get closer."

"Wow. They're golden brown. Not burned." I clap my hands.

"You're rocking this lesson."

My taste buds and smile soar. "What exactly is the lesson?"

Reed scrapes the veggies into a bowl.

"I think it's layered. First, know your characters. They have to be believable, likable, that's even debatable, and don't forget you'll grow the more you write." A throaty chuckle follows. "Second, it's okay to aim for a triple. Don't fall into the perfectionist trap. It'll never be perfect. Nothing ever is."

Okay.

If the lesson is to know my characters, then I need to hear them.

I listen best when I'm writing.

So my book might actually benefit from stepping in closer.

My hands shake as I wipe them along the front of the apron. I'm aware that I don't have a lot of experience with being in a man's kitchen or head, or knowing a lot of good men, but something tells me I won't have to look far for inspiration.

As we combine the final ingredients, Reed and I brainstorm about my character's motivations, desires, and fears. When we sit down, with panzanella, linguini, and prosciutto-wrapped melon, I feel confident I know who Seth Hale is aside from being a chef in love with a woman he can't have.

What surprises me more than eating a meal I didn't ruin is how good it feels to work with another person in this way. A creative way. A partnership.

I start entertaining wild ideas, like maybe I can learn to cook. Maybe I can write from Seth's point of view. Maybe some men do check your arms for burns and patiently show you your potential. And maybe, just maybe, they're the same type of men who don't leave.

✳

REED

The lesson went better than I predicted. No awkwardness, no sign of Rory making excuses. The only awkward thing that happened was the number of times I caught myself checking her out.

She had that apron cinched around her waist. I shouldn't have traced the way it shaped her body in oversized clothing from square to pear, but I'm alive and have eyes.

And another thing. Her eyes. They land like glitter, sticking around long after she's moved on to her next target. I don't know if it's the natural fit she makes in this house or that I'm getting used to having her around, but I'd willingly spend the entire night by her side like a plus-one if that were an option.

We leave our polished-off plates on the table and continue our conversation by the fire. I break out my favorite bottle of bourbon and add logs to the hearth. I'm sitting as close as I can to the flames without being devoured by them. My face tightens from the heat. This is the most relaxed I've felt since I can remember.

I grip the two-finger-full tumbler all the way around, handing a glass to Rory. The surface is warm as it slips from my fingers to hers.

"So you think you're willing to give Seth a voice now?"

"I am."

She's stretched out in front of the fire. The glow makes her eyes hypnotic green. There's no guarantee what will happen if I keep looking straight into them.

"Thank you," she says. "For dinner, for everything. It's been so helpful."

"Hey, don't thank me, it's all you." I focus on the fire. The safer of the two options.

"Well, I take it back then."

We share a laugh, settled on the matter.

"I can't believe I'm going to write multiple points of view and be in a man's head. I have no clue how, but I'm going to try."

I turn back to face her. Our knees knock like bumper cars.

"I think you're doing great. No one else but you could've written this story, and now you have a clear direction to make it shine."

The scent of butterscotch and spiced pecans invades my concentration. I'm all over the place. I want to know more, too curious, too selfish to stop myself.

"Do you have a favorite place you've lived?" I ask. I taste my drink while she formulates her thoughts. The bourbon burns strong and sweet down my throat.

"It's not really a simple answer."

The fire highlights her face in golden hues.

"Is it ever with you?" I say.

"I *can* keep it simple." She's peering down inside her glass, swirling the amber liquid. The flames climb higher.

I lift her chin gently with my finger. Her spine straightens, exposing her neck. "I don't think you need to be anyone but yourself."

A shudder rolls across her shoulders and up to her chin. My body bends forward instinctually as I follow its path to her mouth.

That fucking mouth. That pout—the one that just parted as if she's about to utter "oh" in shock or submission—it's all too close, too comfortable, too convincing. Nothing makes sense anymore.

It's just us, a roasting fire, bourbon-stained lips, and a couple of undefined inches closing in on us.

She reaches up to touch her neck and winces on contact. Air hisses between her teeth.

I push away her hand. "Let me see," I demand.

She lets her head and hair fall back, the fire illuminating her heated skin, so I can get a closer look. There are two red ovals marking her.

I force myself to get up before oxytocin ruins everything she's working toward. She's my mentee. I cannot make her out in my head to be someone she's not allowed to be, even if my body tells a different story. When I return with a potted plant in my hand and kneel down beside her, the flush in her cheeks softens like sorbet—a blend of peach and pink—I want to taste until she melts on my tongue.

Her slightly labored breaths pull my eyes back down to her neck, and I pretend not to notice her racing pulse vibrating in her throat.

"What's that?" she asks.

"An aloe plant. It will help them to heal faster."

"I've never seen it out of the green bottle before. What do I need to do?"

She sits perfectly still as I rub gentle circles over the burns, and blow on them. Her warm exhales graze my chin. Vanilla and violets are permanently branded into my brain now. Her chest rises and falls beneath her shirt.

"There." I pull away and fall back against the legs of an armchair, resting my full body weight on it. I pick up my drink.

"That feels so much better. What can't you do?"

"That's laughable, really." In a moment of intoxicating proximity, I blurt out my truth like a forced confession. "I can't write."

Her lack of expression is unnerving.

"I was on a deadline." I try to explain, but I know I'm not making sense. My eyes sting from the fire, from the memory. It's taking physical strength to get this out. "I was supposed to be there. I gave them my word and I was careless." This isn't something I get to be timid about.

When she looks at me with concern and genuine care, like I'm a good person who deserves her understanding, I do what anyone in my position would do when confronted with someone who relies on you looking at you like their whole sense of what they know to be true in the world is about to come crashing down on them.

I course correct, and the truth bends with it.

"It's been a long day and this bourbon's kicking in. Can we go back to you telling me about your not-simple answer to my simple question?"

"Sure, right, um, I guess it's where I live now." Rory's face processes a range of emotions, from confusion to acceptance, in a matter of seconds.

"Why, Rory?"

"It's been the longest stretch of time of anywhere I've lived."

"That it?"

"I know all its quirks."

She's cute, flustered by my questions, chewing on her bottom lip. "Its quirks."

"Yeah, like it's a great community—people look out for each other. We moved so often I couldn't let myself get attached to places. My childhood wasn't like yours. This is a home. The trophies and pictures, stories and memories. I suppose I always divert-ed my attention from the idea of something I didn't think I could have. Anyway, if I were you, this would be my favorite place."

She searches my eyes, looking for a response I don't have. A father abandoning his daughter. A mother dragging her kid around from zip code to zip code. Guilt throws me, swift like a wild pitch to the gut, how I've gone on and on about my childhood. Not allowing myself to judge Rory's parents, who I don't know, because if I judged them, I'd have to face myself too.

I'm no expert at facial expressions, but I know Rory has a Rolodex of smiles. I've been reluctantly cataloging them since last night. This one might've gone unnoticed if I didn't have a Ph.D. when it comes to recognizing walls. Pain casts a distinct shadow, and it's only because I've lived this reality for the last decade that I see her smile for what it is—a shield.

She's holding up a mirror and all I see is my own remorse and shame about the accident.

"I know I have a lot of thoughts and sometimes those thoughts spiral. When I was young, they had a lot more air time, but I've been learning how to funnel their chatter into something useful, like writing. And it's helped. It's why I'm here. To write the best book I can . . . with you."

She's not the only one learning here.

I grab an ivory wool blanket from the couch and open it up in the air. Its weight lands over her legs like a failed parachute. I know that the more I ask, the more I'll learn, which is helping me to mentor Rory, but it's also complicating things. Does my mouth heed my warning? Not tonight, it doesn't. I sit back down and carry on as

if the thought were never there. *As if there won't be consequences.*
"Rory, I want to ask you something."

22

RORY

"SOMETIMES BREAKING THE RULES IS EXTENDING THE RULES."
—MARY OLIVER

HE SMILES AND I'M certain he could ask me to hide a body right now and I'd pick up a shovel.

"Why would you give up on your writing if you didn't get this mentorship?" His eyes beg for honesty.

After hearing his question, I'd like to use the shovel to dig a hole for myself.

I scan his shoulders and arms, down to his hands, resting between his knees. I follow the pattern his sun-kissed hair makes as it falls in front of his eyes. The longer we stare at one another, the more insulated this space feels, the less I want to be anywhere else.

Reed's told me a lot about himself and I have more questions than ever. Where was he supposed to be? Why can't he write? His soft voice spoke and when it did, something in my heart ached for him, like watching a man walking shackled to his sentencing.

He needed to pause, to stop talking, and I know that feeling all too well. At first, I didn't know if I could trust his words without seeing his actions. He's been inconsistent in the past. But tonight, he took a small chance on me, and I think, as I steal a glance over at him gazing at the fire waiting for my answer, flames flickering over his profile, that I want to take a chance on him too.

My fingertips tingle as Reed runs a hand through his hair, pushing each unruly layer away from his eyes. They settle on top of another, creating a perfect harmony of highlights.

"I spent the summer after college at my mom's, dodging the constant disappointment in her eyes every time she asked me if I'd found 'anything' yet. You know, a desk job with benefits. I was having my coffee at the kitchen table, scanning the classifieds, and saw this ad for 'Largest Romance Book Convention of the Year'—'Love Is In The Air'—'Downtown Boston'—'Mix and Mingle with your Favorite Romance Authors.' I had finished writing my first novel a few weeks before and thought I'd check out a signing, get the lay of the land, scope out authors, maybe network a little. I brought a few books to be signed too."

Reed's attention is on me as he leans against a chair. I think it's safe to keep going.

"The heat that day stands out the most. It was unbearable, and in my rushing, I forgot to bring a jacket, so all I had on was this thin sundress and backpack. I was completely unprepared for how cold it would be inside." I cringe at the memory, the caustic air conditioning still stings as the fluorescent lights burn overhead. I clear my throat and take a sip of my drink.

"It was a maze of unaware people and combating smells. I tried to stand in one line—it wasn't even that long—but everyone kept bumping into me. Maybe it was the bulky backpack. Maybe I was just nervous in a room with my favorite authors. The room began to close in on me, like a tidal wave, from out of nowhere. I ran as fast as I could. I swear, I tripped over a dozen feet to get out of there."

"You don't have to keep going." Reed's jaw is tense, like he's clenching down on every word I'm saying.

I wipe the sleeve of my shirt along my eyes and pull my glasses off, setting them on the ground. "They get foggy."

"Yeah, mine do that too. I can grab a cleaner." He lifts to stand.

I reach out, placing my hand on his knee. "I want to finish."

He sits back down, narrowing his attention to my hand. I yank it back.

"I collapsed into a full-blown anxiety attack. I'd never had one before, not like that. I had experienced isolated symptoms growing up but never the storm. I don't really remember every detail. It comes to me in dreams, so I see it in snapshots, sometimes out of order."

He shakes his head into his lap.

"It's better now. It was so long ago. I guess at the time, it was scary because I thought I was having a heart attack. I couldn't unscramble a single thought. Then this random guy asked me if I was okay, and I freaked out, totally mortified, and ran to the train. I was halfway to my stop when I realized what I'd done."

Reed pauses, his hands clasped between his knees, and he leans forward like he's bracing for the impact that my memory will make. As if he wants to protect me.

The motion is slow and deliberate, but I sense he's devastated and doesn't even know why yet.

"By the time I made it back, the backpack was gone. I checked the front desk and left my number in case anyone returned it. I didn't care about the bag or even the books. Those were replaceable. But my handwritten manuscript, Reed. It was inside. My only copy." Fresh tears spill down my cheeks. "It was so personal—details about my life, inspired by all the feelings I had growing up without my father. I wrote it, unfiltered and raw, a true first draft, not even sure where I was going with it. It wasn't ready to be seen by anyone but me. I wasn't ready to expose myself to the world. It wasn't ready. I wasn't ready."

"Rory. I'm so sorry."

His low voice sparks like a match against my skin. The final word strikes and ignites.

I stop breathing when I realize maybe he's seeing right through this story to the other feelings I've been trying to work through all day. Have I slipped up and shown them somehow in all of my telling?

His lashes lift, and his eyes turn indigo.

My pulse leaps. The lines I've drawn are making their own connections now. One blanket, the cabin in the woods, two writers, and a fire to keep warm. I'd write this scene knowing exactly how it would end. Intertwined legs tangled inside the blanket, consumed by a desire hotter than the smoldering flames beside them.

He raises his eyebrows and I'm positive he's scanned the contents of my brain, discovering my specific scene details. I pick up my glass and finish my drink.

"Over the years, I couldn't show up to write without being accosted by the trauma, and it would spiral into anxiety attacks or weeks of depression. I stopped writing to avoid the flashbacks and disruption, to avoid what I'd done—leaving behind something that meant everything to me."

One, two, three, four.

"The hardest part was waking up every day wondering where it was or if someone had found it and was going to claim it as their own."

Five, six, seven, eight.

"I've made so many mistakes, but the one I regret the most was how naive I'd been not writing my name all over that journal. I can't describe the torture in any sort of clear way. The pain was unbearable for so many years. In time, it became manageable. The nightmares were intermittent, and now, I suppose, it's a story I tell by the fire over drinks."

Reed sits trapped under a spell of smoky air. I'm afraid to know his thoughts.

"It was slow, like molasses, but I did eventually find my way back to my writing. And now to you. I mean, here with you."

He drains his drink. "I'm glad you found your way back." His voice is shaky. "What you've shared with me, Rory, is a gift. You're a gift."

The air is warm. The room sways in my peripheral. There's a weight that's been lifted in sharing my story in a safe space. With Reed.

My head may be light from the bourbon too.

"I did find my way back. You're right. I made it through the hardest days, where I couldn't breathe or get out of bed. Where everything felt broken and lost forever. But I've come so far. So right here, I'm declaring it." I reach over grabbing his hands. "And you'll be my accountability. I'm ready to let it go and to finish my novel. I won't let the past control my future anymore. I never want to think of that journal or backpack or summer day again."

The fire snaps and sizzles. I retreat immediately when I realize I'm holding his hands, uncertain which impulse was instinct and which was restraint.

"And thank you, Reed, because without you pushing me out of my comfort zone, like cooking dinner tonight, I wouldn't have known how much I was holding myself and my story back."

He's searching my eyes. I feel a lasso around my lungs, constricting all the air. The space has shifted to something strong and tight, like time itself has frozen, and one whisper from either of us could destroy the whole thing.

He's become someone I think I understand and who understands me at times better than I seem to understand myself.

We both now seem lost in our inner worlds.

The silence is deafening.

Maybe it's the long day, or the elevating temperature, or our side-by-side meal-making tonight. All the excitement and anticipation from idea generation and outlining. It's creative. It's chemistry. I've never felt so confused and yet clear about what I want.

Reed's eyes darken like a summer storm. Delight tugs at his lips. I want to know what he tastes like. Maybe I went too far and said too much.

I slip my suddenly stone-cold fingers into his enveloping palm. Though he's only physically touching one side of my hand, I feel it in all the places I promised not to.

He laces our fingers together, each pad scraping against my skin.

How can one touch from this one person, with his words and the way he looks at me, like my messy mind, riddled with anxious thoughts and fears, is okay?

"You're here," he says.

Electric currents surge through my body.

I shake my head. *Yes. No. Yes. No. Yes. No.*

I'm collecting each breath and hum of heated silence, shoving them in every open pocket of reasonable thinking.

"You're here," he repeats.

He said he'd leap. Leap right off that cliff.

I didn't mean to be this close.

Yes. No. Yes. No.

I'm caged inside my skin and his mouth is the only thing that will set me free.

I chew on my bottom lip.

Yes. No.

"Rory, we're in this together."

Yes.

I daringly sweep my lips over his, parting them with my tongue.

His kiss is warm and strong, and there isn't an inch of my body that's not responding to him. Reed tortures me with his tongue, soaked in caramel and desire. My arms rope around his neck, and I hang on to keep above water. Breathing him in as he breathes into me is undeniable. He glides his lips over my cheeks and across my jawline. His beard's rough and igniting along my skin.

I whisper into his ear a final truth, because that's all I have left.

A deep pressure on both sides of my face tears me away. My lips burn, desperate to get back. My heavy eyes snap open to find Reed, sharp inhales and heaving chest. His eyes wild with movement. Whatever he's thinking is in direct response to what I whispered. His lips part, swollen, still wet from our kiss.

His voice is strained and resolute. His face, laced with regret.

"We can't, Rory. Please, I need you to hear me out," he mutters, gasping for breath.

It's only then I realize, with my heart in my throat, that I didn't finish answering his original question. *Why was I going to give up on writing?*

Instead, I just dove off that cliff, headfirst, alone.

23

REED

"SOMETIMES THINGS MAKE MORE SENSE THE SECOND TIME AROUND." —RANIA NAIM

THIS ISN'T POSSIBLE.

Years have passed, leaving their mark. Faint lines like crescent-shaped brush strokes paint the edges of her emerald eyes. The severity in her stare slices right through me. I'd be instantly drawn to their glittering flecks of gold in any crowd or decade, and yet, only now do I see it's the same girl—woman.

"I guess we've mastered show versus tell." Rory attempts to divert my attention and I have no idea what to say. I back up, blink, and race to scrutinize every detail, matching each feature to a pile of buried images I have from that day. Sorting through them feels like a game of memory I'm playing and my time is running out.

My hands are digging into my pockets, scrambling for my stone.

"I'm so so so sorry." She speaks before my thoughts fully form. "Bad joke on my part. I'm just trying to fix this, and I know what you're going to say and you're right, and I shouldn't be kissing my mentor, and we can't, and it was impulsive, reckless, and not like me at all."

Rory's voice is raw and scratches inside me.

The desperation in her eyes has not changed. My memory of her has been preserved, frozen in time, waiting to thaw.

I should've figured out who she was sooner.

The story in her journal. I knew her. Well, I knew her feelings, understood them as if they were my own. She came alive on the page, as this real person. Someone I cared for without having ever met.

Over time, I had brushed off how I felt about a total stranger as a side effect of the excessive heat warning that week. Nothing more than remorse for not returning the backpack to its owner.

But seeing Rory now tells me that what I've been holding onto from that day has been something much greater than guilt.

While I was drawing comfort from her written words for a decade, she was being bullied by the most gut-wrenching loss and grief.

Rory's emails—there were so many times her words tugged like familiarity. I thought maybe it was easy to talk to her because she was available and engaging and I knew I'd probably never meet her, so there was protection in that too.

But it wasn't those things alone that pulled me in. She felt like a friend because part of me recognized her voice between the lines.

And now, I have to tell her how the universe has brought us together, not once, but twice.

I should go upstairs right now, grab her journal, and ease her heart. I should do something instead of sitting here staring at her trembling chin resting on her knees.

It's a simple truth, an honest story, yet it doesn't feel like an adequate explanation. How does time take something simple and tie it into double knots?

"Can we please blame this on the fancy bourbon and the altitude and pretend it never happened?" She combs her fingers through her hair, pulling her knees to her chest.

The stone flips between my fingers, reminding me where I am. And where I'm not.

Even if I want to tell her, what purpose will that serve but derail her? The fact is, *she doesn't know me . . .* not how I know her. I'm not going to dump ten years' worth of baggage onto her lap, not now, not after she kissed me like she'd give up her dream to do it again.

I shake my head. The faint smell of ash causes my eyes to water. The bourbon has turned sour in my stomach and the room is closing in.

I swiftly collect our glasses and bring them to the sink.

Fenway follows me out the door.

I'm aware it's a dick move on my part to leave her behind, but that's the least of my problems at the minute. She's safe inside.

The dock creaks under my boots. The reflection of the moon over the lake's surface colors the water amethyst. It hasn't snowed yet here, but I can taste the heaviness in the air. It's only a matter of time.

She wants to erase the last five minutes. She never wants to ever think of the journal or the backpack or that summer day again.

I have so many questions. Why does she give up so easily? On her writing, her feelings. She's a master at backpedaling.

I want to tell her everything, but this isn't about me. For once in my damn life, this is not about me.

Rory also made it pretty clear that kissing me was an impulse she regrets. Not even going to unpack how shitty that feels.

Whoever I was when her journal found me isn't who I am now, damaged beyond repair.

And whatever I felt the moment her lips met mine and I pulled her into my arms . . . and whatever I was trying to say back there, trying to untangle the past . . . none of it matters.

She doesn't remember me. We have a deadline. There are rules for a reason.

I'll wait until the mentorship is over, only a few months. It's nothing short of what I've been doing anyway. I'll keep my thoughts to myself, but now that I know who she is, who she's been all along, and what she tastes like, I have no idea how to keep my distance.

I pull the stone from my pocket and chuck it into the water. It sinks on impact.

Groggy from last night's flat-out failures of both honesty and sleep, I walk the perimeter of the house, processing. Frost bites at the edges of each window. The lake looks nearly frozen. The top layer glistens with sharp bursts of light, like millions of tiny diamonds fell from the sky overnight and stuck on the surface.

I'm carrying the stack of mail from the kitchen counter. The hair on the back of my neck stands up, and I shiver through the chill that penetrates my skin. I should've let Mom shred these. What purpose was there in keeping this? It serves as a shrine symbolizing the misguided vision I once had for a certain version of my life. I held onto it like a form of daily penance. As if I could ever forget how I ruined the lives of so many people, including my own.

Rory's already awake, leaning against the kitchen window when we walk in.

I drop the mail back on the buffet.

"Good morning," she says.

Fenway wags his tail, making his way over to secure all of Rory's attention. While I force myself to focus on anything other than her raspy morning voice and lazy smile.

The coffee smells good. It's gonna be a whole pot kind of day. There's a mug already waiting for me on the counter. I grin as I grab the coffeepot.

I clear my throat. "Hey, good morning."

Rory's eyes have a violet tint beneath the lashes. I'd recognize exhaustion anywhere, as well as my own reflection.

Limited sleep often interrupted by night terrors of Emerson's accident. The crunch the metal door made as EMS cranked it open to pull out her broken body from the lake. Two minutes too late. That's all it took to be stuck behind yellow tape, pounding my fists in the snow until they bled.

"Reed, stop." Rory's voice yanks me from the frozen waters. "Here, here, take these."

She's throwing paper towels and rags at me. It's not until her hands are on mine, taking the coffeepot from me, that I realize I've dumped coffee all over the counter.

"Shit." I step back and survey the damage. All over the counter, down the dishwasher, dripping to the floor.

Rory's back around the counter in her baggy sweats, hair wrapped in a bun on top of her head. She's cleaning up my mess and I'm standing here, useless.

"I'm sorry. You don't have to do that."

"No big deal. I spill things too, as you know. Hazard of being in our imaginations most of the time." She laughs—a generous gesture after leaving her hanging last night.

"Are you okay?" She nods to my white t-shirt, splattered, wet with permanent stains.

I lift it up to check, exposing my chest and abdomen. "No burns." Rory's eyes are on me. I don't have to see them to feel them. When I look up and catch her watching me, she turns around faster than a plot twist and bolts upstairs.

Lesson number one, don't make out with your mentee.

Lesson number two, don't undress in front of your mentee.

I toss the shirt into the washer and go to the bunk room for a fresh one.

Lesson number three, stick to the fucking plan.

Even though the door to my room is open, I knock on it. Rory's reading on my bed, her head resting against the wall.

"Hey, got a minute? I want to show you something."

She closes her book. Her eyes remain on mine. Questioning. Cautious.

"Grab your computer," I instruct.

She doesn't move. I know she's curious about what step is coming next. She just needs some encouragement.

I add some platonic pep to my tone. "Any day now, Wells. Remember? You. Me. Deadline."

She smiles, releasing her bottom lip from between her teeth, and hops off the bed. She carries her stuff and coffee, and follows me down the dimly lit hallway to the door at the end.

I try to ignore how close she's standing, directly behind me, since there's no room anywhere else.

I square my shoulders, planning to use force, but the key turns easily in the lock. The door groans open—a subtle yet unsurprising warning. It's been two years. What did I expect, a red carpet?

Rory walks in as I hold the door open for her to pass.

The room is stale and dry, exactly how I left it. I breathe in long summer days that have died in here. I lean over the desk to crack the window. The cold air strikes across my face as hot as the fire burning within me.

"This is my writing cave. I've written every story here."

Rory's eyes widen in excitement.

She squeals, does a twirl where she stands, then stops mid-revolution, eyes darting between me and the door. "You keep a bed in here?"

"This used to be Carlynn's room. When I was on deadline, it was easier to sleep here than to disturb . . . anyone else."

Her shoulders drop and she clutches her laptop tighter. I think she's going to ask me more about what I meant. Maybe she'll see the pleading in my eyes to drop it.

"Who's Genevieve?" She peeks at me through her full lashes and thick frames.

Nope. She did not recognize it. Not even for a second.

Now that I've been around Rory's voice versus deciphering it through emails, I understand that her frequent line of questioning is a quality of how much she cares, not a reflection of being invasive.

Still, this question cracks open my chest.

Her mouth was on mine less than twelve hours ago. I think we're past dancing around each other, and yet, I want to spin her in circles to avoid this conversation.

I flip around the chair at my desk and sit down, resting my arms over the back.

A deep inhale pushes through my lungs and I run a hand through my hair. Rory tracks my movement and I track her summoning stare, speaking only in an effort to silence my relentless thoughts.

"Gen was my girlfriend. We worked together in the book world." I pick at my cuticles and decide to cross my arms instead. "She introduced me to my agent, and the next thing I knew, my author brand was born. Don't get me wrong, I'm grateful to her and for every opportunity I've had. I didn't have to fight for an agent—I was simply handed one and he liked my book ideas. A specific publishing house we know well was thirsty for a male romance author who was willing to show his face. It was part timing and part luck but mostly strategic marketing. Anyway, the work became front and center in our relationship until it became all of our relationship."

I've probably shared more than she asked for, but I have no clue how to do this. How to be two people at once in my own home.

"That must've been hard. To work with someone you lived with. Didn't the chemistry get in the way?"

"The chemistry between us was convenient, I guess. Maybe even the glue at first. We were both motivated to succeed, focused on our individual goals. But chemistry can only do so much of the heavy lifting. So though we lived together, we were also passing ships. Sometimes, it's easier to stay than it is to go." I shut everyone out after the accident and after Gen left. I didn't need anyone else to poke the sore spots.

"So you two were like the right people, but bad timing?"

She's possibly trying to tie this idea back to her book, so I push my comfort zone. "Genevieve and I functioned more like good friends and productive colleagues. More like, good timing, wrong people."

Rory's eyes linger on mine. When she returns to examining the room and its dust particles, I think we're moving on.

"The thing is," she adds. "I don't know if it's possible to balance the two. You'd either bring work home all the time or carry chemistry and challenges into work. Seems like a lot to manage."

Her doubt feels like a pin sticking into a part of my heart that's been slowly inflating since she arrived.

I don't know how she could dismiss the way that kiss felt.

Maybe I was wrong and she wouldn't give up anything to kiss me again. Maybe I was in that moment alone.

I lick my lower lip, then swallow the memory of her mouth teasing mine. "Did you know that almost a quarter of married couples in the United States meet in the workplace?"

"How many end in divorce?" Rory fires back.

I glance at the floor. *I don't have that statistic.*

A running list of successful artistic collaborations throughout history surfaces in my mind. I cut that train of thought off before it gains traction. What am I even doing? Attempting to convince her that some relationships can thrive professionally and personally.

"I'm sorry, Reed. I don't know why I said that. Ignore me."

Ignoring her is not possible.

She's carrying a heaviness today. I was wrong. Her eyes aren't tired—they're sad. It would be dismissive for me to not acknowledge that it probably has to do with last night. I need to find a way to repair our connection so she's comfortable again.

"There was a part of me that felt like I lost something when Genevieve left, but when I spent some time and pulled it apart, I was more upset with myself. How I was willing to let something I knew wasn't meant to be, go on for so long. It says more about me than her. I got complacent because I was focused on building some kind of bullshit legacy, based on the person I wanted to be for everyone else. I cared about what people thought. Life was easy, and admitting I wasn't in love with her felt like failure."

"But you figured it out and that's what matters." Rory and her optimism move over to the window, taking the longest route to go around me.

"Did you also know humans are the only animals that blush?" I ask.

"Really? You sure are full of random trivia."

I'm running out of ideas here. I want her to feel at ease so we can get to work.

"Mom gives me a different trivia book every year on my birthday. May I offer you one piece of unsolicited mentorish advice?"

"Well, I don't know, it's still pretty early." Her humor is as sharp as ever. I decide, as she holds my mug—it looks good in her hands—and I want her to have it.

"Trust your gut with your decisions, with Seth's chapters. You most likely already have the answers."

"The trouble is knowing the difference between my gut and my anxiety. They sound the same."

I stand and push the chair back in, making my way to where she is, keeping a healthy distance.

"Rory, that's not your anxiety talking to you—that's your intuition. If you listen to it, it will come. Keep practicing."

"I think *it* comes from growing up with parents who love you."

Part of me feels like it's stealing to learn about who she is now without first telling her who I am.

It's easier to exist in compartments, taking rain checks for feelings I'm not ready to deal with. But when she says something like that, and I'm reminded of what she's shared with me and what she's written in her journal, I can't help myself.

"You didn't feel loved as a child?"

"I don't entirely remember. I guess I felt loved at times. But it was inconsistent too. My emotional safety wasn't a priority. What I do know is what I believe—that the greatest thing you can give any child is a childhood. Time and space to become themselves, to grow confidently, to hang dreams on the wall. If you protect the childhood, you don't have to heal the adult. And a healed adult is someone who knows what love is."

She's calm and considerate.

At first, I think she expects me to say something, but her gaze slips to the horizon, to the sun rising, an orange ball ascending. I realize she's talking to the space between us more than to me.

She keeps watch on Berry Lake, its landscape of pine and wet branches, and I keep my eyes fixed on her.

"Writing this novel, Reed, will be my greatest achievement. I have to make it happen, even if it's scares me."

"Someday you'll see what I already see in you."

She does a double take, a flash of recognition in her eyes.

One on the surface where she registers my words, and the other beneath the layers of fear, where the inner child she's exhausted from protecting, might hear me too.

"Listen, last night," I say.

Rory's foot's tapping against the floor. She's playing with the ends of her hair and her eyes are begging me to tread carefully. Before my throat closes, I spit out, "Cooking like that, together, I just thought it would bring you closer to your story and character. To experience how art can inspire art."

"I know." She nods.

I push off the wall and walk back to the door.

"I'm wondering if maybe I'm not the best match to mentor you. Clearly I'm making up the rules as I go, and I think I put you in a difficult position, and I'm sorry for that. I understand if you want to ask for a different mentor. I can call my agent today. No hard feelings or anything."

Rory's cheeks flush and her eyes start to flood. Shit, this isn't helping. I want to help. "It's not about—"

"Listen, Reed." A loose tear falls and she lets it.

I squeeze my fists and shake out my hands. Once, twice, waiting for her to continue. Holding myself back from closing the distance.

"I was matched with you for a reason. I don't want a mentor who tells me generic information I can look up online. I want a mentor who forces me to cook and to think about my story differently. Someone I can trust. Last night happened. I take responsibility for my part in that. We agreed to move on. We have a deadline. And I need to get this entire manuscript converted into first-person. You said you were going to help me. Have you changed your mind?"

I shake my head.

"Good. Because I'm in this room that desperately needs dusting off and I'm ready." Rory pulls back the curtain fully, opening the window to get a true view of the water. "Unreal. This view. I see why you'd write in here. This space is you."

I clear my throat at her suggestion of knowing me. I might be able to keep my mentee making progress on her manuscript, but when it comes to Aurora Wells, I have no plan at all.

24

RORY

"YOUR INTUITION KNOWS WHAT TO WRITE,
SO GET OUT OF THE WAY." —RAY BRADBURY

NOTHING HAS EVER FELT more real. What was I thinking? How could I even say those words? To someone I barely know.

The reality is, nothing about that kiss was real. It was hormones, a hazy moment driven by imagination, weakness, maybe even gratitude. I mistook attention for attraction and almost buried my dream in its intoxication.

I was too embarrassed to even call Kat. So I held my own hair back while I released my shame into the toilet. Reed was outside, unable to face me and, luckily, didn't hear me retching. I had barely any energy, using the last of it to crawl into bed. I fell asleep with two options on my mind. Plan A, never leave this room, or Plan B, pretend it never happened.

At dawn, I put on clothes and made coffee.

Luckily, I also beat him to the punchline. I kissed him. It was my mess to clean up. I saw enough in the straight line of shock across his face. I couldn't let him see my disappointment too. It's better this way. And on the heel of that half-truth I tell myself, I sit down at his writing desk and fire up my laptop.

Staying busy will keep me productive. Productive will keep me out of my head. Out of my head will keep my hands to myself.

Reed returns to the room with rags and a spray bottle of bleach. He wipes down the space and tosses me my manuscript with all of his notes. I thumb through his highlights and tabs. He has an actual system for this.

I don't know why I expected chicken scratches and chaos, but this is color-coded and my compulsive heart does a cartwheel.

He lays on the twin bed in the room, stretching out over a quilt. I will simply ignore his messy hair and ocean eyes.

"The orange tabs are some of the places I think it would be good to see from Seth's perspective as well. I want to read them out loud together. Hear how they feel."

"I don't know what he'd say." I grab a pen and chew on the cap.

"Well . . . we could improv if you want." Reed grabs a baseball off the nightstand and wraps his fingers around the stitching.

"Does that have a story?" I ask.

"Doesn't everything?"

I pull my legs up into the chair and prop my head in both of my hands. Reed's smiling, so I try to relax too, a little.

"Pops caught a fly ball once during a home game. It was coming right toward us behind first base." He points to his head. "I'd have one different-looking mugshot had he not been paying attention. Caught this ball three inches before it made contact with my face."

"That is a story," I exclaim, jumping up and walking over to inspect the evidence.

"Wanna see it?" he asks.

"Yeah I wanna see it."

Reed drops the baseball into my hand.

The surface is smudged with decades-old dirt and the stitching has faded. I bring the leather under my nose. Reed doesn't take his eyes off me, and I wonder if he's kept track of how often I find myself breathing him in too.

"I'm a weirdo."

Reed shrugs his shoulder. "Aren't we all? Anyway, that's the most action that thing's seen in almost thirty years."

I toss the ball back to him like it's on fire and retreat to my side of the room.

Will I ever stop reading into everything? He's talking about his dad and playing baseball and I'm trying to scrub away the tingling sensation my lips feel whenever he speaks.

Maybe I should ask him for the bottle of bleach. A few squirts in the air might do the trick.

"So, page forty-two, look at that sentence, read it, and then tell me how Seth would say it."

My fingers warm in the light of the window. The ray reaches Reed's eyes, turning them into the clearest summer water as it reaches the shore. I shake out my hands to steady my pulse.

I go over the sentence twice. "Okay, how about, '*Yes, our timing sucks, but that doesn't define us. Our choices do.*' Short and simple."

That's most men I know, at least. Limited expressiveness, getting to the point in a fraction of the time it takes me to.

"Is Seth simple?" Reed challenges. *Of course he does.* "What I know about Seth is that he's always projecting and protecting his ego. He likes the spotlight, Rory. Try again."

I know this is supposed to be helping me understand Seth, but it's frustrating to perform for an audience.

"Can you please give me an example? Show me."

Reed frowns but acquiesces. Fenway strolls in and lays at my feet.

"Hey, buddy." I reach to rub his ears, nuzzling a kiss on the top of his head.

"All right, let me think for a sec . . ." Reed clears his throat and rakes his hand through his sun-kissed hair. My heart attempts to leap and I knock the impulse down. *No leaping!*

Reed locks his eyes on me and his voice wobbles, at first, then smooths out.

"Maybe something like, *'Even though it's been years, I've only known her in small increments. How can I risk everything for a love I don't even understand? All I want—need—is for this to be any other time in my life. Though our timing may never be right, she has to make her choices, and I have to make mine.'*"

And I have to remind myself that this is a character talking to another character, which isn't easy to do when he's got a heartbeat and is looking at me like I'm somebody to him.

"Um . . . that was really good," I say, clearing the edge in my throat. To hear him come up with something completely off the cuff like that reminds me of the voice I've always admired in his books. "Maybe you should write this with me?" I suggest, half-teasing, semi-curious, and open to anything at this point.

Reed's eyes widen. His mouth drops open.

"Rory, us brainstorming and sharing dialogue for practice is simply an exercise and is intended for you to flesh out what you already have. To sense your story, delve into who these characters are, what they want and desire, what's holding them back. Becoming them so you can tell their sides. I offered you one possible Seth so that it might motivate you to build your damn own. It was not me sniffing around for a seat at the table."

"I definitely didn't say you were sniffing. I appreciate the exercise, really, I do. It's just that these notes, it's like my words are here, but in a way, so are yours, and they sync. I don't even know where one of us begins and the other ends. It's like a great piece of pie."

"Fuck." Reed stands and paces the room, digging through his hair again.

The window's open and it still smells like him in here. I can't think when my head's clouded in Reed's voice and Seth's intentions.

"Hear me out. I have an idea." I glance up from the pages to Reed's scowl.

"I'm listening."

"Right, well, this scene isn't working," I admit.

"Be more specific," he grits out.

"Okay." I clench my teeth against his request. "Chelsea's hurt. She's furious at Seth for giving up, and she wants to be mad, you know, like, throw her fists into him kind of passionate anger."

Reed drags a chair from across the room and parks next to me at the desk. He leans into my space and I can't stop myself from breathing him in. Sometimes I wonder, with Reed being all tucked away in this house in the middle of the woods, if he isn't a mythical creature with powers that invite you in and can also destroy you. I shiver the thought away and chalk it up to too much vampire fanfic in my twenties.

I spread the scene across the desk, observing his eyes scanning the rows of text. He leans back a little and faces me. This would work better if there were toothpicks holding my eyes open. It's taking physical strength not to succumb to their instinct to close when he's this close.

"What's behind the anger?" he asks.

I sigh, trying to put myself in Chelsea's experience, not mine. "Hurt, maybe, regret, I don't know, no, not regret. She'd do it all over again." I'm rambling, speaking in a stream of consciousness.

"She'd do what all over again?"

Why is he so close to me? Where's a wheelie chair when you need one?

I'm sitting on a solid oak chair that might as well be bolted to the ground.

"She'd love him all over again. She'd go through time just to be with him because he was worth it." I'm so excited about the pieces of the story coming together. I cover my mouth in shock and the chapters in my lap fall down my legs.

Our hands crash into each other in an effort to stop them. Reed scoops up the pages, placing the pile safely back in my lap.

"Be careful."

My thoughts exactly.

"How does she feel here?" he continues, pointing to the page in my hand, and I've stopped clocking the distance between my own heart and Chelsea's. My head's revolving like a merry-go-round.

Chelsea's thoughts. My words.

Chelsea's story. My feelings.

Are they separate? Are they the same?

He presses me again, "What about her physical body, Rory? Is she cold or hot? Shaking or still?"

"She's hot," I blurt out. My skin's damp around my collarbone and above my lip. There's flames everywhere. She's not mad. I look at the paragraph, jotting down notes on how I'll switch this scene to first-person.

The porcelain cup rattles as she places it back on the café table. The memory is old, from a time when the man sitting across from her wasn't a stranger. She had the scars on her skin to prove it. His eyes had aged, too, reflecting a hollowness in his heart that she didn't remember. She wondered what had put it there, what had become of the boy she once stole time with. But some things hadn't changed at all. The pull between them was the same, strong and magnetic, like a stifled spark that finally caught enough air to go up in flames.

"Just hot?" Reed pushes for more.

"She's on fire." I finalize my notes, crossing out what needs to be fixed.

"Are you saying she'd walk through the fire, even though she knows it would hurt her? Give those emotions words. What does she want to say to him?"

He's inches from me now, with his hair falling over his forehead. I'm tracing the lines around his eyes and counting every lash. I get to twenty-seven on top when Chelsea's words strike. I look directly into Reed's eyes.

My throat is raw and open. "You could've handed me the match, told me you were going to hurt me, and I would've lit myself on fire anyway."

My heart and head are racing together.

Seconds pass.

I count rounds of exhales.

The slowest progression of a smile makes its way across Reed's face. He approves? He's amused? He's horrified. He's smiling.

No, no, no . . . don't do that. Not this close.

It's one thousand degrees in this room made up of everything that is Reed. This is how I'm going to die, in flames like Chelsea, consumed by fumes like cognac and black cherry, writing inspiration, and lived-in flannel.

"Window," I gasp.

"Window?"

There's no time to explain. "Open the window more," I demand. "Please," I recover, trying to salvage any shred of dignity I may have left.

Reed hops up, and with a little winterized force, pushes the window fully open.

I'm five seconds from stripping down and throwing myself out of it into the freezing lake.

He lifts his chair with one hand and casually walks it back to his side of the room. "I think you found what you're looking for," he says, sporting a full smile.

Quickly, I get the words on the page. I know he sees me smiling, too, because I feel his eyes still on me. He probably assumes it's pride about the work, and maybe it is, a little, but some of that pride is wrapped up in making Reed Ashton crack a genuine smile. I could get used to being on the receiving end of those, but I shouldn't want to.

I'm sitting on the living room floor setting up a Scrabble board, shaking the tiles, trying to keep my stalking eyes to a minimum. The fake felt bag reminds me of an overly starched dress shirt, uncomfortable in its own skin.

"I saw you posted some new pics on your Instagram. I like them, especially the one of Fenway."

I pass the bag of tiles to Reed while organizing my draw. I'm grateful that my hands are occupied as my heart rolls around on the ground, trying to extinguish the memory from last night in this room.

"Wine?" Reed hops up. He talks to me, facing the wall while opening the bottle. "You did see Fenway wasn't the only one in the pictures?" He turns back around to me with two half-full water glasses. "It's been a while for me. I'm rusty." He slips the glass into my hand and sits back down on the floor, his long legs stretched out in front of him. "Cheers."

My gaze travels to his throat.

The aroma of the wine eventually catches my attention, the dark, spicy currents bringing me back to the present moment. "Yeah, you're in those pics? I hadn't noticed."

I fuss absentmindedly with my tiles.

"I don't need an ego boost, Rory. I wanted to know if they're Instagram-appropriate? Genevieve used to do all of that for me. I don't know—there's got to be a way to share some stuff without putting your life up for grabs."

The fact that he's posting is pretty incredible.

"Yes, the photos are A-plus Instagram-worthy. They're great. Your readers will love it, I'm sure. Your turn."

Reed plays his letters, "T-I-D-A-L. Double letter score. Seven points. Something's on the tip of your tongue. What is it?" he asks.

There's too much happening. I'm trying to avoid the way I want to press fast-forward. The wine's warm and Fenway's snoring trickles in from the kitchen.

I finish placing my word over his. D-E-S-I-R-E.

"My nevers list," I say, focusing on tallying my points.

"Your nevers? You mean like the game, Never Have I Ever?"

Stop asking questions Reed, I internally beg.

"Actually, not at all like that." I meet his stare and then peek back down to arrange the new letters I've collected. C-Y-P-L-E-X.

"It's more like the stuff that isn't going to ever happen." *Like me making a decent next word with this pile of crap letters.*

"What do you mean exactly?" Reed places an I-L-L-Y alongside my S. Triple letter score. Sixteen points.

I'm conflicted because I can't define our friendship, and I don't want to ruin it because there are times I can't catch my breath around him. It's really hard to navigate what I want to say with what I feel like I'm allowed to say.

Reed's watching me unravel in front of him, slowly giving me enough room to let my feelings show themselves.

"Like how I'll never see Pops again?" I meet his compassionate eyes. "Like how you may never meet your father?"

"Yes, Reed, like that."

I lay against the couch, counting my breaths, *one, two, three, four . . . five, six, seven, eight*, focusing on the firelight as it extends across the painted white ceiling and exposed beams. Like a pristine page I want to write on.

"Are you thinking about your father now?" Reed's voice treads softly. Wine in hand. Stained lips.

"Always, a little. I'll never know him and I'm mostly okay with it," I admit.

"I'm sorry, I shouldn't have brought that up." He shakes his head into his lap.

I don't want him to think he's made me sad. "You can bring him up. I'm just trying to make sense of what's happening in my head."

His throat bobs and his eyes stay locked on mine. If pheromones had a scent, they'd be the way this room smells right now, a mix of repressed honesty, merlot, and lake air. When he doesn't say anything, desire floods the space. I don't realize I'm sharing my thoughts until I see their imprint on his perplexed expression.

"I was thinking that I'll never know 'what if?' What if I was never accepted into the program? What if you weren't my mentor and I never came here? What if you and I met some other way? Would we be friends? What if I never finish this book? But I shouldn't ask these questions because *what if* only leads backward."

Expressionless Reed.

Protective-shell Reed.

I recognize this Reed.

My eyes close. Regret sinks in. Not knowing his thoughts is crushing me more than direct rejection ever could.

The warmth of his fingers lacing between mine seizes my spiraling thoughts and arrests my heart. I mean to let go after he firmly squeezes and brushes the pad of his thumb along the top of my hand, but for the first time in my life, while scared, I don't let go first.

In the morning, I find Reed working in the front yard. *Because that feels normal.* We have an emotional night and he gets productive and self-disciplined while I'm slowly drowning my regret in scalding caffeine, two liquid gel caps, and my prescription sunglasses, which I'm unapologetically wearing inside.

The sun definitely hates me.

Reed waves when I step outside, smiling at my approach. The heart-stopping one that reaches his eyes. *It's too early for this shit.*

His smile fades once I'm near enough to stand over his body, and I kinda want it back. I sink into a chair and sip my coffee.

"Hey, roomie," he greets me with a cheerful tone. His playfulness must be from the endorphins.

I'm pretty sure he can see on my face how his cheery disposition is turning me into a raisin. It truly is equal parts attractive and offensive that he's basically walking on sunshine before I've finished my first coffee.

What's gotten into him today?

Reed rests his elbows on his knees, sips his water bottle, and wipes some sweat from his face on the white towel he's holding. He pulls his earbuds out and smiles at me again.

That smile. I look down and am met with a glistening abdomen. I rip my eyes away.

Is sweat supposed to smell good? My coffee is spiked. It's the only reasonable explanation.

"Headache?" he asks.

"Not entirely," I spit out. Extracting this apology is going to be painful but necessary to move on.

"I wanted to say I'm sorry for—"

"Are those new pages in your hand?"

It seems he's completely past last night and in mentor mode. Guess I'm taking this free pass.

"I revised some chapters last night and wanted to know if you'd look at them? Before I keep going. I want to make sure I'm headed in the right direction."

"Sure, yeah, let's see them."

He slaps his knees, stands in one swift movement, and reaches his hand out to help me.

I grab hold and let him pull me onto my feet. Flashes of last night tear through me, uncertain if gravity is on my side. As my body stills, I notice I'm standing because he's still holding my hand. Again.

Our exchange changes from something inspired and playful to fierce.

It only lasts a few seconds, a blink of an eye, but to me, it's like time has slowed down on purpose, laying a roadmap to find my way back.

"These are the pages?" He points to the papers in my hand as I pass them over. "So, you've got both points of view here. Okay." He strokes his beard and that's entirely unfair this early in the morning. How am I supposed to concentrate? "Okay, I'm ready."

"Ready for what?" I step back.

"To read these out loud?"

Not my plan. "Um, well."

"I'll start with Seth." He clears his throat.

I say a silent prayer that I survive this before my coffee's kicked in.

"'Why am I here, Chelsea?' I stare at her with an intensity that throbs. One smile in my direction, one step, one hitch of breath, and nothing will stop me from consuming her right here on this countertop, her bare feet in the air. When I mean nothing will stop me, I mean nothing . . . except her next words.

But they don't come. And then I hear it, the hitch in her breath, skimming through her teeth. I run my fingers up her tanned arms. She trembles beneath my touch.

'I want to hear you say it. I deserve to hear you say it.'
Her skin pebbles and a hot tear of pride releases."

There's a pause.

"Rory," Reed interjects.

"Yes, sorry." I swallow and begin reading Chelsea's section.

"'I'm yours.'"

I stop. I think maybe time has stopped too.

"Rory."

I blink a few times to bring the page into focus, and continue reading.

"A smile and a swear escape his lips. His shoulders fall, taking with them the burden he's been carrying for years. He doesn't waste a single second, crushing his mouth to mine. He tightens his grip on my hips, commanding me to receive him."

I take a gulp of air, and another, checking on Reed, who's encouraging me to continue with a steady smile, his skin shining under a sun that clearly worships him.

I can't read these words out loud to him—he's going to know that part of me is thinking of him. That every shred of inspiration comes from something tangible. He's the one who taught me that.

"The pressure of our kiss matches the force of his fingers. I'm wasted in a haze of Seth, all the time we've missed, all the torture I've put myself through. I melt into the caress of his hands slipping beneath my dress and pressing into my thighs. Our embrace grows powerful and hungry. I'm devoured and, finally, alive."

Chelsea's part ends and Reed picks up where I've left off.

The heat in my chest burns through my skin. I place two fingers over the pulse point on my neck while Reed works through Seth's section. It's just a scene.

One, two, three, four. This isn't about him.

Five, six, seven, eight. This isn't about me.

"I grab her hand and lead Chelsea through the maze of her own house. Her bed is covered in clean sheets, perfectly made, perfectly Chelsea. A deep satisfaction takes hold, knowing we're about to destroy it.

'We're not leaving this room for the entire weekend.' I promise her."

Reed swallows and shakes out his page. "There ya go," his gravelly voice breaks the trance I'm in. "How did that work for you? I think it's great. Seth's really taking shape."

"Yup, it works." Hurrying to gather my coffee and pages. "Have to go . . . feed Fitz—I mean, call Fitz. Call Kat, check on Fitz. Bye."

Last night rolls out in my mind like a map to a scavenger hunt, exposing clues. Reed said something—it was low, in my ear, and throaty, barely above a whisper. Every nerve ending in my body flushes awake when the words appear like an x marking its spot.

When he was holding my hand, he said, *Never say never.*

Did that really happen? Did I write that?

Am I making things up now?

Looks like I'm switching to decaf.

25

—— ❖ ——

REED

"IN ONE KISS, YOU'LL KNOW ALL I HAVEN'T SAID."
—PABLO NERUDA

I SET UP A fully stocked workstation for Rory, including blue and red pens, notecards, water, and a stress ball, leaving her with one simple instruction—to *write.*

No word counts, no pressure. *"While you're here, this room is yours, so make it what you need it to be."*

I gave her permission to write dirt. *"Dirt we can work with. Dirt builds foundations,"* I told her as she stared at me with her negotiating eyes. *"Everything you need is already in your possession. Don't overthink it."*

She made a promise not to fixate on the details and just keep pushing forward. I took her phone and placed it on her bed. She's officially in a distraction-free zone.

And now it's my turn. I linger in the living room, eyeing my laptop on the couch, attempting to mentor myself to lay down my own dirt.

I wasn't sure how the rest of the day would go after last night. I held her hand because she needed a friend. I held her hand because I wanted to. She didn't get hurt, nothing happened to her, but I know I can't keep holding her hand. She's a strong person and has survived without me her entire life. I made a pact with myself. If only I could keep it together.

After Pops died, I felt numb. Everything reminded me of him, but in a dull way, like he was never even here. Nothing held joy.

I hadn't committed to any real plans after that. I stayed close to home for my family and, to be honest, for myself too. I took odd jobs around town, fixing roofs, cleaning out yards, things that kept me busy.

The only thing that made sense during the early days of Pops's death was journaling. Then I met Genevieve and everything happened fast. Then I found Rory's journal.

I tried to write a book about a father and son relationship, but it was too raw to write from the wound. I put it in a drawer.

When interviewers ask me where I get my inspiration, my answer never falters. I grew up knowing what love looks like. I approached every story with the same feeling I'd get watching my parents navigate life.

Though deep down, I always knew Genevieve was not it, I began to have purpose again, funneling my grief into the fantasy of romance. I ran fast, dove into the work, and rarely came up for air. Our relationship progressed and deteriorated somewhere in the middle of that race.

Genevieve cared more about preserving my image than about how I felt as a person.

I hung my hat on the facade that *Reed Ashton* protected me from my personal life, when in reality, it confused things, making it impossible to decipher what was real. I don't want to be two people ever again, marinating in self-hate, the kind that happens when you exploit your identity to sell something.

You can't use a shell for publicity purposes and not expect to eventually discover you've been hollowed out in the process.

I was ashamed. I took my father's and my grandfather's legacy, a lifelong commitment to helping others, and traded it in to get my name on the top of bestseller lists by writing books I stopped believing in.

After Emerson's accident, I fell into a really dark place. I didn't understand it at first because it felt different from when I lost Pops. This loss felt like a hole I buried myself in and didn't care if I survived.

I press my damp palms into my thighs and shut my eyes tight.

Emerson. Shannon. You couldn't help them.

Focus on Rory. Help her.

Aurora and Rory. Two people.

Not just to the outside world, where judgment awaits, but inside, where, I fear for her that the critic is much harsher than anything she would face out here.

Holding the power button down, the screen fades to black, and I tuck the laptop into the bookshelf.

One thing I'm sure about are energy levels. Rory needs to eat, and I should too.

There's a fresh loaf of French bread, so I pull out what I need. While I'm washing the lettuce, my phone rings. I dry my hands off to answer.

"Yeah." My voice cracks more than it clears. "Hello."

"How's my favorite romance author doing?"

I unwrap the provolone and set aside tomatoes to slice.

"The book's coming along. We had a couple minor hiccups, but I can safely say she's writing as we speak."

"Right, right. The mentorship. Good, man. I knew you'd make that work. And anything on your end?"

My hands work double time as I've got the receiver in a headlock between my tense shoulder and irritated face.

"I've got nothing, Cal."

"Nothing as in not a single chapter."

"As in not a single word."

"What do you need from me to work this out? Seriously, man, I'm here. Let me help."

"I don't think you can."

"Are you seeing someone?"

"No," I bark, pushing away the image of Rory's mouth. "I'm not interested in dating."

"I mean counseling."

He's not the first to ask me, but Mom and Carlynn gave up on asking a year ago. "I'm doing okay."

"If you change your mind, I've got someone. She's good and can meet virtually."

"Cool, thanks, but my hands are full. Talk soon." I hang up.

When I knock on the door to the writing room, Rory's lying on the twin bed, looking up at a poster of the Milky Way tacked to the ceiling. She's focused. I don't want to distract her, but she immediately acknowledges of my presence.

"There's a lot of posters of the universe in your house."

"Space and stargazing, it's a thing around here."

"Well, it's giving me something to look at while I try to pin down whether Seth should go to Chelsea's because her daughter sends

him the article or because he randomly comes across it online."
Rory volleys her ideas at me from across the room.

"I brought you a sandwich."

She shoots up. I know that look. Less words. Less rambling.
She's hungry and happy.

"I know it's sometimes easy to forget to eat." I hand over the
plate.

"Thank you. Seriously, you've got a thing for culinary if you ever
decide to add another career to your resume."

"That's what makes it a hobby. Getting to enjoy doing
something without worrying about it. And nothing beats a
made-for-you sandwich. I can't make made-for-you sandwiches
for just anyone." It's definitely its own love language.

We sit and eat. Rory's on the bed and I'm sitting on the floor,
back to the wall, next to the door.

"I have a random request. Well, really, it's my mom requesting
your company, and you can decline and I'll tell her you're working."

"What is it? You're making me nervous."

"I should've asked instead of hyping it up. Our community
theater is hosting an art show, mostly local and regional artists, and
she wanted to know if you'd come. I help with breakdown and
staging at their events, but if you want to hang back, have the place
to yourself for a night, it's all good."

"I'd love to go. What's the dress code?"

"Anything."

"You probably don't want to set those parameters. I'm bound to
show up in reading-romance-on-the-couch attire."

"Come as you are, seriously."

She leans back down on the bed, staring at the poster again.

"Do you also know a lot about science? I was too busy doodling through eighth-grade science class." She laughs.

A chuckle emerges from my throat. "I know a fair amount. What I don't know is how any of us make it through middle school. The stories I could tell . . . truly *life is stranger than fiction.*"

"Ah, a Mark Twain quote." She smiles, alert and eager to engage. She didn't pay attention in science but she knows her literary history. "Did you do a lot of research for your *Cupid* series?"

"A fair amount, though I'd like to write projects that require more."

"Is there a specific story you're working on now?"

I put my plate on the floor, move over to where she's sitting, and park myself next to her on the twin bed.

"There's this one story I can't get out of my head. About a father and son. I began writing it years ago."

"You haven't finished it?"

"I don't think I could, you know, near the end. I couldn't find a way to let it go."

Rory wiggles her head into the pillow. The same pillow I'd spend nights brainstorming on, working through a scene or idea.

Having her in this room, knowing her mind is creating where I've created before . . . grabs hold of something inside my chest and won't let go.

She doesn't hear my thoughts, but I know she's got one sentence after the other waiting in line for checkout.

I'm relieved she's pausing. I'm not positive I could hear her over the thrumming echo of all her words that have taken up residence in my heart for years. Now that I know who she is, I can't stop rereading the journal and reciting lines in my head when she's around—connecting all the dots.

I want to reach out. To push aside the strands of hair covering her face. How do you touch someone when you've trained yourself not to?

"Look at this with me." She scoots over to the edge of the mattress. It squeaks until she settles, her body still against my ribcage as I lay down. I push to the farthest inch this bed will tolerate without collapsing so we aren't brushing against one another.

She's wearing black leggings and an ivory sweater. Violets and vanilla invade my bubble. My eyes close on a deep inhale, and I summon the courage to open them and face her.

"Did you know the Milky Way is made of stars? Billions of stars," I ask.

Her body relaxes and softens the sliver of unoccupied space between us.

"The universe fascinates me. Everything we've yet to discover. All of the wishes it has to remember. Don't you agree?" she asks, likely to persuade me to keep talking, which would be a colossal mistake. I don't trust my heart not to betray my head.

I nod, agreeing with her. The brilliant expanse in this poster reminds me of her eyes, the way they sparkle like the clearest, coldest night, full of every wish I've ever made.

"What are you thinking, and not saying?" she asks.

"I don't want to freak you out with the things I think."

"I like hearing your take on things." She blinks.

"And I like sharing them with you." I smile back.

The late afternoon sun beams through the skylight. Subtle patterns play over her sweater in waves.

"I sometimes compare studying stars to building character arcs. If you think of a constellation like a story, you can make connections between everything. Just like you use a telescope to see what you're looking at in the sky, you've gotta get microscopically close to a person, almost to the point of possible self-destruction, to see their core." My willpower crumbles and I tuck the loose strands of hair safely behind her ear. Her warm skin slides like silk against my knuckles.

"I don't know if we're talking about characters anymore," she whispers.

"We're all our characters to some degree. At least a piece of us is. The center of the Milky Way is its brightest spot, and I'd say the same is true of the human soul. Like stars, we're unique as individuals, but we're collective in what we possess."

"What do you mean? What do we all possess?"

Being this close to Rory is enough to tip the scales. Things left unsaid are building into a storm—one that is desperate to claim everything in its path. "It's our humanity."

I expect her to move, to take cover, but she's as still as a statue. I clear my throat. But she remains. Every ounce of my strength is honing in on her mouth.

"Nature reflects the human form and the human experience. Take for example, the veins on the backs of leaves mirror the lines of a person's mouth," I tell her.

Rory reaches up to touch her lips.

"And the way a tree's branches and limbs are a breathing system, just like our lungs."

Her palm slides down her throat and lands over the rise and fall of her shallow breathing.

My heart hammers in my chest as I complete my thought. "Think about how many things have to come together at the right time and place in this universe."

"I have thought about it—every day," she explains. "I think about who we are and why we're here."

This is torture. I've never wanted to kiss someone as much as I want to pull Rory into my arms right now, letting her soft hair fall over my face. To breathe her in. To devour all of the places on her body that demand exploration. To trace my tongue down her delicate neck while tasting every shiver my silent confession sends through her body. I want to scrape my teeth along her fingertips, the same ones that transport her ideas onto the page. Her written words have brought me to my knees and to a cold shower more times than I can recall.

I'm hooked on how it feels to be close to Rory as she loses her way and discovers it again. She is shelter. She is truth. The kind that sees before it speaks.

The bed is like quicksand, and I remove myself before we sink to a place we can't return from. No matter how good this feels, this isn't about me. I'm not taking advantage of her presence because I've wanted to talk to her this way for a decade. She didn't spend time with my words the way I have with hers.

The air drops a few degrees as the sun fades. The sky deepens from a pale lavender to a dusky plum.

"Mothers often want what's best for their children. The same could be said for children when it comes to their parents," I suggest, staring out the window.

"You have a great mom."

"Yeah, she's wonderful. I don't deserve her."

"Everyone deserves a great mom." Rory exhales long and slow. "Yes, that's it. Of course her daughter would want to help her get her happily ever after. And Chelsea won't find out about it right away. She'll need to stumble into it when she's ready."

"Now you're thinking like a pro." I like to encourage her, though it's entirely unnecessary. I learn as much from her process as she might mine. My pulse has returned to normal and I'm ready to face her again. "Give the readers a little twisty-tie." I link my fingers together in the air like a strawberry Twizzler.

"A little what?" She laughs into the sleeve of her sweater. "Is this a writer's tool I don't know of yet?"

"It's a Reed original."

"You're an original, all right." She shakes her head at me like we're back in middle school and I've just done something completely juvenile to get her attention. *Not that I did.* Not that I wouldn't.

Before I can move out of the way, Rory's standing in front of me, my back pinned against the window.

"Did you know you can't have stars without night?"

Why is she so close to me? I look up, sending silent wishes like rapid fire, one after the other. Be strong. Hang on.

"Except for one," I mutter.

Her bright eyes searching mine sends my heart hammering.

"One?" Her voice is open and dry like a cracked shell abandoned on the shore.

"The sun, Rory. The sun is a star."

Her lips part in delight. She smiles and my heart stops. I don't know what to do, so I keep talking, but the more I speak, the closer she gets.

"Do you know how many cultures have revered the sun?" The window pierces my back. I can't see her mouth anymore, only those eyes. "How many artists are inspired by the sun, sing about it, paint it." My thumbs press into her cheeks, tipping her face up towards me. "It's central to everything. Earth can't help but orbit around its magnetic pull. I spent a long time sleeping through my days, and now, every morning I wake up, and the sun, it's the first thing on my mind. It's all I see."

I don't need to ask if she's okay. The evidence is soaking into my fingertips.

"The sun," she echoes back, surrendering to my touch, to her own will. "Are you saying—"

My mouth captures her words. And she welcomes me in. Her kiss is tender and strong and teasing my tongue. She rakes her fingers through my hair, as I lift her into my arms. Her hands slide down my back and sneak under my shirt, and my hands travel to her hips and squeeze.

Rory moans into my mouth and I freeze.

My lips throb, desperate to return.

"Fuck, Rory." Ripping myself away, I say, "I'm sorry, I—" I stare at her whiplashed expression. I will not ruin this for her. "You and me, in the same space, isn't working."

"Are you asking me to leave?" she exhales.

"We should make a plan."

26

RORY & REED

"THE VERY ESSENCE OF ROMANCE IS UNCERTAINTY."
—OSCAR WILDE

IT'S NOT UNTIL THE cereal selection is down to a quarter of a box of Golden Grahams and no milk of any kind that I realize we've been existing in a creative bubble for a few days.

I know reality is waiting for me on the other side, and that time has arrived in the form of an Ashton family night on the town and my heading back to Boston.

We kissed. *Again.* Then he politely suggested I leave.

I spent last night alternating between packing and combing through all of my mentorship paperwork. Nowhere in the fine print does it state that you can't make out with your mentor.

Technically, there's zero written rules about dating or personal relationships at all. If anything, getting personal is encouraged.

I'm working on a plan of how to tell Reed that I think I've been wrong. Maybe the right people at the right time can make it work.

The phone rings twice and Kat picks up.

"What's up?"

"Hey, I miss Fitz."

"Yeah, he's ready for you to come home."

"Probably gonna head out tomorrow. There's an art show tonight with his family."

"Are you wearing *the* heels?"

"Nope."

"You'll regret this decision on your deathbed."

"If I wear those heels around here, I'll be on my deathbed."

"I'll revoke your espresso privileges if you don't wear those heels."

"No need to play dirty. I'll think about it."

"Thank you."

"You can thank me in the hospital when I slip on the ice and break a leg."

"But more importantly, will you look fab going down?"

We both shout, "That's what she said! Jinx!"

"Grab a pic with Mr. You-Got-Him-Back-On-Instagram, will ya?"

"I didn't get him back online."

"Okay, so he randomly showed up posting pics after two years. That makes sense."

"I'll call you on my drive back."

"Have fun."

My duffel is packed except for what I need for tonight.

I take in his room, in my own way, thanking it for the time I've had here.

The posters and baseball memorabilia, photos, and of course, all his books. I trace the spines, uneven rows of varied thickness and genre. There's no rhyme or reason to the collection here. It's messy, beautifully free, and grounded like Reed.

✳

REED

You'd think it was opening day by the look on Mom's face. Like they're all realizing for the first time that the sun is in fact a star, Rory walks down the stairs, completely unaware of how she affects a room and everyone in it. She's not wearing her typical baggy clothes or messy bun. *She's barely wearing anything at all.* There are long legs attached to curves and wavy brown hair brushing her bare shoulders. It's not that she doesn't look like herself—it's that this version of her catches my heart by surprise, skipping beats like stones across Berry Lake.

"What's that?" I clear my throat, rolling the sleeves of my black button-down shirt up to my elbows.

"What's what?"

"That." I point at her without looking, like being blindfolded during a game of pin the tail on the donkey, hoping to land somewhere in the middle.

"You mean my dress?" She sounds amused, maybe annoyed.

"Yes." I clear the pinch in my throat again.

"It's an LBD." A smile slowly creeps its way to her rosy cheeks. She's wearing contacts and her lips shine like liquid glass.

"What now?" *Dare I ask.*

"Little black dress, Reed. It's versatile."

"You look so lovely, dear," Mom remarks. "Stop gawking, Reed Ashton West."

"I'm not gawking." I'm admiring, avoiding, anything to settle myself down.

"West?" Rory makes the final step and it takes everything I have not to hold her hand and tell her how beautiful she is.

When Mom links her arm through Rory's, smiling and pulling her in close, I shove my hands—traitors—into my pockets. I check Fenway's water bowl and give him some love, though all of my attention is directed at the woman walking out the door with Mom.

They stride like childhood friends reuniting. There's no awkwardness or tension from our kiss or me suggesting that it's time to give us both some breathing room.

The only awkward thing happening is the amount of time I spend looking at Rory. Which means it's likely other people aside from Mom will notice too. I can't help it. It's like I'm finally paying attention to how it feels when she's not in the room. Some people you get to know in ways that slap you across the face. Others, like Rory, creep up on you. It's the small things, like her laugh, how it begins restrained and then erupts into a song that I want to sing along to.

"I thought Ashton was your last name?" Rory comments.

"Ashton is Reed's middle name," Mom explains.

Rory puts her coat on and wraps an oversized scarf around her neck. The tails drape to her knees. She slides her bare feet into her knee-high brown boots, and now, I'm gawking.

"I hadn't considered that you were using a pen name." She looks up at me as I enter the enclosed porch.

"Pops was Reed Ashton West, Senior."

I hold the door to outside open. Lew's waiting in the car to drive us to the theater.

"Our Reed," Mom boasts.

I glower in response to her bold implication as she smiles once more. "He's a Junior."

We buckle up and take down the gravel onto the dirt road.

"You kids comfortable back there?" Mom giggles while Rory and I settle into their compact car.

Nope. I wouldn't use that word exactly.

Each second that passes is taken hostage by Rory's presence.

Her soft curves.

Her sweet scent.

Our escalating body heat.

I want to yank at the collar of my cotton undershirt, sit on my hands. Anything to stop myself from touching her.

I have to put this fire out before I go up in flames.

"I know a piece of random trivia that you don't," she boasts. "You write romance, Reed. I'm honestly shocked you haven't heard of a little black dress before."

I say, clipped through clenched teeth, "I won't forget it."

The one-lane road leads most of the way into town, over the bridge, around the lake, and deep into a thicket of birch trees. We slow around the corner, and the pile of yellow ribbons comes into view, followed by a framed photo.

My chest tightens. I push air through, forcing myself to look, to acknowledge, a mouth full of metal braces tucked behind a set of blunt-cut auburn bangs. That sun-starched teddy bear's still there, having weathered two summers.

I can barely bring myself to breathe as we drive past, like I'm leaving her behind, again and again and again.

My fingers tap on top of my thigh, the rough denim resisting the dance.

"So many ribbons," Rory whispers, leaning over my side as we pass. "That poor girl. Knowing she'll be that age forever. She deserved more time."

I exhale hard, angry at Rory's lack of perception, spitting out whatever she feels, whenever she feels it, and pissed at myself for inviting my mentee and her little black dress in the first place.

It's getting dark enough outside that I can't see inside the car well enough to know whether she's figured me out. How her grief over a girl she doesn't even know is directly tied to everything she wants to know about me.

Lew parks by Carlynn's van and we enter through the theater's main door. What I'm not prepared for is how to surface-level socialize after days of intimacy with Rory and years of avoiding small talk. I hadn't considered how harshly a room full of voices and live music would greet me.

We drop our coats off at the check-in and I hold onto our tickets. I force my eyes to stay open when Rory's hair brushes my chin as she turns to walk inside.

RORY

"You look stunning," Reed whispers above my ear. The warmth of his voice tickles my neck. His hand falls to the small of my back without touching it as he gently leads us into the main lobby area.

"Kat convinced me to wear it."

"I like Kat." His voice sticks in the air like smoke.

Reed alternates his glances between me and the crowd. The room is small, covered in children's art and local show performance posters. Some people are formally dressed, while others wear jeans and sweaters. It's an eclectic mix and mingle, and it's unmistakably welcoming.

"You clean up well yourself, Junior."

His smile is refrained and acknowledging, but not easy like the other day. He's uncomfortable with me here. I'm visibly the only stranger among them.

"I'm going to grab us drinks. What can I get for you?"

"Seltzer is good, with a lemon, please."

Reed weaves through a few hurdles to reach the bar on the opposite side of the room. I've written about this before. The tense eyes, the serious mouth, the escorting arm. It's like Seth's character, except I never felt Seth's attention land in soft caresses over my body to the exposed places my dress doesn't cover.

I know Reed sees me and I don't doubt that he has my back, but he's acting like he can't stand being in the same space as me right now.

When he asked me to join his family tonight, was he asking as my mentor? My friend? My chaperone? And when I said yes, was I saying yes to the man? The bestselling author? My mentor?

Why ask me, if he didn't want me here? It registers that inviting me was Meryl's idea, not Reed's.

My line of questioning pauses when two guys and a girl approach me to introduce themselves.

"Hey, I'm Ashley," she states, with a summer glow in winter, pointing to two bearded, casually dressed men beside her. "This is Sully and Ryan. We saw you come in with our buddy."

"Hello." I wave in return. "I'm Rory. I'm visiting from Boston."

"Nice, we love Beantown," Sully adds. "So how'd you get that one out of the house on a school night?"

"Oh, no, not me." I'm searching to see if Reed's on his way back, but I've lost him. I don't see Meryl or Emmy or anyone else I recognize.

"I gotta tell you, Rory," Ashley adds, "it's really good to see him."

"Yes, amongst the living," Ryan chimes in.

A pianist is playing in the corner and the room's filling up.

I nod my head a few times, not knowing what to say.

"We didn't think it was ever going to happen." Sully pulls a swig from his beer bottle.

"After the accident, and with Gen bouncing." Sully keeps talking like he needs to get something off his chest. "We told him it wasn't his fault."

"Over and over," Ashley adds.

My eyes squint, maybe from the fluorescent lights above. There's a lot of noise and movement. I'm a part of a conversation that isn't meant for me.

"You mean Emerson?" My voice cracks.

"And Shannon," Ryan informs me. He crosses his fingers over his chest and tips his head up to the sky.

Adrenaline leaps into my chest, leaving little room for oxygen. I follow everyone's line of sight to the ceiling and am met with a pale Reed holding two sweating drinks in his hands.

"Sorry, man, we were just talking about how good it is to see you," Sully covers their tracks, nudging Reed's elbow.

"Hey, Rory, good to meet ya. Reed, let's shred it up soon, 'kay?" Ryan squeezes Reed's shoulder, the tightening cords of his forearms cloud my vision.

There's so much history here that I'm not understanding. So much about Reed that I don't understand either.

He passes me my drink, we find his family, and don't exchange more than a few civilities for the rest of the night.

✳

REED

Until last night, I hadn't thought about how lucky I've been to have parents who built a life together. I've always had an unwavering security to fall back on. I had advantages and privileges that Rory never did. I took more risks because I knew there was a landing pad beneath me. So, when Rory takes risks, she's putting everything on the line.

I don't know what my friends said to her, but she's barely spoken two words to me since that huddle. This is not the way I planned to spend our last night. I don't want her to return to Boston with a strain between us. I want her to get back home and focus on finishing the edits so we can revise and get it in shape to query. I know Eden doesn't require us to go past the revision and query letter prep, but I want to help see her through to landing an agent, and I have some connections that might put her book on the top of an agent's pile.

Rory leaving is the smartest move, even if it's my least favorite option. I'm doing the right thing—for her.

"Looks like you could use one of these." Will slides a cold beer into my hand, acknowledging who I'm focusing on.

"Thanks." I relax a little, momentarily out of my head.

"Something going on there?" he asks. Rory's laughing with Car-lynn and Emmy, assessing some abstract painting with piles of primary colors that are senseless to me.

"Off-limits territory."

"That's too bad. We like her. She's—"

"She's extraordinary."

She's also your mentee and just a friend.

I'll repeat those words on a loop until she leaves tomorrow or until I believe them. Whichever comes first.

27

— · —

RORY & REED

"ONLY THOSE WHO WILL RISK GOING TOO FAR CAN POSSIBLY FIND OUT HOW FAR IT IS POSSIBLE TO GO." —T.S. ELIOT

"WAKE UP, REED. YOU'RE shaking. Wake up." I'm shouting, my hands slipping off his slick skin. I fumble in the moonlight for the switch to the tiny wall lamp while blocking Reed's thrashing arms from flying across my face. "You're safe, Reed." I repeat, "Open your eyes. It's not real. Open your eyes."

"What?!" His eyes respond. "I'm fine, Gen. Go back to bed."

"Reed, it's Rory. You're having a nightmare." I place my hand in the center of his chest like a weight. "I want you to take a deep breath."

I release his shoulder and hold his hand over mine. "Again, Reed, slowly inhale a breath and as far as you can. And we'll count together. One, two, three, four . . . and exhale, five, six, seven, eight."

His shaking steadies.

"And again, one, two, three, four . . . and exhale, five, six, seven, eight."

His breath lifts our hands, as they rise on the inhale and sink on his exhale.

"Tell me what you see."

"I see your emeralds. I mean, your eyes."

"Yes, I see your eyes too, good." I smile. Keeping my voice even, I ask another grounding question. "What do you hear?"

He closes his eyes before responding. "The heater rattling and your voice."

"Good. I hear Fenway snoring and your breathing. What do you smell?"

"Vanilla and my toothpaste."

"The vanilla is me."

His eyes open, flickering over my face. "Yes, I know."

I clear my dry throat. "And last," I ask. "What do you feel?"

He's not averting his gaze or avoiding my touch, but he's also not answering the question.

Normally I'd start nervously rambling during this type of silence, but spending time here, where everything is slower, has forced me to be patient. Bracing myself for the impact of whatever he has to tell me, whether I'll like it or not.

"I feel too much." He runs his hands through his hair, then rests his head against the wall behind him.

"I understand what that's like. Do you want to tell me what's going on? I'm here for you if you want me to be."

Reed's abrupt laugh startles me.

Oh, right. I'm the last person he wants around. This is embarrassing.

"I'll go." I push the mattress with my hand to stand and stop when his fingers wrap around my wrist.

"Rory, I'm failing miserably here."

"I don't understand."

"All I want, is you here. I'm trying not to. I'm failing."

My pulse races. I flip over each word with a highlighter in my mind, counting the syllables like they'll help me solve for x.

"Thank you for helping me," he says, revealing his intention, clearing the air of uncertainty stretching between us.

"Of course." I reluctantly let his hand ease from my wrist.

I should go now. *Stand up, Rory. Walk across the bridge, back to your side of the house.*

Reed straightens the blankets. He points to the open space he's created next to him. I convince myself that I'll leave once he's settled. I'm not thinking of what my choices will lead to. I'm leaving tomorrow. I've already kissed him so sliding next to him for a horizontal hug doesn't seem too reckless.

Before I can beat myself up about the decision I've already made, I crawl into his bed, resting my head on his heated chest.

Unsure of where my limbs should go, I wait until his breathing has tempered and he snakes his knee between my thighs, and pulls me in closer.

Then I find my place in his arms like maybe I could belong here, even if just for tonight.

He plays with my hair, looping his fingers around the ends as the raw vibration of his voice rattles beneath my ear.

"I was on deadline that week."

He squeezes my hip. My heartbeats grow feverish, anticipating his next words. I slide my hand back over his heart.

"It'd been a relentless winter. Hidden black ice and snowbanks built up high enough to bury all visibility, especially near the water. It was impossible to tell where the road ended and the lake began. If you didn't live here, forget about finding your way. Usually Genevieve took care of everything when I was on deadline. She kept my life running while I locked myself in my cave. Some weeks I'd sleep and eat in there, only taking breaks to shake out my hands.

"That week, though, she was away at her sister's bachelorette party in Austin. Carlynn had asked me if I could pick up Emmy after ballet. She was taking night classes to get her CNA certification and there was a test for class, so she said it might run long and she didn't want to worry about being late to get Em. It wasn't a problem. I'd planned to get some writing done in the afternoon and then go into town to get her."

Maybe, it's better if I don't know.

"I lost track of the light when it started to snow, and then I lost track of time altogether."

The despair in his tone crushes my heart.

Reed runs his hands through my hair and releases a shaky exhale. "I let my phone die, Rory." His pain peels off each word.

"It wasn't until my mom came to the house that I even looked up from my laptop. When I didn't show up on time, Emmy asked her friend Shannon for a ride home. Shannon was sixteen. A kid behind the wheel, doing a kind thing by driving a younger kid home in a snowstorm."

Shannon. Her name is an epiphany I swallow. A question I already have the answer to.

"They couldn't see an inch in front of them. The snow was heavy, the wind was hard. That corner was an ice rink. That tree was too big, the car too small, the lake too quiet." Loose tears spill from his eyes and land on my cheek. "By the time the sheriff and paramedics got there, it was too late for Shannon. I couldn't do anything but stand on the sidelines as they pulled my half-broken niece out of the water."

"Reed. I can't even imagine, I . . . " I lose my words in my throat.

"Now Emerson won't walk, won't ever dance again. And Shannon, Shannon," he cries out. His head drops and a desperate sob breaks free from his gut. The walls shake around us.

I pull him into me, wrap my arms as tight as I can.

He's placing so much blame on himself. This is why he isn't writing. He's punishing himself.

If Emmy wasn't able to live her dream, if Shannon wasn't able to live, Reed wasn't going to allow himself to live either. I slip my hands through his hair. I rub his trembling back. He scoops me up and we hold one another until his internal storm subsides.

"It wasn't your fault," I say. "It was a horrible accident. A bend in the universe. No one could've known. I see the way your family looks at you, with love, real love, wrapped in devotion and forgiveness."

"How am I supposed to carry on with my own aspirations when Emmy's are over?"

"They aren't over. They're starting over. A new beginning." My tone escalates like I'm preparing for battle. "And because you don't get to stop living."

"I'm sorry I didn't tell you. I'm sorry this is how you found out."

"You've been through so much."

"I'm sure you have questions."

"I don't see how they matter," I say.

"She didn't leave me—she chose herself. I wasn't good for anyone."

My head shakes in disagreement.

"Rory, I wasn't going to let her stay, with or without the accident."

"I don't know how you can say that. We don't get to abandon people because it's inconvenient or hard." I know this isn't all about Genevieve anymore because it doesn't feel like thirty-year-old Rory is talking.

✳

REED

There may be a metaphorical mentorship wall between Rory and me right now, but I've never felt closer to her than I do in this moment. Sometimes, you need an actual wall to hold you up while you let someone in.

Every time she wrote in character, I couldn't help myself. I felt her words like they were meant for me. There were times I couldn't tell if the characters were talking or if we were. And my words reached out for her when I didn't dare to. But we aren't characters, and those words were born from something creative, borrowed from the imagination.

What's happening right now, I couldn't have written. You can't write something you won't let yourself dream of.

Her hand is a warm compress, a gentle weight over the most sensitive part of my chest. My thundering heart steadies beneath her protective touch. I lace my fingers through hers, joining our hands like mosaic pieces that fit together, bound by a shared brokenness, and the strength of this bond.

She comforts me like I've never hurt a soul. She sees the real me. Not the versions of myself I lend to others. But the core of who I am. One breath closer and nothing will ever be the same.

RORY

He steals away my spiraling thoughts with his mouth. His soft addictive mouth pulls me out of my head and into the moment.

He kisses me to heal something inside each of us.

He kisses me to prove something to the both of us.

And I take every breath he gives me.

Our intensity grows into a yearning wish for the other to extinguish the grief we both share.

He fists my hair behind my shoulders and tugs to expose my neck. Our racing pulses and shallow breaths collide, fighting for us to work through this.

We search one another's eyes as we try to rescue the parts of ourselves stuck in the past.

REED

Our kiss is like slipping through wet sand, only to have the ocean come and sweep it away. Over and over again.

I want to memorize every part of Rory that's been off-limits to me. Her mouth tastes like an exhilarating turbulent storm. It's deep, alive, and threatens to take everything with it.

Together, we've become permanently blurred, yet what I want has never been clearer.

RORY

"Can you hear it?" I whisper.

"What, hear what?" Reed replies.

I motion with my eyes to the window behind us. The bed creeks as we tilt our heads to look at the fluffy white powder twisting in the air.

Reed smiles at the sky, then back at me. "The first of the season."

"I kinda have a thing for firsts," I remind him.

"I know."

REED

My eyes snap open to my second favorite smell. Bacon. I throw on pants and am halfway down the stairs when I stop. Rory's in the kitchen, making breakfast. Coffee's brewing, the air is sizzling, and she's reaching on her tiptoes for a bowl in the cabinet. An apron is cinched around her waist over a simple oversized shirt. If I'm not dreaming, this must be the afterlife. I scrub my hands over my face to find she's still there, and it's all very real.

"Morning." Rory waves. "Hungry?"

I make my way down the rest of the stairs and over to her.

"Morning." I kiss the top of her head. *I could get used to this.*

She grabs plates from the counter, carrying three stacked up on her left arm and one in her right hand. There's sliced tomatoes, oranges, and bacon, and she didn't . . .

"I wasn't sure how you take your eggs."

She did and there it is, in all its glory, the perfect grilled cheese sandwich. Lightly toasted on the outside, warm and melty on the inside. She returns with two cups of coffee, sitting down next to me. *Next to me.*

"You made me a grilled cheese."

She shrugs, like it's no big deal.

"Don't blow my cover, Reed. Kat thinks I can't cook, and she'll cut off my scone supply if she finds out."

I can't decide if it's her morning voice, raspy and sweet, the perfect melody laughing at her own joke, or if it's the pinch of pink in her cheeks that my presence may have put there. If this weren't the most sincere gesture of kindness, I'd sacrifice the sandwich and have Rory for breakfast instead.

"Anyway." She clears her throat. "I wanted to surprise you."

She still doesn't get it. I'd go a lifetime without grilled cheese if it meant I could replay even once what she did for me last night.

"You always surprise me."

"Well, go ahead."

"We have a lot to talk about."

"It'll get cold," she encourages.

I slide my hand over to hers and squeeze. "Thank you."

She raises the mug to the edge of her lips, smiling into the steam.

Then I take the first bite and it goes straight to my heart.

RORY

My journal's open and I'm surveying the damage.

Pros vs. cons.

My bag's still tucked away in the corner. The plan was to go. But that was before. Before last night. Before Reed said that we had to talk. Before I decided there was something I needed to do too.

I've been thinking about the way my anxiety has manifested itself over the years and how it's informed every decision I've made and avoided. And this time up here with Reed has been full of high stakes and risk and uncertainty.

We have these moments that feel like we're speaking through our characters. The rush. The heart palpitations. The kissing. The same inevitable self-doubt. They've all been present in the mix, so how do I know for sure if this is real or pretend? Sometimes, what feels real to me is a symptom or a story I tell myself.

I might not be one-hundred-percent clear about my feelings for Reed, but I deserve to know, to give myself the chance to talk to Reed, without a mentorship or my characters getting in the way. My phone lights up as I make the call.

"Eden Books, Allison Healy speaking."

"Hi, Ms. Healy. This is Rory Wells from the mentorship program."

"Of course. Hello, Rory. Good to hear from you. How's everything going?"

"That's why I'm calling. I'd like to ask if it's possible to be assigned to another mentor."

28

REED & RORY

"CHEMISTRY. YOU CAN'T BEAT CHEMISTRY."
—LAUREN BACALL

WHO KNEW THE FORMULA for a solid night's sleep was a good cry, a snowstorm, and lying in Rory's arms.

The grilled cheese and hot shower sealed the deal. I haven't felt this clear-headed in a long time.

It occurs to me that I may have confused last night's connection with commiseration, but I won't know unless I directly ask her. And there's more I need to say.

She's standing by the window in my room in a tank top and jeans, looking out at the blanket of snow. The air hangs heavy like an early morning fog when it settles a foot above the sea. I'm hovering in the doorway when a text comes in from Cal.

"Hey," she says, spotting me.

"Hi," I reply, peeking down at his message. There's an instant brick in my stomach and the air has been sucked from the room as I read his words.

CAL: You're off the hook. Your mentee asked to be reassigned. Let's get lunch soon and talk about your plans.

Slowly my chest constricts and my jaw locks. *I fucked up.* She's so desperate to leave, her bag's already packed, and she ended the mentorship without telling me.

How . . . What do I . . . Can I even say?

Her mouth on mine.

The way she held me.

How did I misread this?

"Did you want to talk now?" She moves to the middle of the room, and I drag my feet to meet her.

"Yeah, Rory. Listen, I'm really sorry about last night, if I made you uncomfortable or feel unsafe in any way. I know things are blurry sometimes between us, but I wanted you to finish this. I wanted to be here to help you."

"What? I wasn't uncomfortable at all. I feel more safe here with you than almost anywhere. I don't understand. Why did you say 'wanted?'"

My head's spinning. Why can't people say what they mean and mean what they say?

"You requested a replacement, Rory, without even talking to me about it. How am I supposed to take that?"

She covers her mouth with one hand and takes my hand with the other.

"I didn't ask for a new mentor because we did anything wrong or because I'm upset about last night. I asked because I don't want our lines to be blurred anymore. I want them to be crystal clear. And I also asked because I'm impatient and tired of being down the hall from you and wondering about my nevers list, and tired of being tired, and tired of being scared."

She's moving at lightning speed. I'm relieved to hear she wasn't feeling unsafe, and a little shocked that she just sprung this on me, and still unclear as to what she wants.

"Be specific, Rory. Say exactly what you mean." I hold her delicate chin in my palm, sweeping my thumb back and forth along her jawline. "What's your damn elevator pitch?"

Her breath is shaky but she keeps her eyes steady on mine.

"You're no longer my mentor, Reed, but I'm open to private lessons, if those are on the table."

My smile is my answer. But just to be absolutely transparent here, I tell her exactly what I'm thinking. "Fuck yes, they are."

And then I pull her into my arms.

RORY

Reed's body molds into mine as his arms curl around my waist, locking my back into place against his protective chest. His jawline tickles my neck, causing me to shudder in his embrace.

"Are you cold?"

My skin tightens as he scrapes his fingers over my arms and kisses my bare shoulders.

My lips part. Tiny gasps of air expel at his caress.

My insides are an inferno of flames, racing, rioting, running into each other.

Reed's fingers brush under my chin, gently guiding me to turn and face his gaze.

He leans his forehead on mine and leaves a soft kiss on the tip of my nose.

My teeth tap together and chatter.

"What's happening?" He searches my eyes for answers.

"I'm scared." A warm tear escapes, streaking my heated cheek.

"We don't have to do anything. We can just talk. I've got you."

"It's not that. I don't entirely know why I'm scared."

"Can we be scared together?" Reed whispers against my lips.

I nod my head, and my eyes surrender as my hands explore, tracing the lines and angles of his face that I've come to know by heart.

His body is responding, succumbing to my touch. I break his sealed lips with my tongue, caving to the hunger of wanting him.

Lifting his shirt over his head, I leave a trail of secrets against his skin, confessing one truth after another.

"Lesson one. Reality is so much better than fantasy."

Kissing the base of his throat, I remove his shirt entirely and let the fabric fall to the floor.

My lips move down to his chest, lingering over his heart. "Lesson two. Being in your arms is where I feel safe."

Lowering to my knees, I pepper whispers over his abdomen, as his hands run through my hair. "Lesson three. Less is more."

I slide his belt buckle open and unlatch the top button of his pants, savoring the expanse of his long and defined torso.

My smile slides lower and I stop spilling secrets.

With the force of a riptide I'm not expecting, Reed's arms slip around me, cradling me into his warm chest. He lifts me up, and my legs wrap around his waist. He holds me like he's never letting go.

"What if we lose what we already have," he growls into my neck.

I sigh, comforted by his honesty.

"What if we don't?"

He pulls back. Quiet amusement plays on his lips. Not knowing what he'll say next is a cruel way to pass the time. Reed shakes his head and inches us back toward his bed.

We're submerged in anticipation, trust, and racing pulses. The pressure penetrates all of the oxygen in the room.

"I don't deserve this, Rory, but I'm going to savor every second you'll give me."

"This isn't a competition. We can both win here." I take his bottom lip in between my teeth.

He lays me down on the bed like a present he plans to take his time unwrapping.

I sink beneath Reed's weight pressing firmly between my legs. He slowly lowers on top of me. Painstakingly slow. His forearms are stone pillars on both sides of my face. My core winds tight like a ball of strangled yarn.

My skin pebbles at his touch.

"Yes?" he asks.

"Yes."

Reed dives for my mouth like it's the deep end of the ocean and has no plans of us returning alive.

We give in.

We let go.

We collide.

He gasps for air and I beg for more.

Every graze sends shocks, powerful surges ripping through me. I lose my mind in his fierce desire, discovering my own.

He touches my body and I respond in moans and words I've never spoken aloud before. We explore each other with eagerness, drenched and strung out like a wave burying into itself.

"This whole time. It's been you." Reed's telling me things I don't fully comprehend.

He slides his hands beneath my shirt and down to my hips. Rows of chilled stars erupt all over my skin. In one easy motion, my shirt and bralette are over my head, finding their rightful place on the floor.

My timid smile appears in the reflection of his eyes, as he feverishly drags his gaze over the parts of me he's never seen before, wanting him to like what he sees. His hard, feral stare is undeniable. We're both caged animals, waiting to be fed. Stalking each other's bodies, staking the pieces we plan to consume first.

I press my body against his, getting closer, growing wilder. Our connection is like fire, up in flames, an overpowering desire.

He extinguishes my thoughts with his mouth, licking my abdomen. I suck in air and grip the sheets between my fingers. His kisses hit every nerve as his beard marks my sensitive skin. I squirm and stretch against his unpredictable path. His lips are a roaming target I thrust my hips into as his affectionate mouth claims me.

I drag my fingers through his silky hair as he teases his lips up my legs. A strong current builds beneath the ocean floor.

The heat between our bodies tethers to one another. I push down the thoughts that call for my attention, a foghorn off the coast.

Rory, don't go that deep—you could drown.

Reed's warm breath hits between my thighs. His thick tongue presses into me, and whatever doubts were trying to force their way in vanish. His mouth meticulously tortures me while his hands steady my thrashing thighs. His strokes are gentle and tormenting. He's licking and sucking every last syllable of his name from my core. I can't catch my breath, in the best way possible. His unrelenting stamina sends my spirit from my body into some kind of heaven where lust and libido live.

Reed's pace slows to a stop, stealing his warmth from me and replacing his mouth with the pad of his thumb, waltzing small circles in place. My begging breaks into whimpers.

His kisses return to my stomach, drawing a path with his tongue to the places he hasn't dedicated himself to yet. Their pebbled peaks stand on edge, wet from his devout attention.

Our bodies are covering the parts of him I'm anxious to devote myself to.

"You taste incredible," he whispers without missing a beat.

White light filters in through the window onto the bed. I study his face like a masterpiece. Every line, each freckle from the sun, the curve of his cheeks and chin, the fullness in his lips. He's beautiful, fragile beneath the surface, and all I wanted last night was to be there for him.

We kiss for ages, maybe moments, time stands still.

Breaking our seal, I tell him, "I didn't know it could feel like this. Like wishes and dreams and—"

Reed's lips land on mine like a desperate plea for mercy, imploring me to believe.

I hadn't planned on any of this. It wasn't supposed to happen, but somehow it was.

The sheer intensity of his presence and my overwhelming desire for him takes over. I wrap my arms and legs around his competitive nature. Touching him has already become a habit, a necessity, a coping mechanism. Every second feels like a war between aching and relief.

I don't recognize the person inside of me speaking out, demanding my own pleasure from another person.

Our chemistry is being sculpted into something defined, a tangible choice we're making together.

He reaches over to the nightstand, and pulls out a condom from the drawer.

You'd think I'd never seen something like this before, with how I'm reveling in his every move. Nothing could've prepared me for how hot Reed is right now, taking care of us both, and seeing him exposed this way, anticipating him, might be the end, and the beginning—of everything.

"Keep your eyes open," he commands. "I want us to remember this."

He leans back in and kisses me like it's the first time.

Then he keeps his word, and I lose all of mine.

REED

I've never known anyone like Rory, who sees me the way she does, making me feel alive and understood.

She doesn't run or hide from anything I throw her way. She embraces it all.

I've waited for too damn long, and she's even more beautiful than I ever imagined. Her natural curves, the faint smile lines around her eyes, her flushed skin, the way she stood before me, nervous as hell yet offering all of herself. My feelings are too much to fight anymore.

It's not until I begin to slowly rock back and forth into Rory that I allow myself to exhale. Our breathing pattern syncs with the rhythm of our bodies. My chest expands as we uncover each other in layers of sweat and shadows.

RORY

My heart cracks with each beat that passes through it. The promise itself is too much. The way it grows inside a person, all the pieces, admiration, care, excitement, the collective minutes, memories, time spent together and apart, then the joining of spirits. It's everything I'd ever wished for, yet, in all of its strength and fragility, it strips you down, tearing apart your insides, and then glues you back together, forever changed.

My own delayed comprehension stuns me.

Reed kisses my tears, stilling his body, pushing up onto his arms. The open space between us hits like hail, sharp and cold. I reassure him, pulling him back down into us, sucking salt from his lips. I fight to keep my eyes open.

We hold onto each other as the wave swells and rages, lifts into the air, high above our head to their highest point.

I am here. Shallow breaths.

He is here. Crashing bodies.

Falling fast. Holding on.

Together, we come undone.

*

Laying blissfully wasted in each other's arms, my hand holds his over his glistening stomach as I count each inhale, *one, two, three, four*. Reed's chest rises and falls. And exhale, *five, six, seven, eight*.

"You okay, Rory?"

"I'm happy."

He brushes wild strands of hair away from my face and holds his lips to my hairline, whispering, "I don't want to question why the universe brought me to you or you to me. It's something I won't ever be able to explain. The answer doesn't seem to matter when I'm close to you this way."

REED

I always thought it would be impossible to experience love if it was one-sided. How could it be real if it wasn't shared? I was ashamed to care about someone I only knew through words.

For years, I didn't tell anyone about Rory's journal or how often I visited it to be understood. Eventually, when I hadn't proposed to Genevieve, my mom asked me if there was someone else. I told her there wasn't, but I was lying to myself.

All those times when I needed a friend, she was there without even knowing it. Her thoughts were a guardian angel that made the solitude less lonely.

I know there's more to learn about Rory. Things I'm only discovering now, like how her peach skin streaks pink when she breathlessly whimpers my name, or how her mind finally caves in and quiets while her body shakes beneath mine. There's still so much I don't understand. And I never want to stop learning about her. I never want to stop being someone she can be completely herself with.

But first, I have to tell her everything.

This moment with Rory may just be this, and not to keep.

And I'll take the time I'm given because I found something real here with her.

We're both imperfect, a little broken, and those are the pieces that fit the closest. I see that now more than ever.

I found courage in the space between our words. I've never truly given up the fantasy that there exists that deep kind of forever love out there, like Pops and Mom had. The kind that paints the sky in stars. The kind that makes its own rules and doesn't conform. The kind of love born of friendship and respect, that grows into a passion, one that burns well past a lifetime. The kind that invigorates and soothes. Lake air and warm wind that moves freely, and earth that's rich enough to grow roots.

Somewhere in time, that kind of love is meant for everyone. Maybe even for me.

RORY

Sometimes, it's simple. The best life has to offer usually is. Like a surprise conversation, the way the air smells after it's rained, the first sip of a margarita on a summer day, or a stamp in my passport. Today, it's a familiar yet brand-new gratitude that brings me joy. I turn on my side to face Reed and trace my thumb along his eyebrow, down across his cheekbone, and over his smile.

"When I was little, I used to believe that when it rained, it meant that the universe was crying for all the suffering in the world. That it knew my pain and cried for me, so I didn't have to carry the burden anymore. And all those tears would nourish the soil for spring."

"Rory." Reed lifts my hands and brings them to his smiling lips.

"I believe in something bigger than any of us. Perhaps, the universe speaks its own language. All those little coincidences, the signs, the feelings deep in our gut that we can't explain or deny. Exactly how it felt when we first met. It was as scary and as sacred as any experience I've ever had."

Reed kisses me softly. "Talking to you has been like talking to a friend I've known my whole life."

I snuggle into his neck, focusing on our recovering heartbeats, and I think about something he told me once during one of our talks. We'd been discussing boundaries and desire in writing characters. He asked me, "Is there a real difference between fantasy and reality? My experience is that the only differences are the limits you place on yourself. These may be healthy limits, but the fact remains."

It's probably not the right moment to tell him everything I'm feeling. Maybe I can keep trying to show him. "Hey, I hear practice makes perfect. Up for testing the theory?"

He chuckles and squeezes me against his chest. I'd do just about anything to be in his arms every day.

Before I let myself get lost in what this all means, his gaze turns scorching. The intention behind his heated stare burrows itself into my heart. Reed moves up onto his arms and leans himself on top of me, pinning my hands over my head.

His mouth hovers above mine. His face splits into a playful grin.

"Challenge accepted."

29

RORY

"It's the trying that heals you. That's all you have to do. Just try." —Katherine Center

It's cold enough by the lake that I'm wearing someone's random gloves from the borrow bin.

We're sitting at the end of the dock, Reed and I, each nestled in an Adirondack chair, a plaid blanket draped over my legs, making the most of the view and our last sunset together before I head back to Boston.

The ground's covered in fractured patches of ice and snow. Traces of thawing earth settle over us.

"There's this little brick courtyard with a wrought iron bench outside of Down and Route. I'd have my lunch there and talk to my characters. I definitely don't miss that job, but I do miss the ritual." I admit to Reed, "I've loved shaking things up, but I also need consistency."

"I know. I know," he repeats with an understanding smile. "Have you heard who your new mentor is yet?"

I sip my cider, sweet and refreshing. "Ms. Healy said she'd get back to me with a name next week."

Reed sighs. "It wasn't all a waste for you, was it?"

"Are you kidding?" I almost crack a joke when I'm met with a sober stare.

He isn't kidding.

"This story wouldn't be what it's going to be without this experience, without you. And . . . it's not that I don't love your lessons, because I do, but have you looked at yourself in the mirror lately?" I reach over and run my fingers over his jaw. "You're distracting."

Reed laughs from his gut and it makes me happy.

"Well, Ms. Wells, I know I wasn't a perfect mentor, but I'm really glad you're in my life."

"Perfection is a myth too many of us spend our lives chasing. I breathe easier around you. I definitely eat better. I even sleep better. You never needed to be anything but yourself."

"I haven't slept this well in a long time." He shakes his head.

I always want to know what he's thinking. But especially in this moment, when his face is painted in defeat.

"Pops would've really liked you, Rory. I wish you could've met him." Reed tips his head to the sky.

My gaze follows his, to the sun melting behind the pines. "Me too."

"Try this." He passes me his bottle. "It's local."

I take a sip and wince. "That's so bitter. I don't know how you tolerate an ounce of that."

He smirks at me like we're sharing a secret, a lingering memory from an hour ago, and I smile into my cider.

"You're drinking a juice box," Reed replies, quickly dipping a finger into my bottle, then sticking it in his mouth. I follow the curve of his lips as they close in.

He returns his hand to his own drink. "That's nothing but liquid candy."

"And here I've been, under the false impression that you enjoy the taste of sweet things."

Now I'm smirking at the way he's squirming in his seat.

His playful stare drops as he leans over the arms of our chairs. Warm whispers graze my skin.

"I think I'm going to need another sample, to be sure."

I push him back to his side. "Get outta here. I'm finishing this cider."

The silence is enveloping. Being here with Reed, on this lake, it all fits somehow. I want to tell Reed what it is that I want, but I'm holding back, afraid my feelings are of a magnitude much larger than either of us are prepared for.

It's not like me to stray from finding the right words.

While some kids were digging for the toy buried in the center of the cereal box, I was reading the back. Words have always bridged the gap between my imagination and my life, which, at one point, I needed to survive.

I didn't expect to somehow infuse my feelings into the characters I wrote. Like a gentle gravitational pull. I wrote, and those words brought me into the orbit of another person. Maybe even before I knew he existed.

"So, what about your writing?" I ask.

"I can't write anymore, Rory." His face is all hard lines and lies.

I put my bottle down between my legs. He'll die on this hill if someone doesn't push him off it. I drag in a few deep breaths.

"I call bullshit. I've read the articles. I've read your books. You can write but you're choosing not to. You ask me to believe in myself yet you're giving up on yourself. You're not paying a penance, Reed. You're taking the easy way out."

The pained expression pulling between his eyes tells me that maybe I've gone too far, but I can't accept this is it, for his writing, for his dreams.

"Some days, I sit out here and force myself to face it, to sit in the truth of what I've done. But it's never that simple. And though writing is who I am, I won't allow myself access to my words. Because to write, Rory, is to feel. And I'm not ready to confront what that will bring."

The bottle and blanket land gently on the dock as I climb onto Reed's lap. We slink to the back of the chair. I pepper slow kisses on his forehead, sending messages to that mind of his, which isn't always kind to itself, about how he deserves to be living and creating. I make my way down his throat, where the vibration of his increasingly staggered breaths rumbles against my tongue.

"I don't know how you do it."

"What?" I smile against his skin.

"You know me and still like me, even after everything I've done."

My lips pause. I pull back to face him. *How can he not see something that's so clear to me?* Everything he went through, and the way he selflessly shows up for his family and this town, and for me—that is bravery. He's honest and patient. Thinking about his lessons makes me smile, and when I was open with him about my anxiety and history, he was empathetic and supportive. I know the past few years have felt like a string of strikeouts, but I also know if anyone can build something from that grief, it's Reed. He just needs someone who sees the best in him. He needs to know that some people stay, even when it's hard.

He wipes the emotion from my cheeks.

"You let me in, and have shown me who you are. And being yourself with another person, I can't imagine there is anything more valuable in this life than that. So, yes, I like you. I care about you. All of you. Including the parts you don't like about yourself."

Reed holds me and I let him because I want him to and because he feels like home.

*

Fenway skips up the ramp to the kitchen and goes straight to his water bowl. Reed walks into the living room to check on the fire.

I bend down and touch my right arm to my left toes, and raise to center, then reach for the opposite foot. I'm windmilling, stretching out my frozen body.

"What do we have here?" he chuckles, standing directly in front of me. I peek up, my head between my legs.

"I'm crossing the midline."

"I see that. Why?"

"Well, it's one of the many tools I use, helping my brain and body to communicate better."

"Don't let me get in the way of this view." He smirks, stepping back a few feet.

"Hey, this is no free show." I straighten out, hands on my hips. "Paying customers only."

Reed closes the distance between us and brings my mouth to his. This kissing him business is the best part of losing him as a mentor.

"I've got a question for you," I say.

"Shoot."

I chew on my lip a little, trusting he'll be okay with my digging a little deeper. "Have you been diagnosed yet?"

His shoulders slack. "No."

"So, how long have you been self-managing your anxiety?"

"They're night terrors mostly."

"I see it now—the distraction, the mood swings, not sleeping." I hold his hand. "Mine started when I was thirteen, mostly as stomach pain. Can you remember when it started for you?"

"It wasn't obvious, really. I guess high school. It started as a compulsive need to protect my image and to not let anyone down, and it grew into issues with self-structuring, indecision, and sometimes isolation. I started getting headaches randomly, too, before big games."

"Yeah, I get them too when I'm really stressed."

Reed kisses my fingers.

"I didn't understand it as panic, at least not in the way you've described yours, until after Pops was gone. My heart would race at the apprehension of anyone leaving. I was okay for a few years when I was writing romance, and then you know the rest. No one in my family suffers from it, so I didn't have a name or label."

"Society fails at prioritizing mental health. We are only beginning to talk about it the way we should. I'm working on the approach of embracing my anxiety, even welcoming it. When the symptoms are debilitating, I have to ride them out, but mostly, I manage through breathing and grounding tools. I guess I appreciate that I'm different in this way. Accepting this is a part of me, like someone who has trouble seeing without corrective lenses. Anxiety may make things blurry for me, but it also has strengthened all of my other senses. Maybe it's my superpower."

"You're super something." He draws me into a hug and holds me. Really holds me. And I start making plans in my mind.

"There's so many ways to get support. Can I help?"

"You've helped more than you could possibly know."

Chills roll down my arms.

"You're freezing. I'm gonna start the big shower down here if you want to warm up."

"Yes. Yes, I do. Hold that thought, though. I'm going to grab my stuff," I say, then run up the stairs.

I dig through my duffel, to the sound of falling water, searching for my toiletries, remembering that all my clothes are dirty. And my emergency sunflower pants are back in Boston. It's inconvenient, but I'm feeling too much excitement and gratitude right now to be bothered by anything. The manuscript has a plan. I'll be meeting with my new mentor. Being close to Reed. I haven't thought about health insurance or the fight with my mom. I haven't been dwelling. I've just been present, here. And I want to make the most of our time together, before I have to leave.

I blow out a reflective sigh and think quickly. I'll just borrow something of his.

Score. The hoodie Reed lent me is hanging on the rocking chair where I left it.

I peel off my sweater and leave my tank on. The air is biting cold, so I throw on the hoodie and check Reed's dresser drawers for bottoms. They're stuffed full of denim and sweaters, and I need something with an elastic waist. *Maybe he keeps his sweats in the closet.* I walk around the bed and unlatch the door. It's one of those cabin closets, smelling of cedar and built like a scalene triangular coffin. I fish around for the light on the wall and take a step in, colliding with a string. I catch the pull-cord switch as it swipes across my face.

There's no way I'm about to unlock a trap door and get a hot iron to the face, so with caution, I yank the pull-cord and jump back at the same time.

The light flickers on and the cord violently swings like a pendulum. I reach to stop it so I can assess if there's anything I can wear in here.

I step into the dim light and look up, fixing my eyes on hangers, on rows of shelves, on the top shelf, to a familiar flash of gold fabric on the top shelf, a beloved friend, screaming my name ... The shelf is screaming. "No. No. No. No. No." I am screaming.

My skin sets fire, a rush of adrenaline knocks the breath from my lungs, bile stings the back of my throat, my gut plummets. I use the door frame to hold myself up.

I can't think. I can't breathe.

Something vital inside me snaps.

My vision goes red.

30

—·—

RORY

"No matter how many words we get, there's always going to be the last one, and one word is never enough."
—Amy Harmon

"Hey there," Reed calls, coming up the stairs, "did I lose you?" He finishes toweling off his hair.

I'm sitting on his bed, in his hoodie, heartbroken.

All the color drains from his face and neck when he sees me clutching the backpack to my chest. "Let me explain."

Every book, every article of clothing, everything not attached to the walls lays on the floor in a swimming pile of my wrath. His room is destroyed and I have no regrets.

"Answer one question. How long?"

"It's not that simple, Rory. I know what you're thinking."

"You can't possibly know what I'm thinking. Answer me. How long have you known? How fucking long?"

When Reed hesitates, I grab my duffel and push past him, running down the stairs.

"Rory, wait, let me put on some fucking pants."

I look for Fenway to say goodbye, but I can't find him and my glasses are foggy.

Get yourself out of here. Shit, he's already downstairs.

"Listen, I didn't want to derail you. I was trying to protect you. I'll try my best to explain, but it's dark and you can't drive when you're like this. I won't let you."

"Let me. Yeah, I see how you feel like you can make all my decisions for me. But I don't want your help. I don't want anything from you."

"If you're going to go, at least wait until you're not shaking. It's not safe to drive. Can I please make you some tea? And then you can go."

I hate that he's right. I can't drive in the dark when I can hardly see a foot in front of me as it is. Reluctantly, I drop into a chair at the kitchen table. "One cup."

When Reed sits across from me, I force myself to confront his deceiving eyes. He will not see how much pain I'm in. He clears his throat, pulling a thumb-sized stone from his pocket and turning it over in his hand.

"I don't even know where to start."

If I speak, it will send me back into the red, a flipping-the-table throwing-scalding-cups-of-tea rage. I also don't care that he doesn't know where to start. Not my problem.

"I guess it starts with Genevieve."

Of course it does. Blame it on the person who isn't here to defend herself.

"I mean, right before I began writing my first romance, Genevieve brought me to a romance convention at a hotel in Boston. It was summer and unbearably hot. Boston was mine and Pops's thing. Especially during baseball season. I hadn't been feeling like myself that day, missing him more than usual. Maybe it was an aftershock of my grief. Those were happening more back then. I went outside to catch my breath while I emptied my mind. But it seemed fate had other plans for me, as it put this emotionally distraught, beautiful girl outside of the same hotel, at the same time, on the same day, trying to catch her breath too."

His eyes fill as a soft sigh slips from his lips.

"Whenever I needed a place to retreat, on the days I missed Pops so much I could barely breathe, or the days I struggled with this new author identity, that journal—your words—were there for me. At first, I kept it because no one claimed it. And then I couldn't let it go because it was you in those pages. Your heart, your passion, your search for self . . . I visited those pages so damn often I left my fingerprints on them.

"And that lasted for years. Then Emmy's accident flipped our world upside down, and I'm barely holding on, when I get an email that pisses me off. You think that'd be a bad thing, right? But I hadn't felt anything other than a hollow emptiness in two years. I was irritated, but I was also motivated. Each email was an intrusion, a necessary invasion of the walls I'd built up. And then one day, those aggravating words, those digging questions, and the caring person behind them had gotten under my skin.

"And here's the part I really need you to hear me out on, Aurora Wells."

He rubs his hands over his face.

"Like a complete fucking miracle, journal girl and my mentee are the same person. But you have to understand that I didn't know at first. I should've known by the rhythm of your language on the page, but I've been numb to my instinct, suppressing it, and it wasn't until the night by the fire when you told me your story and we kissed that I knew who you were. In the same breath you also told me you never wanted to speak of the past again. And I made a call. What seemed like the best decision at the time. And I'm deeply sorry because you are the last person in the world I want to hurt." The conviction in his voice softens.

At some point, the echo of my name settles between my ears and registers. *He called me Aurora.*

His hair's still wet and my hands seek the relief they grew used to having. I squeeze them together into a fist on my lap. I know how easily we could slip right through each other's fingers if we let it.

My bag at my feet and the cold cup of tea tell me it's time.

I face him on my inhale. "I'm going back to Boston." Reed's tortured expression threatens my resolve. Chills rush along my spine. I'm suffocating in this house. I can't think clearly while I'm here.

His lips smack together. "You've got questions, ask them. I'm an open book."

There's an undefeated grappling in his voice.

"You're an open book? Since when?" I huff.

He goes to respond and I cut him off, not because I want to, but because the dam is broken now, my nerves are shot, and the wires in my brain aren't sending complete messages. I free-for-all into jagged waters.

"Were you an open book when you refused to return my emails and answer my questions?"

"I didn't know who you were then. I was in a different place. This mentorship, as you know, was thrown in my lap."

I can't even believe my ears. "How about you not trusting me enough to tell me all of the truth? Never giving me the benefit of the doubt, that maybe I'd still choose to be here. You're so scared of everything. Of feeling, of living, of letting someone in who cares about you."

I was certain I found something special here with Reed, amongst the confusion of creative chemistry.

I spit out my anger, a combination of unplanned words and salty betrayal. "I was some naive rookie you used for what, entertainment? An ego boost? An orgasm? A temporary way to harness inspiration? Seeing how far you could take this thing before I cracked the case that I was the only one being honest?"

"You're not being fair, Rory."

"You're right. None of this is fair," I bite back and strain my eyes staring at an impossibly silent lake.

"Keeping you temporarily in the dark had a purpose, Rory." He's out of his seat and kneeling in front of me now, the warmth from his shower pouring off his body. "You told me you didn't want to talk about it ever again. I wanted to respect your wishes. In hindsight, terrible choice on my part, but while I was in that moment, all that mattered was keeping my promise to you, to get you query-ready. The past had waited for ten years—it could wait another few months. And it killed me. Don't think for one second this has been easy for me."

I turn to him, which is a mistake because he's close enough for me to slap or kiss, and my mind refuses to make a decision.

"It's not about you, though, is it? Or maybe it is. Maybe, this has been about you all along, and I was some joyride you took to get your spark back."

"No."

"You're just like him, same skeleton masquerading in fancier clothes."

I'm holding the wall, but my chin is quivering and my teeth are tapping. Reed's face is like stone.

"I'm sorry he left you. But I'm not him. I'm here. Rory, you've always been whole and worthy of unconditional love. You were an innocent child who deserved to have a free childhood without the cost of adult worries and responsibilities. I've been trying to tell you that you've always been good enough. Good enough to be loved and adored and valued. You never needed to prove yourself or your worth to anyone. It was about his issues. And for all of the disappointment your parents have been to you, you are not a disappointment. And at any age, if we had met, I would've seen you and given you my whole heart."

He searches my eyes to see if his sentiments are making contact. A tornado is passing between us and I can't reconcile all the versions of Reed I'm sorting through.

"Did it ever once occur to you how important my book was to me?" My eyes burn and sting. I refuse to cry and give him any more of myself than I already have. His face is becoming a blurry target somewhere in the middle of blinding pain.

"You weren't even writing," I screech. My throat is raw and throbbing. "I can't believe I didn't piece it all together. Explaining *just* enough to distract me. You controlled the narrative of us the entire time, everything on your time, your schedule, your emotional availability. And to what end, Reed? For your own self-preservation?" I'm disgusted at how I let this happen. "How am I ever supposed to believe anything you tell me? I'll always be looking for plot holes."

Reed slowly backs up, farther away from where I sit in scorching flames.

"All your lessons, your words, you made me think you believed in me, in us."

Reed stands before me, barefoot and barely making a sound. His fists are shoved in his pockets, and his white t-shirt waves in front of me. I expect Reed to fall to the floor in a pile of dust and be swept away for good. But he comes back in, closer this time.

My heart's pounding out of my chest and my vise-grip on my anger is loosening the closer he gets.

"Hear me, Rory . . . I saw in you a way back to myself, and I don't care if that meant running through fire. You've been a light on my path when I've needed it the most and when I didn't know what I needed at all. When life surprised me with a girl in a coral dress, now a woman, with her runaway ideas and unforgettable mouth." He tucks a piece of my hair behind my ear. "I won't let you push me away."

I swat at his hand and miss. He holds my wrist and links his hand through mine.

"It's so easy for you, isn't it? We don't all grow up with the luxury of forgiveness and family. Look at this incredible life you have right in front of you, and you haven't even appreciated how lucky you are. Your family loves and wants to support you. And instead of doing the hard work and facing your regret, you threw your whole career and life away."

My tank is running on fumes. I want to collapse and melt into nothingness.

"I'm trying. I'm asking you to stay so we can do the hard work."

"You think us being together is going to fix things? I can't be responsible for the game of limbo you play between your past and your present." The projection doesn't hit me until I've said it to him. *I have to get out of here.* Standing up, I yank my hand from his and reach for my bag.

"So that's it? Feels like you're burning a bridge because you're too afraid to cross it." His face hardens.

"It feels like self-preservation to me," I confess. "You should recognize this move."

Reed's head falls to his hands. He speaks quietly, but every word makes impact. "How can the things we've said, the things we've done, have meant nothing to you? I was careless in the past in so many ways. Shit came easy to me and I didn't understand the gravity of my actions." He blows out a frustrated breath. "Dammit, Rory, I don't think we should be careless with this. We were brought back together for a reason. This, you and me, is a gift. Can you see that?"

His resolve is slipping into a ravine where I'm not there to catch him. And yes, the universe found a way to intersect our lives twice and throwing it away feels egregious, but my mind is folding in on itself and I don't have the tools to repair it. I've got to separate fact from fiction, and that's not something I can do in his presence.

"You think I wanted to feel this way for someone who doesn't believe he deserves happiness?" I throw up my hands. "We're two broken people playing a dangerous game of make-believe. When you chose to hide parts of yourself from me, we both lost."

His bruised heart is exposed and I keep punching it and he keeps rising back up, each time slower.

"What would you have me do? I was your mentor. I had an obligation and I wanted you to succeed. Maybe I didn't express how I felt or tell you everything the way you wanted to hear it, but that doesn't mean it's not real."

My eyes blur. "I don't know what to do." My voice cracks.

"Oh, Rory." When he reaches for me, I step back again. I know the minute we connect, it will break me, and I'll lose the strength I need.

"Don't go. Not like this."

I hold out my hand to stop him. Acute shock flashes in his eyes.

"I needed a mentor, Reed."

"You never needed a mentor."

"Yes, I did."

"Why do you not see what the rest of us do? You already have it all in you. Everything you need to write this story is already in your power. You never needed me, but selfishly, I wanted to be here to witness you soar."

He takes a cautious step forward and places my hand over his rapidly beating heart, gently flattening his hand on top of mine.

"I hid it from myself. It wasn't ever about me not wanting to let you in. It was about you being the only damn person who looked at me without sympathy. Who looked at me like I was enough." He removes his hand and brings it to my bottom lip, stroking my worried pout with the pad of his thumb. My knees and chest cave in at the same time. I crumble into his arms. He's holding me, someone I haven't known for long, but I instantly knew his heart.

"I'm sorry that I didn't look harder to find out who you were and that I didn't tell you sooner once I knew, but I won't be sorry about us. You see me. I see you. It can be that simple." He forces me to look into his eyes, a place I won't survive at this point.

"Rory, we know the parts of each other that matter. And I refuse to let you go without a fight. I want you. I want you like I want naps and grilled cheese and stories and Scrabble. I want to listen to night games on the radio under the stars and leap off the highest rock on Founders Day into the water with you. I want a chance at what I think could be the best risk of our lives. I want to choose you. Let me."

He's handing me all of his torn-up pieces, and all he's asking from me in return is to help him put them back together.

I make my way to the door. My hand stills on the cool metal.

Reed stands behind me. His voice bleeds like a neglected wound.

"This may not be the best timing or convenient. It may not be what you're ready for. It may not be the exact things you're used to hearing and it wasn't easy for me to share my feelings. It may not look real to you. It may scare you. And you might leave, never believing a word I say again, but I promise you, it was, and is, and always has been real to me."

The doorknob in my hand feels as cold as my heart. My wrist locks. There's not enough strength left to turn the knob. I can't call for help through the well of tears jammed in my throat.

Reed leans into me.

My eyes squeeze shut in violent protest as his arm grazes over my arm. His hand reaches my hand. He holds our palms together, two rotations to the right, and then pulls the door open like it's a feather and we are the breeze.

"It's never been a fantasy to me," Reed vocalizes with finality.

"Maybe that's true," I confess, over my shoulder, my words pathetically hanging in the air, not even convinced of themselves, "but it's become my worst nightmare."

I carry myself out each unlocked door, over the gravel, and to Kat's car. As I pull down the drive, Reed walks inside. His shadow, cast by the dim porch light, dutifully follows, and I swallow the instinct to throw the car in reverse, to run to him, to pound my fists into his chest, and bury this day in the ground. A sudden wave of fear that this is the last time I'll ever see him or hold him is acidic coming back up.

It's not until I cross state lines that remorse swoops in, and grief takes over, as I release the silent screams of my own six-year-old, and now self-inflicted, shattered heart.

31

RORY

"OFTEN WE MISTAKE KNOWLEDGE FOR TRUTH."
—ELOISE RISTAD

THE CITY SOUNDTRACK THAT once comforted me is gone, replaced by a numbness to everything. The apartment's as dark as it can be and it's still not enough to shut out a world that moves on with or without you.

I was relying on Boston's busyness to drown out the stillness, silence, and mountain air . . . of the Reed I knew before I opened my eyes to a complete stranger who sells half-truths.

Lies catch up.

In a closet on top of a shelf.

In an email exchange.

In the mirror.

They'll find you. *Especially the ones you tell yourself.*

The truth has become an estranged friend I'm fighting to face. Memories haunt me when I'm awake. I cannot escape their persistence.

When I think . . .

I'm dragged under, asphyxiating in regret and shame.

All the time I spent with Reed was high-stakes.

The rush, the heart palpitations, the constant flush in my chest and cheeks, waking up at dawn to see him, the anticipation, the closeness. It was a constant state of being on alert, wasted away in adrenaline fatigue at the end of each day. So I cry.

When I cry . . .

Grief soaks into the pillow, unable to forget the euphoria of his touch, his smile, our creative chemistry, cooking together, sharing ideas or opposing opinions. The music, the words, the walks, the closeness. It's been impossible for me to know what was real and what was pretend.

So I sleep.

When I wake again from another think-cry-sleep cycle, I remind myself that people who love you don't lie. Once trust is severed, whether it's a paper cut or a gaping wound, it bleeds into everything. *It was all a lie, Rory. He wasn't real. Reed didn't care about you.*

I flip my pillow over and find a dry spot to lay my head on.

There's nowhere else to go and no one to hide from anymore. Bile threatens the back of my throat, and I cough and cry and bury this part of my story into the wrinkled pillowcase.

I have to break from what I wanted to be true. I wanted to believe I meant the world to him. That what we were experiencing was a once-in-a-lifetime miracle.

When I saw the backpack in the closet, my navigation system spun out. I regressed into Rory the child, where everything is acute and aches.

Fitz begging to be fed pulls me from the bed. I drag my feet across the cold hardwood to refresh his water bowl and pour food into the feeder. The fridge is empty except for a few cans of ginger ale.

I haven't even charged my phone since I made it back last week.

I take a ginger ale and a glass from the drying rack.

The crack of the can and then the pour. The bubbles sparkle and burst on impact against my lips. The fizz fades down my throat. It would be better if it were mixed with bourbon. *Scratch that. I hate bourbon now.* All it did was make me reach for a connection. It clouded my judgment.

But I need something, anything, to dilute the flashbacks enough so they get lost in the shuffle of my shopping list, the cat puke stain on the rug that needs scrubbing out, and my characters fighting for airtime in my head.

My bed feels better each day that passes. It's the only place I want to be.

Trying to make sense of this is a fool's errand.

I'm running in sideways eights. Ruminating is the weapon of choice I use to gut myself. Combing through every detail. What I said. What he said. And he said so many words.

Words who'd been companions my whole life now felt like fair-weather friends. They betrayed me. They made me believe he cared.

Words were fucking liars. He was too.

Someone who put on a show and sold me a story.

Like a researcher who manipulates his data, or a family man who publicly places his wife on a pedestal while simultaneously promising himself to an inbox full of women (he collects on the side), or a bestselling author who holds your manuscript hostage, or a parent who leaves a child behind.

As with all great actors, I accepted Reed's performance at face value. I gambled on him. And I lost.

Back in Boston, miles and miles away from the stage and the performer, and everything still has his imprint on it, including his hoodie that I haven't taken off. I pull the fabric up to my nose and breathe in.

One, two, three, four.

✳

It could be night or day. Could be today or tomorrow. The orange glow behind my eyes tries to warn me. I thought I'd closed all the curtains. *I hate the sun.*

"Aurora." A soft familiar voice reaches me.

Not another dream. I grab my pillow and smash my head between the mattress and the filling. Now I'm manifesting him calling my name. *This is not improving.*

My hand burns as the pillow is ripped from it, stolen into thin air. I leap up, cursing at figments of my imagination.

"Rory. Breathe."

I rub my eyes and shake my head. "Mom . . . What are you doing here?"

She's sitting on the edge of the bed in a pristine cream trouser and sweater set. Two round pearls are peeking out from her low chignon. She's so graceful, beautiful, like an angel who raided Audrey Hepburn's closet, and I have so many questions, like did she see Holly Golightly's iconic little black dress, and also, how did she get into my apartment?

Her cool hand feels good placed against my forehead.

She brushes my hair away from my face. "Kat called me. I borrowed her key. She was worried about you. Frankly, so am I."

Awareness settles over me. It's the first time I've been touched since his arms were around me. I follow Mom's gaze to the floor, littered with tissues, where the duffel sits, unpacked.

"Mom, did you have to open every curtain?"

"Have you left the apartment at all? You're pale and your eyes, baby girl, they're so red and swollen."

"Is this rundown of my disgraceful appearance supposed to be helping? What day is it?"

"When was the last time that you ate something?"

"I think I ate. I don't remember. There's stuff in the fridge. Don't worry, I wasn't going to starve. I'm just tired."

"A bottle of ketchup and soda. I checked. Real food, Rory, like a meal. You need to get up."

I roll my eyes, pulling the covers up to my chin.

"You want to talk about it?"

"There's nothing to say." My chin quivers, and my eyes instantly flood, like they do every time I think. "I thought Reed was one person and he turned out to be someone else entirely. I handed him my heart and he broke it. And then I handled it poorly, and now, I'm behind even more on my deadline, and I have no idea what I'm gonna do. So you win. I failed."

"Win? My daughter is hurt. That is not me winning." She pulls me into her hold and I sob hot, heavy tears. My inner child shakes in her arms, crumbling, full of shame and regret and rejection.

She rocks me until my shaking subsides.

"So he's no longer your mentor?" she asks.

"Nope. I'm so embarrassed."

"Were you yourself?"

"Yes."

"Then you have nothing to be embarrassed about. I'm here. I'm here." She slides her hands over mine.

"I shared so much of myself, my ideas, my wishes, my fears." *My body.* "I got too excited, too quick, and forgot to slow down. I'd never met someone like this. I was so unprepared. It felt so real."

"Sometimes, we only get and give versions of ourselves. Sometimes, we don't know what something is when we're in the center of it. Sometimes, we think we know the whole of someone when we only know a sliver. I know what it's like to chase a thing, a person, bending a little here and there, until you look down and realize you're the only one in pieces."

"How could I be so wrong about this?"

"Come, baby, let's get out of bed."

"I want to sleep," I say, shivering.

"I know it hurts."

"I trusted him."

"Yes, you did, and that only makes you brave."

"He had my story, Mom." My body is shaking, my eyes are too swollen to blink back fresh tears. "He had everything for years, knew it was mine. He was pretending to care about me, pretending to be . . ." I'm at a loss for words. Saying it out loud snaps my bones and brings on a pounding headache.

Mom's sweep of blush goes crimson. She looks down at her watch, then stands up. "He still has your shit?"

"I left it behind."

"What's his address?" She's one click away from firing up GPS, so I shoot up, wobbling and weak, and cover her screen with my hand.

"No. Don't. It doesn't matter."

She grabs onto me so I don't fall over.

"Knowing where it is now doesn't change that I let it go a long time ago."

"I want to give this guy a piece of my mind."

"Mom, help me to the bathroom."

She lends her arm for me to lean on as we enter the bathroom. Mom flips on the light and runs her fingers through my hair while I brush my teeth.

"And writing?" she asks.

Writing reminds me of him. He reminds me of writing. I'm playing chicken between writer's block and emotional bullets.

I shake my head.

"Okay then, what's the plan now?"

"I haven't thought that far ahead yet. I'm not ready for people to have opinions about my situation, so I've been keeping to myself, trying to sort it all out."

"That's a good start. Can I make a suggestion?"

"Will my saying no stop you?"

"Probably not. Let's write down a few goals, beginning with step one."

"What's step one?" I ask, turning around, leaning against the bathroom sink, my stomach growling as the knots loosen.

Mom turns on the shower and passes me a towel. "Step one, shower. Step one and a half, pizza."

✳

A few weeks later, I'm sitting with Arty at the dining room table, eating bagels and cream cheese, coffee cake, scrambled eggs, and freshly sliced tomatoes. Mom's on the phone, selling raffle tickets, marching up and down the stairs like a badass magenta and gold warrior, sweatband crown included. I see her shiny blond head whip past on a lap around the foyer.

"She's getting her steps in," Arty notes, smirking.

"She's committed."

Our laughter rattles the forks on our plates.

Mom quirks an eyebrow as she pops her head into the room, pointing to the earbud in her ear, instructing us kids to quiet down.

I haven't laughed this hard since I was with Reed's family. It's been one month since I left New Hampshire. It still hurts. I'm able to think of them without crying, but the ache is ever present. It wasn't only Reed that I was attached to. It was his world—the house, his family, their history, and the lake.

Arty's digging into his brunch and following Mom with his smiling eyes.

"You have laser vision for that woman."

"Didn't you know it's my superpower?" he whispers. "She's the first person I see in any room." As if scripted, Mom walks by and blows him a kiss.

How have I never noticed their affection before?

"If you want to raise money, she's your person. Her persuasion efforts are trophy worthy," I remark, admiring how easily she moves through social situations. A natural waltzer.

Arty's voice reaches my ear. "Nothing she wouldn't do for her girls."

I huff. "I don't know about that," slips out through my mouthful of bagel.

"Don't you?" He sounds surprised with a dash of protectiveness. "Then you don't know your mom because to that woman," he nods toward her perfectly blown out hair that seems impervious to the speed walking, "her children are everything."

I wonder if we're talking about the same woman.

Sometimes, I think Arty sees Mom through a rose-colored lens with a post-nineties filter. He knew her after I knew her. And that's okay, but it doesn't paint the full picture. I'm not here to alter his image of her, but it's like they all live in a copy print, and I've got the original stored back at my place.

"How long did it take you to know Mom was it for you?"

He chuckles. "Not long. Six days. But I waited six months to ask her to marry me so I wouldn't scare her off. But I knew almost immediately."

"So, you weren't nervous about marrying someone you barely knew?" There's a lot about Arty I've never taken the time to learn. That's been an oversight on my part.

"Nerves are a part of the package when any kind of vulnerability is involved. But love doesn't live in the black and white, Rory. Every relationship has its own trajectory."

"So, did you always want to own hotels?" I change the subject, picking at the crumble topping of Mom's coffee cake.

"Me?" He chuckles. Laugh lines appear at the corners of his mouth and fade like a frown. "I wanted to be a high school history teacher."

"Really? Like tweed coat and everything?"

"The whole shebang. I liked sports growing up, but I wasn't ever going to be a professional athlete. I would've been happy being a teacher, but things change."

"What changed?" The topping is demolished.

"I see writing a novel has reawakened your investigative spirit."

My shoulders sag. I do sound like a journalist when I ask questions. I swallow the memory of someone else who thought so too.

"Ever hear of the playwright George Bernard Shaw?"

"Sure I have. Youth *is* wasted on the young."

"The very one." Arty sighs, adding, "To a degree, I get his point, but I believe youth is a privilege of being young. There's more time to try and fail and try again. I made some good investments and purchased my first hotel as a fixer-upper, and soon it became the change."

"But what about teaching? Do you regret not doing it?" My head hurts when I think of Arty's dream getting lost in the shuffle of the rat race.

"Regret is wasteful at any age, Rory. Change is inevitable and necessary. Our dreams sometimes grow outside of ourselves. Would I have loved teaching history? Sure. But the trade-off? I got to live a life most people dream of. I take vacations wherever I want. I can send you and your sister to college. It brought me to your mom. How can I regret any of that? Life is good because I spent each day appreciating it while I was living it."

If I close my eyes I'll cry, and I'm not ruining a good breakfast. Sometimes, you gotta bench your own feelings.

"You know, I think seeing me is your superpower too," I say.

Arty leans in and holds my hand like I've always been his. "I believe in you, Rory. Hold on a sec. I want to get something for you."

When Arty leaves the room, I blot the corners of my eyes with a linen napkin and sip my warm coffee.

He returns, placing a white box on the table.

"Your mom wanted to make sure you kept this somewhere safe."

Mom's waving her hands everywhere like she's throwing out handfuls of confetti, oblivious to us watching her.

"She's so embarrassing."

"She's unapologetically herself, isn't she," Arty replies, winking. "I know someone else who deserves to embrace that about herself too."

I think about the way life had to twist and turn to get them together. And if one of those turns hadn't worked out the way they did, we wouldn't be sitting here today. And I'm glad we are. Because I'm lucky to belong to Arty. He's the best person for my mom and us girls.

I've spent my life deeply hurt that my father left before I was born, didn't even give us a chance, didn't give himself a chance at being my dad.

When I've wished for moments with my father, I've overlooked the one I have. The man who always sits to my left and knows how I'm feeling. The man who chose me despite my rough edges.

Maybe my father leaving was in the plan all along.

"I love you," I say. "Even if I don't always show it."

"I love you too, sweetheart. Remember, we all get to our destinations in our own time." He nods over to Mom. "Even parents."

At my apartment, Fitz hops onto the couch to chew the crimson and ivory string as I unwrap the gift box. There's weight to it and the contents shift a little as I pull the lid off.

Tissue paper covers the top. I fold back each layer and gasp.

The wrapping and box fall to the floor as my shaky hands grasp the cool metal frame. It's simple, silver, with clean lines, and I can see my shocked expression reflecting off its polished surface.

Once again, I'm knocked on my ass. My grip on what I know to be true is slipping away right before my eyes. A notecard written in Mom's block letter handwriting lays on top of the sheet of glass.

Aurora,
Can't wait to make everyone buy your book.
You've Got This! Proud of you!
Love, Mom

She saved my acceptance letter from Eden and framed it. The note is dated the week I left Boston to go to New Hampshire. She's always believed in me. Fitz nudges warm tears from my upturned chin. It's safe to say my feelings are back, have suited up, and are taking swings in the on-deck circle.

I rush through the apartment, grabbing rags and cleaner, bypassing the bleach, a feather duster, and a travel-sized tool kit from the hall closet. There's no more time to waste. My desk has become a disheveled dumping ground. I sweep off the clutter, recycle the miscellaneous papers, and dust and wipe down where needed until my workspace shines. I turn on my laptop. While it's loading, I take a nail and hammer it into the wall. I hang my acceptance letter above my desk and tape Mom's note next to the frame.

The computer finally wakes up.

The wall comes alive.

And I get to work.

32

REED

"WRITE YOUR STORY AS IT NEEDS TO BE WRITTEN. WRITE IT HONESTLY AND TELL IT AS BEST YOU CAN. I'M NOT SURE THAT THERE ARE ANY OTHER RULES. NOT ONES THAT MATTER."
—NEIL GAIMAN

CARLYNN AND WILL ARE horrified when they walk through the door. Emmy is curious. Lew nods his head a few times while passing through to claim his spot on the couch. And Mom puts the tangerine casserole dish on the counter, unable to step past the pile of debris on the kitchen floor.

"Doing some light remodeling, Junior?"

I push my safety glasses on top of my head.

Will gives me a good-luck-buddy (digging yourself from this hole) smirk and seeks refuge with Lew. I've been ditched by the only two people who'd back me up here.

Emmy laughs and looks at Carlynn. "Does this mean we can order pizza?"

"Are you saying you don't want my lasagna?" Mom throws a hand on her hip.

"Gram, we have no kitchen to cook in."

"Hey now, there's a kitchen, just no cupboards," I clarify.

"Emmy, tell Dad we're ordering from King Subs."

"Really? Thanks, Mom," she squeals and wheels around my mess into the living room.

Then there were two.

I chug some water and face the music.

"Sorry, I should've let you know."

"Yeah, Reed, a little heads up. I could've baked it at home and brought it over warm."

"Reed, seriously, what's going on here?" Carlynn adds.

"I've waited too long to get these in shape. They're peeled and warped. The paint's outdated. I had some extra time on my hands is all." Their identical lifted brows and tilted heads of curls suggest to me they're not satisfied with my story. "I've put things off that need to get done."

"Sure, and had we known, we could've called in some favors. You didn't have to do it solo," Carlynn counters.

I stretch my hands out and shake my head. "I started late last night. I wasn't calling anyone."

"Not sleeping?" Mom infers. "Reed, I agree this needed to be done, but I don't appreciate that you didn't consult us about it first either. You're tearing something down that's been a part of this family, so I'd have liked a family discussion first."

She's right. It's her house. It was an impulse and once the first hinge came off, I couldn't stop until it all came crashing down. I take stock around me, at the bare shelving, and regret sinks in. My hands tremble.

"Mom, Car, this is your home too and Dad's memory. I can't believe I demolished this without including you. For so long I haven't so much as replaced a nail. I was afraid to change anything because changing things might erase memories, but then Rory left and I got it in my head that change would somehow fix everything I've done to everyone. I've ruined so much for the people I care about. I'm so sorry."

"Things aren't what give people or memories meaning," Mom says. "Sometimes, we hold onto them because we think it's all we have left. Honestly, I'm happy to see new cabinets, but after all these years, I was in shock and a bit triggered."

I hop off the counter, stepping over a pile of wood, to give my mom and Carlynn a hug.

Carlynn pulls back with misty eyes. "You have to let go of this guilt. It's eating you alive. It's stolen your writing, your relationships, your enthusiasm for life. And when Rory was here, that light flickered on. We didn't just lose Shannon or Emmy's ability to walk after the accident—we lost you. Whatever you and Rory are or aren't, for a minute there, I saw you coming back to us. And I'm terrified you'll slip away again now that she's gone." She leaps back into my arms.

My heart shreds as I hug Carlynn. Mom rubs slow circles on my back, and I practice what Rory taught me, breathing in, *one, two, three, four,* and exhaling, *five, six, seven, eight.*

After our eyes are dry, Carlynn looks up at me and says, "Emmy loves you. We love you. Life doesn't always give us the answers to why terrible things happen. It sucked. Some days, we get to be angry about that, but we aren't going to let it rob our lives either. My little girl has a beautiful future ahead of her, and she needs grown-ups who can show her what it means to accept what's out of our control. How to forgive others and how to forgive ourselves. Otherwise, there's no point to anything we do to strengthen her body or support her progress."

If only Pops could see us now, standing in a construction zone in the heart of the house, amongst so many of our shared memories. Here, we've lost, we've loved, we've welcomed and said goodbye, like we always have done, as a family. I don't think there's anything else in this life he wanted more than to know we were all okay and happy.

Battling anxious thoughts has broken me so many times. It has made me afraid of love and failure, so I've avoided both, but I can't ignore my feelings. Whether they make my pulse race in fear or in excitement, I won't lock them up anymore.

Emmy grabs my attention with her soft voice and smile. "Will Rory be coming back?" she asks, and before I can squash the emotion rising from my gut to my chest, I choose to express it.

"I don't think so, Em."

"She's a great Scrabble player, and I miss having her here."

Mom kisses Emmy on the head, and Carlynn jabs me in the side with her pointer.

"Okay, yes, she is, and I miss her too," I admit. When I confessed to Rory how I was feeling the night she left, that was the most honest I'd been with somebody in my entire life. It was brave to honor my feelings and brave to have shared them, even if they weren't returned.

But those were just words and my words had deceived her. We're writers who know words are pliable. They can be bent out of shape to fit any narrative we want them to. Words weren't going to repair the damage I'd done. Though they weren't the solution, they were a start.

And as she once professed to me in the passenger seat of my truck, Rory Wells believes in beginnings.

✳

"Wallet, keys, watch, hat." I recite my checklist while confirming by touch: my back pocket, hands, wrist, and head.

"Reed," Mom says, sweeping the last remaining piles of dust from the floor. "Can you spare a minute before you head out?"

I check the time. "I've got all of town needing a plow. I should get going."

Her less than amused shift from smile to scowl tells me I've miraculously found a few minutes to spare.

Mom hands me a thermos of coffee. "I love the way the cabinets turned out. The sky blue, green, and preserving some of the original yellow, you really nailed Tuscany here. It's so warm. Pops would love it."

I pull a scalding sip from the lip. "Thanks, Ma." This might be the first time I've taken the time to appreciate the work we all did. I suggested a traditional Tuscan design and everyone was on board. We hung up new cabinets, painted them olive green and blue, and added sunflower and cinnamon red accents. We added a floral tile backsplash incorporating the color palette, bringing Italian landscape into the space.

"You haven't stopped in weeks, Reed."

"It had to get done."

"Okay, well, do you *have* to plow tonight?"

"I said I would."

"You going to tell me what happened with Rory?" she asks, wiping her hands on her apron.

Rory's hair was pulled back, exposing her ivory skin. She'd been standing in the kitchen beside me, nervously dropping noodles into a rolling boil, when the impact splashed water, grazing her neck. Then the fire. The aloe. Our first kiss.

"Surprised to see you two at odds." Mom's voice pulls me back to our conversation.

If she knew everything, she might not be.

There's nothing I can do. Visions of Rory linger in every corner of this house. Remodeling didn't erase the past, or the memories of the night she walked away from me.

"Remember the journal, the stories from that girl on the bench?" I reach into my pocket, bypassing my key, flipping over the stone.

"You told me about your breakup with Genevieve around the same time you told me about that girl. What's this got to do with Rory?" She wipes her glasses on the inside of the apron.

"Rory is the girl. The journal is hers. And when I realized it, I decided to wait to tell her for reasons that aren't good enough, and that was a mistake. She's black and white about rules. And I broke one. There was so much between us in the gray. I get why she left. She didn't deserve how I handled this whole situation from the very beginning."

Mom's expression is all shock. "It's astonishing that you knew her before."

"Disappointed in me?" I look at my laces tied up tight.

"I like Rory and I'm sorry to hear that your actions hurt her. But I'm really glad we can talk about it. And I think she wouldn't ever wish for you to be so hard on yourself. You should call or email her or whatever you kids do, text, video . . ."

"Okay, okay." Laughing, the tension in my shoulders melts a little. I release the stone. "Definitely not emailing her ever again.

I haven't found the right time and she deserves peace. I don't want to disrupt her life anymore."

"There's never a right time, only right now."

"She's probably finishing up her mentorship, and I told her how I felt before. I don't know if I can risk myself in that way while I'm trying to get better."

"You know what Pops would say, right?"

"Baseball or courtroom analogy?"

"Well, I'm probably going to butcher this, but let's try."

Mom pulls out Pops's chair at the table. The legs scrape along the floor. She sits down while lowering the register of her voice.

"Well, Junior. There's risk in everything we do. Doesn't stop you from getting on with living. When you're young, there's lots of chances to experience the unexpected. Some are tough losses, but most are sweet, and if we're lucky, somethin' special. This one life is an adventure. Don't forget, I saw your first home run, cheered on every big win. I was even there the time you let a girl knock your concentration, the bat slipping from your grip. As you get older, life's firsts happen less and less. And that's why you gotta open your eyes while you're still in the game."

I nod and smile and kiss her on her warm cheek.

"So, I did pretty good, huh?"

"You did great. Thank you, Ma. Love ya."

"Love you too, honey." She pushes the chair back in. "I'm going to take this trash out. You need anything thrown out?" Her eyes dart over to the counter by the door.

We both look at the stack of mail.

"Did you ever get a look inside the journal Lew brought over?" she asks.

"Not yet," I reply, gathering the mail in both hands.

"Could be worth a look."

"Yeah, I'll get to it." My exhale is slow and deliberate as I gather the stack of mail off the counter. "I have a feeling I'm going to need a crowbar of an apology to get Rory to hear me out."

"What's that piece of advice you're always yammering on about? Show versus tell. Put yourself in her shoes." Mom follows me into the living room.

She reaches down to rub Fenway's belly as he's sprawled out in front of a small fire. Though it's early spring, the night air still drops low.

"Does this animal ever move? He's one pile of snuggling naps. You don't even feel Grams giving you love." Mom turns to me, saying in a low chuckle, "He cracks me up. He can sleep through anything."

"Except thunderstorms."

The flames go up and the sound of crinkling paper and plastic spit out their final crackles.

"Are you saying I should somehow show Rory?"

"Actions speak louder than words," she reminds me. "One time, I was so furious with your dad, he'd been working late hours and in Boston more than home and I missed him, really missed him. Raising two kids all week was not always easy, and it was a season where Carlynn was extra fussy at night and I wasn't getting much sleep. He couldn't drop his clients and I knew it, but I was feeling neglected. Wouldn't listen to a word he had to say."

"How did you two work it out?"

"Well, Pops had your grandparents watch you kids for the weekend. He picked me up and took me to a hotel in Mount Washington. Made me sleep for twelve hours straight, and then we spent the rest of the weekend together."

"Such a romantic."

"He was, but he also showed me he knew what mattered to me. I was sleep deprived and exhausted. That's what love is. And then, it took me time to learn how to not be resentful when he had to work long hours."

Mom's face flushes from the roaring fire, maybe from the memory too.

She was so busy showing her resiliency, I never considered a version of Mom where she felt forgotten. Sitting across from her now, I see her. She's not just the woman who cared for me and put us kids first, she's always been the strength behind her roles.

"I got there eventually. We had choices. Grow together or grow apart. It had its moments, but I wouldn't change a thing, because it was a beautiful life, and it was ours."

She never leaves Pops behind. He's definitely with us tonight. The sky outside is littered with stars. I can feel him shooting an arrow, kicking my ass at how I've dragged my feet with Rory.

Of course I have to *show* her, especially since I haven't said a single thing to convince her that I'm not a total fraud. She needs proof that I'm someone she can trust.

I don't linger on that thought. Instead, I focus on the fuel it provides. To want something again. I haven't allowed myself to want anything in so long. Unlike the unopened mail turning to ash in the fading fire, I'm ignited with inspiration.

Tingling-fingers. Heart-racing.

Soul-calling inspiration.

To write.

I shoot off a text asking Will if he'll grab the plow and take a run for me, and I'll go over it in the morning. He agrees with a smile emoji.

"Gotta go, Ma."

Right in front of her approving smile, I dart up the steps, two at a time, to the second floor of the house. The floorboards beneath my feet don't even have time to creak. I push through the door at the end of the hallway, switching on the floor lamp in the corner of the room, and approach my desk.

"Sorry I left for so long," I whisper, wiping the keys gently with the bottom of my t-shirt. As the screen wakes up, my blood pumps fast and my heart floods with impatient anticipation. The white page accosts me like a slap to the face, and I avert my eyes from its illumination.

I drag my hands over my face and blow out a sigh, sending a silent wish to Pops, and to Rory. *It's now or never.* That's all it takes for the dam to break.

Dialogue scrambles onto the page. The characters are screaming for their turn.

I can't type fast enough. My hands ravage the keys with determination. Stroke after stroke until my knuckles ache. I push through the pain. Creative release is a full-body experience, and it doesn't take long for my muscle memory to kick in.

My fingers pound the keyboard, black ink spreading across the screen in a blur. A web of sentences growing page after page. Each consonant and vowel falling in line, one by one, until they all stand side by side, holding their place.

Trained soldiers.

A battlefield's worth.

Hours pass until morning. I write until my forearms grow numb and my eyes happily burn, on fire too. I reward every muscle that's working for me tonight with thoughts of praise and gratitude.

I don't stop until there's nothing left, and when the last key I press down releases back up, slow and deliberate, the final popping sound it makes tears me from my trance, causing my hands to pull away from the keyboard and drop down to each side of my body like dead weights. I drive my chair back with force, as far away from the desk as wood against wood will allow in one determined motion.

My breaths are heavy and stacked. Something has transpired in this room tonight, and I'm pretty sure the evidence is a few feet in front of me, patiently waiting for spell-check. My legs feel like mature tree stumps as they hold me upright. I'm afraid to confront what will happen when I peel my weary body from this chair and face what I've written.

The damp staleness that accosted me when I entered the room earlier has been replaced by a surge of adrenaline and ideas. My skin sticks to my shirt. After all this time, how easily the words welcomed me back into their sheltered embrace.

There's buzzing all around me in the stillness of this empty room. In the creative expression that has transpired here. I press my hands firmly into the tops of my thighs to settle the aftershock. Now that the inspiration I was running on has processed through me, I'm wiped out.

I drag myself over to the twin bed.

Memories surface, and I let them in, allowing the pieces to finally put themselves back together.

The haunting sound of steel scraping open against the broken ice.

Emerson's agonizing screams as she's pulled from the water.

Carlynn's fists bashing into my chest, burying her face against me, trembling, a mother's mouth full of hot tears and terror.

The impossibility of the waiting room, its harsh lighting.

Everyone's suffering, on display as darkness slips into day.

A new day, where the life we knew is over and all that remains is the aftertaste of my selfishness and irresponsibility.

"Reed, there was nothing you could have done," Mom whispers. "It wasn't your fault, Reed."

It's not until I notice the moisture drying on my eyelashes that I realize I'm talking out loud, atoning to an empty room.

Mom's words replay in my head, like an absolving chant, until my throat is raw and I can't speak them anymore.

It wasn't my fault. It wasn't my fault. It wasn't my fault.

Warm air blows in, caressing my cheek. I lean into the pillow, imagining the way she touched me.

I rub my eyes with the palms of my hands. The screen's bright light has faded, allowing visibility out the window, through an early thaw, onto Berry Lake. Its deep purple hue turns iridescent, claiming the canvas of glittering stars, persistent and powerful, rising up to greet the moon. I watch until I see her peek out from the horizon.

There you are. I sigh.

A sight I've come to long for. A sight I've come to know even before she arrives.

Every muscle in my body burns brighter than the sun. I, too, have been here all along.

33

—— · ——

RORY

"HAVE ENOUGH COURAGE TO TRUST LOVE ONE MORE TIME AND
ALWAYS ONE MORE TIME." —MAYA ANGELOU

THE SECONDHAND STORE IS an easy two-block walk down the
street from Memory Lane. My plan is to head there first, then see
Kat.

"Hello, hun, need any help?" The clerk behind the register greets
me upon entering.

"Yes, please. I'm here to consign."

"Great, why don't ya go and see if there's something ya want and
I'll meet ya back here." I hand her the bag I'm carrying and she
places it on the counter.

Her name tag reads *CeCe's Closet*, and below that line, *Owner*.
I check around, scoping out a pair of winter boots that resemble
Carlynn's. There isn't so much as a scuff or a speck of dirt on them.
A knowing grin takes over my face. The little ways the universe
likes to remind me she's in charge. My instinct is to call Reed and
tell him all about the identical pair, reaching for my phone. An
internal fire alarm sounds off. "*You don't do that anymore.*"

Reed's still like a reflex to me. The habit of having him in my life
was the hardest to break those first few weeks after I left. In such a

short time, he became the person I wanted to share all the details of my day with. Who I thought of when I woke up and who I wanted to dream with.

I still haven't recovered from walking away from the wish that had planted itself beneath my ribcage. That sharp sliver that burrowed so deep it became a part of me. But it's been months now, and the ache has dulled, new habits and routines have formed. The world moved on.

"These have been well-loved," CeCe observes, giving my boots a once-over.

"If they're too damaged to consign, I can take them back," I offer.

"Nah, they just need a little polish. I'll find them a good home, don't worry."

I watch CeCe fold my boots back into the bag. "Bye, boots." They've been good to me.

"All right, so ya wanna exchange these brown boots for credit toward these hiking boots you were looking at?"

"Well, I was wondering if you carry any refurbished record players?"

Kat's morning rush has dispersed, so she's free to chat when I arrive. I put my bag on the armchair and set the box on the table.

I haven't been back here to write at all. Now that my desk and workspace is cleared off, I'm focused when I'm writing. My mentor has helped me become better at self-structuring. She's been instrumental in shaping my manuscript and getting me query-ready. We haven't met yet in person even though she's local, but we email every day and she's always checking in to see what I'm working on. Now that I'm in the querying trenches, she's also encouraged me to start my next book.

"It's been busy lately." Kat plops down across from me.

"That's a good thing? Or not?"

"I could definitely use another part-timer. Thinking about taking a breather over summer, maybe do a couple road trips."

"Love that idea. Let me know how I can help."

"Thanks, Ror. So, what's this?" Kat asks, eyeing the cardboard box.

"What's what?"

Her voice raises. "Um, this huge box that's breaking my tea table."

My throat vibrates as I keep a straight face.

"Aurora Wells," Kat warns.

"Guess you're gonna have to open it." I'm so excited to see her face.

"You're kinda freaking me out."

We laugh as Kat looks inside. Her gaze turns serious. Her jaw drops.

"How did you? How could you? This is not easy to find!"

"Yeah, well, I don't know anything about it, but my new friend CeCe told me it was steal."

Kat's bouncing from one foot to the next. Her smile's glowing.

"This turntable is iconic, Rory. It's in stunning condition. I cannot wait to play Stevie on this. Seriously, I don't even know what to say. Thank you so much." She leans down and hugs my head. Cinnamon and strong coffee embrace me.

While I was busy with my inner world, I've made myself unavailable to the lives around me, to the people who matter most to me.

"I'm sorry I've been MIA and super Rory-centric. I've been so focused and also completely unaware. Our friendship is important to me, and you're always the one crossing the bridge to meet me on my end. I want us to meet in the middle. I'm so grateful for you. Thanks for always being a latte and phone call away."

"Bridge? I have no idea what you're carrying on about, but I love ya."

I help her lift the turntable, and walk it over to the corner.

"Speaking of calling people, have you heard from Mr. I-Shall-Not-Mention-His-Name-But-I-Think-Maybe-We-Should-Talk-About-It?"

I shake my head.

"Have *you* reached out?"

I shake my head again. "I deleted his number from my phone."

"That seems proactive." Kat adds, "Maybe a little impulsive."

"It was too hard knowing I could contact him at any time. I didn't trust myself."

Kat clears a pile of vinyls to make room for the turntable.

"The thing is, Rory, I'm still fuzzy as to why you wouldn't try and work through this with him. I know he lied, and I'm NOT defending his shitty actions, but you are the most caring person I know— you're a fighter—and you don't go down without trying when something really matters to you. Aren't you the one always reminding me that our condition in life as humans is a carousel of fucking up, fumbling, rebounding, and recovering?"

She's repeating back to me a phrase I learned in therapy about healing and letting go.

Then she goes to the wall and returns with a quote. "Read it."

I take the torn paper from her hands.

"Out loud," she insists.

I clear my throat, *"Love settles for less than perfection, and makes allowances for human weaknesses. Ann Landers."*

Kat's making kissy faces at me.

"So what's the plan?" she asks.

Even if Arty and Mom and Reed's parents knew quickly, that doesn't make it everyone's story. I let myself indulge in the fantasy that there might've been something special between us. But our time has passed, and I don't know how to go back.

"We barely knew each other. This is no insta-love or whatever."

"Who made up that rule? That's a pretty limited viewpoint, you know, for a romance author." Kat shakes her head at me because she knows, deep down where it matters, I don't want a word of what I'm saying to be true. But time has shown me over and over again that love isn't always enough. It's not the only answer.

"It's irrelevant, Kat. I'll never know what was us and what was some kind of made-up creative chemistry. It was too messy."

"You might not be able to explain this to yourself in a way that makes sense, but I'd hate to see you walk away from something real because it didn't play out on paper the way you would've written it."

Reed isn't a bad person and I know he had the best of intentions, but I realized that too late after I burned the bridge to keep myself safe.

Though I continue to make excuses for why he and I shouldn't be together, that feeling, the one I can't explain to anyone, never goes away.

"He's not him, you know. Your father is a coward, but Reed, I think he might be worth a second chance. Right? We all get those?"

"Maybe," I admit.

"What I know is that you're not the same person since you came back. It's like you left part of your heart up North. I was really worried about you this winter, but now that you're getting your footing back, I wanna say something." Kat lifts her old record player and places it into the cardboard box.

"Why not? You're on a roll."

"Glad you see it that way." She pats my cheek. "There's a million unknowns in this life. That's why we have music and books and art dedicated to working out this crazy thing. It'd be a shame if you didn't give what you have together the real shot it deserves."

"What did I do in this life to deserve you?" I whimper.

"You'll get me back in the next one."

The Victrola is ready and Kat grabs a *Fleetwood Mac* album.

"Hear how clear that sounds?"

"So good. Haven't heard this song in forever."

"This is nothing serious, so don't make a big deal about it, but I have some news." We return to our spot and barely sit before my eyes jump out of my head.

"I promise I'll try to not make a fuss."

"Okay, well, remember how I met your office friend at your going away party?"

"Yes." Nodding in confirmation and pulling at the ends of my hair.

"Gavin stopped by the café a couple of times after that on his way to work."

"What? Why didn't you say anything?"

My disbelief is the size of a magnifying glass.

"Because he's a customer and all we did was exchange money for pastries. And you were in New Hampshire."

"You went from pastries to—"

"Slow your roll. I'm getting there."

I shut my mouth.

"He started coming by on the weekends during my slow time, and we'd talk about music and comedians, Irish roots, favorite sitcoms, regular stuff. And it turns out we have a lot in common. A couple of weeks ago, we met up for dinner in the North End and ended up back at his place. It was all PG. We watched reruns of *The Office* and he kissed me. A great first kiss."

I clap my hands together like a matchmaking mother.

"Can I be your Maid of Honor?"

"Rory," she shouts playfully.

"Okay, okay, but why didn't you tell me sooner? You could've messaged me."

"Honestly, when was I going to tell you? We haven't gotten to hang out at all recently."

She's right. I'm finally in a good place, but I wasn't before.

"I want you to know, Gavin's my friend. You're my best friend. I love that you two are hanging out, and I can't believe I didn't think of it myself."

Kat pulls me into a side hug. "I needed to make sure it was going somewhere before I shared it with anyone. Even with best friends, we get to have some things that are just for ourselves."

A few months ago, the idea that Kat would keep something from me would've made me question our friendship and go into a sad spiral about Reed, but I've had so much time to reflect.

I joined a weekly group for survivors of parental neglect, so I'm learning about how trauma has driven my impulsive need to control everything around me. I'm practicing being kinder to myself. I'm a rough draft, embracing the revision process.

"So, how would you feel about spending some more time together, on the clock?"

"Sign me up," Kat replies.

The sky is covered in freshly wrung clouds, their gray giving into the sun breaking through. The view out the window is as bright as ever. The sidewalk is full of closing umbrellas, floral dresses, and baseball caps.

I send out a wish into the world, a sentiment of gratitude, with an intended recipient in mind, and hope that wherever he is at this exact moment, he's smiling too.

34

RORY

"AND NOW THAT YOU DON'T HAVE TO BE PERFECT,
YOU CAN BE GOOD." —JOHN STEINBECK

"THANK YOU FOR SEEING me today." Meryl explores Memory Lane, smiling warmly at the records and memorabilia on the walls. "I'm sure you're busy."

"Can I get you something to drink? We have water, coffee, tea, these little fruity sparkling drinks Kat keeps in the back."

"Earl Grey is great, thanks, dear."

I go behind the counter to prepare Meryl's tea and plate a few scones. I carry them over to a nearby table and we take a seat opposite each other.

One, two, three, four. The silence itches.

I don't know why she's come all this way, and it's impossible to look at her and not see him. *Five, six, seven, eight.*

"How's the rest of the program going?"

Meryl pauses while drinking her tea.

The stillness in her presence makes me want to share every thought I've had since leaving New Hampshire.

"The program ended this spring. My mentor is great."

I straighten out my tie dye apron.

Meryl's gentle smile is a balm to my nerves. I smile back and settle.

"We have a lovely friendship. Bonded over our shared love of regency romance. And she's been so supportive. I'm writing a new story now. We'll see how it goes. And I've submitted my book to three agents."

"Well, that sounds fantastic. I know you'll make a mark in this world."

"Thank you." Tears well behind my eyes. "That means so much to me."

"I'm happy for you, Rory."

I hadn't realized how much I relied on Reed when he was my mentor, needing his validation, not trusting my instinct.

I doubted myself so much that I unintentionally used Reed as a crutch. If he helped me with every decision, then if I failed, I could somehow blame him too.

All his lessons and activities, getting me out of my comfort zone and challenging me to understand my characters—it was a mirror he was trying to hold up for me.

"These blueberry scones are pretty good." Meryl breaks one in half. She examines its texture.

"I'm Kat's unofficial baked goods compost pile. I won't tell her yours are better, though."

"Best not to." Meryl smiles at me with a fondness that makes me long for one of her hugs. "So, aside from writing, how've you been?" She picks up a crumb from her lap and puts it on the plate.

"I'm well. Been working part-time with Kat and hanging out with my family. I'm taking my sister on a girls' spa trip to Portland next weekend."

"Reed would love to hear how you're doing. Is it okay if I tell him?" she asks. His name still tugs at the deepest part of my heart.

I didn't plan on things falling apart with us, but I understand now that they had to—so I could finally take care of myself. I couldn't do that or even see it under the microscope of my enmeshed feelings for him.

My anxiety often reacts before I can respond. I'm working on forgiving myself for how I handled things. For not saying goodbye to his family. For not appreciating how much of himself Reed really did share with me. How he was trying to make sense of his own feelings. He was trying to protect me from reliving the past while I was trying to work toward my future.

"Please let him know I kept my promise to myself." I smile.

"Of course. Thank you, Rory." She reaches out and squeezes my hand.

"I'm pretty certain I let him down, but I think I let myself down the most," I confess, through blurry vision. We release our hands and I get up and grab a tissue. "How's everyone doing?"

"You know, not much changes in Berry. Reed's doing well. He's seeing someone, finally. She's been really good for him." My mind slows to a stop as I blow my nose. The tissue in my hand weighs ten pounds. *Reed's seeing someone?* My pulse is in my throat. Meryl carries on talking to my back. "He's been writing too. It's helping him work through some of the loss and grief he's been carrying."

I toss the tissue in the trash and breathe deeply as I turn to face the rest of my punishment, having to endure hearing how he's his best self now, without me.

"Reed never really processed Pops's death. He felt this responsibility to take care of his family after he passed, but he was still so young, and it made him more anxious than he'd ever been. Instead of sharing that with us, he buried it, kept it locked away, and suffered in private, and then with Emmy, it all became too much again. He was always a great builder as a kid—sandcastles, Lego cities, snow forts, imaginary worlds, you name it," Meryl sighs. "After Emmy, I think he built a fortress around his mind to keep guard of his heart."

My eyes fall to the floor, and I beg my heart to find someone else to beat for.

"But you know, Rory, you made a difference. Your compassion. He felt like he could be himself with you. He laughs more. He even joined a softball league." She lets out a light laugh. "I'm proud of him." A pause sits between us. "I'm also proud of you."

I nod so I don't speak. I don't speak to avoid bawling.

I'm determined to hang onto the last shred of dignity I've got left. What did I expect, that he'd wait forever?

"We sure do miss seeing you, especially Emmy."

"I miss you all so much," I choke out, followed by a crumbling dam of feelings.

Even if people aren't in your day-to-day life, it doesn't mean they aren't still crowding the corners of your heart.

I've been downplaying how hard it's been not having them in my life.

Meryl moves over to me. Her hand glides over my head and hair and down my back. "So, maybe you'll come up? You know, blueberry season is upon us."

"I don't know if that's the best idea," I admit. "Reed and I haven't spoken in seven months."

"Well, I'm also your friend. That hasn't changed."

"I grew up thinking things were hidden from me all the time. It developed into a general mistrust of the world. I was always waiting around for the worst possible outcome."

The inside of my cheek burns between my teeth. I never imagined I'd be talking this openly with Meryl about her son.

"Our childhoods truly shape us in ways we can't always see, including Reed's. He might not acknowledge this, but he was a worrier from the time he was in kindergarten. He'd worry if his friends would play with him, if his socks matched, or if the homework assignment was complete. And I should've paid closer attention. I was raising the kids by myself while Pops was in town, and Reed was always doing things and was popular, so I neglected to see what he was burying beneath the busyness. If I had gotten him the support he needed, I could've helped him know he didn't have to tough it out himself."

"There's twenty million people living with anxiety disorders. Society didn't accept or understand it until recently." I try to comfort her.

"Yes, but still, children need to know that their feelings don't make them weak."

"Oh, Meryl, Reed knows how much you love him."

"Thank you, Rory. Most of the time, all any of us can do is love people the best way we know how to. Reed knows it was wrong of him to keep things from you. It wasn't fair of him to continue your friendship without being transparent. And for what it's worth, I'm sorry you were hurt."

Everyone deserves a Meryl in their lives. Whether things will work out and we'll remain friends or not, at this moment, everything is okay. And I'm holding onto that.

She stands suddenly and I stand too. "Do you believe that it's possible to deeply care about someone and also make a mistake?"

I nod, following the yellow bricks she's laying out for me. "I do."

She heads over to the door, then turns and wraps her arms around me. "I think so too." She pats my back once more.

It isn't fair that Meryl was married to a lawyer for forty years. She's mastered the art of leading the witness.

"He wanted me to give these to you." From her bag, she pulls out a brown paper sack and hands me a coffee mug. "You know where to find us. Don't be a stranger."

When Meryl leaves, I collapse on the couch to the left of the door. Luckily, it's almost closing time and no one is here but me. My eyes sting from crying and my nose is raw. I'm a mess processing my conversation with Meryl and what that brought up for me about a chapter of my life I was sure had ended. My hand grazes the side of the paper bag. It reminds me of a packed school lunch, the way the seal rolls into itself. I imagine Reed's hands where mine are now. I open the bag, dumping the contents into my lap. My heart pounds in my ears as I run my fingers over the soft cover, turning my journal over and peeking inside. A reunion I never thought would happen.

Then I pick up a thick stack of crisp white pages. My eyes flood as I read the note written beneath the title.

Dear Rory, It was never about me helping you. Your words, your heart, gave me the courage to stop hiding and to finish the story I was too afraid to let go. They say write to one person, and this one, Aurora Wells, is for you. Reed

A series of thoughts about my time with Reed shoot at me, like a succession of steps I'm running down, racing toward the end. I land at the bottom with a final realization. It knocks the air from my lungs.

I've been so fixated on one lie that I've missed all the truths around me. The truth is, I'm never going to be able to predict how things will work out. The truth is, Reed wasn't the only one not facing themselves. As I hold both mine and Reed's first novels side by side, while the misshapen coffee mug I fell so much in love with in New Hampshire rests in my lap, I'm convinced that you can have everything you thought you ever wanted and be missing the one thing you truly need.

35

RORY

I USE MY KEY and walk in the front door to my mom's house. I hang my bag on the hall tree and head into the kitchen.

"Hey, Mom."

"Come in, Rory, come in. This is a surprise."

"I'm sorry to show up without calling first."

"What are you talking about? You don't have to call first. This is home. Grab an apron."

"Did you just call me Rory?" I walk over to take the apron from the hook on the wall.

"I call you Rory."

"Um, when?"

"When I talk about you, honey."

"But you always call me Aurora when you speak to me."

"It's a beautiful name."

I sit across from her at the kitchen island and toss a slice of cucumber into my mouth.

"And I call you both. Where's this coming from?"

"I think I've gotten it wrong for a long time. And I want to say I'm so so so sorry for placing all of my anger onto you. I know you did your best and you love me." My chin quivers, but it's no use. I've spent a lot of time crying lately, years' worth of repressed feelings. April, my therapist, calls it shedding and says that soon, I'll feel lighter. These tears fall quickly, drying on the way down. They remind me of maple leaves in autumn, the way they know when it's their time and simply let go.

Mom comes around the island and pulls me against her shoulder. We hold onto each other for a while.

My face stains her pink chiffon blouse. "I'm sorry about your shirt."

She whispers, "You stay right here. It was never your fault. None of it. He left because he only wanted what came easy. He left because he couldn't face himself. You were perfect and it's entirely his loss."

"It used to hurt so much. Wondering if he'd ever return and want me."

"Oh, Rory. I tried to shield you from it. Tried to find a better life in any way I could. Everything you went through was hard. You're a survivor. You're my hero, baby girl."

I lift my head in disbelief. My words stagger. "I'm not a mistake?"

"No! Not for a moment. I made mistakes, but that doesn't mean I wouldn't do everything the exact same way, knowing that it brought you into my life. Not having you, not knowing you, is not a world I want to be in. You are all of the best parts of me and him. I've never been more proud of anything I've done in this life as I am watching you conquer your dreams."

I smile and my eyes burn, still puffy from crying and forgiveness and healing. My thoughts come out jagged and heavy.

"I sort of get why he left, but it really messed me up. My graduation picture might hang on the wall in this house, but I leave my coat on the hall tree like all the other guests. I've been a child in many ways, envious of the relationship you have with Lexie. I love her so much, but she gets this version of you, special trips, tucking her in at night. You got to be the best you for her. I didn't realize how much that stuff meant until I sat on the sidelines watching you provide it for someone else."

"I would've given you all of that. And though we did have fun, I understand now what I didn't know then. That a child needs attention and stability. I didn't give that to you because I couldn't, but I want to give that to you now if you'll let me."

I press my palms into my swollen eyes and laugh. "I think I'm a little old for tucking in."

"Nonsense, never. You know, we don't always get to confront the people who hurt us. So we have to do that work inside by facing the pain ourselves."

I didn't get the chance to tell my father how his leaving made me feel like I wasn't enough. And how a part of me has always been stuck in that role as a young child, waiting for her father to accept her. I need to stop letting his choices define my worth.

Maybe it's too late for me and Reed to rebuild, but it's not too late for me and my mom.

"Did I ever tell you he was a poet?"

"Really?" I blink, clearing my vision.

"That's what lured me in." She smiles, slipping into a place in time, only she has access to. "Well, that and his charming, easy way with people. That man was such a crowd pleaser. Great smile. Gentle eyes. Beautiful voice. I first saw him play during the underground days of grunge. I followed him and his guitar all the way to Alaska." Mom hands me another cucumber.

"So, he was a writer too."

"He was. And I'm going to dig through some old boxes to find song sheets and poems of his that I might have. I'm sorry it's taken me so long to do that for you. For years I was mad, and wanted to protect you from anything connecting to him. I made a mistake, not sharing those with you and giving you the agency to make your own decision."

Knowing my father expressed himself creatively, that this part of me came from somewhere . . . I can carry that. It is enough.

Mom whips something into shape in her cherry red bowl.

"For the record, we did include you on mother-daughter trips together—don't forget."

"Yeah, in winter, to the snow, yuck." I laugh.

"Listen to me, you have a selective memory. Sometimes, it scares me when I see you chase shadows the way you do. You remember the pain of the past more than you remember the good times."

"That's the hardest part of living with anxiety. It likes to keep me in the dark."

"We didn't always travel to snow. Do you remember the summer we went to Nantucket? Right after the wedding."

The memory surfaces like an early morning dew; I can't see through the fog yet.

"Arty and I thought it would be a good idea to take a vacation together before Lexie arrived. He knew how much you loved the ocean. We had a great week. Don't you remember? You even discovered your first big crush that summer." Mom sips her coffee, leaving mauve lipstick marks on the edge of the mug. "You were absolutely smitten. Enamored. I think that boy was a few years older than you. Great smile. Eyes like the water."

She shares her anecdotes with fondness, recalling something I'm still uncovering. Like she can see clear across the shoreline, and I'm barely opening my eyes.

"What was it now?" she ponders, tapping her nails on the counter. "Oh yes, he worked at the activities rental booth on the beach, and you dragged us there every morning, at the crack of dawn, to try a new activity."

"Me? Activities?" I question. The picture is drawing closer. I can feel the warm sand and taste the salt air.

Mom digs until my hippocampus starts to recognize the lost memory.

"First it was bodyboarding, then it was snorkeling, and kayaking too. And you didn't say a word, not to him or to us. You were completely lovestruck. You would fall off that board, over and over again, all to get that boy's attention." She laughs.

"What? Well, did it work? Did I get his attention?"

"How could you not, gorgeous child of mine. He was there every morning to help you."

"Stop it. What was his name?" I whisper.

"That was so long ago, who knows." She continues to tap.

The fog is lifting, as I riffle through details, the rocky sand and humid sun are coming in clear now.

"Do you remember anything about him?"

My feet were hot and I'd dance around to keep them from burning.

"Oh yes, I do recall the older gentlemen he was with. They both were wearing coordinating Sox jerseys, and I remember them because they had a personalization stitched across the back. I thought it was sweet."

My pulse is in my throat. I start to make out a face, youthful and carefree. His smile. Those sparkling eyes I'd know anywhere.

"Mom," I screech, my heart now banging down the walls of my chest, "what did they say? What did the jerseys say?"

"It was really very cute. One read, Senior, and the other, Junior. So clever, I remember thinking."

The room spins. My fingers go numb. I'm frozen, just like the moment in time where I first laid eyes on him.

"Hey, Junior. This young lady needs some help with her bodyboard," the man in the Red Sox jersey with the bright smile calls over his shoulder. He looks down at me, parked in the hot sand, fussing with the zipper of my wetsuit with the tags still on. "Don't worry, my son will take good care of you. Have fun out there, kid."

"Thank you," I say, grateful, squinting from the sun overhead. Hope this guy knows how to administer CPR, because I'm definitely going to need it taking on those waves.

Heat presses on the tops of my shoulders and scorches my knees. I finally secure the zipper when a protective shadow hovers above me, bending at the waist. Matching jersey. Matching smile. Ocean eyes.

"Hey there." He reaches down and cuts the tags from the top of the zipper. "Ever used one of these boards before?"

Lips sealed, covering my mouth full of braces, I shake my head no.

"Well then." He chuckles. "Let's get you comfortable on land first." He extends a tanned and toned arm, offering me his hand. "I've got you."

"Aurora, what's happening? Are you okay?"

The memory is crystal clear now and full of ghosts I wasn't prepared to disturb.

✳

Kat's legs dangle off my bed and I'm scrolling through my phone. "I'm thinking I want to take a vacay. Maybe to Ireland."

"I owe us that trip. We should do it," I return with unbridled enthusiasm.

"Gavin wants to come too. It could be fun with the three of us. Maybe you'll meet some sexy strapping Irish lad and make an honest man of him."

I bite my lip and fantasize about fresh scones instead. "No way. I'm not crashing a couple's trip."

"What if I get there, see what's been missing my whole life, and never leave?"

I wouldn't put it past her to try—I've heard Ireland calls people home like that.

"C'mon, Rory, it would be a perfect excuse to get some book inspiration."

"Yeah," I say, and shrug. I'm taking a little breather from new sources of inspiration.

I read once somewhere that perfection is the enemy of good. And yet, here I've been my entire life, striving for that unattainable point. To be good enough to be chosen. I'd forgotten that I have a choice too.

My parents are people, just like me, figuring it out while trying to fill their roles in life.

It doesn't mean what happened to me didn't count. It does mean that I don't have to own it anymore.

When I met Reed, I didn't realize that by holding onto what I believed to be true, I was limiting myself from growing into who I was meant to become. If everything always ended up according to my plan, I would've missed out on so many great experiences and people. I would've missed out on Arty, writing my book, winter hikes, falling in love, and finding myself.

I thought if I focused on the future I'd make it there safely. I've come to realize the destination is inevitable, but the journey is definitely the point.

It's exhausting living in limbo between two places in time that don't exist. I don't want to regret anything anymore. I want to learn from everything. The stars, the failed chapters, the loss, and the wins.

Not only did I meet Reed by the bench that day and then again for the mentorship, but I also met him before he lost his dad. I got to see that version of Reed, the one not yet touched by grief. This is a gift I didn't know I wanted.

Maybe I use words to build things, but I also use them to break things too.

I thought if I left, I'd be able to sever the space between us. But sometimes things don't work that way. Sometimes a person loves you so deeply that it's too quiet to hear when you're not listening, and catches up to you when you least expect it.

I wrestle with the impulse inside me that says I still have time and the realist who holds out her hand and stops me in my tracks, reminding me, *you pushed him away.*

"Rory, you need to make a decision," Kat demands.

"I don't know what to wear." I stand in my room, staring at my uninspired closet. Nothing is calling my name and saying *guest speaker panel attire.*

"Well, I suggest anything other than the towel you're in. Though . . . it could be a great marketing strategy to get people to read your book, once it's out there."

"You think PR would be cool with promoting above the knee?" I laugh.

"Be yourself, Rory. These people are excited like you were, interested in Eden's mentorship program, and maybe whatever you say will give them that push to apply. They don't care what you're wearing."

"You're right." I smile, straightening my spine. "He also might be there," I disclose.

"He might."

"I'm not sure I'm ready to see him with a girlfriend in tow."

"You've spent months working so hard, in every way. You'll keep your head high."

"What if he doesn't want to talk to me?"

"What if he does?"

"What if he's still mad at me for leaving the way I did?"

"What if he isn't?"

Kat, the eternal lemonade to my lemons.

"What if he's madly in love now with some other person, and I never get to explain?"

"Do you want an opportunity to explain?"

My arms flail in every which way as I try to find something to wear and think about other than this. "I've been telling myself all the reasons why I'm okay. And I'm okay. I can live this way."

"But?"

"But I want to be more than okay—with him. Imagine how large this planet is, and I've crossed paths with Reed three separate times. I think it's a sign."

"You two have certainly gone out of your way to find each other in one lifetime."

My eyes close at the thought of us happy together.

"Do you know what you want to say?"

"Everything," I mutter. The words that matter the most and the feelings that never extinguish.

I know I've grown over the past few months. I know this because my footprint is lighter. My anxiety doesn't linger as long. I rebound quicker, I sleep better, and I'm writing. I know I've healed some parts of myself, but that doesn't mean I don't feel the stakes creeping around the corner.

On a deep inhale, I pluck the coral sundress off its hanger for old times' sake—and any luck that I can get.

36

—— · ——

RORY

"WE LOSE OURSELVES IN BOOKS.
WE FIND OURSELVES THERE TOO." —ANONYMOUS

PLANNING AN EXIT STRATEGY typically goes one of two ways. Successful or horribly wrong.

A surefire way to guarantee success is to have a plan. So that's what I've always done.

I'd start off small, in the silent scenario stage, and let the scenes unfold that way first. Then I'd take pen to paper and create lists and color-coded sister lists for the lists. After I'd mapped out multiple scenarios and potential escape routes, I was ready.

Now that I'm embracing living in the present, I only set one intention this Saturday afternoon.

A rookie move, perhaps, as I prepared the best I could, but I chose not to plan for any of it.

Could I be lounging by the hotel pool with a romance novel? Sure. Maybe I will, later. There's freedom in flexibility, and I'm working on enjoying my life without a detailed itinerary for every single step.

So here I am, back at the annual LITA conference—a decade later—in my tropical dress and linen blazer, sporting heels that Kat insisted I wear, and staring at the event program with my name in it.

There are a few of us "graduated mentees" that have been invited to speak on a panel about the mentorship program. I haven't been in this room before. It's small with one long table in the front, six chairs tucked behind it, and eight rows of ten chairs on each side, creating the illusion of a runway down the middle.

A woman with long blonde hair is leaning against the table. There's a man beside her, their hands entwined. The way her head surrenders against his arm is an intimate act. I collect the details and open my notes app. She looks up at him, her eyes close a little and a sigh slips from her pink-stained lips. She releases the weight of the world and he shoulders it. I'm lost in their exchange. I jot down, *To be a part of someone. Can we ever truly be someone else's? They fit, in that sort of silent way, that inspires artists to paint, musicians to make music, and writers to create stories.*

I put my phone away and scan the rest of the room. There's a few people lingering around the audience chairs, and I see a couple of people have joined by the front table. I steady my breath and make my way up the aisle, my heels pressing into the thick carpet.

A high-pitched hello comes from behind me. I turn to find Ms. Healy in all her glory, rocking a tangerine blouse with matching lips.

"Rory, you're here. I'm thrilled." She leans in and gives me a side kiss on the cheek that doesn't quite land. I quickly rub the spot anyway after she turns around to face the group. The seats are beginning to fill up. *One, two, three, four.*

"Okay, Rory, take the seat at the end here." Ms. Healy places my name card in front of the spot she points to. Each seat has a water bottle and notepad with a Pelham Hotel ballpoint pen. I unscrew my water bottle cap and take a sip while she instructs the three of us sitting down, "This is going to be great. We'll have the mentees on the left and the mentors on the right." She claps her hands together, tangerine nails tapping against each other.

I spit out my water onto my crisp, lined legal pad of paper. It crinkles instantly, wincing in embarrassment. I want to crawl under the table and wither away.

My panel comrades look at me, wide eyes for miles, and Ms. Healy approaches the end of the table. She whispers, "Can I help you?"

I clear my throat and dab the top of the paper with the corner of my blazer. This is horrifically awkward. "I'm sorry, I misunderstood you. I think you said," I pause to steady my pulse, "on the opposite side," I point discreetly to the three empty seats at the other end of the table, "those are for the mentors?"

"Yes, you heard me correctly. The panel is for the entire program, which includes both our new writers and our established authors."

"Um, so, are these mentors selected at random or something? Is Avery going to be here?" I nod my head.

Ms. Healy chuckles at me as if my struggle is adorable.

"No, it's not random. It's who you were matched with. Didn't you know?"

NO. I DID NOT KNOW. I scream, inwardly.

I shake my head and chew on my lower lip.

"Avery couldn't make it last minute, so Reed offered to attend in her place. We'll make sure to grab a pic of the three of us when the panel is done."

I want to vomit.

"Great," I say, with more gusto than necessary, "we'll do that."
My voice is a high-pitched frantic squeal like a pissed-off squirrel.

I rummage in my bag and pull out my phone, texting Kat.

ME: MAY DAY - Reed's on the Panel today!

ME: Maybe, I can escape and no one will notice.

KAT: Rory Wells, keep your ass at the conference.

KAT: You deserve to be there.

KAT: Maybe don't make eye contact. Oh, and breathe.

I can do this. *Five, six, seven, eight.*

The girl next to me nudges my arm. "Hey, they're here," she says.

My eyes snap like an elastic band released in the direction of the aisle to three people walking. I only notice the last one. The one.

A submerged feeling washes over me as I focus intently, losing myself in imagery. Tingles trickle down my spine and my mind grows fuzzy as I shift into a memory of the first time I saw Reed. It lives deep in my imagination, where all the sacred ones are kept.

My heart cannot be trusted—it's wild with stomping beats and dropped mics.

He stalks my gaze as he makes his way to the other end of the table. My lips remember. The way they used to graze along the lines of his face, brushing over his mouth, until he'd catch my lower lip with his teeth. I know there were other people in this room twenty seconds ago, but I can't see or hear any of them now.

Reed sends me a faint smile, a brief vanishing gesture I may have imagined.

Into the microphone, Ms. Healy's voice takes over the entire room, and I come to realize that everyone else is still here and we are, in fact, not alone. "Looks like we're waiting on a few sessions that are running late. We want to give everyone an opportunity to join us, so we'll begin in fifteen minutes."

The girl, whose name I still don't know, nudges me again. "Hey, I think this is going to be a well-attended session. I'm Ricky by the way."

"Hi." Grateful for the distraction. "Rory. Nice to meet you."

"I hear there's a well-stocked martini bar. Wanna check it out?"

"Actually, I'm going to step outside and get some air."

"In that heat?" She laughs, grabbing her bag and standing. "Good luck."

If she only knew. I need to regroup. I gather my things and feelings as fast as I can and run out of the room.

Even with the addition of a blazer, I'm shivering, thanks to the hotel's industrial-sized air-conditioning unit that is unfortunately still operating.

I make my way outside, choking on caustic air, moisture collecting at the base of my neck. And then I smile because I see it, sitting there—its smooth solid oak—impervious to time.

I claim a spot on the bench and soak in the summer sun. I think this season must be Boston's favorite. The traffic's humming and people are coming and going.

It's a mystery to me, how time changes both everything and nothing—how all the cells in my body still light up when Reed walks into a room. How my heart soars even with my feet firmly planted on the hot pavement.

I reach into my pocket when a deep voice projects from behind me.

"Rory."

I turn my attention over my shoulder to see Reed, hand covering his eyes, shielding his face from the sun. "Nice dress."

He remembers. "Hey."

"Can we talk?" he asks.

My reply is a silent slide on the bench, making room for two. When he sits down, my stomach sinks.

"It's good to see you."

I squirm a little in my seat, trying to quiet the rush of words pounding on the door to get out. Playing it cool so I don't frighten him off with all of my feelings at once.

"Just to let you know, I didn't realize we'd both be on this panel today. I was—"

"Are you seeing someone?" I blurt out unapologetically. I can't sit here and pretend like pleasantries or anything else matters.

Confusion spreads across his face, and a stunned stare settles above his eyes. "Seeing someone?"

"Yes." I look directly at him even though I'm scared to hear the answer. "You were seeing someone this spring, your mom told me she was really helping you, and I'm asking if you still are, you know, taken?" I steady my shaking knees by pressing my hands into a balled fist on top of my thighs.

"Ah, right." It clicks. "She was probably referring to Lauren."

"Lauren?" I echo her name like I won't believe him until he provides a confirmation number.

"I'm still seeing Lauren, yes, on Tuesdays at ten o'clock. She's great. Mom's right, she's really helped me work through Emmy's accident and losing Pops. You'd like her—she specializes in post-traumatic stress and anxiety disorders."

"I don't understand."

The math doesn't make sense. "Wait. The person you're seeing, the one who has been so good for you—"

"She's my therapist, Rory," he completes my thought.

Months of wasted worrying rushes to my head so fast, I might pass out. "That's so great. I'm so happy for you." *Please don't cry, Rory, please don't cry.* I squeeze my fist.

He stuns my thoughts into silence with his smile, the tender one I know is reserved for me, like the way a rainbow only appears after it's poured.

"Bravo, by the way. I've heard great things about your book from Ms. Healy."

First, he throws me off, waltzing into that panel room like the guiding light he's always been. Now I'm simply trying to process the fact that he's not in a relationship, and all I can focus on is how incredible he looks and smells. His beard is gone and replaced with stubble. The linear line of his jaw and the way the light accentuates it has me crossing my ankles. There's so much I want to say, but my mouth has other plans.

"And I've got a question for you, but first, will you please sign my program, right here by your name? I was hoping to avoid the line." He winks.

"Give it here." My cheeks pinch from their quick ascent into a beaming smile.

He hands me a pen and I write down a personal note. I pass the pamphlet and pen back to him and he tucks them into his jacket pocket. The cyan color he's wearing channels memories of that summer sky, and the sea, and it brings me back to my sixteen-year-old self, completely lost in their clarity. I look around, not sure where we go from here. I clasp my hands together.

"Before we get back in there . . ." he trails off. "It's just that, well, being this close to you, I'm scared I'm going to mess this up." He clears his throat and takes my hands in his, rubbing the top of my palms with the coarse pads of his thumbs. Every swipe strikes. "I love you, Rory Wells. Let's make that absolutely clear."

Tears fall down my heated cheeks and I don't even care that I'm making a scene. These feelings that terrified me for so long have only been waiting months and days and hours and minutes, to have this chance to finally listen to him.

"I've had a lot of time to think, and I've realized something about us, Rory, something I've missed so much. The mentorship may have brought us together, but it was our friendship that mattered, from the beginning. And it's special because it's never been the taking kind. It's always given. It gave back to me a deeper understanding of myself, how incredibly valuable time is, and how loss can help us grow to love even more. I see that now. Because in your absence, all I've ever wanted is the best for you. To know that you were happy."

The top button of his shirt is undone, exposing his throat sticking as he swallows. I dig my toes into the soles of my shoes, accepting the flood of fresh tears.

"After what happened to Emmy, I didn't think I deserved to be happy when those around me were struggling. But hiding didn't protect me, and I know I'm the last person to figure this out, but I needed time to forgive myself. I needed to do that before I could tell you what I came here to say." He steals a tear from my cheek.

"Aurora."

My name on his lips is a question, a caress, a vow. I nod my head yes, and let his words wash over us.

"I didn't mean to find love here and make our friendship and lives more complicated. I didn't ever want to sacrifice your work for my feelings, but some things in life are out of our control."

Reed runs his hand through his hair, like he does because it's always hanging in front of his face. I don't know how much longer I can sit here without climbing into his lap.

"There's a million things we could've done. But what's the use in tearing ourselves to shreds over the past? We're here now. You've been the most unexpected adventure of my life. I've had no roadmap here. In the entire world, out of all of the people, in all the possibilities that fate and timing could play out, I met you, not once, but twice," he says, then smiles.

He cups my face in his hands and drops his forehead to mine. The tips of our noses touch and all I want is to taste his words. Every syllable. Every consonant. Every vowel.

Reed's warm breath whispers over my lips as he adds, "And when you showed up on my doorstep, like an answer to a wish that simply lost its way . . . I felt it, the hope of you, and I haven't stopped believing since."

His words puncture the center of my chest and curve back around, tying a knot inside. I should say something, anything, so he doesn't misunderstand my silence, but I can't speak.

Reed releases my face, turning his focus to the street. "I understand." The tone of his voice drops from his throat to his gut.

How can two people, broken in different ways, fit the way we do? How can he speak to me like he's known all along?

I'm unable to move, like a statue sculpted with an open mouth, wanting to scream, to keep him close. To possibly keep him forever.

"All right." He blows out a long exhale and places his hand on the arm of the bench. "It's okay, Rory."

My fingers reach for Reed and wrap around his wrist. His racing pulse matches my own.

He shakes his head in confusion, peeling my fingers off his wrist and then prying them open to reveal what I'm holding.

"Where'd you get that?" he asks.

"Sometimes, I carry them," I clarify through a smile of relief.

"Why do you carry stones, Rory?"

"It's silly." I bite on my salty bottom lip.

"As you're well aware of, I don't ask questions I don't want the answers to."

Admitting this isn't easy, but being vulnerable with Reed has always been the only choice for me. "The stones keep me close to a time where I felt brave and most like myself."

"That all?"

I shake my head. "They keep me close to you."

Reed pulls me into his arms and takes complete hold of me, pressing his warm palms into my spine. He squeezes the fabric of my dress as I fold into his chest like a deck of well-shuffled cards that know their place. I bury my cheek into the soft cotton of his dress shirt and breathe him in.

We lean on each other, two forces reuniting through the stagnant summer air.

Being with Reed, wrapped in his arms, the truth dancing all around us. This person who sees me and understands.

"I've missed you so much," he cries into my hair. "Promise me we'll always talk things through, especially when you're scared?"

I squeeze tighter around his waist. "I promise."

He kisses the top of my head, the tip of my nose, and brings my mouth to his.

Nutmeg and cider, fresh air and old books, rush my senses. *He's always been here.*

Reed kisses me long and hard. With each brief pause between our embrace, I make a new promise to myself to always show Reed how loved he is.

I spent my whole life trying to belong until I figured out that it isn't about what hangs on the walls or how you fit in. Belonging is about the people you love, who love you back, and finding home in each other.

"Did you seriously think I was taken by anyone other than you?" he asks. His eyes are wet and searching.

"I *may* have misunderstood your mom when she shared that you were seeing someone."

He laughs a deep, hearty sound of pure amusement.

"It's an honest mistake anyone would've made," I insist.

"Of course you did." He smiles and kisses me again, but this kiss is steady and soft. "What do you say we get back in there and show them what a creative partnership looks like?"

"Should I start by suggesting excessively worded emails on day one?" I laugh at my next thought and look up to see a twinkle of recognition in his eyes. "Or better yet—"

We say in unison, "Ice-breakers."

"Definitely ice-breakers," I add.

Reed surrenders his smile to a serious gaze.

"I love you, Rory. All of you. You understand that."

"I love you, Reed Ashton West Junior. And don't you forget it."

"I have a feeling you won't let me," he says, grinning against my lips.

"I have a feeling you're okay with that." I smile into his.

We stand and head out of the heat. He takes my hand in his and they sway together. I slip the stone back into my pocket.

"By the way, I've got a great story for you."

"Oh yeah?" He tilts his head toward me. "Your tone suggests this is one of those moments where I need to read between the lines." Reed laughs at himself, unfiltered and bold, and it envelops me like a warm surf.

Reed and I, we found our love in the space between our words. Not a love to fear or to keep locked away. The kind you want to share because you know it will always come back to you.

If I wasn't a writer, I'd say you can't make this stuff up. Who knew that along the path of make-believe, we'd find our story? I like to think that something bigger than we could ever explain brought Reed and me together. Maybe the Milky Way had something to do with it. Reed is convinced Pops pulled some strings for us too. None of our theories are guaranteed, but what I do know is that I'd hoped for him too. It wasn't the smoothest road. It was more like we tripped over our feet, rolled down a muddy hill, and crawled through a valley to get here, back to our bench and the reliable summer sun. I guess when you believe that deeply in something or someone, what you look for is what you'll find.

Reed holds open the door to the conference room, and I slip under his arm, lifting on my tiptoes. I whisper into his ear, "How well do you remember the summer you spent in Nantucket when you were eighteen?"

I lean my head back just enough to catch a nostalgic glow behind his eyes, brightening them from the center of the ocean blue, to a cloudless sky that I want to spend my days laying under.

"My mom told me this one."

"Is it a love story?" he asks.

"Aren't they all?"

EPILOGUE - REED

"LOVE IS THE MOST IMPORTANT THING IN THE WORLD, BUT BASEBALL IS PRETTY GOOD, TOO." —YOGI BERRA

WINTER

I'VE GIVEN EVERYONE EXPLICIT instructions. Not a single peep. They're all in the living room waiting for us to arrive from watching the sun set over the White Mountains.

"The house is so dark, hun. You didn't leave any lights on?"

I don't want her to get too nervous, but for the few minutes it takes to get to the front door, it'll be worth it. This woman has a radar for surprises. She sniffs out clues better than Fenway. I've had this day planned for a while now, and it's been the longest stretch of time in my life, keeping a secret from her. I had to coordinate Boston people and New Hampshire people, and party planning is really not my thing. Luckily, everyone was on board and pitched in.

"Just a few more steps, babe. Hold my hand."

"I know I'm going to trip over something."

"All right, woman." I swoop her up into my arms.

She yelps. "You're not seriously carrying me."

"Oh, yes, I am. Stop squirming. I'm no spring chicken."

"This is kinda hot." She nuzzles into my neck. *Not a good time, Aurora.* I take the two last steps to the door and open it. I place her down on the kitchen floor and pretend to struggle to find the light.

"This switch isn't working. Will you go turn the lamp on in the living room?"

"Why did we leave our phones at home? This is rid—"

All the lights flash on and everyone shouts, "Surprise! Happy birthday, Rory!" The room's decorated in green and gold, streamers and balloons, and is full of the people she loves.

First, Rory screams.

Then she grabs her chest. *Which makes me smile.*

Then she comes to and jumps up and down, runs into the room, and hugs everyone, one at a time.

"How did you guys pull this off? This is amazing. Thank you so much."

I lean against the door frame and watch her happiness float around the room like a kid chasing a stream of bubbles at her birthday party, with no empty seats and people who know her favorite color is periwinkle and that she's allergic to almonds. She turns back to me and mouths, "I love you."

"Happy birthday, amore mio," I say.

Mom and Tillie have a spread that could make a grown man weep. I swear everything is wrapped in bacon.

We all gather around the table and celebrate the day this beautiful, creative, one-of-a-kind woman came into this world, and I feel especially lucky because I get to spend the rest of my life loving her. *That is if she says yes.* But that's later. For now, we're simply enjoying today.

✳

"What's this?" Rory asks after everyone is asleep, scattered throughout the house. She's lying against my chest in our bed, holding a journal with an envelope enclosed in it.

"It's your birthday present." I kiss the top of her head.

"The party was my gift. It's enough," she protests.

I hold the line until she gives in.

"I guess one more will be all right." She giggles.

Turns out Rory Wells loves presents. I think it's okay to make up for lost time, and I love the way her face lights up. Except, she's not smiling. I think she may be in shock.

"This journal, is it yours?" She's curious, confused, thumbing through the pages.

"Lew gave me that journal for inspiration when I wasn't writing. It's all the letters I wrote to him when I lived in Italy. Since that was before Pops died, I thought you might enjoy knowing that piece of me. It will be fun to read through them again once we get there."

"What do you mean, once we get there?" She turns around, and climbs on top of me. The sheet pools at her waist and I've momentarily forgotten her question.

"Open the envelope."

She rips it open and stops breathing.

"Rory, breathe." She closes her mouth and inhales deeply.

"Wait, how are we gonna do this? Work? Fenway? Fitz? Emmy?"

I smile at her thoughts running a mile a minute. I lean in and kiss her quiet. "It's taken care of. Fenway and Fitz are going to Carlynn's, and Mom's helping with Emmy. And we're writers Aurora—we can work from anywhere."

"From Italy," she shrieks. "From Amsterdam," she shrieks louder.

"You're gonna wake everyone up," I burst out, laughing.

"Are we really doing this? Three months in Europe. Is this even real life?"

"It's real to me if it's real to you."

"It's always been real to me."

I lean in to kiss her again. She submits and then pulls away.

"This journal is so special. I'll cherish it. And do you know what this means? Amsterdam in the winter," she exclaims.

"I planned on it."

"We're going to see the northern lights." The tickets fly in the air as Rory bounces up and down, straddling my stomach.

She still has no idea what she does to me—to all of me. Okay, her grin would suggest that maybe she has a clue.

"We're also going to eat copious amounts of baked goods in France," I add.

Her smile sours into a frown. I know this one.

"Flying," she states.

I run my hands through her hair, down her arms, then squeeze her thighs. "I booked a night flight. You'll have help from your Xanax if you need it, and a front row seat to the stars."

Rory nods and exhales. The frown fades.

"The stars," she whispers. "And what if I get scared, or can't breathe, or start spiraling?"

"You have me. I've got you."

"How do I deserve this, Reed?"

"It took us four times to finally figure out how to be together."

"True."

"I think we owe the universe a little thank you by taking this time, you and me, on one giant inspiration date."

After Rory falls asleep, I climb out of bed, gather the tickets, tuck them inside the journal, and place them on our bookshelf. Tonight's winter sky is a sparkling canvas. And without fail, there's one star shining the brightest.

"I've got it from here, Pops. Love ya. Go Sox."

I'm so grateful for the time we had, the lessons he taught me with unconditional love. The place inside myself, Rory reminded me, was always there. Knowing Rory met Pops that summer in Nantucket has brought me so much happiness. It's funny, the way the stars align, answering wishes before you know to make them.

Rory's steady breathing is my evening soundtrack, and as she lays in our bed, in our room, surrounded by our books lined up together, this is where I'm at peace.

I flick on the lamp by the window and dry my eyes. I scan the rows on the shelf, touching the spines, feeling a deep sense of pride, something healed and whole again. Cal sold that first story, the one of a father's love. It's releasing next year.

Rory's time-travel debut, *Synchronicity*, is out on submission. She landed an agent who fiercely believes in her voice, and having that relationship has been an exciting step for her career. I know if she catches me staring at her this way, it will send her into hiding. She never wants any praise or spotlight. She prefers to write in her quiet corner with the best view of the lake while Fenway and Fitz snore at her feet. But fuck that. I will shout this woman's praises and accomplishments. I've never stopped being in awe of her resilience and capacity to care. She still makes me feel like I'm the only person in any room.

And she got here all on her own merit. I was the lucky one she chose to share the journey with, even after how misguided I was, thinking that if I did everything I could to help her, somehow it'd make amends for a past that was haunting me.

I pull Rory's original journal off the shelf and hold it, sliding out the program I asked her to sign that day before I knew if she'd forgiven me. Seconds before I confessed how much I loved her. I run my fingers over the ink.

It whisks me back to our bench. To her nervous smile and curious eyes. My heart swells in place every time as I anticipate her words. I see our story in Polaroids, one after the other, frozen lakes and fallen leaves, sandy beaches and cobblestone streets, merged together multiple times over the course of our lives. I then envision our future together and absolute joy comes over me.

I don't have to know what lies ahead in order to trust its purpose. All I can do is what I've been doing all along, hoping she's ready for the only plan I'll ever have, which is to love her with all that I am, each day, like it's the first, the only, and the last.

Dear Reed,
Whatever your question is,
my answer will always be, yes.
I love you more than I knew was possible.
More than scones and coffee and every star in the sky.
I love you more than words.
Rory the Writer

Official Memo

TO	**All Employees**
FROM	**Allison Healy**
DATE	**December 12, 2019**
SUBJECT	**Publishing Deal – Aurora Wells**

We are happy to announce that Aurora Wells's time-travel debut will be releasing next winter. Many thanks to the editors and team who made this all possible.

Digital: Fiction: Women's/Romance

Synchronicity

We have invited the author, and her fiancé, along with her agent, to join us at our annual holiday party to celebrate. Thank you for all your hard work.

6006 Montgomery Street,
Boston, MA 02128

www.edenbooks.com

EDEN BOOKS

BOOK TWO

COMING NEXT!
Sign up for book news & to receive an excerpt:
CHAPTER ONE of *SYNCHRONICITY*
Read how it all begins for Chelsea and Seth
Book Two – In the Stars Duet
A timeless love story by S.L. Astor

Sign up available @ https://www.AuthorSLAstor.com/

Reviews help authors and books.
Please consider taking a moment to leave an Amazon review.

DEAR READER

Berry Lake is a fictional town, but it, and the setting in Rory's chapters, were modeled after the years I spent living in the beautiful states of New Hampshire and Massachusetts. I loved celebrating places close to my heart. If you haven't been, I hope this story puts those places on the map for you. I definitely recommend going in the Fall, early enough to catch both the foliage and a game at Fenway Park.

As a reader, fated love has always been one of my favorite fictional worlds to get lost in. I get giddy for all the details that conspire together towards an HEA. As a writer, it proved trickier than I anticipated to tie in those moments without being too obvious or seemingly careless. I hope you enjoyed picking up on the ways Rory and Reed were connected even when they didn't "know" it. If you didn't notice and still enjoyed the story, then I did my job better than planned. I had a blast weaving the details in.

I also had a ton of fun exploring blurred boundaries in a creative partnership in fiction—in reality though, boundaries are a crucial component to establishing and maintaining a safe and successful working relationship.

If you're a writer seeking guidance, coaching, and mentorship, or if you're looking for information regarding the self-publishing and/or querying process, I highly encourage you to be diligent in your selection.

Ask for testimonials from past mentees/clients. Request samples of previous work. Shop around before you hand over your manuscript or ideas. Below, I've listed a few recommendations for reputable coaches and programs. Please do your research to ensure the best fit for you.

Author Mentor Match https://authormentormatch.com
HappyWriter Coaching http://happywriter.co/coaching
Parker Peevyhouse https://www.parkerpeevyhouse.com
Stacy Frazer https://www.writeitscared.co

There's no "one" sure-fire method or "right" way to write. If you're like Rory, eager to share your story and bit lost in the shuffle, looking for insight into the publishing and writing worlds of both traditional and self-published authors, Emily Henry and Rachel Griffin have a wealth of information saved to their Instagram *Highlights*, and both, Amy Harmon's *Word of the Week* Series, and Kandi Steiner's *Wrangling the Writer,* are available on their Instagram pages too.

I've spent years listening to podcasts. Some of my favorites are: *How Writers Write, The Shit No One Tells You About Writing*, and *Unpublished.* Specific to the romance genre, check out romance authors, Cat Wynn & S.J. Tilly, at *Tall, Dark & Fictional.*

I've also had the opportunity to be a part of *Quill & Cup*, a women's writing group, where you'll find dedicated writers in an uplifting and safe community. We all start somewhere.

I'm rooting for you! xo Sam

ACKNOWLEDGMENTS

There's something special about the self-publishing and indie bookverse. I met perfect strangers—other writers, readers, creators—and somewhere in all of this, they've become cherished friends. So even though this book began as a single inspired idea, it ended up as a collective effort within a collaborative community. And after three years, there's a whole lot of people to thank (and inevitably, I'll miss some), but it is my sincerest hope to express my gratitude to everyone behind the scenes—whose investment in this story, and in me, cannot be adequately measured in words. But I'm going to try anyway.

To the incredible storytellers out there, you set the bar high, and I'm grateful for it. Your words brought me back to reading fiction, and your kindness and willingness to share your knowledge with readers and writers has made a difference in my life. I've learned so much from you. Thank you.

Every book has a first draft, and lucky for me, this story also had a patient and thoughtful first reader. Sunshine Kamaloni, you've been a champion of Rory and Reed from the start, when I was still getting to know them, and settling into my voice. Thank you for believing in me and for seeing me through to "the end". For always digging with me to the heart of "story" and humanity.

My developmental editor, Emily Martin. I gave you a lost version of this manuscript, and you graciously guided me to make this story something worth reading. Thank you for your insight and encouragement.

To my thoughtful and talented friends, Allie, Em, Lori, MK, and Sarah, who beta read and answered a million questions—I cannot thank each of you enough. You were the eyes and ears this book so desperately needed.

I'm fully convinced there is magic in editing. Lilly Schneider, it's the smallest of changes that often have the largest impact. You made this story shine. Thank you.

And Sarah Peachey, simply put, this manuscript would not be in existence without your expertise and care. You are brilliant. Thank you, for everything.

Thank you to my proofreader, Sarah Rosenbarker. I'm so grateful to have had your final touch on these pages.

Murphy Rae, you designed the absolute most perfect cover for this book. Thank you for your vision and patience. Seeing the cover for the first time made this whole dream (all these years and tears) feel real.

Meredith Schorr, thank you for your valuable mentorship experience perspective. Your account is the aspiration I have for anyone who enters a creative partnership.

Krysann and Sarah, my BFF CP's, thank you for taking writing to the next level and sharing your love of language and the human condition, with me. I'm in awe of you both, and beyond thankful for your friendship.

To my booksta-fam—I told myself I wasn't going to write out a list of names, because in many ways it feels impersonal, but I changed my mind, because how can I not try to thank each of you, and let you know that whether we've had one conversation or we talk regularly, our conversation(s) have meant so much to me. Allie, Amber, Amy, Ania, April, Ashley, Crystal, Em, Elaine, Enni, Eve, Hannah, Jamie, James, Joel, Jordan, Julie, Kate, Kelsey, Kristen, Korrie, Lexie, Lilly, Lindsey, Lori, Loren, Mandy, Maria, Megan, Megs, Melissa, Penelope, Sara, Tammy, and Trilina—(If I forgot to include your name, and you don't know how much I heart you, please know how much I appreciate you, but that my writer/mom/human brain sometimes needs an assist)! What in the world? You've all welcomed me, making me feel right at home—thank you for graciously sharing your time and thoughts with me. We might solely communicate in memes or talk about parenting or fur babies or our favorite books, I'm just grateful for you. Thank you for supporting my fictional historical hero habit, encouraging my work, and sharing your lives, creativity, and stories with me. You're the most wonderfully supportive people out there.

To the 2020 Shenanigans crew . . . Book Club was a blast. Thank you for teaching me all about the romance genre when I knew nothing. In an impossible year for the world, we carved out a space that made a positive impact.

Thank you to the women of "Quill & Cup" for opening up your Hedgie House and hearts to me. I've grown in my craft and made true friendships.

Navigating the business side of self-publishing has been a steep learning curve, and I couldn't have done it without HELP. Thank you to the established authors (you know who you are) who continue to hold my shaky hand and lead the way. You're the absolute best of the best.

MK, I'd still be lost in pages of backstory, if it weren't for you. One day, there will be a kitchen floor, with wine, homemade pasta, and our names on it. You've made me a better writer. Thank you, for everything.

Jen, thank you for walking the writing and parenting paths with me, for brainstorming sessions, and for your friendship. You make this community, world, and my bookshelf, a better place. I'm excited for our future adventures and the stories they'll tell.

Lindsey, getting to experience a debut year with you and swap "the few" similarities we share—has been the gift that keeps on giving. Hallmark season is upon us. Always here to cheer you on and laugh together.

Diana, thank you for all of the pep-talks and/or chill pills I've needed over the years. For reminding me that it's okay to go at my own pace. It has been such a touchstone for me to have your generous spirit and support. Thank you for saving Ch. 35! You + Me + PEI.

Laurie, 2,923 miles is nothing when you share a brain. Thank you for the chapters you provided feedback on and the voicemails you endured. For fiercely believing in me. And for being you. Margaritas, please.

THANK YOU to my sprinting besties, Bea, Cat, Elaine, Gabby, and S.J., turned true bosom friends, for taking the time to review scenes, blurbs, and talk about anything and everything with me. Your feedback and friendship have been an essential piece of the puzzle. I hope I've been able to give back to you a fraction of what you've given me. I've never sprinted a day in my life, but I'm glad that didn't stop me from tagging along. You're all stuck with me, and Anne Shirley, now.

To my friends who are family: *The Hope of You,* is as much a love letter to a writer's journey as it is to the power of friendship. The decades have been too short. I hope you find a little bit of those years in Rory and Kat & Reed and Meryl. They were by far the scenes I felt most at home in.

Chrissy, Linda, Margo, and Sara, I cannot thank you enough for loving my kiddos and taking care of them during the times I was stuck behind the computer or on a deadline. It takes a village, and I'm grateful for ours.

Thank you, Paula, Sophie, and Finn, for your presence. It's been the support I didn't know I needed, and wouldn't be here without.

Thank you to my family for all of the encouragement along the way, and to my *ride-or-die*—you've always believed in me, reminding me that my words matter, and make a difference. I'm not me without you.

To my husband, you make our beautiful life and my dream possible in every way. Ten years of marriage, and I think I've finally mastered the differences between Star Wars and Star Trek. Quiz me later. xo

And to my children—it's been through your childhood and magical sense of wonder, that I reconnected with my voice. I love you to the moon and back, and yes, now you can tell every random person we meet on the street that your mom's an "auffor". Thank you for sharing your mommy with my world of make-believe.

When it came to writing this story, there were lots of walks, late nights, and a constant soundtrack in my ears. I'm especially thankful to Mumford and Sons. The *Babel* and *Sigh No More* albums were my *Guiding Light*.

To the creative hearts out there, I hope you found some comfort in these pages. It was you I was thinking of the entire time.

And finally, to the team of ARC readers, and to you, dear reader, thank you for taking a chance on this writer and debut book. Thank you for sharing and supporting my art. I made a promise to myself, and I kept it. The next chapter of this story doesn't exist without you. She's all yours now.

Take good care of her, yourselves, and one another.

ABOUT THE AUTHOR

S.L. ASTOR writes emotionally driven stories with characters who love big and don't always play by the rules. She lives (and bakes) in NorCal with her husband and their cookie enthusiast children. When she's not in meetings with her chatty imaginary heroines and heroes, you'll find Sam on the beach, reading and dreaming, with an iced latte in hand. Sam loves hearing from readers. She mostly hangs out on Instagram. The Hope of You is her first novel.

🅾 https://www.instagram.com/sl.astor.writes/

Printed in Great Britain
by Amazon

87312577R00239